INTO
THE INFERNO

INTO THE INFERNO

EARL EMERSON

Ballantine Books
New York

A Ballantine Book
Published by The Ballantine Publishing Group

www.ballantinebooks.com

LIBRARY OF CONGRESS CATALOGING-IN-PUBLICATION DATA
Emerson, Earl W.
Into the inferno : a novel of suspense / Earl Emerson.—1st ed.
p.   cm.
ISBN 0-345-44591-0
I. Title.

PS3555.M39 I67 2003
813'.54—dc21   2002074747

Manufactured in the United States of America

First Edition: March 2003

10 9 8 7 6 5 4 3 2 1

The good die first . . .
                          —William Wordsworth

Life, in my estimation, is a biological misadventure that we terminate on the shoulders of six strange men whose only objective is to make a hole in one with you.
                          —Fred Allen

INTO
THE INFERNO

1. JUNE—NEAR THE END

I'm a mad dog. Utterly mad.

If you knew my circumstances, you'd trust me when I tell you I'm as crazy as they come. And growing madder by the minute.

Nobody out there in the dark doubts me. I can see a few of the uniforms in the shadows, fingers tightening on their triggers, scopes zeroed in on my heart. I can hear the whispering. Most can barely wait to begin pumping rounds into the night. Into me. Any excuse. Any little twitch on my part will provoke a bloodbath.

You think I'm kidding?

Consider this. . . .

I'm standing on the roof of a police cruiser screaming at twenty police officers to keep their distance. My mouth looks like the bloody maw of hell. Several of my teeth have been loosened and quite a few others are missing entirely. I have a cell phone in one hand, a pistol in the other. The cell phone is pressed to my left ear. The gun to my right ear. During most of the last twenty minutes I've been threatening to put a bullet through my brain. If that's not enough, I'm naked as a jaybird.

I'm crazy as a shithouse rat and they know it. Destined for a jail cell, a straitjacket, or, more likely, to end up dancing the funky chicken in a fusillade of bullets.

Don't waste your time feeling sorry for me. You're headed there, too. That's what I've learned in the last week. Maybe not the nuthouse or a fusillade of bullets, but you're headed for the dirt. Same as me. Same as every last one of us. Eventually everybody lands in the dirt.

I don't care anymore.

You can't fake my kind of insanity. They know I mean business. They know I'm a mad dog.

That's the whole point.

All I have to do is make a move and they'll kill me. Don't think I'm not tempted.

Suppose I move.

They'd shoot.

And they'd keep on shooting.

Maybe I should do it and end all this. In seven days I've turned into a lunatic, my life expectancy dropping from years to hours to minutes.

Running into Holly Riggs was the end for a bunch of us.

2. FEBRUARY—THE BEGINNING; OR, A YOUNG GREEN-EYED WOMAN IN TIGHT JEANS SCREAMS SHRILLY AT RELIGIOUS CHICKENS

The first time I saw Holly Riggs, she was standing in the left lane of Interstate 90 up to her knees in Bibles. Three hundred Bibles. Eight hundred chickens. It was ten o'clock at night, and already a good many of the birds had absconded for parts unknown, others sauntering away more slowly than any animal with a brain would. Some of the chickens were frozen to the roadway like art projects in a school for the mentally challenged.

As more emergency vehicles arrived, dozens of birds scampered off into the snow. Up the hill, teenage boys on their way home from night skiing got out of their cars and chased fryers, a shabby sport at best, for the birds were easily overtaken, even more easily bagged, and the boys had no use for their prey once captured.

Holly Riggs. Anyone who'd come over Snoqualmie Pass in an eighteen-wheeler in the middle of February on the iciest roads the state had experienced in almost a decade—you had to give her points for spunk.

For a week the Pacific Northwest had been dancing with a freeze-thaw cycle. The iced-over road surface on I-90 was polished and melted each day by the sun and by cars with chains and studded tires. When night fell and the roadway refroze, it became so slippery, a person could barely stand on it. Washington State wasn't like Minnesota or North Dakota, where the roads were frozen all winter and the state knew how to deal with them; our region's fleet of DOT sanding trucks had been swamped from the onset.

It was a few minutes after ten when my pager went off, when Mrs. Neumann stagger-stepped through the frozen field between our houses like a stork wrapped in an afghan. She would look after my girls while I responded to the accident, was still knocking the snow out of the treads in her galoshes when I pulled out of the drive.

The accident happened on the last downslope from the pass, prior

3

to North Bend, just before the Truck Town exit, where a huge field lay between the eastbound and westbound lanes of I-90. It was in this field that several of the smaller vehicles and one of the big trucks had come to rest.

Parking on the eastbound shoulder, I followed two sets of footprints across the crusted snow. I knew this meant I was only the third fire department employee on the scene.

I could see Chief Newcastle up on the roadway speaking into his portable radio, Jackie Feldbaum beside him. We were all EMTs—emergency medical technicians.

Even though North Bend was growing like a tumor on a nuclear facilities inspector, it was still a small town, and cleaning up road accidents was just one of the taxes shouldered by any small-town fire department situated next to a major highway.

I-90 was unidirectional, so the impact speeds weren't as high as they might have been, the injuries not as severe. Including the two big trucks that started it, fourteen vehicles were involved. A heap of work for a mostly volunteer department, but Chief Newcastle ran the operation like the seasoned veteran he was.

Having retired as a captain after thirty years of working for Portland Fire, Newcastle's trademark at emergencies was remaining so cool and unencumbered you would think he was about to take a nap. Jackie, one of our volunteers, was already beginning to triage patients. A ten-year volunteer, she was one of those people who needed both hands while watching brain surgery on the cable medical channel, one for draining Budweiser after Budweiser and the other for taking notes just in case she might have to reenact the procedure in the field someday. We called her the Fire Plug behind her back, which wasn't a reference to her firefighting history so much as a testament to her figure.

Marching across the slippery road surface in her sure-grip Klondike boots, Jackie yelled like a crazed football mom. Before the night was over, she would videotape the wrecked vehicles for her home library. Her job tonight was to count up the casualties and begin assigning the injured to incoming personnel in order of priority. It was called triage, from the French word *trier*, to sort. Jackie might have been better at it if she hadn't been in the tavern when her pager fired, though we didn't find out she was half-crocked until later.

I guess I should have been suspicious when Newcastle asked me to check out the two big rigs and their drivers. That's when Jackie Feldbaum winked at me and said, "You might want to get the phone number of that second driver. She's just your type."

"What's my type?" I asked without stopping.

"Still breathing." Jackie's cigarette voice erupted into a guttural laugh like a dog coughing up a fish bone. Everybody in the department, volunteers and paid both, had their fun kidding me about women. I didn't mind.

The guy from the chicken truck was chasing chickens up and down the highway; he told me he didn't need medical attention. His truck was facing backward on the freeway, the trailer on its flank, he had blood running down his face, but he said he didn't need medical attention. Fine. I left him alone.

Somewhere on the long curve down the last of the foothills into North Bend, just after the point where the State Patrol liked to sit with their radar guns, the chicken truck had jackknifed into the middle lane, sideswiping the second truck and sweeping it down the icy highway like a push broom sweeping chestnuts. The driver of the chicken truck later said he thought everything was okay until he glanced out his window and noticed his own trailer passing him on the left. After that, all he remembered was screeching metal, squawking chickens, and feathers in his teeth.

Just to make the whole scene even more demented, some radical vegan activist appeared out of the line of idling cars and used a screwdriver to pry open a bunch of chicken cages. She released at least eighty birds to join those with their feet already frozen to the roadway before she was stopped by Jackie Feldbaum, who called her a chicken fucker. The Fire Plug had a mouth on her.

The second truck had skidded on the ice for several hundred yards, then, after spewing part of its load into the snow, came to rest on the edge of the field, the tractor upright, the trailer on its side, rear doors burst open.

Inside the cockeyed trailer, I found a young woman shouting at a trio of escaped chickens. There were the Bibles, several bales of comic books, some jeans that had spilled out of their boxes, and a tacky substance we later identified as Coca-Cola syrup. Most of the truck drivers we saw coming through North Bend could spit out the window and clear two lanes of traffic; Holly was different.

"You need help?" I asked, realizing that I'd gone from a scene of public cacophony to one of utmost intimacy, just the two of us in this echoing cubicle. My God, she had beautiful eyes.

"Yes, I need help."

"You hurt?"

"No."

"That blood on your knees?"

She looked down at her jeans and said, "I'm okay. There must be people who're really hurt. Anybody killed?"

"No."

"Thank God for that."

"You driving this rig?"

"Yes."

"You got an MSDS?"

She handed me the Material Safety Data Sheet. There was nothing dangerous on board.

When I got closer, she stuck out her hand and said, "Holly Riggs."

"Jim Swope." As we shook hands, our eyes met in the quivering light from our respective flashlights. I was wearing heavy firefighting gloves; hers were made of goatskin. Still, there was something provocative, almost sensual, about the handshake.

Holly Riggs had short strawberry-blond hair, an upturned nose with a wash of freckles across it, sparkly eyes she enhanced with green contacts, and a tiny waist that accentuated what Chief Newcastle later called her childbearing hips. At five-two, she was more than a foot shorter than me.

"I suppose you're going to take her out and ruin her life," Newcastle joked that night at the accident site, when he found out I'd gotten her phone number.

"I've never ruined anyone's life," I said. "Besides, I'm not even sure I'll call. It just happened after we started talking that we have a lot in common."

"I just bet you do," Newcastle joked. "Have a lot in common. You have a lot in common with every good-looking woman you've ever met." Newcastle laughed until he was sick with it. Sometimes I thought he was going to have a heart attack laughing at me. Nobody liked a joke more than Harry Newcastle. I didn't mind the ribbing. I really didn't.

He was wrong about me, though. To tell you the truth, I had the worst luck when it came to women. Think about this—three years ago my wife cleaned out our bank account and ran away with the mayor. To make it worse, everybody in town knew about it before I did.

3. A BRIEF AFFAIR OF ALMOST NO CONSEQUENCE

It took almost two hours that night to get traffic rolling.

Ambulances and extra aid units came from Issaquah and Bellevue, respectively fifteen miles and twenty miles up the icebound highway. We ended up with thirteen volunteers and four paid guys, seven ambulances, two aid cars, four tow trucks, six State Patrol vehicles, dozens of road flares, and two miles of irate drivers backed up toward Snoqualmie Pass. It was almost twelve-thirty before the last of the injured were on their way home or to a local hospital. I took Holly aside and bandaged her knees, rolling her pant legs up and taping four-by-fours neatly in place. She said the way I worked reminded her of her sister, who was a doctor.

Toward the end, I got the brilliant idea that when we finished with our patients we might all hop in the back of Holly's truck and help straighten it out.

Shuffled into the mix of comic books, Bibles, Levi's, and Coca-Cola canisters we found the occasional escaped or liberated fryer. Six of us assisted in the cleanup: myself, Stan Beebe, Chief Newcastle, Jackie Feldbaum, Karrie Haston, and Joel McCain.

Afterward I was surprised when Holly agreed to have coffee with me in a nearby Truck Town restaurant while the wreckers righted her truck. But I guess I'm always surprised when an attractive woman agrees to spend time with me.

As we walked across the frozen field toward my pickup, I couldn't help thinking this was almost like a date, the two of us walking hand in hand, the moonlight, the crunch of snow under our boots, the dentist-drill sound of tires spinning on the icy highway behind us.

We tried to ignore all the dead or dying chickens, some already flattened in the eastbound lanes.

Holly was as pleasant as a tropical breeze. She was twenty-eight, six years younger than me, had never been married, and two years earlier had escaped a dead-end relationship and hitchhiked to Washington State from California to learn to drive a truck. She'd been doing short-haul mostly, but this trip, one of her longest, had originated in Tennessee.

I noticed when she took her parka off the sight of her strawberry-blond hair turned heads in the restaurant. I notice things like that.

Newcastle could joke all he wanted, but Holly and I did have a lot in common. We'd both immigrated to Washington from California—she originally from Ohio. I'd been raised here and then fled to San Diego, where I ended up in the army. We'd both come out of long-term relationships that ended when we were deserted. During an airport layover, her boyfriend ran away to New Jersey to join a religious cult. Like I already said, my ex ran away with the mayor, cleaning out our bank account and selling our car on her way out of town. Holly's boyfriend had slipped her engagement ring off her finger while she slept. My wife had emptied our younger daughter's piggy bank. Stealing from her own child was what convinced me she was back on drugs.

In the three years she'd been gone, I'd heard from Lorie only a handful of times, twice to ask for bail money and always on Christmas Eve, when she wanted to speak to the girls.

Neither of us had a backup chute. Holly's parents had died in a traffic accident. My father was in a nursing home. The last time I heard from my mother, she was on a fly-through from Cape Horn to Japan with a flaxen-haired suitor twenty-five years her junior in tow. I had no brothers or sisters. Holly's only sibling practiced medicine in Ohio and was so full of herself, Holly was lucky to get a phone call on her birthday.

"Gosh," she said. "I can't believe how much we have in common."

"It is amazing."

Holly and I spoke on the phone a few times in March and then got together in April, dating off and on for about a month and a half. She ended up with the funny notion we were going to get married somewhere down the line. Odd how two people who'd started out sharing so much could have gotten their signals crossed like that.

DAY ONE

4. I'M A RAT BASTARD

Okay. I admit it.

I'm a bastard.

On Monday that day in June when people saw me sprinting through the fire station, they thought so, too. Everybody did. I'd spotted Holly's red Pontiac in the bank parking lot catty-corner from the fire station. I hadn't fled because I was a jerk. God knows I'm not a jerk. It was just that I didn't like being stalked by a former girlfriend.

The truth of the matter was, Holly had a whole roster of psychological baggage she kept trying to push off on me, and even though I'd last seen her a month earlier, I didn't have the nerve to face her.

Not today.

North Bend Fire and Rescue had been going through some tough times, and Holly was like a disease you thought you'd kicked, only to wake up in the morning with the symptoms back in place. I couldn't suffer through another of those interminable conversations. The last had been a never-ending phone call during which I'd fallen asleep. Okay, I guess that sounds bad, but you had to be there. See, I was really just too nice. Maybe I should have told her to forget the *friends* thing, that we simply weren't suited for each other, that I didn't *ever* want to see her again. But, tell me, how could I do a thing like that?

If I'd been smart, I would have gone through the empty apparatus bay where we keep the station's gym equipment, but I dashed past the watch office, blurting out instructions to Karrie Haston, the newest paid member of our rapidly shrinking department. "Tell her anything. Tell her I'm out of town for a week."

"Tell who?"

"You'll see."

"No way I'm going to lie for you again, Jim," said Karrie. Moments later I heard the two women's voices and I knew that, despite her instincts, Karrie was following my directions.

Upstairs I concealed myself alongside a window in the station's living quarters and waited for Holly to leave.

*　*　*

It was true. I was a bastard.

I didn't learn about the literal aspect of my bastardy until I was twenty-seven and my father, or the man I thought was my father, returned from a ten-year sojourn in Arizona determined to patch up our relationship. You had to give him points for trying, even if he was the one who'd mucked up our relationship in the first place. He'd just buried his third wife. It was the last of four marriages, including two to my mother.

One of the benefits of having my father nearby after so many years was that he told me all sorts of things about our history I had forgotten or never knew. The biggest surprise was discovering he'd married my mother when she was eight and a half months pregnant—to save her soul and bring her to Jesus, who died on the cross to pay for her sins, my father said—and that he never knew who my actual father was, never cared, never asked.

Until then I'd had no reason not to believe James Swope, Sr., wasn't my biological father; I'd lived with him until I was sixteen, and neither he nor my mother had ever given a hint we weren't related. Despite the fact that we'd lived all those years in the commune at Six Points when I was growing up, my parents reiterated the nuclear family mantra ad nauseam, reminding me how lucky I was not to be the spawn of a divorce, how important it was to stick with the religion of my birth, how happy we all were.

Even though from my earliest days I'd suspected there was something wrong at the core of our little triumvirate, it wasn't until I ran away from home and lied my way into Uncle Sam's army that I began to realize the true strangeness of our family. My mother, who, by her own admission, had endured a misspent youth, had also, ironically, run away from home at age sixteen. Hidebound by a vague ambition that seemed to have fizzled in middle age, my father had taken a more traditional route and graduated from the University of Washington Engineering School.

After the news sank in, I was able to look back over my life and see a thousand little pinpricks of light where before there had been only confusion and darkness. I ended up tall and, some said, handsome, while James Swope, Sr., was medium height with knobby features that might have been chipped off the side of an old apple tree. That alone should have given me a clue. I'd always thought my father hated me—if truth be known, my mother, too—as much as any father could hate a son while telling him he loved him, and now I believed I knew why. Illegitimacy was the spark in the motor of that dislike. Illegitimacy propelled those late-night quarrels between my parents. Illegitimacy was the hoarfrost on our relationship from day one.

A few years ago, when my mother showed up at the airport on her way through the Northwest, dragging around her latest bleach-blond ex–surf bum, it became obvious from the far-off look in her eyes that she didn't want to chew the fat with me over our history. The upshot of our conversation was that whatever had taken place in her life before she met my father was now locked away forever.

When I said I had a right to know who my real father was, Mother tossed a flag of dyed-black hair away from her face, sighed, and said, "They say a human body replaces all its cells every seven years. I'm not the woman I was then. I'm not even the woman I was when I left your father. You're *my* son. That's what matters. You know that, don't you?"

"I just want to know who my father is."

"God is your father."

"So it was an immaculate conception?"

"Don't be insolent. I told you all I'm going to tell."

It was that simple.

I was a bastard.

Moreover, I got the queasy feeling had she dropped a hook into the waters of memory for a name, she wouldn't be able to produce one, that I was the by-product of some impulsive heated liaison in the backseat of somebody's father's Chevrolet or the back room at a party. Mother had been wild in her youth. Everybody knew that. What nobody ever knew was how wild.

There were only three of us on duty that day late in June: myself; Karrie, who was downstairs telling lies for me; and Stan Beebe, who turned out was lurking in the shadows on a bunk not ten feet away. I hadn't noticed him and jumped when he spoke. "Woman trouble?" he barked.

"No. Of course not. Why do you say that?"

"Because A: you *always* have woman trouble, and B: you look like you're about to shit a brick."

"I do not."

"Do not what? Look like you're about to shit a brick or always have woman trouble?"

"What makes you think it's a woman?"

"What else would make you so nervous?"

"Come on, Stan."

"I'm tellin' the truth. You need to see yourself the way you are so you can change."

When I looked down at my hands, I detected a slight tremor. It was the weirdest sensation, one I couldn't remember feeling before. My hands had begun trembling the moment I spotted the Pontiac.

Jamming both fists into my uniform pants pockets to quiet them, I peered out the window. The Pontiac was still baking under the June sun in the bank parking lot.

"Who's chasin' you? Suzanne?"

"I told you I'm not going with her anymore."

"The other Suzanne? The one you met at the river?"

"It's the truck driver."

"The short-hauler? Kelly?"

"Holly."

"I liked Holly. You never should have dumped her."

"I didn't dump her. It was mutual. Or just about."

"She carrying a pair of tin snips?"

"What would she need those for?"

Beebe laughed. "Sooner or later one of 'em's going to take your family jewels. Call 'em spoils of war."

A few minutes later I saw the Pontiac door closing. She'd walked from the station to the car while I was talking to Stan. Unable to see past the reflections on her windshield, I ducked back behind the window.

It was over, but she couldn't accept that. I hoped she wasn't here to tell me she was pregnant. Just when you think you've got your life straightened out, up jumps the devil with a dead rabbit in his hand. I already had two perfectly legitimate kids and, God knows, we certainly didn't need any more bastards like me in the family.

"You think we're jinxed?" Beebe asked from the bunk. He had his hands behind his head, legs crossed on top of the bedspread.

"I'm beginning to think *I'm* jinxed. At least where women are concerned."

"No. I mean the fire department?"

"There's no such thing as a jinx."

"You just said *you* were jinxed."

"Well, there's no such thing."

"I could make a case that we're jinxed bad. That we're going to die. All of us."

"Everybody's going to die."

"No, I'm talking about here in this department. This summer."

"You serious?"

"Within the next ... say ... few weeks. I mean you, me, Karrie, maybe even Click and Clack."

"That's crazy."

"That's what Marsha keeps telling me."

"She's right."

"No she isn't. I'm dying. I got a syndrome."

I turned from the window. "You serious?"

"Serious as a heart attack."

"You seen a doctor?"

"Three of 'em. Brashears and the two specialists he sent me to."

"What did they say?"

"Said something's going on. Some sort of syndrome. They don't know what. They ran tests. I'll get the results next week."

"There you go."

"There I don't go. By next week I'll be dead."

"You can't know that."

"But I do know it. They told the Fire Plug she was all right, too."

"Jackie had a car wreck."

It was true that North Bend Fire and Rescue had been suffering a string of bad luck. A month ago Chief Newcastle had set out on a week-long solo hike, trying to get in shape for an ascent of Mount Rainier he was planning with a group of volunteers. Eventually the rangers found his pickup at a trailhead in the Alpine Lakes Wilderness. Four days after that, a quartet of hikers found Newcastle's body facedown alongside a spur trail near Painter Creek, just below Icicle Ridge. Except for some small animal bites, there wasn't a mark on him. He'd been fifty-six. The autopsy concluded he'd died of hypothermia. A close friend and coworker dies sudden like that, it scares you.

A few days after the funeral, Jackie Feldbaum managed to drive her Miata sports car under the rear of a tractor-trailer rig on I-90, where she missed being decapitated by inches. She was now living—if you could call it living—in room 107 at Alpine Estates Nursing Home.

Ten days after Newcastle's funeral and seven days after Jackie's accident, Joel McCain, one of our other permanent-position firefighters, fell off his roof while pressure-washing moss off his shingles. Joel's family had been keeping him under wraps for the last month. I couldn't fathom the reasoning, though Beebe, who was friendly with the family, explained they were Christian Scientists and didn't want any "mortal thought" to keep them from a "demonstration."

"Three down, three to go," Beebe said. "Newcastle, Joel, and the Fire Plug. You, me, and Karrie. We're next."

"Ridiculous. Newcastle probably had a CVA. And Jackie . . . you know she drank more in a week than you or I ever put down in a year. She's lucky she didn't hurt somebody else. Joel never was good with heights. He'll be back."

"Joel's not coming back."

"His wife said he was."

"One of the volunteers ran into his brother-in-law in the store. He said Joel can't even follow cartoons on the TV. No way he's coming back. Trust me."

"That's just a rumor."

"Maybe."

Beebe had a tendency to blow things out of proportion. On top of that, I'd noticed when things began to go wrong he tended to slip into a vortex of self-pity, his mood precipitating more problems than the events spurring it.

"I'm scared," he said.

"Of what?"

"Of falling off a roof. Dying in the woods. Crashing my car. Drowning in the tub. Think about it. They all lost control. All three of them."

"You're right about that."

"Damn right."

Stan Beebe was one of the few African Americans in the valley. These days we had urban commuters coming out our ears, but not too many years ago the town had been primarily made up of forest workers and their families, many of whom migrated to the Northwest after the timber ran out in the Southeast, bringing their Southern redneck attitudes with them. Crackers, Newcastle called them. Beebe managed to win them over to a man.

Beebe was a big man, the color of dark chocolate, round through the chest, with biceps like ham hocks and forearms thicker than a pecker-wood's neck; he routinely did repeats on the bench press downstairs with four hundred pounds. Occasionally he overheard a rude comment or got a look from one of the local crackers, but he was so good-natured, if it bothered him he never let anyone know, although a year ago Chief New-castle sent him to Dr. Brashears for what he described as clinical depression. Beebe came back with a prescription for Zoloft and seemed better after that.

As titular head of the fire department, it would be my duty to send him back for more treatment if this current depression he seemed to have fallen into became incapacitating. Even if you weren't listening to what he said, you could hear it in his voice.

"Jim?" he said. "Anything happens, I want you to look after my wife and kids."

"Nothing's going to happen."

Before we could finish, the bell hit and the pagers on our belts fired. We jogged down the stairs to the apparatus floor. Normally there were five responders in the station, but the medic unit had driven to Overlake Hospital with a patient, so there were only three of us.

Although most of the other small towns in the area contracted their fire services from the county, North Bend still ran its own department, the mainstay of which had always been the volunteers. Currently there were only six paid members.

Beebe drove the aid car while I got behind the wheel of the pumper, Karrie, who was still in her probationary period, alongside me. Technically, with our two senior officers, Harry Newcastle and Joel McCain, out of the picture, the mayor and I were running the department, but the mayor seemed uninterested, so I was running things myself.

North Bend Fire and Rescue had always been shorthanded, but these days we were limping along like a three-legged dog, depending heavily on the cadre of volunteers Newcastle had recruited and nurtured during the five years he'd been in command.

The report for our alarm came in as "man choking."

5. EVERYBODY KNOWS BRAIN DEATH FROM LACK OF OXYGEN OCCURS IN FOUR TO SIX MINUTES

Chief Newcastle's oft-repeated dictum on response speed through town was clear: "There's no point in killing a carful of kids on your way to a Dumpster fire." Everybody followed the precept except Click and Clack, who were usually too wired on caffeine, adrenaline, and do-goodism to slow down.

Siren whirring, we lumbered through traffic as we headed for a small subdivision just east of town on property that, until ten years ago, had been a golf course. Bulldoze the flora and fauna and slap up houses, bring in new citizens by the busload, sell them a car and two trucks apiece, and pave any greenery that's left. It was the standard urban recipe. No planning. Just cram us rats in until we're all giving each other the bird at every four-way stop in town.

As soon as the house number came across the radio from the dispatcher, I said, "Joel McCain lives in that cul-de-sac."

Karrie looked at me. "That his house number?"

"Couldn't tell you."

Karrie was a tall, slender young woman who had decided to become a firefighter when she was six years old, after taking a school field trip into downtown Seattle, where she'd spotted a woman riding a fire rig.

"You realize your girlfriend is following us," Karrie said.

"What girlfriend?"

"How many girlfriends do you have chasing you around town?" I glanced into the tall rearview mirrors on either side of the cab but couldn't see beyond the boxy aid car behind us. "She's back there."

"Don't worry. She'll go away."

"How much do you want to bet?"

Watching the town slide past, I tried to let it go. What the heck did Holly want now? I decided she either was pregnant or had a bug. Not from me, though. Not a sexually transmitted disease, at any rate. I was clean on that score. However, it was just possible she was pregnant. On top of all my other bills, all I needed was a child support payment. Christ, maybe she'd come to tell me *she* had given *me* a bug.

To my way of thinking, North Bend was one of the ugliest little towns in the state, a prime example of what happens in a municipality when what little vision there is becomes polluted with second and third and fourth opinions bought and paid for by developers working duplicitous schemes they'd already honed to perfection on other communities, schemes designed to pull the wool over the eyes of planning boards and all those small-town politicians willing to dabble with the devil to expand their tax base. Controlled growth, they called it. Nobody ever had the nerve or the brains to ask for or think about zero growth. Developers knew they could wear down the protest groups with endless "dialogues." Talk was good. Keep 'em talking. Eventually each new project broke ground before we all realized we'd lost another battle.

Along with the fairly recent blight of suburban sprawl, our town was pockmarked with oases of backwardness from the days when everyone was a logger or the offspring of a logger and locals felt their birthright was to park on their front lawns, burn unseasoned wood in their woodstoves until the town was murky with the stink, and shoot their neighbor's dog with .22 shorts if he barked too much.

In the piecemeal central business area, we had a Bavarian motif on a Chinese restaurant and across from that a condemned building. We had a gas station converted into a coffeehouse across from a car dealership on the main drag. There was a minimart service station proudly displaying a hundred feet of blank wall to the main street, even more proudly approved by the planning board. We had planters in the middle of North Bend Way, designed years ago, but not built until traffic was already so bad the loss of the center lane jammed all the intersections.

Half a mile away on the floodplain of the South Fork was the Nintendo factory and the South Fork interchange with an outlet factory mall, McDonald's, Taco Time, Arby's, gas stations, and minimarts sucking in skiers, hikers, and rock climbers off the freeway. The outlet mall brought ten thousand cars a day. Busloads of old gummers showed up every day at eleven to shop for bargains. Local burglaries and car breakins had skyrocketed.

"It's Joel's house, all right," Karrie said as we pulled up.

We'd been here before. It was a house Joel could ill afford on a firefighter's salary, though he managed with the extra money from his wife's job as a legal secretary in Seattle. More money came in from his wife's retired mother, who had moved in with them after her husband died. I knew this house. At the fire station Christmas party this past year, Karrie and I spent an hour downstairs on the couch in the dark, an episode we were both trying to forget. I never knew why I did things like that.

"You think it's Joel?" Karrie asked. "The radio report said man choking."

"Gotta be somebody else. Joel likes to chew his food."

Joel's mother-in-law, a slightly more rickety version of his slender wife, answered the door in a faded housedress and sturdy black shoes with thick soles of the type I hadn't seen since the last time I was in Sunday school. Wringing her hands, she led us under high ceilings and past an open staircase that led up to the second story. The McCains didn't have children, so the furniture was clean, not a stick out of place, three lazy cats lounging about.

The old woman's hands fluttered about her head as she spoke. "All I did was give him a little slice of apple. A Braeburn. When I came back in the room, he was like this. I thought he would like the taste. They're from New Zealand."

Our old compadre was in a motorized hospital bed, the section under his knees and back elevated, though he looked a whole lot less than comfortable. He was thinner than the last time I'd seen him, his face a blue-black color, mottled with beard growth, eyes bulging, neck veins distended. His jaw was open and he was gasping for air. When I shone a light down his throat, I could just make out a foreign object next to his tonsils.

He was barely getting enough air to support life.

I put my finger down his throat and did a finger sweep the way we'd been taught. "He was okay before you gave him the apple?" I asked over my shoulder.

"Fine. I was reading to him from the Scientific Statement of Being."

A finger sweep wasn't going to work.

Stan and I hauled McCain off the bed, and Stan turned him around, gripped him from behind, pressed his fists together under his sternum, and compressed violently three times. On the last compression an object flew out of McCain's mouth past my shoulder and skidded across the floor like a hockey puck. A slice of Braeburn. From New Zealand. Sweet and tangy at the same time. Eager to conceal incriminating evidence, the old woman knelt quickly and put it in the pocket of her housedress.

It was about the size you would feed a plow horse.

Now, slumped in Beebe's thick arms, Joel was gasping for air as if he would never get enough. When it became clear that he wasn't physically capable of getting his feet beneath him, Beebe, Karrie, and I laid him back on the bed. We tugged his pajama bottoms back up and put a nasal cannula on his face and administered 0_2. The pajama bottoms bothered all three of us; what bothered us even more was that he was wearing an adult diaper under them. He hadn't moved a limb on his own since we got there, hadn't twitched a finger, hadn't said squat. He hadn't stopped drooling, and the damp bib tied around his neck told us he wasn't going to. Karrie straightened it and patted some of his hair into place, as if she might mother him into normalcy.

"Hey, Joel," I said amiably. "What the hell? You're not supposed to swallow the whole thing. Just a bite at a time. How you doin', buddy?"

No answer. No eye contact.

The setup was Spartan, to say the least. The hospital bed was in the center of the living room and had a rack over it with bars for the patient to use when repositioning himself, though I gotta tell you I couldn't see any evidence that Joel had the capacity to use them. Beside the bed was a single straight-backed chair and, alongside that, a small table. No phone, radio, television, or magazines. No flowers, nothing to indicate it was a sickroom except the hospital bed, the lack of furniture, and, of course, the goggle-eyed patient.

There was a single item on the table next to the chair, a small book with a leather cover, *Science and Health with Key to the Scriptures* by Mary Baker Eddy. The book was open, a purple ribbon marking the page, several paragraphs limned with blue chalk, as if they'd been read repeatedly.

"Let's get a BP and a rate," I said. I called for a medic unit on our portable radio. The dispatcher confirmed my request and stated the medics would be responding from Bellevue. Normally a choking victim came around as soon as the obstruction was removed, but there was something wrong here.

Brain death from lack of oxygen occurs in four to six minutes. We all knew that. It had taken us four minutes to get here.

"How long was he choking before you called?" I asked.

Joel's mother-in-law wrung her hands and stared at me. "I don't know." She'd been making a point of not looking at Joel, as if not looking at him would make things better. "We'd been praying together, and I thought I saw an improvement, so I went into the kitchen and peeled that apple. I gave him a bite, and then the phone rang and I went back to the kitchen to answer it. When I came back, he was like you saw."

"And you called us right away?"

"I prayed first."

"How long did that take?"

"We said the Scientific Statement of Being a couple of times."

"How long did that take?"

"A couple of minutes."

"We? You said *we* were praying?"

"Joel and I."

"He was able to pray with you?" Karrie asked.

"It was a silent prayer." She was a diminutive woman, maybe a hundred fifteen pounds.

She burst into tears when Beebe said, "What'd you do, push it down his throat with a broom handle?"

"It's all right." I put my arm around her heaving shoulders and shot Stan a look. "What we need to know is how long from the time he started choking until you called us."

"I don't know. It might have been five minutes."

Five minutes added to our four-minute response time was enough for some serious brain damage. But then, he'd been getting some air all along or he wouldn't have been conscious when we arrived, although what we'd seen when we got here and were seeing now was a pretty relaxed definition of conscious.

"What's the history here?" I asked. "He on any medication?"

"No. Of course not. Joel doesn't take medicine. We don't believe in it."

"So why's he in bed? Why were you feeding him?"

"He can't eat by himself."

"From falling off the roof?"

"I guess."

"He has a head injury?"

"The doctors don't know what he's got. Doesn't that tell you something about material medicine? Even the doctors can't do anything."

"We heard he got banged up pretty good from the fall."

"No. He only had a few scratches."

"So why's he wearing a diaper?"

"Mary likes it on him. It's easier to clean up."

"So he's incontinent?"

"It's been a difficult demonstration. We thought he would have a healing before this."

"He's been this way for a month?" I asked, picking up Joel's right arm. It fell limply when I dropped it.

She nodded.

"Jesus," I said.

Stan Beebe was taking Joel's blood pressure on his other arm. "What'd the doctors say was wrong with him?" Beebe asked.

"As I said before, they didn't tell us."

"Could have been an ischemic attack," I said. "Could have been a lot of things. Head injury? Spinal column? They must have said something. They weren't keeping him in the hospital just to jack up the bill. These days they release patients as soon as they can."

"The doctors told us we'd have to wait to find out what was wrong. That was when Mary and I decided to bring him home and rely on Christian Science."

"He's been like this for a month?" Karrie said. "Why didn't you tell somebody?"

The old woman, who was crying again, didn't reply.

I got on the radio and advised the medic unit what we had. Near as I could tell, Joel was brain-dead. Had been for a month. The doctors couldn't fix him, and the Christian Scientists were feeding him apples.

The old woman told us they'd hired a nurse but that she'd been called away and this was her first time alone with him. "Mary told me nothing but juice, but I was just so sure he was better, I guess I pushed things. That apple was just mortal mind trying to stop the healing. It was never part of the real Joel. It was the Adam apple."

"Didn't come out of there like the Adam apple," Beebe said. "Came out of there like a cannonball. We should have worn eye protection."

"The real Joel is the perfect son of God. Always has been and always will be."

Beebe was hovering over Joel now, begging him to move his hand, a leg, anything. Mary was the godmother of Stan's youngest child. Stan and Joel were both adherents of minority religions, Joel a Christian Scientist, Stan a Seventh-Day Adventist. I'd kept out of their frequent dialogues on religion, although there was plenty I might have brought to the table.

Beebe couldn't get a blood pressure, tried twice more, and handed the ears to Karrie. It wasn't like Stan to fumble a blood pressure, and I could tell he felt bad about it. Tears jeweled the corners of his dark eyes when he handed Karrie the stethoscope.

"Look at his hands," said Beebe, presenting his own for comparison. Joel's looked as if they'd been dipped in wax. Beebe's looked similar, though because of his dark skin, they were a slightly different hue.

"Chapped?" I asked.

"Guess again," Beebe said.

The medics showed up, looked Joel over, phoned his doctor, and agreed with what we'd already concluded. Joel wasn't any different this afternoon than he had been yesterday afternoon.

The medics had just driven away and we were putting our aid kits away when the red Pontiac pulled up in the cul-de-sac.

The driver of the Pontiac got out and stalked around the front of the car, her movements looking so much like those of an assassin, I actually caught myself checking to see if she had a gun. When somebody walks toward you that deliberately, you're usually in some sort of trouble.

"You asshole," she said. "You dirty coward."

Stan Beebe was on the other side of the rig. I could hear him chuckling.

6. SISTERS OF JILTED WOMEN CASTRATING MEN

Until she was ten feet away, I believed the woman coming at me like a missile was Holly Riggs, my former lover. I also believed I knew what she was going to say.

That I was a jerk. That I'd behaved badly. That I deserved her hatred. Most of which was no doubt true.

Although this woman was trim, short, pretty, and impeccably groomed, she was not Holly. For one thing, she was feistier. For another, she had a mouth on her like a snakebit sailor.

The fine lines around her eyes and brow suggested she was around thirty, maybe three or four years younger than me, the same strawberry-blond hair as Holly, though I'd never seen Holly band hers into a ponytail. I couldn't figure out what she was doing with Holly's car until her pale dusty-blue eyes focused angrily on me.

"You bastard," she said.

"Don't turn on the charm machine just for me."

"I saw you running away from me in the parking lot."

"You must be Stephanie, Holly's sister." It was a stupid remark, given their resemblance and the fact that she was driving Holly's car, but it was all I could think of.

She'd moved closer now. We were almost touching, hate emanating off her like steam off a racehorse. To make matters worse, she was wearing the same brand of perfume as Holly. You can't blame me for thinking of sex when I smelled it.

"I didn't run."

"The hell you didn't. You thought I was Holly."

"But you're not." This was so typical of me. One incredibly scintillating comment after another.

"You thought I was. You led her on and then didn't have the decency to admit what you'd done. This innocent act of yours doesn't surprise me. She said you could be dumber than a bag of hammers when you wanted."

"Holly said that?"

"You don't even want to know what Holly said."

"What do you want?"

"I guess I came to see what a dirtbag looks like."

"Okay. You've seen me." She didn't move, just stood close and stared into my eyes. After a few moments, I said, "I didn't lead anyone on. And I don't see what business it is of yours anyway. Holly and I dated for a while. Then we broke up. People break up all the time."

For a moment, my words gave her pause. I wasn't particularly quick-witted and almost never thought up a reply to this sort of thing until my opponent was long gone, but, damn it, she didn't know anything about my relationship with Holly.

By now Karrie was laughing on the far side of the rig along with Beebe.

"She thought you wanted to marry her."

"It was never even on my mind. I mean, think about it. Who gets married after a month? You know as well as I do, one person in a relationship always takes things more seriously than the other. Believe me, I never did anything to make it turn out that way. I felt as bad about the breakup as Holly."

"You think so?"

"Look, I'm on duty and we're not exactly having the best day around here. Why don't you come back to the station and we'll talk over coffee? Out of the sun."

"It's taken me all morning to corner you. I'm not going to let you slip away now."

"Come back to the station and we'll talk. How is Holly?" When I saw her eyes relax, I said, "Where is she?"

"As if you cared."

"I've always wanted her to be happy. Holly's a sweet person. She deserves the best."

"Which was definitely not you."

"I never pretended it was."

She waited a few beats and continued. "When was the last time you saw my sister?"

"I don't know. Somewhere around the first of May."

"When was the last time you spoke?"

"She called once after that."

"Try six times. She called six times after that. She caught you home twice, and the other calls were never returned."

"There was nothing left to say."

"You don't know where this is leading, do you?"

"No."

"Holly said you weren't too bright."

More laughter from behind the truck.

Stephanie was a little taller than Holly—prettier, angrier, crueler. Even at her angriest and most heartbroken, Holly had never shouted at me. Holly was a whiner, a weeper, and, in bed, a moaner—the best sex ever—but one thing she never did and never would do was make a scene in public.

Across the street, two of McCain's neighbors came outside, attracted no doubt by the flashing red lights and our large lime-green truck. "You're even more of a coward than I thought you were," said Holly's sister, who then climbed into the Pontiac and left.

You can understand I didn't like getting braced by this pugnacious woman while two of my coworkers hid on the other side of the rig sniggering. I was a firefighter and had been for twelve years. My family and friends thought of me as a regular guy. There were even times on the job when people thought I'd displayed some bravery. Still, it was going to be a while before they stopped joking about this around the station.

When I climbed into the rig next to Karrie, my hands were trembling.

7. WELCOME TO THE CASTRATI

It was after dinner and I was driving to Tacoma, switching the truck radio between talk shows to keep myself distracted, when I noticed my hands were trembling again.

It had happened three times today, and each time Stephanie Riggs had been at the root of it, which made me wonder about her. You meet a woman and your hands start shaking, was that the same as chemistry? There were a lot of reasons why nothing would come of our meeting tonight. First of all, she was Holly's sister. Second, she was a ball-buster. The original ice queen. And the worst part of it was that she was a whole lot smarter than I was.

My standard operating procedure was to shun smart women. It only made sense.

North Bend to Tacoma. An hour each way, the two-way trek would consume the meat of the evening. It was Monday night and I had to work again in the morning, had been putting in seven days a week since Joel McCain's accident, and I didn't need additional distractions. Neither did my daughters, Britney and Allyson, who were used to having me home in the evenings and begged me not to make this trip.

I was retracing the same route I'd used for a month in the spring when I was seeing Holly, who lived in Tacoma and who, from the beginning, had required more attention than a naughty kitten.

With luck I would get back in time to play a board game with the girls. Currently they were hot on Monopoly, which, for them, was a blood sport. It was an unusual game when I didn't go bankrupt first, rarer still when either of my lovable little connivers showed me any mercy.

The phone call had come while I was preparing dinner. "Who?" I said.

"Stephanie Riggs."

"Oh, yes. Weren't you the one called me a bastard? No, wait. That might have been the lady at the bank. I get confused."

"I called to apologize."

"For telling me I was a bastard or for making me a laughingstock at work?"

Britney looked up at me with her brown eyes and said, "Somebody said a bad word." I kissed the top of her head and put my finger to my lips.

"I'm sorry for all of that. I've had a difficult visit, and I'm scheduled to fly back home day after tomorrow."

"Gee, we're going to miss you."

"You're not making this easy."

"Sorry about that. I had a tough day. I met the original she-bitch from hell."

The line was silent for a moment. "Okay. I deserved that. I was wondering if you could come to Tacoma so we could talk."

"We're talking right *now*."

"I'd come back up there, but I'm stuck at work. There are some issues I need to go over with you. In person. Please?"

"I don't even know you, lady."

"You knew my sister."

"That's over with."

"Just please come?"

"She going to be there?"

"My sister won't even know you were in town."

"Okay. Sure. Maybe we'll videotape it for when I have friends at the house. Some of my pals missed your remarks this afternoon."

"This morning when I saw you, it surprised me. Holly said you were a nice guy."

"I thought she said I was a bastard."

"I'm so *not* like today. I couldn't even believe I said those things."

"Neither could I."

Despite everything I was feeling, her conversation had the hint of promise to it. I couldn't tell whether she was flirting or I was only imagining that she was flirting. In the past I'd thought women were coming on to me when they weren't. As outlandish as it may sound to you, I found myself entertaining lascivious visions of a summertime fling with my ex-girlfriend's sister. Was this an invitation, as in *invitation*, or was this a setup so her favorite rugby team could knock me down and put the boots to me?

"You really took it well, I thought, considering. You were a darling." The word oozed out of her mouth like maple syrup. *Darling*. Next to *cute* or *sweet* it was one of the major tip-off words that a woman liked you. I didn't know much, but I knew that.

"I suppose I can drive down," I said, mentally kicking myself for being a sap.

"I'm at Tacoma General until midnight. On the third floor."

As I was on my way out the door, Allyson said, "Is she foxy, Dad?"

"This is business."

"Oh, yeah? So her house is on fire?"

"Okay, she's foxy."

"That's what I thought." The girls exchanged looks while the baby-sitter put on a mood like a coat. My girls had solved the conundrum I couldn't solve: why I was wasting my time.

All day I'd fumed over Stephanie's verbal assault. It didn't help that Click and Clack had gotten wind of it—Ian Hjorth and Ben Arden reporting to work that afternoon to take up the slack after Stan Beebe went home sick, sick of heart over our friend Joel. Click and Clack commentated on my love life with remarks that alternated between the lewd and the hilariously lewd.

Normally they were a positive addition to the atmosphere, poking fun at everything, including themselves. But their favorite target was my love life. To hear them rehash it, my tongue-lashing at the hands of Holly's sister was the funniest thing ever. At one point, Ben got a sympathetic look on his face, turned to me, and sang to a melody of his own invention, "Somebody got a spanking." Ian laughed so hard, his knees buckled. I suppose after what we'd learned about Joel McCain, our department needed a diversion.

Downtown Tacoma sat on a hill overlooking Commencement Bay. On top of the hill, a block or so from Wright Park and fronting Martin Luther King Junior Way, stood Tacoma General Hospital.

It was almost eight o'clock and still light out when I approached the nurses' station on three. A barrel-chested woman with eyebrows plucked too thin gave me a questioning look from behind the counter, then reached over to thumb the intercom. She drew her hand back, glanced past my shoulder, and said, "There she is."

She wore clogs and hospital scrubs with a stethoscope draped around her neck, her hair shoulder-length and loose. She wasn't wearing a name tag, and it was a split second before I remembered how proud Holly had been of her older sister.

"You're a doctor," I said.

"Don't act so stunned." Any hint of flirtation in her demeanor had vanished.

"Holly said you worked back east somewhere."

"Ohio. I've been volunteering here for a few weeks."

"Terrific. Most people on vacation would never think of volunteering."

"No, I suppose they wouldn't."

Holly had been proud of her older sister, said she was smart as a whip, had graduated from high school a year early and did the same in college, even though she had to work the whole time because their parents were dead. Their mother died of cancer. Six weeks later Holly came home from middle school and found their father hanging by his neck in the garage. Stephanie had been in her last year of high school.

Turning away from me, she said, "I have a patient to check on. Come along?"

"You sure it's okay?" She walked away without replying.

When I caught her, she said, "Funny how all hospitals are pretty much alike. Don't you think? You get inside and you could be in New York or Toronto or Timbuktu."

The breeze from our pace brought tears to her eyes. She stopped at a patient's room, glanced at the chart on the wall, pushed the door open with her fingertips, and went in. After a moment alone in the hallway, I followed.

It was a small room with one bed, the foot toward the door, a dark television high on a bracket on the wall. The only light was provided by the evening twilight whispering in through the blinds. The patient was silent and motionless. From where I stood, I could see only a swatch of lusterless hair on the pillow.

"I'd better leave," I whispered.

"No. Stay."

"You sure I'm not . . . ?"

"Take a look. You don't recognize her?"

"I don't know anybody in Tacoma."

"Oh, I think you do." It was at this point I realized all the sweet talk on the phone had been part of a ruse. I was always slow on the uptake, which explained why I was attracted to dim females, females who couldn't fool me, but I'd never been this slow. On the drive down, I'd alternated between euphoria and apprehension, seesawing between the thought that she'd summoned me either to slake her lust or to de-man me with a scalpel. I could tell now by the sudden edge in her voice I was scalpel-bound. "Step around here. You've seen patients before. You're a big brave fireman. Take a look."

She moved aside to make room for me. It was a woman, older, faded, devoid of makeup, her features flavored with that lack of vitality a long-term patient acquires, her body so tiny and frail and motionless, I had to look twice to be certain she was breathing. When I turned to Stephanie, her eyes were like blue lasers.

"You don't know her?"

I turned back to the patient. "I don't think so."

"Look again. Sometimes it's difficult to recognize a person when they're horizontal. But you've seen her on her back before. That was the whole point, wasn't it? Getting her horizontal?"

It was with a queasy feeling that I realized we were standing over Stephanie's sister, Holly. I'd cherished Holly, made love to Holly, woken up beside her, and yet I barely recognized the skeleton she'd become. "Oh, God."

"Her doctors don't think so, but I believe she hears everything around her. I believe she's listening to us right now. You know how a stroke victim can hear what you say but can't respond. You ask them to move their hand, their brain sends the signal, but the signal never arrives. It's got to be the most frustrating feeling on earth."

"What happened?"

"A cerebrovascular accident, although so far nobody's been able to figure out exactly what caused it. We think she had an aneurysm."

"This is incredible."

"Is it?"

"She's the second person I've seen today in basically this same situation."

"I'm sorry you're having such a bad day."

"That's not what I meant."

"I know what you meant."

"I don't get it. She's twenty-eight. People her age don't have strokes."

"Not unless there are special circumstances. I was hoping you might be able to shed some light on what those circumstances might have been."

"That's why you came to North Bend? If I'd known she was sick, I never would have . . . Holly was in perfect health the last time I saw her."

"Perfect mental health?"

"What are you getting at?"

She reached under the blanket for her sister's hand. "We think she tried to kill herself. You wouldn't know anything about that, would you?"

8. FREAK ME OUT

Nothing she might have said could have rendered me quite so speechless.

At least now I knew the primary source of her antipathy toward me: Stephanie Riggs thought I had driven her sister to suicide—and a botched job at that.

Ten years ago our department responded to a young man who'd tried to hang himself in the woods; he was found minutes later by his brothers, who revived him so that he could spend the rest of his life in a vegetative state. We all thought about that patient from time to time. All of us who'd been on the alarm thought about him. There were endings worse than death.

What had happened to Holly, for instance. It was one thing to be ninety and have a stroke—live a couple more years. It was quite another to be twenty-eight and have a stroke, consigned to a bed for another half century.

"This was because of you," Stephanie Riggs said. "Because of your shabby affair."

Our relationship had fizzled after Holly discovered I was seeing one of the Suzannes. I *had* treated her shabbily.

"I can't believe Holly would kill herself. I certainly never saw any hint of depression or—"

"Not until you dumped her. They found her forty-some hours after you last spoke. As far as we could ascertain, she didn't speak to anyone else or leave the house after that last phone call with you."

I remembered it.

The conversation had been one-sided and rambling, an hour during which Holly had cried over the fact that we were no longer an item, as if two people had never decided to go their separate ways before. Looking back on it, I could see now that our breakup had been my fault. What's tricky to explain without making me sound like a jerk, and what I would never admit to her sister, who already thought I was a jerk, was that during our last phone conversation I'd nodded off.

Twice.

Fallen asleep. I felt bad about it even as it was happening, but as was Holly's custom, she'd phoned late, after the girls were in bed, after I was

in bed, having lost sleep the night before fighting one of North Bend's infrequent house fires. I don't believe she'd been threatening suicide. Still,
there were a number of minutes during that conversation when I didn't
participate.

"I remember the call," I said.

"Not that you're going to answer me truthfully, but how did Holly
sound?"

Boring, I thought. The way any jilted lover sounds when she pisses
and moans and tries to rationalize her partner back into a relationship
the partner wants no part of. "If you're asking if she threatened suicide,
the answer is no. She wasn't happy we were breaking up, but she never
hinted she was going to do anything like this."

"What would you say if I told you she wrote in her journal she'd been
talking to you about killing herself?"

Holly had never mentioned a journal and Stephanie's question was
most likely a subterfuge, but I had no way of knowing for certain. She
hadn't said Holly's journal included mention of suicide, had only asked
what I would say if it had. It was a trick trial attorneys and cops used, one
my father had often wielded on me as a child, one the elders in our
church had used on him and my mother both, on all the adults in the
commune, a contrivance I was thoroughly familiar with. The secret was
to not let the other person buffalo you into admitting something there
was no proof of.

As far as I knew, during the minutes of that phone call when I was
asleep Holly had continued talking about our relationship, nothing else.
It had been a ghastly hour, though I gotta say the current one was stack-
ing up to be worse.

In the days and weeks after that phone call, Holly had gradually
faded from my thoughts and I believed I'd faded from hers.

All the while she'd been right here.

Comatose.

From the look of her, she hadn't thought about anything during the
past month, least of all me.

"The electric meter reader went to the rear of her duplex and spotted
her on the floor. He called the police, who called the fire department. By
then she'd been on the floor God knows how long. Naked. Hypothermic.
We think she went down right after that phone call with you."

Okay, I admit it was all too easy to visualize Holly naked on the floor of her house. To my embarrassment the first time we'd made love popped into my mind. It had been right there on her kitchen floor. We'd been too entranced with each other to do anything but kiss and drop to the linoleum after we came through her back door. The second time on her floor was the last time we made love, a desperate tryst instigated by Holly and calculated, I later realized, to replicate the circumstances of our first lovemaking, as if the cold kitchen linoleum would rekindle my ardor. Except for my sore knees, the sex had been good, but the affection had not returned. I wondered if she hadn't planned to be found on that floor as some sort of message to me.

Feeling my legs beginning to give way, I made a fierce effort to remain standing—nothing would be worse than fainting in front of this man-eater.

She hadn't brought me here to tell me about her sister. She could have done that in North Bend. Or on the phone. She'd brought me here to shock and humiliate me, and then to use that to extract information.

She brought me here to see me in pain.

This was turning out to be a summer in hell. Chief Newcastle's hiking accident, Joel McCain's fall, Jackie Feldbaum's car wreck. Me running into this cannibal.

Holly.

If Holly's current condition had anything to do with me, I would never forgive myself. Holly was a sweet woman, natural and unaffected, and for a time I'd genuinely loved her. For a variety of reasons it hadn't worked out, perhaps because she'd been too clingy. Or because I'd been unfaithful.

"She loved your little girls, and she loved you," Stephanie said. "For some reason she thought you felt the same about her. But then, that was before she found out you were sleeping with another woman."

"We never said we were exclusive. As far as I knew, she could have been seeing other people, too."

"You know she wasn't!"

"She could have been! We never made any rules."

Stephanie Riggs looked at her sister. "It's strange how much you recreational womanizers don't know about women. It's strange that no matter what you want to believe, women are never quite the sluts you men are."

For half a second I thought this was a sick joke the two of them had concocted, that any minute Holly would jump out of bed and laugh at me. But it was too intricate and grim to be a joke. To begin with, Holly had lost an enormous amount of weight. She'd lost color, too, which I didn't think could be faked.

I jammed my trembling hands into my pockets to keep Stephanie from seeing them. I could run into a house fire no problem; angry women took my breath away. I wanted Holly's sister to like me more than I'd ever wanted anybody on this planet to like me, but it was not going to happen.

Not now and not ever.

"Why did you bring me here?"

When she spoke, her voice, which had been rising steadily since my arrival, returned to the quiet, thoughtful tones of our conversation on the phone over an hour earlier. "We believe whatever caused this is systemic, some sort of sophisticated poison, something that has affected her brain and nervous system at a basic cellular level. I thought she might have had access to industrial solvents, insecticides, that sort of thing. I looked all over her house. I even went back through all the shipping manifests to see what she'd been hauling. I was hoping you might have some ideas. Was there some prescription medication that came up missing from your place? I know she hadn't been there recently, but before?"

"I have two little girls. I don't even keep Weed and Feed around my place. I need drain cleaner, I use it and throw the can away."

It hadn't occurred to her that I was capable of loving anyone, much less two anyones. You could see it by the look on her face. "Did you ever talk to Holly about poisons? Or ways people might commit suicide? You ever discuss suicide at all?"

"No. Didn't she leave a note?"

"I haven't found one."

"Then how do you know it was a suicide attempt?"

"I know." Stephanie Riggs turned her attention away from her sister and looked at me. "Except for trace amounts of fluoxetine hydrochloride, which she'd been taking for the last year, the toxicologist's report came up negative. My last hope was she'd left some clue with you during that phone call."

"What's fluo—?"

"Prozac."

The sketchy details of our phone call were coming back like pricks from a bed of nails. During the conversation she'd dissected our relationship from the time we met until she discovered, through a stupid slip of the tongue—mine—that I'd been seeing another woman.

After we broke up, she'd begged to be friends and I'd tried hard to accommodate her, but you couldn't be friends with someone you'd been intimate with a week earlier. One of you was bound to be hurt. Besides, she didn't really want to be friends; she wanted to be married.

In the end, she'd gotten so desperate, her attitude alone became the barrier against getting back together. It wasn't anything I could have told her sister—that Holly had been a whiner.

Anyway. Holly wasn't whining now.

Another thing I didn't want to tell her sister was that a few days after I'd made the final break, she'd said something that had stuck with me. "What kind of life am I going to have without you? I won't have *any* life without you."

Suicide must have crossed my mind at the time, because I'd worried that the guys at work would find out a woman had killed herself over me. As if my embarrassment would have been the worst of it. Then I'd quickly put the whole thing out of my mind.

The trouble with emotional blackmail was once you let it start, there was no way to make it stop. I knew all about it.

Lorie had been a seasoned pro.

Now Holly was in a coma, drool oozing down her face, a pool of it on the sheet next to her.

I would give anything to deliver her out of this.

Maybe I'd been wrong to dust her off. Maybe I really was the heartless heel her sister thought I was.

I couldn't get over the astonishing coincidence that Joel McCain and Holly Riggs were both bedridden. Two people who'd been close to me. Had Stephanie told me the truth in the cul-de-sac outside Joel's house, I might have learned of their fate within minutes of each other.

What were the odds, I wondered, that these two situations would be almost identical?

It freaked me out.

9. POOR BABY, TELL AUNT MARGE

A few minutes later, clad in a svelte navy business suit, Margery DiMaggio swept into the room as if she were about to accept an Oscar from the Academy, which, to the best of my memory, was how she swept into most rooms. DiMaggio was Holly and Stephanie's aunt, sister to their deceased mother.

I'd met her twice before, and each time we'd gotten along famously.

"God, this is all my fault," she said melodramatically. "If I was a Catholic, I'd confess to a whole roomful of priests. If they could tear themselves away from their little altar boys. Oh, what a detestable thing to say. I'm sorry, Steph. I just get so depressed coming here. I thought she was happier in the hospice. They played that music. I know you didn't like it, but it *was* soothing."

"I didn't mind the music, Marge. Or the hospice. We needed to run more tests. This was the place to do it."

As they hugged, the remnants of a family standing over its youngest living member, Stephanie looked over the older woman's shoulder at the ceiling before her eyes lowered to me. I'd been brought here for interrogation and retribution, and now my presence had become offensive. Stephanie had used me the way she'd accused me of using her sister. Worse, for I'd never intentionally set out to hurt anyone. If people got hurt because of my actions, it was strictly on account of my own ignorance, stupidity, or lack of grace or because of *their* unrealistic expectations. Stephanie, on the other hand, had planned this assault like a four-star general.

I started for the door.

"Oh, Jim, honey," DiMaggio said, speaking as if we'd last seen each other only yesterday. "Good of you to come. You didn't hear what I said, did you? I hope you're not Catholic."

"I'm not anything. I'm sorry the circumstances have to be so . . ."

"I feel like it's all my fault. She came to Washington because of me. This is my fault. Every bit of it."

"Aunt Marge, don't be silly," said Stephanie, glaring at me. "It's not your fault."

"I feel so bad for you," Marge said. "At least I can go home. You have to go back to Holly's little place, where you're surrounded by her things. Even her cat. This whole experience must be so dreadful for you."

"I like being surrounded by Holly's things. In fact, I've been wearing her clothes just to feel closer to her. It's Holly we have to be concerned for. Getting her back to her old self."

"You're not still hoping for a miracle?"

"Of course I am."

Two months ago when Holly and I had been seeing each other, I'd met Marge DiMaggio at an auction to raise money for muscular dystrophy research, an affair for which I'd had to dig up my tuxedo from the darkest part of my closet. Marge DiMaggio had been thrilled to death to see her niece out on the town with, as she'd put it, "a handsome and eligible fireman," describing me in terms of marriage, the way so many women described men, as if that was our primary function in life, to be married to them. Marge liked me from the moment she set eyes on me. I guess she thought she was looking at a future nephew-in-law, though you'd better believe she didn't get the idea from me.

Even though she was twenty years older than I was, Marge had flirted with me and with every other male that night, a mannerism I attributed at the time to habit and alcohol rather than ambition and inclination; she'd gone on to belie her flirtations with self-deprecating remarks about being too busy to think about a private life. Marge was chic, smart, candid, and seductive in a sophisticated manner that went way over my head. My impression was that she was one of those older women who had always been a coquette and just couldn't stop.

DiMaggio was the CEO of an Eastside research company. She'd explained it to me once, but the details were fuzzy. Having resigned a profitable position as an executive in a New York department store chain ten years earlier, Marge had joined her husband's fledgling research outfit. Then, out of respect for her husband's memory, she'd stayed on with the company after his death. According to Holly, Canyon View now held patents that aided scientists across the country in gene and DNA research, patents that had enticed megacorporations to pump big bucks into Canyon View's coffers.

When Stephanie and Aunt Marge turned to me, I could see the family resemblance. They were both relatively short, the older woman a couple of inches taller than her niece, both with slightly squarish faces, a trace of freckles, light-colored eyes. Marge displayed an openness I found comforting under the circumstances, perhaps because there was already so much guile and manipulation in the room. "Jim . . ." she said.

"It's such a shock to see her like this. I—"

"A shock?" Stephanie said loudly. "You sonofabitch. The only thing Holly ever meant to you was a romp in the hay."

"Despite what you may believe, Dr. Riggs, I feel awful. She's the second friend I've seen like this today."

"Yes, you've already told me how you're having such a bad day," Stephanie mocked. "Poor baby."

"Okay. Sure. I could have treated your sister better. You probably could have, too. And maybe Aunt Marge could have. Maybe *everybody* could treat everybody better. But at least I don't take my guilt out on total strangers."

I stalked out the doorway.

For a moment Stephanie was speechless; then she yelled at my back and her shrieking voice told me how close I'd gotten to the heart of the matter. "Get out! Don't ever come back! Get out! Get out of here, you stupid bastard!"

I was halfway down the corridor when I realized Marge DiMaggio was following me.

"Jim. Don't listen to her. She's been out of sorts. She cried for two days when she first got here."

DiMaggio stopped in front of me and hugged me, and after a few moments I could feel her heaving against my chest as she wept. She was fashionably New York thin, the flesh of her arms and back stringy and soft. "Jim, I can't get over how good it is to see you. It was wonderful of you to come. And never mind Steph. You want to see Holly, you come any time."

It was hard to see a point in a second visit. Holly hadn't known I was here tonight and would hardly jump up to greet me if I came again.

"I'll come as often as I can. I would have been down here sooner if I'd known."

"I know, dear." Standing close, Marge DiMaggio held my elbows. She was about the same age as my mother, her hair dyed the same stark black as my mother's, though, as far as I know, my mother hadn't yet resorted to cosmetic surgery the way DiMaggio obviously had. "I feel so bad about all of this."

"It's not your fault."

"No, it is. I should have done more for Holly. She came up here from California because I was the only family she had on the West Coast. At first I gave her a job with my company, but she didn't want to work indoors. And she had no skills. So then when this truck-driving idea developed, I treated her to the driver's school. I even threw work her way. That company she drove for in Seattle? It belongs to an old friend of mine. In fact, you two wouldn't even have met if it hadn't been for me."

"Really? How do you figure that?"

"She was on her way to Canyon View to drop off a couple of boxes of books we'd ordered from back east. Now tell me. You said you had a friend who was ill?"

"A firefighter I worked with. Finding out about him was a shock, but then to find out Holly's in basically the same condition . . . I don't even know what the odds of that are. I've been trying to reconcile this whole—"

"He tried to commit suicide? Your friend?"

"Fell off a roof. Marge, I feel so sick about Holly. She had her whole lifetime ahead of her."

"Tell me about your friend."

"I . . ."

"I know how this works, Jim, and you need to talk this one out. I know exactly what you're going through. Tell Aunt Marge all about it. I'm not going to take no for an answer."

I told her about our alarm to Joel McCain's house, about his choking, about the family's religious objections to medical intervention. At one point I must have mentioned Stan Beebe's disjointed theories, because she homed in on it. "Syndrome? You say somebody out there thinks there's some sort of disease going around that all these people are catching? And it's a syndrome?"

"Stan Beebe. One of our full-time department employees. He's a good firefighter, but every once in a while he comes up with something a little wacky."

During our chat I watched the door to Holly's room down the hallway, lest Stephanie come sprinting out to rip me a new asshole. I'd been an idiot to drive all the way down here.

Maybe it was the way she listened or the way her gray-blue eyes stared up at me so relentlessly, but talking to Marge DiMaggio made me feel much better. Strange how tragedies can unite comparative strangers.

10. TAKING IN THE BIG PICTURE

It was not quite dark when I got onto I-5 and began driving north. Beyond the water park I took Highway 18 and headed east by northeast, the Douglas firs on either side of the narrow highway opening up to an occasional view of a housing development or shopping mall.

It occurred to me that had Holly been considering suicide, she would have used the threat during our last phone conversation to lever concessions from me.

But she hadn't.

At least not while I was awake.

I'd made the mistake of telling someone at the firehouse I'd drifted off during that last phone call, and now whenever I got a call at work Click or Clack would announce over the station intercom, "Telephone for Jim Swope. Lieutenant Swope? Nap time."

I felt enough guilt over that call without finding out I was the last person Holly spoke to.

She deserved better than me. Better than that bed in the hospital. Better than her angry sister even. When you thought about it, most of the women I'd been seeing in the past couple of years deserved better than me. Maybe Stephanie Riggs was right. Maybe her sister tried to kill herself because of the way I'd treated her.

It was mind-boggling, because underneath I was basically a pretty decent guy.

Today had been a double whammy. Joel's predicament had been a jolt for us all. Joel and I, at fifteen years and twelve years of time in the department respectively, had known each other longer than any of the other full-timers. Having made lieutenant a year before I did, he often joked that he was my superior, though in fact we'd worked as equals until he was obligated to take over the department's administrative duties following Newcastle's death.

Never one to volunteer for extra paperwork or meetings, Joel hadn't been happy holding the reins of the fire department. When he fell off his roof, I'd made a bad joke that he'd done it on purpose in order to get out of running the department.

Now the whole enchilada rested on my shoulders.

After our call to Joel's house, Karrie had wept openly. Stan Beebe had gone home sick. I might have done either or both, but at the time I was too upset about my meeting with the cannibal to think straight. You meet a man-eater like that, it disturbs you.

What happened to Joel and Holly was the type of thing you could put off thinking about if you were thirty-four like I was. You could tell yourself you didn't need to think about it for another forty years. I didn't even have a corner of my brain where I kept problems like that.

Three years earlier when my father had a stroke, I'd calculated that I had forty-six years before I needed to worry about it myself. Now I faced the inescapable fact that people my age were not exempt—were, in fact, dropping like flies.

I was not exempt.

It was something you always knew but tried not to face, in the same way teenagers knew they could die if they drove recklessly but, nonetheless, still drove as if they were invincible, which of course was why so many teenagers died in automobile accidents.

None of us knew for certain whether Joel McCain's brain was still functioning. Or Holly's. To be able to think but not speak. To be able to itch but not scratch.

You got like that, it had to be hell on earth.

Stan Beebe had told me he'd rather be dead.

I would rather be dead.

Life was such a simple thing when you sat down and thought about it. You were conceived, born, lived for a few years, mated, had children, grew old, and then you died and fed the worms. Afterward, your offspring duplicated the process.

Same as any animal.

Same as a kernel of corn.

My life was no different from anybody else's. My days passed pretty much like everybody else's. I got up in the morning and looked in the cupboard for a box of cereal. Thought about the fact that I needed to take the girls shopping for school clothes, that I'd forgotten to write a check for the phone bill. That the car needed gas. I found my wallet empty and went to the cash machine. Like those around me, I was consumed with the minutiae of daily life, by the fact that the driver in the next lane cut me off, by how much of a raise the fire department might expect from the city next year. Crap, all of it. Absolute crap.

Rarely did anything that mattered touch my thoughts.

The downpour of daily trifles was so constant and so steady I rarely had time to look up at the sky.

It sounds foolish to say it, but the feeling of my own impending death seemed to fill the pickup truck. Some philosopher said that when we feel sad for somebody else's death, we are actually mourning our own. He might have been writing about me.

When I rolled down the window, the cool night air tossed around some papers on the seat beside me right before it brought tears to my eyes.

DAY TWO

11. WEAK LEGS, MILD HEADACHE, THE HANDS TAKE ON A WAXY APPEARANCE

I woke up unable to breathe.

When I opened my eyes, a seven-year-old was sitting on my chest, a nine-year-old alongside straddling my pillow as if it were a horse. Britney was skinny as a pencil. She'd been bugging me to cut her hair, which was the same shade of red her mother's had been as a child. Her older sister, Allyson, had black hair that fell just beyond her shoulders, almost the same color as mine; she thought she wanted to keep hers long. Or short. Alternating opinions by the hour. Allyson was already beginning to stretch out into the elegant young woman she would become.

Even though I discouraged it, Allyson had taken up the unofficial mantle of mother in the family, striving to be the voice of reason in any familial endeavor or discussion. Allyson had become the sober one, taking after my father and myself, Britney the free spirit, as Lorie had been, as my mother had been in her youth and now was again.

The three of us had stayed up late playing Monopoly and listening to a Britney Spears CD. "Come on, Dad," Britney said. "Your alarm's been going off for hours. You have to wake up. Time to go to work."

"Oh, yeah?"

I'd slept like a rock, which was unusual because I was generally a light sleeper, especially after a day as fraught with emotional scenes as yesterday. Now I had a headache. I wondered if I'd picked up a bug at Tacoma General. But then, I doubted a bug I'd picked up last night could strike so quickly.

"It's ten after seven," Britney said. "You're not going to have time for breakfast."

"The alarm go off? I didn't hear it."

"Been buzzing for hours," said Allyson, as if already bored with the day, rearranging my hair with one hand.

"Your alarm woke us up, and we were all the way in the other room," said Britney. "We're just little. We're supposed to sleep through anything."

"Know what else?" Allyson asked.

"What?"

"If you're going to find a really good stepmother for us, you're going to have to stop wasting your time on bimbos."

"What makes you think I was with a bimbo last night?"

"You said yourself she was foxy."

"I meant foxlike. As in sharp teeth." I gnashed my teeth. They laughed.

"You always say we'd sleep through a *nuclear saster*," said Britney.

"Nuclear disaster, honey. And I didn't hear my alarm."

"Buzzing for *hours*," said Allyson.

"Yup," confirmed Britney, sighing. "I don't know what you're going to do about breakfast."

"I'll grab a bite at the station."

"Dad, what happened to your hands?" Allyson picked up my right hand and showed it Britney.

"Oh, ick," said Britney as the front doorbell rang. "Looks like you got into the Elmer's Glue." She rolled off the bed and sprinted for the front door. "That's Morgan."

"Don't open up to strangers," I said.

"You know who it is, Dad," Allyson said.

Morgan was sixteen and lived next door. Baby-sitting for me was an easy-money summer job for her and a pleasant experience for my girls, partly because she looked on them as contemporaries and shared her secrets about boys and high school, partly because she brought over makeup and showed them how to apply it. Seven and nine, going on seventeen and nineteen, my girls shared a thousand little confidences with Morgan that I wasn't supposed to know about, including the fact that Morgan had a crush on me.

We were in the same house the girls and I had lived in with Lorie, a rambler on two and a half acres just north of the main section of town. A fixer-upper that had taken five years to bang into shape. When the girls came along, Lorie quit work and our budget became strained at about the same pace as our relationship.

We'd never had water in the basement, but for the last three years during the spring or early winter the Snoqualmie River, normally two hundred yards distant, flooded the road in front of our house. Three years ago when it flooded, I bunked at the firehouse, Lorie and the girls at the mayor's place on the other side of town. That was when I should have guessed about the mayor and Lorie.

We lived at the end of a short dirt road. Morgan Neumann and her mother lived next door on five acres, a well-worn path between the houses. A vacant field buffered us from the two-lane paved road. To the south there were horses on leased land, untended apple trees squatting here and there in the surrounding fields, a few alders, and at least one tall pine.

Our most recent topic of conversation around the dinner table was whether or not Allyson could have a horse. At nine, I didn't feel she was old enough to take care of it, and with two girls and Eustace, our cat, under my wing already, I didn't need the extra chores. Still, the folks at work had a pool going that there'd be a horse in our pasture before the year was out. Sometimes I thought the guys at work knew me better than I knew myself.

When I climbed out of bed, my legs felt weak and jittery, as if I'd been running uphill all night, but then after I got moving my thighs began to regain some of their strength. My head was throbbing.

Standing over the toilet bowl, I saw that the backs of both hands were scaly, as if they'd been sunburned and were peeling, except they weren't. I washed and dried my hands, but the waxy-looking substance wouldn't come off. Hand lotion didn't help.

"Morning, Mr. Swope," said Morgan Neumann when I went downstairs, still rubbing my hands.

"Morning, Morgan. There's twenty dollars on the fridge if you need groceries. I'll be at the station if you want to get hold of me. Unemployment Beach is not okay, but a video from Blockbuster is. G or PG."

"Daddy, I want to go to the beach," Allyson said.

"Not without me. That current's faster than it looks. It'll sweep you away like a bug on a rug."

"We don't need no video, Daddy," Britney said.

"You don't need *a* video."

"That's what I said. We're going to play house."

"No, we aren't," Allyson said. "We're going to mop the kitchen floor, and then I'm going to read my book. Morgan's going to surf the Internet."

"I am not," Morgan protested.

"It's okay, Morgan. Just don't let the house burn down."

"Thank you, Mr. Swope. You're the greatest." Knowing Morgan had a pinch of Eddie Haskell in her, I was always a little leery when she turned on the applause spigot.

At the station I had Click and Karrie working with me, plus the two medics the city contracted from Bellevue.

Stan Beebe, who was still on disability leave, showed up in civilian clothes around ten o'clock, eyes bloodshot, unsteady on his feet, reeking of alcohol.

We sat him down in the kitchen and poured him a mug of black coffee. Normally Stan drank coffee by the bucketful, but this morning he only sipped it and played with the handle of the mug.

Click stood in the corner with his arms across his chest.

Wearing jeans and an open-necked shirt, Stan Beebe cupped the coffee mug in his thick hands and stared at the surface of the liquid. His hair was cropped short and peppered with lint. There was animal hair on his pant leg, food stains on his shirt.

Ordinarily, Stan was as meticulous as a parson's cat.

I had never seen him drunk.

In fact, I couldn't recall ever seeing Stan do anything more than hold a paper cup of malt liquor, not even at the wildest department party ever, which we'd had last year at Joel McCain's place. Click and Clack had gotten into a playful tousle and ended up smashing Mary McCain's tea table. Jackie had gotten so juiced, she took a leak in the corner of the spare bedroom and fell asleep on the floor by the dog dish. I spent an hour in the dark on the sofa downstairs with Karrie. The volunteers yukked it up and tossed horseshoes over parked cars, my pickup included.

Mary McCain grew so disgusted with the drunken antics that she made her husband break up the party early.

"You look like you've had a couple, Stan," I said.

"A couple? Man, I'm smashed."

"We all feel bad about Joel."

"It's not about Joel. Tell me something, Jim. What's the worst thing you can imagine? How about you're here, but you're not here. You're dead, or close enough that only a few people can tell the difference. You're miserable to the nth degree, plus your existence makes your loved ones miserable, too. What I don't understand is why they don't have the best medical care for Joel. I know they have that religion, but when somebody's life is at stake, you'd think—Would you? Jim? Back when you were religious, would you have been willing to die for your beliefs?"

"Probably. When I was a kid, I almost drowned in Lake Washington stepping off a dock. Went down like a piece of angle iron. I had just turned eight, and I'd been told if I had enough faith, I could walk on water. Some big kids pulled me out."

Beebe placed his lips on the rim of the coffee mug and inhaled the aroma. He set the mug down on the table and slowly spun it around in his hands. "Mary McCain's just like you were stepping off that dock. I called her last night. She thinks Joel's going to be healed. Jesus healed, and Christian Scientists think they can heal, too. See, they feel the majority of world thought is against them—"

"It is."

"—that the majority of thought on this earth is causing the problem. Joel once said if everybody believed the way he did, there would be no sickness or evil. 'Course Joel told me there wasn't any matter, either." Stan pinched himself. "No matter. We're all spiritual beings. Everything else is false."

"You mean we're really floating around in ether like ghosts?"

"Something like that. Joel said you had to demonstrate these things a step at a time. You wake up from the dream one step at a time."

"Look, Stan, I've been around zealots all my life, and if there's anything a religious freak is good at, it's seeing what he wants to see and ignoring everything else."

"Don't call Joel a freak."

"I didn't mean it that way. Or maybe I did. His mother-in-law stuffed half an apple down his gullet because she thought he was healed. You think she's tuned in to reality?"

Stan's eyes met mine for the first time in over a minute. We broke into simultaneous laughter as we thought about the apple sliding across the floor. His mood quickly grew dark again.

"You going to be all right, Stan?"

"Yesterday I told you I was dying. Now you ask if I'm going to be all right. That's the trouble with you, Jim. We have to spell everything out for you. Let me say it one more time—I'm dying. Just like Joel. But I'm not going to end up choking on apples. Not this buckaroo. No sirree. Not in *my* future."

"I guess you're right. I guess you do have to spell it out. What are you saying, Stan?"

"I'm saying I have twenty-four hours to kill myself."

"You're not thinking about suicide?"

"No, I'm not thinking about it. I'm going to do it."

"This is silly. Joel fell off a roof. He doesn't have any disease. He hit his head."

Beebe looked at my hands, grabbed one of them, then dropped it. "Christ! You got it, too!"

"Got what?"

"You have the shakes yesterday?"

"That woman chasing me all over town made me nervous."

"Newcastle had the shakes. He goes out by himself on a seven-day hike. Dies of exposure. They figured he was on his way back when he went down. Day seven."

"What do you mean, when he went down?"

"Same way Joel went down. Same way Jackie went down. It's a syndrome, man."

"I don't see a syndrome. All I'm seeing is a whole lot of bad luck."

"Newcastle . . . I figure it took about two days for him to die. They said from the look of him, he was on the ground the whole time. Some animal bit half his ear off, and he didn't do anything about it."

"I hadn't heard that. Stan, you're not really thinking about killing yourself?"

"I got a copy of the autopsy report. He had the hands, too. Like yours."

"We've probably been using some bad detergent around here."

"It's not no soap. We been poisoned."

"Is that what your doctor's testing you for, poison?"

Beebe's laugh had a hysterical component to it. He turned and looked into my eyes. "I'm going to be just like the Fire Plug over there in Alpine Estates."

"Jackie got drunk and crashed her car."

"Well, I'm drunk. Maybe I'll do a better job of crashing my car than she did."

"Joel slipped and fell off his roof."

54

"Not how that happened, either."

"Newcastle had a heart attack. He shouldn't have been out in the woods alone."

"My guess is we were all exposed to it on an alarm. Chemical or biological. It doesn't matter. Once it's through with you, you're helpless. You want to end up like Joel, fine. But it ain't for me."

12. A BARREL ROLLS OFF A TRUCK

"Look," said Stan. "Remember that story Newcastle told us? Happened in California twenty or thirty years ago? A barrel rolls off a truck onto the highway somewhere? They send a company of volunteers to check it out. The barrel doesn't have any markings, so they roll it off the freeway and call the highway department to pick it up. It's been smacked by a couple of cars and it's leaking. Nobody wears any PPE. It turns out the barrel's full of undiluted insecticide. The chemical enters their nervous systems through their skin, and seven of the nine responders end up in nursing homes. Brain-dead."

"We've all heard that story," I said. "But we haven't investigated any barrels on the highway."

"We did *something*."

Stan's morbid pessimism was beginning to get on my nerves. Worse than that, down deep somewhere I was starting to buy into this harebrained hypothesis.

Ian Hjorth had been so quiet I'd almost forgotten he was there, arms crossed in front of his muscular chest, listening quietly. A tall man in his late twenties with thinning blond hair and a penchant for pranks, Ian was well-read but not overly opinionated, intelligent but not particularly ambitious. Because of his fun-loving nature, and despite the fact that he teased me ruthlessly about my love life, Ian was one of my favorite people. He had a wife who was young and pretty and who worked for the city. They had a little girl with big brown teddy bear eyes. Britney called her Pimmy.

Ian said, "I don't buy it, Stan. Newcastle died over a month ago. Joel fell off his roof a week later. Then Jackie had her accident. Okay. Maybe those things happened around the same time. But now we're a month later. If you guys got this on the same alarm, don't you think all five of you would come down with it together?"

"There's nothing says it has to happen that way," said Beebe. "You heard about the state patrolman who was at the hazardous materials spill directing traffic, accidentally got some chemicals on his trousers, went home, and his wife washed his pants in the same load with his kid's baby blanket. The baby ended up dying. The patrolman never even got sick. If he'd forgotten those pants in the bottom of his locker and taken them home half a year later the baby would have died six months after the incident and the death never even would have been connected to the hazmat spill. This could be something with a built-in time factor we're all tripping in our own way."

"Jesus," said Ian, with a sly grin. "If I was dying, I wouldn't spend my last day with a mug like me or a lady-killer like Jim. I'd be home with my family. Or in Jim's case, at a whorehouse." He looked at me and laughed.

"Thought I'd get on the computer and compose my epitaph," Stan replied grimly. " 'He lived a life—he had a wife—he did his best—now he's at rest.' What do you think?"

I'd never heard anybody feel so sorry for himself, not even me when I'd dipped into the swamps of self-pity after Lorie ran away. Stan was doing everything but sizing himself for a coffin. If it hadn't been so pathetic, it would have been almost comical.

"You feeling sick?" I asked Beebe, thinking about the headache I'd woken up with this morning.

"You don't have to feel sick to be dying."

"What made you go to the doctor in the first place?" Ian Hjorth asked.

"Three days ago I started falling down. I had this junk on my hands. I knew Joel and Jackie had the hands, so I started investigating."

"I never noticed Jackie's hands," Ian said. "And Joel's wife wouldn't let anybody in."

"She let me in," Stan said. "I dug up the autopsy report on Newcastle. Same thing. A whitish discoloration of the hands. Then I started thinking about Joel going off that roof. I'd been on a roof when I fell, I mighta got hurt. I'd been driving like Jackie, I mighta crashed. Out in the woods like Newcastle, dead. So I went to Dr. Brashears. He's the one treated Jackie."

"What'd he say?"

"He started running tests."

"And?" I asked.

"He sent my blood away to some special lab in Texas. He sent some hair samples and tissue to Washington, D.C. Won't find out anything until next week. It's a pisser, 'cause I won't be around next week."

"Of course you will."

"Don't believe me, Jim. It's no never mind to me. But remember what I'm telling you, because after you realize you have it, you'll wish you'd listened. It's a seven-day cycle. Who knows what triggers it, but from the minute it starts to the time you sign off . . . seven days. Get your affairs in order. Say good-bye to the people you love."

"Don't be telling me I have seven days left."

"You *don't*. You have six. The waxy hands come on day two."

I couldn't help doing the math. Today was Tuesday. If Stan was right, sometime on Sunday night I'd become a vegetable. Maybe if a team of doctors were telling me this, I might believe it; but this was Stan.

Aware that he had no way of knowing about my headache or the weak feeling in my legs, I asked him to list the symptoms.

"The first day, yesterday for you, the hands start shaking for no reason. Day two: trembling legs, pressure on your frontal lobe, usually in the form of a mild headache, the backs of the hands take on a waxy look."

He'd pegged the last two days perfectly.

I'd never truly believed all the horrors visiting our department could have been coincidences. On top of that, I'd been living with a feeling of impending doom since visiting Holly. I'd seen too much misfortune land on innocent people in the past few days, and now I was bowing to the all-too-human propensity to concoct a sinister plot to account for it. Grief always went down better if you could follow it with a healthy dose of conspiracy.

I didn't want to believe Stan, but he'd pointed out my symptoms like a bird dog pointed out a dead pheasant.

"You driving today?" I asked. Tears were dribbling down his cheeks.

"I live out the Mount Si Road. Of course I'm driving."

"You shouldn't."

"I'm on day six, man. I'm going down anyway." He was crying full out now. It was hard to know what to do for him.

"Jesus, Stan. I'm not going to let you drive."

"Okay. I'll kill myself here."

"You're not going to kill yourself, Stan."

He looked directly at me for the first time in a couple of minutes, held my gaze, and said, "Don't try to stop me. You stop me, you'll be doing the worst thing you've ever done."

"Stan, I'm not going to stand by and—"

Never one to miss out on a melodramatic moment, Mayor Steve Haston suddenly appeared in the doorway behind Stan Beebe, wildly gesticulating and silently mouthing some kind of urgent message to me. I had to assume his daughter, Karrie, had called him and told him about Stan.

I excused myself and left Stan pouring salty tears into his coffee. At the other end of the corridor, Steve Haston whispered, "I hear he's talking about killing himself."

"That's what he says. He was depressed a couple of years ago, too. Newcastle sent him to a doctor and they put him on something. Prozac, I think it was. He needs a doctor. When the medics get back we'll have them take him."

"Has he got a gun?"

"Not that I know of."

"We've got to do something."

"That's what I just said."

"What do you think we should do?"

"How about . . . we have the medics take him to the ER?"

"You think that'll work?"

Just then the bell hit. It was a medic call, which meant we would take the aid car and engine, and the medics, who were out of quarters, would respond from their current location, probably somewhere between Overlake Hospital and North Bend. It would be a good little while before they showed up.

"Listen, Steve. We've got a call. We need somebody to stay with him."

"Me?"

"I don't see anyone else in the station."

"I've got an appointment in fifteen minutes."

"Steve. A man is talking about committing suicide here. A friend of ours. I don't want to come back and find him hanging in the hose tower."

"Oh, yeah. Sure. I guess I can stick around until somebody shows up."

"Until the medics show up. Or we come back. Don't be turning him over to the mailman, and don't leave him alone."

"Of course not," Haston said, heading for the beanery with an air of confusion about him.

The dispatcher sent us to Edgewick Road. Ian Hjorth drove the aid car; I drove the engine.

As we headed south through town and toward the freeway, Karrie said, "You think he's going to be all right?"

"I think so. He was pretty depressed a few years ago. He snapped out of that one."

"There's a lot to be depressed about. The chief. Joel. Yesterday was terrible."

"I know."

A few moments later Karrie looked into the mirror on her side and said, "I think she's following us again."

"Who?"

"That woman from yesterday."

Now even the probies were mocking me.

13. STICKING A PINKIE IN BEN'S COFFEE

On our way to the alarm, I tried to convince myself Stan Beebe was off base about whatever it was he thought we were all coming down with. He was a nice guy, but we all knew he was not exactly a brain surgeon. He'd gotten the facts wrong. Had to have.

I tried to distract myself by focusing on North Bend as we raced through town. It was a funny little place. The dinky downtown district had at one time been bisected by the major east–west route that traversed the Cascade Mountain Range, which separated the dry half of the state from the wet half, where we lived. These days Interstate 90 skirted the town by a good quarter mile. The old highway was now the main drag in town, the speed limit twenty-five MPH.

When Lorie and I first moved here as newlyweds, the occasional stray dog could be observed sleeping undisturbed in the middle of any of the side streets. Most locals didn't even bother to honk their horns—knew the dogs and the owners, just pulled around or waited for the pooch to wake up and move. The town was small enough then (under twenty-five hundred people) that we all felt like neighbors. Then came the outlet mall and fast-food chains next to the freeway and later the up-scale housing developments.

These days people drove faster, meaner, gunned their engines at stop-lights, rode your bumper, gave you the bone. Just like everywhere else.

The fire station was a block north of North Bend Way, on a street still quiet enough that sometimes in the summer we dragged fold-ing chairs out in front of the station and drank iced tea. Immediately north of the station was a small cluster of housing, a stray apartment building, and the North Bend branch of the King County Library. Far-ther north, things became rural, although new houses were going up all the time.

My daughters and I lived farther north, our lot snug under Mount Si, the four-thousand-foot monolith rising almost straight up from the flat valley floor.

Mount Si was the first vista strangers saw driving into town and the last one they saw upon leaving. The mountain never failed to inspire awe, especially in the winter, when the top third was encapsulated in snow and ice. The west face, the face that hovered over town, was almost a sheer cliff. In the still of the night we could sometimes hear rock slides rumbling down the face like cannon fire, taking out trees, forging long, rocky chutes above my house.

There were ancient boulders in the field next to our house, evidence of rockfalls that surely would have swept away our home had it been there five hundred years earlier. In the middle of the night, when we heard the mountain rumbling, the girls would climb into my bed. Helen Neumann from next door would call and ask in a tremulous voice if we were evacuating. We never were.

To the west of town, the South Fork of the Snoqualmie River ran near the heavily guarded Nintendo plant. There was a winery that had burned down years earlier, pastureland that developers and the town were squabbling over. As always, the developers would prevail. I had no doubt of it.

East of the city center, a golf course had been cut up, paved over, and converted into minuscule lots with monstrous houses sitting on them. Joel McCain lived in one of these. More houses and planned developments could be found off the Mount Si Road, which ran parallel with the pass highway. Clusters of new housing surrounded Truck Town farther east.

Just as the freeway began working its way up the foothills to three-thousand-foot Snoqualmie Pass, Edgewick Road took off south and snaked into the hills, dead-ending near the Cedar River Watershed, which fed freshwater to a good portion of the Seattle metro area. Generally, people didn't take Edgewick Road unless they knew somebody up there.

That was where we were headed.

Our alarm had been phoned in by Max Caputo.

We'd seen Caputo before. He'd lived in North Bend all his life, could barely read, and if he could write, I didn't know anybody who had proof of it. His grandfather, father, and uncles had come to the region fifty years ago looking for trees to cut down, but now that the logging industry was dying, the older Caputos had retired and the younger ones had turned to more traditional blue-collar occupations: butcher, house builder, auto mechanic, and, in Max's case, floral deliveryman, along with the occasional petty theft.

Caputo lived on wooded property in a double-wide trailer that was in a constant state of disrepair. He was one of those men who had so much trouble staying organized, he would be living on the streets if not from the periodic help of family. Besides burglaries, Max Caputo had been arrested for shooting deer out of season, bearbaiting, and allegedly killing one of his neighbor's dogs by feeding it a quarter stick of dynamite.

You had a neighbor like Caputo, you kept the police on auto-dial.

He lived like a hermit, taking in the occasional unkempt live-in girlfriend, most of whom didn't last more than a week and served mostly as drinking companions or drug connections. He was a small, wizened man who appeared to be in his midfifties but who, at thirty-three, was actually a year younger than me.

When I pulled the fire engine into the circular dirt drive, Caputo's two Dobermans tried to hang themselves on their chains, standing on their hind legs, barking, two of the most vicious dogs you would ever see. Two years earlier one of our volunteers had been bitten when we'd come out here after Caputo somehow put a crossbow dart through his thigh. Caputo claimed the dog had only *grabbed* the volunteer, prompting Newcastle to quip that he didn't know Dobeys had opposable thumbs. Six months later when Caputo accidentally shot himself with a handgun, another volunteer got bit.

Today Caputo was shirtless, covered in blood, sitting on the front step of his trailer home holding his left hand, his fist wrapped in a bloody white T-shirt. A table saw was still powered up and whirring in the yard. When the weather allowed, Caputo kept his power equipment on wooden blocks in the front yard, fending off the rain with tarps stamped UNIFIED FISHING TACKLE. If you're missing a table saw, we know where it is.

"I think we were followed," Ian Hjorth said, glancing out the driveway at the road.

"Karrie already tried that one."

"No. I really think we were followed." Nobody could play straight man better than Hjorth.

It was hard to hear anything between Caputo's yelling at the dogs and their barking.

Max Caputo had sliced off the last three fingers on his left hand. By the time he'd gotten his dogs chained up and phoned us, he'd deposited a pretty fair blood trail.

When Karrie took his blood pressure, Caputo fainted. And then, as if the barking had all been a show for their master, the dogs grew silent.

Ian stanched the flow of blood while I retrieved the fingers from the table saw and dropped them into a plastic bag. After the medics arrived, we helped them get a line into Caputo and put him onto the stretcher.

We cleaned up the blood on the floor of the trailer, unplugged the table saw, turned off the radio and two TVs that were blaring inside the trailer, fed the dogs, and locked up.

Before we left, Ian said, "I wonder if I could get those fingers back. You know? If they're not going to sew them back on?"

"What do you want with them?"

"Well, two of 'em I'd tie on a string and hang in the doorway of the garage for the cat to play with. The pinkie I want to put in Ben's coffee."

Karrie said, "Ugh! That's sickening."

I couldn't help laughing, not at the joke, but at the demented Jack Nicholson look on Ian's face.

The station was empty when we got back, no sign of Stan Beebe or his truck. Or of the mayor. I couldn't believe it.

After we scrubbed down, I dialed Beebe's house, but nobody answered. I told Ian where I was going and took a portable radio, intending to seek out Mayor Haston in the city offices next door to the fire station.

"What happened?" I asked Haston in his office. "Where's Stan?"

"He wanted to leave."

"And?"

Haston shrugged. "He wanted to leave."

"You let him?"

"Yes." Even at the best of times, Haston and I had never been friends. I hadn't hung out with him when he was a volunteer, and after Chief Newcastle threw him out of the department, I didn't miss him. His ex-wife and mine had been friendly, so we'd seen each other socially from time to time. In fact, we'd been studiously avoiding each other since our respective divorces. When he showed up to talk with me about Stan, it was the first time he'd been in the station since Newcastle died.

"Where did he go?" I asked.

"He didn't say."

"Did you even ask him?"

"No."

"He just got up and walked out?"

"What did you want me to do? Wrestle him? I wasn't going to wrestle him."

"Did you even try to stop him? Shit, Steve. This is priceless. I just hope to God he's okay."

"Sure, he's okay. He's just a little down. I get down all the time."

I went back to the station, pissed. I'd had some time to think about it and figured Stan Beebe's theory was a good dose of paranoia induced by a vastly overactive imagination. I would never have said this aloud, because I liked Stan for both his good-humored nature and his eagerness to work hard, but he had never been the sharpest pencil in the box.

I was no genius myself, but at least I knew bunk when I heard it. It was bunk that there was a syndrome, and it was probably bunk that he was going to kill himself.

While I disbelieved his theory, it frustrated me to no end that I couldn't definitively prove it wrong, that I couldn't think up even one fact to refute it. What bothered me most was that he'd ticked off every symptom I had. After speaking with Haston, I went back to the station and asked around, hoping perhaps it was the summer flu making the rounds—but nobody had heard of a bug going around.

Trying not to look at my own flaking waxy hands as I dialed, I called Tacoma General hoping to get a description of Holly's hands, but nobody would talk to me about her condition.

Reluctantly I called Holly's home number, where I knew Stephanie Riggs was staying. I got Holly's answering machine, Holly's voice still on the tape. "Hi. If this is somebody with good news or money, please leave a message. Everybody else call back." She'd been cute in all things, having taken her phone message from the play *A Thousand Clowns*.

It was sad and a little bit eerie to hear her voice again.

I stewed about it for a while and then went into the officers' room and began filling out next month's night and weekend schedule. Our station was staffed with full-timers until five in the afternoon each day, volunteers the rest of the night; sleepers, we called them. The same thing on weekends. It was a complicated business keeping the station staffed, and I was worried about what might happen to our ability to do so once Beebe began spreading rumors that we were all dropping from exposure to some unidentified substance. It was a fruitcake theory, but rumors had a way of taking on a life of their own.

An hour later as the medic unit returned to the station, the bell hit for the second time that morning, an MVA on I-90 between the old winery and town, eastbound. It was promising to be a busy shift.

Three vehicles involved. Persons trapped. This might be good.

14. MOI—THE MECHANISM OF INJURY

The stretch of freeway where the accident had taken place ran straight for maybe a mile, firs on either side, a slope on the right, a distant glimpse of the blue mountains down at the end where the highway made a left sweep toward North Bend.

By the time we arrived, citizens were putting out road flares. The Bellevue medics, Rachel Heimeriz and Dan Logan, were peering into two of the wrecked vehicles, a car and a truck, the truck crossways in the center of the highway, the Volkswagen near the left shoulder. They were separated by about two hundred feet, the roadway a pastiche of broken glass, plastic parts, oil, and streaks of green antifreeze.

A third vehicle had gone off the highway into the trees on the right shoulder. If there was anybody still inside that one, we couldn't tell from the road.

I told Karrie to get the pump running and lay a precautionary hose line, while I walked across the now-closed highway in front of the rows of waiting vehicles to see what the medics had.

"Sure you want a hose line?" Karrie asked.

"You ever see a trapped person burn to death in a car?"

One of Karrie's weak points was her questioning of authority. It wasn't so bad around the station when she asked if you *really* wanted the floor mopped, as if you might change your mind and decide to do it yourself, but fighting fire was a paramilitary activity and obeying orders in the field without hesitation was a vital part of the contract.

After surviving an initial training period at the state training center, Karrie was now seven months into a one-year probationary cycle. Her primary supervising officer, Joel McCain, had given her a poor evaluation the month previous, not because of lacking skills but because of her attitude, and warned her that if she didn't modify her behavior, her job would be in jeopardy. It was something I would have to deal with now. Something I'd been trying to ignore.

The paramedics had split up, one to a vehicle. The pickup truck had rolled over on the driver's side, and the roof was caved in, the passenger's side door crumpled. What remained of the windshield space had been compressed until the gap was too small to extricate a patient. There were two males inside, both conscious and talking. In fact, one of them wouldn't stop.

The other vehicle was a new Volkswagen Beetle, crumpled all the way around; the driver, a tearful young woman in her early twenties, had gotten out on her own. "My graduation present," she said. "I just waxed it."

The medic was taking her blood pressure and trying to get her to sit down, while an excited male witness in glasses and a button-down shirt explained how the Beetle had nearly missed the wreck altogether, that it had been zigzagging through the tangle of swerving cars and only got clipped at the last minute, spinning around like a shot glass on a table. There were two other damaged cars up the road on the shoulder. The witness said he'd spoken to the drivers and neither was injured. We would check later ourselves.

As Ian dragged a hose line across the highway, I said to him, "The driver of that truck needs to be extricated and put on a backboard—we'll have to take the roof off and bring him out the top—the passenger's lower leg is pinned. It's going to take awhile to get him out."

"I'll get the jaws," Ian said.

"I'll be with you as soon as I go up here to see what else we've got. I've already asked for more help on the radio. Snoqualmie should be showing in a few minutes." I turned to the closest medic, Dan Logan, and said, "You guys check the vehicle in the woods?"

"Not yet."

Karrie and Ian were off-loading the Hurst power unit for the jaws, a two-person carry unless you were Stan Beebe, who took pride in toting it alone. It would have been nice to have him here today. As shorthanded as we were, it would have been nice to have anybody here.

Heedful of the slippery antifreeze on the road, I jogged along the freeway and stepped off the shoulder, crossed the ditch, and hiked up into the trees. Judging by the skid marks, the third vehicle had crossed several lanes, then shot up into the grass, up the slight embankment, and buried itself in the thick firs.

The first thing I saw was the International Association of Firefighters union sticker hanging off what was left of the rear window. Whoever was inside was either a firefighter or a relative of one. It was a black Ford pickup truck, still hot and stinking of burned rubber, spilled gasoline, and engine fumes. The truck had snapped off enough fir trees that the whole area smelled like a Christmas tree lot.

Squeezing past a bright yellow swatch of blooming Scotch broom, I moved along the driver's side of the vehicle.

The driver's door was intact but wouldn't open. The glass was broken out of the window, the windshield popped out, the air bag in the center of the steering wheel deployed and sagging. No driver in sight. Maybe he was one of the Good Samaritans setting out flares on the highway behind me.

I stuck my head in the window.

When my eyes adjusted to the shadows, I spotted him on the floor, his torso and head crushed under a ball of crumpled sheet metal, the twisted seat hiding the rest of him. Or her. Whoever it was hadn't been wearing a seat belt. Body fluids were already congealing on the floor. The vehicle had struck a tree about twenty inches in diameter, shoving the engine through the dashboard.

"How is it up there?" Ian asked, when I got back to the road.

"DOA."

"Just the one?"

"Unless somebody got ejected. We'd better have some of these lookiloos run around in the trees to make sure."

I turned to one of the men who'd been putting out road flares. "Maybe you could gather up a couple of these guys and do a search of the woods? Make certain there aren't any victims we're not seeing?"

"You got it."

"Thanks. And don't touch anything in the truck."

"No, sir."

I loved it when they called me *sir*.

15. FIVE KNUCKLES TO THE SNOT LOCKER

s firefighters, we're used to the uproar of extrications, but it usually rattles the patients. Our primary tool, after the ten- and fifteen-pound pry bars, is the hydraulic unit we'd purchased from Hurst—the Jaws of Life.

The unit consisted of a heavy gasoline-powered pump with twenty feet of double hydraulic hoses coming off it, each set of hoses powering a single handheld unit.

We have a pair of spreaders, a huge, plierlike tool we insert into crevices on a wreck to pry the surfaces apart. It also squeezes like pliers and can compact or crush jagged flanges. Along with the cutting unit resembling crab claws, it was the extension used most often. With these tools we can take a car down until it's only a pile of tin.

Unless circumstances dictated otherwise, the strategy we'd been using the past couple of years with trapped occupants was this: We laid a hose line in case of fire. We calmed the patients as best we could and explained what we were doing. We treated them through the openings if necessary and put blankets or tarps around them to protect them from glass and flying sparks. We stabilized the vehicle so it wouldn't roll, usually by flattening the tires. We removed the windshield, cut the posts that held the roof on, and either folded the roof back or cut it completely off. We put notches in the outer frame at the base of the dashboard and pulled the dash away with our hydraulic tools. Often that was the point at which a firefighter climbed into the backseat to stabilize the head and neck of a patient in the front seat. We cut the doors off, cut the seat loose, pulled the steering wheel out of the way, and at this point, if not before, we were generally able to extricate the patient and slide him onto a backboard.

The driver of the rolled pickup, who had alcohol on his breath, was removed without much hassle, especially after the crew from Snoqualmie arrived to help; but the passenger had a broken femur, was pinned in the wreckage. He screamed every time our tools touched the truck. It took twenty-five minutes to extricate him.

"Dirtbags," Ian Hjorth said. "Drunk as skunks. They killed that guy up in the trees. I hope they go to jail forever."

We'd packed both patients from the truck into transport units and were walking up the slope to the third vehicle in the woods. Ian and I had been carrying the heavy Hurst power unit between us, Snoqualmie firefighters picking up the cables and tools and following like a wedding train. The medics had already confirmed our next patient was dead. The State Patrol had finished taking photographs and measurements. The medical examiner's people were on scene. Our job now was to pull out the body.

"Shit," Ian said as we set the power unit on the ground. "This looks like Stan's truck."

What had I been thinking? Stan talks about death all week. Stan comes to the station drunk. An hour and a half later we get a call to an MVA, and there's a truck that looks like Stan's with an IAFF union sticker in the window.

And yours truly doesn't connect the dots.

I put my head and shoulders through the window until I could see his hands in the shadows on the floor. The skin was dark, the backs of the fingers covered in a waxy-looking substance.

Just like mine.

Just exactly like mine. It was Stan all right.

I couldn't help thinking we might have saved him. We couldn't have, but the idea wouldn't go away. It proved to be hogwash after we dismantled the truck, because Stan's chest and head had been crushed when the impact pushed the motor back through the fire wall. Stan was dead before we left the station.

Weeping, Karrie said, "We were just talking to him."

We were all in shock. It hit us, as Stan would have said, like five knuckles to the snot locker. The firefighters from Snoqualmie. Even the state troopers, when they found out who it was. What made it worse was the guilt I felt over not having taken Stan under my wing earlier. I should have tapped us out of service the minute the word *suicide* came out of his mouth. We could have driven him to the hospital ourselves in the aid wagon.

Had I taken his truck ignition key, an option that hadn't even occurred to me until now, he might be alive still.

The lieutenant riding the rig from Snoqualmie, a man named Meyers, came over while Ian and I were carrying Stan to the medical examiner's gurney, and said, "This is going to be a hard one. Telling his wife."

I placed one of Stan's shoes next to him on the gurney, thinking that stray misshapen shoe was about the saddest thing I'd ever seen.

"It's going to be tough telling her," Meyers repeated.

My brain seemed to be lagging behind everyone else's. As the senior officer of North Bend Fire and Rescue, it fell on me to inform Stan's wife. In another town the chief or the mayor might do it, but we didn't have a chief and our mayor was pretty much worthless for that sort of thing—had in fact already proved himself useless in regard to Stan today. There'd been a lot of bad news doled out in North Bend the past few months, and Steve Haston had done even more ducking and weaving than I had when it came time to appoint bearers of bad news. The Mountain Rescue Team had pulled the short straw after they found Harold Newcastle's body. When Jackie Feldbaum nearly decapitated herself in her Miata, Joel Mc-Cain bit the bullet and told Jackie's old man at the lumber mill.

Yesterday Stephanie Riggs told me about her sister, but if I used her methodology, I would be dragging the stretcher into Marsha Beebe's living room and saying, "Hey, take a look under the blanket."

Before we left the site, I located the state trooper in charge of the investigation and asked how it had happened.

"To tell you the truth," said the trooper, "your friend caused it. Veering all across the freeway, from one side to another. All our witnesses are in agreement."

"The truck in the woods caused the accident?"

"These guys over here have been drinking, but it was your friend. Witnesses say it looked like he purposely tangled with one of those eighteen-wheelers. Knocked him to one side. That's when he bumped into all these other people."

16. WE'RE ALL GOING TO BE ZOMBIES

My intention was to dither around the station and solicit opinions on how to do this, to recruit an aide-de-camp with experience in dispensing bad news or maybe even to find someone who would volunteer to take the load off my shoulders, but the longer I delayed, the more likely it was that Marsha would learn of her husband's death through the grapevine.

And that was not going to happen. Not on my watch.

Three years ago, when I learned my wife was having an affair, everybody else in town knew it before I did. The grapevine had been hot with the electricity of someone else's misfortune. Mine. Nothing was uglier than realizing the whole town had worn out your bad news before you even got to try it on.

Fearing I would ask him to tag along, Ian had been avoiding me since we got back to the station. I told him to find a replacement to fill my slot for a few hours. Then I signed out of the daybook and walked around the corner in the sunshine, pushing open the tall glass door to the mayor's office. Shirtsleeves rolled up, Steven Haston was leaning on a countertop, having returned once again from his tax and accounting business on North Bend Way to catch up on city obligations.

Haston was almost six feet, seven inches, lantern-jawed and lugubrious, born in Norway, a catch for any woman who didn't mind a man who never laughed.

I mean never.

Despite the dilemmas confronting the fire department these past few weeks, until this morning nobody in the department had seen or heard from Haston since Harold Newcastle's funeral. It was okay with me. He and I made a point of avoiding each other.

"Steve," I said. "Wonder if you have a minute?"

"What's going on?"

"Stan Beebe has just been killed out on I-90. I'm driving over to tell his wife."

The secretary in the back of the room gasped. Haston said, "What?"

"You were supposed to be baby-sitting him."

"I didn't know how to stop him."

"Well, he's dead now."

"She home? His wife?"

"I don't know. I'm not going to call to find out if she's there and end up having to say hold up that trip to the QFC; I'm coming over with some bad news."

"I know what you mean. Thing is, I've got some meetings and there's no way I can get out of them. People are coming in from Seattle."

"Seattle," I said, surprised at the indignation in my voice. "My God, Seattle! We wouldn't want to put someone from Seattle out because one of our friends is dead, would we?"

I stormed out of the office.

Defying logic, tradition, and reason, the town council had agreed to let Steve Haston serve out the remainder of his wife's mayoral term after she left town in the middle of the night, even though he'd shown no interest whatsoever in politics before that. When that broken first term ended, he was reelected. He'd run unopposed until the last minute, when a write-in candidate suddenly appeared, a man who claimed citizenship in North Bend because he lived in his van and parked it under the South Fork Bridge, which meant in our tiny democracy that if you were voting for him, you needed to borrow a pencil from the polling officials in order to write his name in. When Haston came to vote that day, we crossed paths—he saw me returning my pencil. I don't think he ever forgot it.

I was still steamed at Haston when I got to my truck and found a Big Gulp container sitting on the roof. I stepped up into the cab and reached over to remove what I was sure was the latest installment in a series of jokes perpetuated by Ian Hjorth, who made a habit of decorating my truck with various and sundry geegaws. His favorite—a reservoir-tipped condom pulled tight over my trailer hitch.

The cup was glued down. I couldn't get it off.

Clearly, Ian had done it before the accident, because nobody was in a joking mood now. The cup and the general air of camaraderie it represented—the first prank I could remember since Chief Newcastle's death—was a spark of life in a deeply disturbed department.

It was a short drive to the Beebes', the high-noon traffic thick with local workers dashing out to lunch. Jeeps creeping along North Bend Way with mountain bikes in racks. Isuzus gassing up at the Shell station, kayaks strapped on top. Scott's Dairy Freeze was filled to capacity, the girls in bikini tops, guys bare-chested, their vehicles looking top-heavy with fat truck inner tubes strapped on for play in the river, everybody laughing and showing off, nothing to think about but the opposite sex and where to meet tonight. I would have given a lot to go back to that time.

But then, my teen years hadn't been nearly that carefree. At fifteen I'd been pushing religion on the sidewalks of Seattle. By the time I was seventeen, I was in the army, cussing a blue streak and getting laid twice a month, after taking the San Diego trolley to a ten-dollar whorehouse in Tijuana, where I eventually caught the clap from a woman old enough to be my mother. There'd been nothing carefree about any of it.

Mount Si Road was a two-lane country road that ran along the base of the mountain next to the Middle Fork of the Snoqualmie River, which was low and boulder-strewn. At the bridge, fifty or sixty cars were parked along the roadway, hikers with kids and brightly colored day packs, looking for the Little Si trail.

Stan lived at the end of a long stone-and-gravel driveway just off the road, maybe two miles from the Little Si trailhead. I turned into the drive, proceeding slowly, the driveway shaded by fir trees and underbrush.

Near the house two brown-skinned children were clambering over a play set constructed of logs and pipes, a boy and a girl, maybe six and eight years old. The boy was a clone of Stan, except lighter-skinned. The children paid no attention to me when I parked behind a Ford Escort station wagon. After the two mongrel dogs were done sniffing my crotch, I walked to the front porch.

It was a single-story house made of logs, its long wooden porch decorated with children's toys, four or five curious cats, and an array of thoroughly gnawed dog bones.

Marsha opened the door before I had a chance to gather my wits.

"Oh, God! What's wrong?"

"May I come in?"

"Get your ass in here. Sit down. Something happened, didn't it?"

In polite company Marsha Beebe used words I would never use in my worst nightmare. My army cussing had been scandalous by the standards of my upbringing, but battery acid and Arctic lightning came out of Marsha's mouth on a regular basis. Like a thermonuclear blast, her cussing could melt your eyeballs from ten miles away.

At department social functions I found myself calculating where she was going to spend the majority of her time so I might spend mine elsewhere. It wasn't that I didn't like her—it was more that I didn't understand her, or trust her willingness to treat me with civility or respect. Stan was the nicest guy in the world, but Marsha took the current of good-natured ribbing the guys around the station bathed me in and turned it into abuse, especially after she'd downed a few drinks.

Short, stout, white, and downright ugly, as opposed to merely homely, she was the last woman you'd pick up at a bar, if you went to bars, and probably had been the last woman in the bar thirteen years ago, when she and Stan met there. Her hair was short and curly, her skin anemic-looking, her dark eyes fierce and determined. She wore a ring on every finger, several necklaces, ornate earrings that dangled alongside her jaw and made her head look about the size of an orange. Okay, so these were not particularly generous observations to be making about the wife of a coworker who'd died less than an hour ago, but I couldn't help it. Marsha terrified me.

As soon as the door closed behind us and I was certain we were alone, I said, "I'm sorry to have to tell you this, Marsha, but Stan is dead."

Having watched a fair number of individuals receive this kind of news over the years, I knew this was not only the quickest but also the kindest way to say it. No equivocating, no stalling, no euphemisms. The last thing you wanted was to be forced to deliver news like this twice because you said something like "we lost him," or "he's passed on," or worse, "he's no longer with us."

Hands at her sides, Marsha sat heavily on the sofa.

I gave her the particulars as I knew them and told her how sorry I was. "Marsha, if there's anything I can do, tell me. I mean that. Stan was one of my favorite people. We're all going to miss him. Terribly."

"Was it suicide?"

"I don't know for sure. He was talking about it earlier."

"He was so afraid people would think it was suicide and we wouldn't get his policy. He kept saying the life insurance doesn't pay off in the event of a suicide."

Her dark-blue eyes remained unfocused. Marsha tucked her arms between her thick legs—she was wearing black leggings and a loose-fitting white blouse that concealed most of her figure. "Stan thought there was something going on with the department. Then one day he got the shakes and told me he was dying. I said he was full of shit up to his eyebrows. A few days later he got dizzy and told me he had a headache—join the club—and thought he was doomed. I tried to convince him he was a whadoyacallit . . . ?"

"Hypochondriac?"

"Yeah. He spent so much time at the nursing home with Jackie, I thought he was laying pipe with a nurse there. God. I can't believe he's dead."

It was at that moment, sitting in Stan's living room listening to his wife, that I began to believe all of Stan's theories.

Stan had had the shakes, same as me. He'd had the waxy hands, same as me. And then he'd died on the freeway the way Jackie Feldbaum had almost died. The question was: If he hadn't died, would he have ended up like Joel?

"Well," Marsha said, standing. "Thanks for telling me. I'll get the kids together and go over to my brother's."

"Do me a favor, Marsha. Call the fire station and leave a number where we can reach you."

"Sure."

"I'll find out what the city and state owe him. Get his package together. I'll call the pension office in Olympia. Get out his insurance policies from work. And I'll collect his stuff from the station."

"Thank you, Jim." I certainly didn't want to hug her, but if there was ever a time, this was it. I opened my arms and she stepped into them. She hadn't shed a tear. A minute later I was almost out the door when she said, "Wait."

She left the room and moments later reappeared with a small white envelope, my name across it in Stan's crabby printing.

"What's this?"

"I don't know. Stan said you'd be here today and I was to give it to you. He said it was the most important thing."

"He told you I would be here today?"

"Said sometime after lunch."

Outside in my truck, I opened the envelope with a deliberation verging on dread.

Inside I found a small sheet of paper torn off a stationery pad. The note said: *Jim, my friend. Your turn to carry the torch.* A three-by-five card fell out of the envelope, one side blank. The other side had a hand-printed list:

Day 1: Tingly hands that shake.
Day 2: Waxy hands, weak legs, and mild headache.
Day 3: Worse headache, dizziness, falling down.
Day 4: Headache goes away, cannot keep food down.
Day 5: Stomach problems disappear. Blurred vision, ringing in ears, syncope.
Day 6: Everything seems fine except the ringing in ears is louder.
Day 7: Now you a zombie.
Good luck, my friend.

It was signed: Stan.
I said, "Good luck to you, too, my friend."

17. SEVEN SACRED DAYS INSIDE STAN'S LOCKER

Somebody convinces you you're going to be brain-dead in a week, believe me, it gets the gears whirring. They can get to whirring pretty fast. For a few seconds there on the drive home, I thought I was going crazy.

A million courses of action raced through my mind. I wanted to call Jackie Feldbaum's common-law husband and ask whether in the days immediately preceding her car accident Jackie had experienced any of the symptoms from Stan's list. I wanted to ask Mary McCain about the circumstances of Joel's fall.

Now that I thought about it, Joel's roof was practically flat. How do you fall off a flat roof?

I'd scoffed at Stan's theories, but now I knew why. From the first there had been a strain of truth to what he'd proposed. *Ye shall know the truth and the truth shall kill you.*

If Stan's theory was correct, I was on day two of my last week as a recognizable human being.

Apprehension and dread were beginning to make my stomach queasy.

I wanted to convene a presidential commission to investigate. I wanted to call the FBI, the CIA. I wanted the Vatican in on it. I wanted somebody important to tell me this was all a mistake.

Whether Stan's end had been a self-fulfilling prophecy or an inescapable bullet of destiny I could not say. Stan obviously felt getting crushed under the wheels of an eighteen-wheeler was preferable to years with a brain that functioned below the level of that of your common house cat. But was that really where his brain had been headed? On the other hand, maybe he'd turned into a zombie out there on the highway. Maybe losing his mind had caused the accident.

If Stan's hypothesis did nothing else, it introduced a comprehensive theory of what had been happening to North Bend Fire and Rescue in the past weeks. The *only* comprehensive theory I'd heard.

Parking across the street from the station, I got out of my truck just as one of the volunteers showed up, a community college student named

Jeb Parker, a happy-go-lucky young man who reveled in the camaraderie of our little fire department.

"Forgot your Big Gulp?" he said, laughing at the large cup still glued to my roof.

I went into the station, jogged up the stairs past Ian and Karrie, who both asked, "How'd it go?," and found Stan's clothing locker in the bunk room. Padlocked. I jogged back downstairs to the apparatus bay and retrieved a pair of bolt cutters from a side compartment on the engine.

"Pretty bad?" Ian asked, having followed me upstairs the second time.

"He's been telling her something was going to happen all week."

"What do you mean, 'something was going to happen'? Like what?"

"Like what happened."

"You're kidding."

"Nope."

Squeezing the bolt cutters, I watched the shackle on the lock split in half and fall to the floor. All of Stan's clothing had been removed from the locker, the remaining articles arranged neatly: two cans of soup on the top shelf, a pair of sunglasses, a pencil, several three-by-five cards, and a manila envelope labeled in Stan's cramped lettering: HAROLD LEVY NEWCASTLE AUTOPSY REPORT. Poor Stan had squandered a portion of his last week making certain nobody had to clean up after him.

The cards appeared to be earlier drafts of the list Marsha had given me. Most were labeled *Seven Sacred Days*, no doubt Stan's idea of a joke, but he'd inadvertently transposed a couple of letters and wrote *Seven Scared Days* on one. In either case, I knew what he meant. The closer I got to the details of Stan's final hours, the more I realized they might also be the details of *my* last hours.

If Stan was wrong about a syndrome, there were a hell of a lot of coincidences operating in North Bend. Chief Newcastle. Joel McCain. Jackie Feldbaum. Stan. My own symptoms. One might even include Holly in the list.

Poring over the various cards, I could see how he'd rearranged the order of the symptoms as his information base and his own condition altered. On two of the cards the list was six days instead of seven. The more I read, the more I became convinced the list I'd received from his wife was the final compendium. For starters, it was the only one that had the first two days precisely as I'd experienced them.

Ian Hjorth peered around my shoulder into the locker. "Don't you think he was traveling a little light?"

"Look, Ian. I'm checking out for the day. Keep Jeb on for the rest of the shift."

"He can only stay a couple of hours."

"Then find somebody else. I'm outa here."

"Sure. Of course. None of us feel much like working."

Brushing past Ian on my way out of the station, I said, "Thanks for the Big Gulp. That was actually pretty funny."

He was chasing me across the street to my car as I left. "Oh, Jesus. I forgot. I put it up there before our alarm. You don't think I ran out there and put it on your roof after we came back from the freeway, do you? Oh, shit. You had to drive around like that? I'm sorry. I'll take it off right now."

I ignored him, was already turning the key in the ignition and buckling the seat belt.

"Come on, Lieut," Ian said. "Let me get that off there. You don't want to be driving around like that. At least let me take the straw out. It's got juice in it. Ben thought it would be funnier with juice in it. Look, I'll climb up—"

I shot gravel out from my rear tires peeling out of the parking area. It wasn't often one of Ian's gags backfired on him. Leaving the Big Gulp container on my roof and pretending to be pissed might be the last joke I ever played.

Alpine Estates Nursing Home was a white single-story concrete-block building three blocks from the fire station. I parked and went inside, found myself being chased down the hallway by a short Hispanic woman in white pants and one of those kiddie-print smocklike tops nurses wear these days that look more suited to a nursery school than a medical facility. This one was all teddy bears or lollipops or some such thing.

"Can we help you?" she asked for about the fourth time. "You want to visit a patient?" I must have been daydreaming.

"Jackie Feldbaum."

She went back to her cubicle and picked up several sheets of paper stapled together. "Not here. Nope. No. Wait. Rolanda Feldbaum. Could that be her?" I nodded. "One-oh-seven. Down at the end of this hall. Turn left."

The room was what you'd expect. Two patients, two beds, a curtain between them, photos and personal touches on the nightstand alongside each bed, and next to the sink a TV that looked as if it'd been underwater for about a year. Jackie's roommate, a small humpbacked, masculine-looking woman with close-cropped hair and no teeth, looked to be about a hundred fifty and was absorbed in a Spanish-language game show I had the feeling she didn't understand a word of.

Jackie was in bed on her back, her hair cut with straight Moe Howard bangs. Both hands were above the blankets, both covered in a waxy-looking patina.

"Jackie?"

"She don't talk," said the roommate.

"Ever?"

"Not since I been here."

"What *does* she do?"

"She farts."

"That's it?"

"That's about all. Yes sirree. They don't smell so great, neither."

Tuning out the racket from the television, I sat in the only free chair in the room and tried to ignore the stench of ammonia pervading the room. I opened the manila envelope I'd been carrying and scanned Harold Newcastle's autopsy report. It took a while to pinpoint what I was looking for. *The palms appear to be normal, but the backs of both hands extending from the fingernails to the ulnar styloid process are spotted with a whitish substance of indeterminate origin.*

When I tried to push myself up out of the chair, my legs felt weak.

"You leaving?" the hundred-year-old woman asked.

I nodded.

"Whatsa matter? She do a pooper?"

"No. She's okay. Just time to go."

"Have a good day, mister."

"I can't see it getting any worse."

18. WANNA BET?

Room 111 was just down the corridor. I couldn't tell you what made me stop there. It wasn't proximity, because during the past three years I'd been proximate plenty of times without stopping in.

On the wall next to the door were two easily disposable paper labels: FUJIMOTO—SWOPE.

I pushed the door open.

Again, two beds, minimal personal effects, some newspaper clippings on the walls, a few photos cut out of magazines. Your basic jailhouse decor.

My father was slumped in a wheelchair next to the window at the foot of the second bed. His roommate was out playing paddleball or racing wheelchairs up the halls, chasing the nurses. Whatever.

My father's back was to the window, his face squared up with the heat register. The window behind him afforded an awkward view of some shrubbery. A few tall shafts of June sunlight penetrated the thicket and lit up the windowpane. There was little difference between my father and Jackie. Thirty years was all.

I squatted until we were at eye level. I don't know what scared me more, the possibility that he would look at me or the possibility that he *couldn't* look at me.

"Dad? It's me: Jim. It's been awhile."

After a minute it became clear that he wasn't going to reply.

Not long after moving to North Bend to be near his granddaughters, my father had suffered a CVA and had, after a brief hospital stay, been incarcerated here. As far as I knew, during his entire three-year tenure he'd never received a visitor. I'd certainly not been here before.

After a few minutes of silence, the day began caving in on me. I thought about how insubstantial were my reasons for not visiting sooner, about Stan's death, Joel McCain's condition, Holly's coma, about my own future or lack of same. If my worst fears came true, I'd end up staring at a wall, too. Except it wouldn't happen when I was seventy-six; it would happen at the end of the week. At age thirty-four.

Somebody had taped a clipping from the local newspaper to the wall over the heat register. It was this article my father was facing, as if study-ing it, which of course, he was not. It included a black-and-white photo of me in my fire-fighting gear kneeling alongside two toddlers; there was a second photo of a burned-out Ford Explorer.

I'd forgotten about the article. About the incident. There had been a clipping in the fire station for a while, but eventually it had been thrown out with the trash. It was one of those embarrassing moments when the newspapers proclaimed you a hero for doing your job. I'd been driving my private vehicle, spotted a car fire on North Bend Way, and did noth-ing more than open the back door and remove two toddlers while their mother and a bunch of bystanders ran around in a panic. Because I'd re-ceived some minor burns, they called me a hero. It was bullshit, the result of a small-town newspaper reporter jacked up on caffeine with nothing to write about.

Kneeling on the floor beside my father's wheelchair, I said, " 'Hear me when I call, O God of my righteousness: thou has enlarged me when I was in distress: have mercy upon me, and hear my prayer.' "

I thought about what I was doing and began to laugh. How many prayers had I uttered during my first sixteen years of life? Thousands? Hundreds of thousands? And how many times during those years had I prayed alongside my father? A better question was how many of those prayers had been answered? Certainly fewer than the laws of probability would suggest—which had caused me to conclude long ago that if I needed something, I was actually better off not informing God about it.

I reached out and put my hand on my father's knee. "In the name of Jesus Christ and William P. Markham, rise up and walk. Leave this wheel-chair. Reclaim your senses. Bid good riddance to this institution of de-spair. In the name of William P. Markham, rise up and be a man again."

I'd like to be able to tell you that my father stood up and said, "Thank you, Son. I needed that little three-year rest. Thanks for bringing me around. Now I can go get a fine potato salad lunch with crab legs and French mustard and a cream soda and be on about the Lord's work."

But you and I both know my father didn't budge. My father wasn't getting out of his wheelchair on his own steam because I'd knelt on the floor beside him and uttered words from Psalms. My father was never getting out of that chair on his own steam.

Faith was what made prayers work. At least that was the conclusion I'd reached over the years. Religion needed to be backed up with faith, and the remnants of my faith had eroded eighteen years earlier.

From the day I was old enough to talk, I'd said prayers over break-fast, lunch, and dinner. I'd prayed next to my father. I'd prayed next to my mother. At bedtime. Upon rising. We'd prayed aloud on the street, and we'd prayed while strangers gawked. Even if I hadn't dodged a life of belief eighteen years earlier, the past few years would have shaken my faith.

How could I pray to a God who let Lorie abandon our two beautiful children? Or a God who'd allowed my father, surely the most righteous of individuals, to end up staring at a heat register for ten hours at a pop? How could I pray to a God who would let Joel McCain and Holly Riggs live out their lives as vegetables? Or who'd let Stan Beebe's four kids be-come fatherless in the blink of an eye. Maybe you could believe in God if all that had happened, but I couldn't.

I couldn't drum up a thimbleful of faith to save my life.

19. THE SIXTH ELEMENT OF THE SAINTS OF CHRIST;OR, HOW TO PRAY FOR ABSOLUTELY ANYTHING AND NOT GET IT

My mind was racing as I climbed into my truck and headed for Tacoma, the visit to my father igniting the wildfires of memory.

Until I ran away from home at sixteen, we'd lived on Capitol Hill in a huge, rambling showplace initially owned and built by one of the Mercers, an early pioneer family who now had a traffic-clogged Seattle street named after them.

A doctor owned the mansion today, but when we lived there it was called Six Points and was the official residence of the staff and founder of the Sixth Element of the Saints of Christ, the minimalist cult religion my father had adopted in his late twenties and clung to until the church virtually disintegrated around him like a cheap suit in the jungle. In those days the neighborhood was riddled with Saints, eight or ten families—the cognoscenti—living in the mansion at any given time, additional acolytes in nearby houses.

It was only a week after my father met my mother that he quit his engineering job at Boeing, sold his house, his car, his personal belongings down to his Boy Scout knife, and signed the proceeds over to William P. Markham, simultaneously becoming a pauper and a board member of the church. As with many religions, the engine of the Sixth Element was fueled by cold, hard cash.

My father had been toying with the notion for months, maybe years. For reasons that were never clear, my mother embraced the religion, too, and they moved into Six Points.

It took decades for me to figure out my father's interest in religion was predicated on a fear of death, on an unwillingness to believe death would be the end for him, his initial donation part of a long religious tradition of paying now for a cushy spot in the afterlife. Nobody feared death more than my father, and Markham had convinced his followers he knew the secret of everlasting life.

Being raised around Markham was like living with Santa Claus, the Easter Bunny, and one of the apostles all rolled into one. Until I was sixteen, my stolen glimpses into the real world had been sporadic and taken with much guilt and little stealth.

It was only years later that I found out William P. Markham had been a functionary in a tent revival show in his youth, a religious circus of sorts that toured the Deep South fleecing suckers who felt in need of salvation. Markham had been a child healer and an infant prodigy who knew how to fire up a crowd of religious enthusiasts the way a pyro knew how to fire up a warehouse.

In his teens, he left his uncle's revival group under cloudy circumstances and attended UCLA on a scholarship that was later discovered to have belonged to another student. He majored in economics there and at times alluded to spending his middle years drifting from town to town working elaborate con games. He also alluded to living off a succession of wealthy widows. Why these confessions should have endeared him to his followers baffled me, for even as a child I believed they were closer to the bone of his character than the charade he put on as a saint.

The religion's primary textbook was penned by Markham: *Dreams of the Afterlife with the Lord Jesus Christ.* Even as an old man, long after the church's demise, my father could, and frequently did, quote long passages verbatim from this tome.

Members of the Sixth Element of the Saints of Christ were encouraged to be model citizens. We talked about the devil, but the evil in people's hearts was implied more than spelled out, as was the end product of that evil, which of course included punishment after death, punishment that we as adherents of the *real truth* would not suffer.

Just as we were destined for a heaven beyond comprehension if we conscientiously followed William P. Markham's interpretation of the Bible and obeyed his tenets, *everybody else on earth* was headed for hell, of which there were, according to Markham, twenty-seven degrees. My father harped on the twenty-seven degrees endlessly and believed Catholics and Democrats would occupy the lowest rungs in Hades.

In many ways, ours had been the most comfortable view of the universe possible. We were God's chosen. The elite of the elite. We were going to embrace everlasting life and grace. Nobody else was. Imagine a world of billions where only a few hundred are destined to escape the fires of hell. Later I realized virtually no religion was immune from the conceit that they had The Truth and no one else did.

My father often announced his belief that only a few dozen true believers would end up in heaven with us. I never could figure out why he wanted heaven to be so exclusive. Sounded boring as hell.

Typically, we spent two or three hours a day in prayer meetings, although at times of church or world crisis a decree from Markham might double or treble that. One hour before breakfast; Bible lessons after school; a prayer meeting each evening. Saturdays and Wednesdays were relegated to recruitment. Until I was twelve, I followed either my father or my mother as they went door-to-door or positioned themselves in some public place where they could proselytize. Virtually nobody but the dimwits, the mentally ill, or people trying to convert us to *their* religion stopped to listen.

Even though they were almost 100 percent ineffectual, our annual hours on the streets were pie-charted and color-coded on a wall near the front door and were a source of great pride and discussion among the members.

This ritual, done without complaint or question by all the followers of Markham, annoyed and humiliated me more than anything else. What particularly galled me were the jeers, whispered criticisms, sour looks, and outright squabbles with other street Bible scholars, of which there seemed a limitless supply. My father loved debate, and the arguments pitched him into his element.

My mother's good looks were a net for the weak and profligate, the lustful and fallen, the needy and the spiritually barren—usually geeky males who would attend one or two of our services and then, when my mother no longer showed any interest in them, would vanish forever. Shy by nature, I never got used to parading my faith before strangers, though from my earliest years I was expected to be a participant, and even though it cut across the basic grain of my personality, as a youngster I'd been fairly effective. As I grew older I became sullen and rebellious and manufactured a hundred small tricks to sabotage recruitment efforts or to be elsewhere when my father debated Scripture in public.

The most embarrassing moment of my life up until the day Lorie left me was when Marcie Birkenheimer and her mother walked past us on a corner of Tenth Avenue East as my father regaled indifferent passersby with quotations from the Scriptures and from *Dreams of the Afterlife.* I was in eighth grade and had nursed a crush on Marcie all term. The look of abject pity she bestowed on me humbled me down to the fillings in my teeth.

The Saints' children went to public schools and were expected to be at the top of the class in all academic subjects, a goal I never achieved. Because of my faltering grades I was perpetually in hot water with Markham and was tutored by one aspiring Saint after another. During my early teens my tutor was a woman named Constance Desmond, sweet-natured and unaffected, a body to kill for, with a complete absence of pretense. She had a way of leaning against my arm as we looked over one of my papers so that the heat of her breast sent a fever straight to my brain. Under the table I would invariably achieve an erection. Except for the boners, Constance's tutelage served no purpose, and my grades grew worse. We were both punished for this, she by being repeatedly reassigned as my tutor, me with additional hours on the street.

I was in love with Constance, and since by then virtually all of my assigned proselytizing time was secretly spent at the downtown public library, where I habitually broke Markham's injunction against reading literature about other religions, I took the punishment stoically.

Several times during this period, one of the elders ordered me to wear a cardboard sign around my neck: IF I TRIED HARDER, I'D BE SMARTER, or, MY GRADES ARE BAD, I AM SAD. There was a synagogue down the street that had dozens of my signs hidden behind it.

These were long miserable months laced with exhilarating minutes with Constance, whose beautiful brown eyes flooded with tears whenever she saw a cardboard sign around my neck. In later years, I realized Constance had been struggling with her own demons, that the accidental pressure of her breast against my arm might not have been so accidental after all. Her husband, a huge, greasy, balding man, would have done almost anything to reach Sainthood, including, I often speculated, cutting off his own pecker, though Markham did not have a basketful of peckers in the back room.

That I knew of.

In later years, I came to the realization that Constance had been as lonely as I was.

And perhaps almost as horny.

Nothing ever happened between us. The emotional fallout from such a liaison would have destroyed Constance and certainly would have paralyzed me.

My affiliation with Six Points left me feeling like an oddball, as if there were constant parties and friendships going on around me to which I not only wasn't invited, but which I didn't even know about. It wasn't until I'd been in the fire department in North Bend for a good ten years and had two daughters that I truly overcame the sense of being an outsider.

My father, a natural-born lackey and former engineer, quickly became an indispensable cog of the inner circle. Mother was a tad too candid in recounting her wilding years during our weekly Confessions, a recounting that probably kept her from attaining the inner circle with my father. Their disparity of status as Saints was a source of much friction between them, as were the misspent years of my mother's youth.

Then, abruptly and without warning, when I was eight, my mother disappeared from Six Points and from my life.

My father was not normally a cruel man, but one night he told me my mother had left because I wasn't following the tenets of the Sixth Element of the Saints of Christ to her standards, that my malfeasance had sparked her desertion. Even at eight, I found the story unlikely and barely credible, but after he repeated it enough, part of me believed him. It might have been that I was a symbol of her sexual congress with other men. It might have been that he was trying to shift the blame for her departure onto someone else. Or maybe he was merely trying to make me a better Saint.

Whatever the reason for his cruelty, for years I strove to be a better Saint in the hopes it would bring my mother back. I even tried to walk on water. Can you imagine a more pathetic kid?

Four years later, almost to the week, my mother reappeared as suddenly and as inexplicably as she'd vanished, taking up the space in our lives she'd filled previously as if she'd never been gone. Nobody talked about it except Constance, who once intimated that while my mother was physically a strong woman, there was some moral weakness she needed to overcome. I never learned where my mother spent those four years, or what she'd done, or who she'd done it with. I don't believe my father ever found out, either. Were I to hazard a guess, I would say she ran off with a man—a practice that became a habit later in life—perhaps someone she'd met on the street while hawking religion.

My first sixteen years we lived in rooms on the third floor at Six Points, sharing a bath down the hall and eating downstairs with the others in a communal dining hall. Three weeks after my sixteenth birthday, I ran away and spoke to an army recruiter in San Diego. I hadn't done well in school, but I must have learned something in the public library, because after they tested me, they decided I was army material. A forged parental signature and a fake ID with a backdated birth date completed my induction. I spent four years in the army, during which my only contact with my past was an infrequent exchange of letters with Constance Desmond. Years after she left Six Points and remarried, she sent me a photo of herself with three small children, all of them looking happier than crooked politicians. It made me feel good to know she'd finally found her place in the world.

My mother left my father again, this time for good. The church eventually disintegrated, and my father moved to the Southwest. When his third wife died in a car accident, he moved from Arizona to North Bend. Later, I failed to tell Allyson and Britney he'd had a stroke. It was only one of my bad decisions in the past few years.

I couldn't help wondering who might visit if *I* were in 111. My girls, of course. But children grew bored easily, and were I in the same state as Joel McCain or Holly, they wouldn't come back often. The guys from work might show up, but their stopovers would be perfunctory and less frequent as time wore on. Karrie would visit once or twice, no doubt thinking about the Christmas party at McCain's, when we'd had too many drinks and ended up on the sofa in the basement.

Aside from my girls, there was really no one who cared.

My friends in the department were mostly gone. And as far as women went . . . I'd buzzed from one to another like a wasp moving from plate to plate at a picnic. Newcastle said I was searching for the mother I never had. "Men with abandonment issues," he said, "like to dump women before the women dump them." At the time, I'd thought his pronouncement ridiculous.

Until she ran out on me, Lorie had been the only woman in my life, but this year alone there'd been Karrie, Suzanne, Holly, Heather, Mary Kay, the other Suzanne, Tricia, and Tina, still friends all. Except for Karrie, I'd made love with all of them and then dumped them. Karrie and I had not consummated the relationship, though we'd come as close as you could without actually having intercourse.

At the time I'd had my reasons for dumping all those women, but right now I couldn't think what they were.

20. FIELD & STREAM, LADIES' HOME JOURNAL, ARCHITECTURAL DIGEST

It was tougher finding a parking spot near Tacoma General during the day. On the third floor I asked about Holly. A practical nurse with dark eyes looked at me and said, "Your name Swope?"

"That's right."

"We have instructions. You're not to visit any patient on this floor."

"Dr. Riggs in the hospital? I'd like to speak to her."

The nurse turned abruptly and went through a door behind the counter, where I could hear her speaking to someone. When she returned, she said, "Dr. Riggs is not available."

"Tell her I drove an hour to see her."

After a moment a second nurse emerged from the back room, closing the door behind her. The first nurse began shuffling paperwork on the desk. The other one turned her back to me. When an Asian man with the look of a lifelong menial worker came down the hallway and stepped behind the counter, I said, "Excuse me. Can you please go back there and tell Dr. Riggs I'm going to wait out here until hell freezes over?"

He glanced at the two nurses quizzically.

That was when I began singing. At the top of my lungs. "Peggy Sue. Peggy Sue. Pretty, pretty, pretty, pretty Peggy Sue. Oh, Pegggggy, my Peggy Sue-ue-ue-ue-ue . . ." Under ordinary circumstances I was a credible singer, but today my screeching was horribly off-key.

Stephanie Riggs popped out of the door like a cork out of a bottle, face compressed in anger, strawberry-blond hair down around her shoulders. Several more nurses and aides showed up behind her at the counter.

"You're making a scene," Riggs said.

"I can make a bigger one."

"Call Security."

"I know what's wrong with your sister."

"Bullshit. Call Security."

I thrust out my hands. "She have this?"

"Hold up," Stephanie said to the nurse who was dialing Security.

Stephanie stepped around the counter, took one of my hands in hers, turned it over, then walked brusquely down the corridor in the direction of Holly's room.

When I followed, the nurse with the phone said, "You still want me to call?" Stephanie didn't hear her.

As soon as we got to the room, I lost all my zip. Holly was in a wheelchair, head sagging at an angle that looked painful. Nothing else in the room had changed. Her eyes were open and unfocused. Her sister leaned over and kissed Holly's brow, a move that provoked no reaction from my former girlfriend.

Stephanie Riggs reached under the blankets and brought her sister's right hand out.

It was pale and waxy-looking, just like mine.

"Was it like that from the beginning?" I asked.

"From a few days before she went down. At least according to this." Stephanie produced a small black journal from the pocket of her lab coat. I found it touching that she carried her sister's diary on her person. God only knew what was written about me in there.

I handed her the card I'd been carrying.

She sat down, the three-by-five card in one hand, her sister's diary in the other, comparing the itinerary of Stan Beebe's last few days with that of her sister's. Brahms played in the background.

"Where'd you get this?" Stephanie asked, looking up with a new openness and sincerity in her dusty-blue eyes. In a heartbeat we'd gone from squabbling like archenemies to whispering like lovers. "These symptoms are almost exactly what my sister reported. Where'd you get it?"

It took ten minutes to explain about Stan Beebe, Joel McCain, Chief Newcastle, and Jackie Feldbaum.

When I finished, Stephanie caressed her sister's hair and pocketed the journal, my list of symptoms tucked into the pages. She took both my hands in hers. "They weren't like this yesterday, were they? Your hands didn't have this crust yesterday."

"No. But Stan Beebe's did."

"Why didn't you tell me about your friends?"

"I did."

"Do you know what this means?"

"It means my life is over."

"Yes. That. And I'm sorry. But it means my sister didn't try to kill herself. That probably doesn't seem important to you, but our father killed himself. I thought . . ."

"It might be a family thing?"

"Yes. You have any other symptoms?"

"Yesterday I had the shakes."

"Bad?"

I held out one hand and demonstrated.

"And today?"

"A headache. My legs feel weak."

"You're describing the symptoms my sister documented in her diary. You mind if we run some blood tests? I'd like a dermatologist to take a look at your hands. He said he'd never encountered anything like Holly's before. If yours are the same . . ."

"Back in late May we found a methamphetamine lab in the woods. Most of those meth cooks don't live past their midforties. We tried to be careful—even had a private company come in and do the cleanup—but most of the people who've had this thing were there. Maybe all of them. I'd have to go back and check the daybook."

"Did you see Holly around that time?"

"No. We were only speaking on the phone by then. What we're looking for, I guess, is some event that connects Joel McCain; our chief, who went down like Holly; and Jackie Feldbaum. And of course, Stan."

"Jackie? What happened to him?"

"Her. Slammed into the rear of an eighteen-wheeler in her sports car."

"She was a firefighter?"

"A volunteer. I just can't believe we didn't all incur this together. We had to have. Don't you think?"

"I do think. Is there any place where you all were at the same time?"

"Only that truck accident in February, where Holly and I met."

"All of you?"

"I think so. That would make the truck accident the most likely source, wouldn't it?"

"I've spoken at length to a neurologist in San Francisco, a doctor named Parker. He thinks Holly went down as a result of exposure to an insecticide. He said the pathophysiology of it affects the CNS, causing euphoria, dizziness, confusion, CNS depression, headache, vertigo, hallucinations, seizures, ataxia, tinnitus, stupor, and ultimately coma. That's not exactly the way it happened with Holly, but close enough. The way I'm thinking about this, if it were just people from your fire department, it could have been anything. But you cross-reference it with the fact that Holly got it, too, and nobody else in Washington or even on the West Coast has it, it narrows down the possibilities."

"The truck accident. That's the hypothesis I should work from."

"I agree. But you're off by one pronoun. It's the hypothesis *we* should work from. I'm in on this, too."

"Trouble is, there wasn't anything hazardous in either of those trucks."

"That you recall."

"One truck had nothing but chickens. The other truck was the one Holly drove, and as I remember, it had a pretty standard array of items. Lots of cartons and packages. Some comic books. Bibles. Coca-Cola extract. It was a sticky mess."

"The chickens interest me. H5N1. That was the Hong Kong virus. Birds have spread disease to humans before. I'll do some research. The trouble is, these aren't flu symptoms you guys are coming down with, and that's what H5N1 presents as. Flu symptoms." She looked at me and I saw flickers of the compassion that must have originally attracted Stephanie Riggs to medicine. Maybe she wasn't such a bitch after all. "You ready to run some tests?"

"Now?"

"We don't have a whole lot of time."

I felt like a man being dragged down the corridor to the gas chamber. I could only hope Stephanie couldn't sense my terror. In fact, I was almost more afraid of her finding out how afraid I was than I was of the syndrome. For reasons I had trouble explaining to myself, I wanted her to like me more than I'd ever wanted any woman to like me. Jesus, I thought. I still had the steely taste of vanity in my mouth even when they were hauling me to the boneyard. Maybe I *was* a prick like everybody said.

"As far as I'm concerned, and until we find out otherwise, you and my sister have the same thing."

"Which is?"

"I don't have a clue. Neither does any doctor I've consulted. I'm hoping, because you're still up and walking around, you'll present differently. If you'll let me test you, it just might be enough to give us the missing parts to the puzzle. You all right? You look a little pale."

"You find out what it is, you think you'll be able to reverse it?"

"Maybe for you. Holly had a brain aneurysm. I'm afraid there's no going back."

"But you told your aunt you were still hoping for a miracle."

"You're a patient. I have to tell you the truth, even if I don't want to face it myself."

"Run the tests."

The rest of my day was spent on an examining table or in a waiting room flipping through magazines: *Field & Stream, Ladies' Home Journal, Architectural Digest.* Stephanie Riggs drew blood, and then in a back room a technician drew more; a few hours later, Dr. Riggs drew blood again. The probing was the worst, umpteen feet of coil with a miniature camera on the end of it shoved up my rectum like a plumber's snake. I was X-rayed, given CT scans. Nothing is more exhausting than lounging around a hospital all day with your heart in your mouth. Samples of my hair, urine, sputum, stool, fingernails, and skin were taken away.

Just before eight that evening, Stephanie came into the lounge area where I was waiting and told me I was free to go home.

"What'd you find?" I asked, trying on a smile I knew was a little tight.

"Too soon for most of it. Your X rays and CT scan were fine. The blood workups haven't told us a thing. You're slightly anemic, but that may be normal for you. The dermatologist says the growth on your hands is the same as Holly has on her hands. I'll be here most of the night. I want to hand-carry some of these samples through the lab, watch the tests myself. You take care of yourself. Stay hydrated. Get lots of rest. If anything changes tonight or tomorrow morning, call me. If I don't hear from you, I'll be in touch tomorrow morning." She gave me a slip of paper with her cell phone number on it. "You have somebody who can watch out for you?"

"My girls."

"I mean an adult."

"They'll do."

"Okay."

I'd been feeling anxious in North Bend, but the dramatic change in Stephanie Riggs was bothersome to say the least. I'd driven down here thinking I *might* have some contagion, but now a knowledgeable doctor thought I was going to be a vegetable. She hadn't said it outright, but you could see it in her face.

She thought I was headed **for the** same fate as her sister.

I'd been hopeful on the drive down, but that was before we found out my symptoms and those on Stan's list correlated with what Holly had documented in her diary. Odds were if Stan hadn't died on I-90, he would have ended up in the brain ward—just as he feared. Odds were I would be forced to make the same decision Stan had: turn into a vegetable or commit suicide. Trouble was, I didn't know if I had the guts to kill myself. Would you? I mean, one day I'm walking around worried about weeds in the yard; the next I'm trying to figure out if I should kill myself. It was too weird.

I was trying to figure out which option was better for my daughters. Which did I *not* want to put them through?

"I'm sorry about your sister," I said. "I wish things had turned out differently."

"Let's not talk about it."

"I'm a firefighter. I signed up for a bad ending. I didn't think anything was going to happen, but in the back of my mind I always knew it might. Holly didn't sign up for anything more than sweetness and light. That's what she deserved."

When tears began creeping down Stephanie's face, I said good-bye and got out of Dodge.

DAY THREE

21. BAD HEADACHE, DIZZINESS, FALLING DOWN

Disoriented and somewhat confused, I came fully awake on the floor next to the bed. I was clad in pajama bottoms and a T-shirt, my usual nighttime attire, but it was morning, the sky bright and blue outside my bedroom window.

Wednesday.

Day three.

I knew I hadn't stumbled or tripped but had simply lost my balance on the way to the pissoir, and not with a topsy-turvy feeling of light-headedness as in a faint, but as if I'd been caught by a trip wire.

I'd gone down like a sack of shit falling off the back of a manure truck.

The on-again off-again headache from yesterday had returned with a vengeance. Headache, dizziness, falling down—it occurred to me with a jolt that I had all of the symptoms for day three.

When I spotted the cotton ball taped to the inside of my arm, the events of the previous day flooded my consciousness.

Arriving back in North Bend the night before, I'd driven straight to the mayor's house. Haston lived on the eastern edge of town, three hundred feet down the road from the ranger station, in a small yellow house with a modest yard. A neighbor's dog barked at me from inside a chain-link fence. Two desolate wooden planters sat on the concrete stoop but contained only weeds. They must have been Gloria's.

Aside from a single phone call when we initially discovered the extent of our joint betrayal, Steve Haston and I never sat down and discussed what had happened between our former wives. Though neither of us had said it aloud, Steve thought I was responsible for the mess, while I thought he was.

When Lorie and Gloria decided to leave town together, Gloria stripped Steve of his spare cash, emptied their bank account, cashed out their certificates of deposit, stole the Land Cruiser, and sold their schnauzer. The dog was the only thing he got back.

On our side of town, Lorie swiped Britney's piggy bank—Britney had been four at the time. I managed to replace it before she figured out what happened. When I accused her on the phone, Lorie claimed Gloria must have taken it. I hated the thought that Gloria Haston had been prowling my house and making love to my wife while I was a mile away at work.

For some reason the two women had filled themselves with enough venom to justify anything. Maybe it was the rain. North Bend was a beautiful town, green as hell, but it rained more than a hundred inches a year, and the clouds and moisture drove people mad. Later, somebody from the FBI called my home trying to get a line on Lorie, told me she was kiting checks all over the Midwest.

"Mind if I come in?" I asked Haston. It wasn't that I was afraid people would overhear us on the stoop; it was more that my legs needed a rest.

"The place is a mess. Sit down anywhere." Despite his demurrals, Haston's housekeeping was impeccable. He told a lot of little lies like that, falsehoods designed to make you doubt your own eyes. I confess I hate people who do that. I took the sofa, while he perched across from me in a leather armchair that looked as if he'd taken furniture polish to it. "Terrible about Stan. Just terrible."

"Especially in light of how easily it could have been avoided."

Haston ignored my sarcasm. "Everyone in town's talking about it. They're starting to call it the Bad Luck Fire Department."

"There's more coming."

"What do you mean?"

"You heard Joel McCain's a vegetable?"

"Karrie told me about him."

"Jackie Feldbaum's a vegetable, too."

"Well, yes. We knew that. The accident."

"Stan thought they all had the same disease. He thought Newcastle died out in the woods as a vegetable. I've been with a doctor in Tacoma all day and she thinks they were part of an epidemic."

"Good God!"

Without telling him about my own symptoms or about Holly, I filled him in on Stan Beebe's theories, adding facts I'd gleaned on my own. By failing to mention Holly I'd left out a lot, including the truck accident in February. There hadn't been much up there but snowballs, chickens, and Coca-Cola extract. I didn't want to have to admit that to Haston.

In presenting my case as a fire department issue, I'd left it in a neat little package, stressing my concern for the families of Stan, Joel, Jackie, and Chief Newcastle. I had another rationale for not talking about my own symptoms. Like a child hiding under the blankets, for some nonsensical reason I felt as if not talking about my involvement would somehow make the symptoms less real. But this wasn't like a cold, where I could resign myself to riding out the symptoms and knew I would be better in a week.

"You think all these people have arsenic poisoning or something?"

"Nobody's exhibiting the symptoms of arsenic poisoning. Or cyanide or anything else the doctors are familiar with. This is a whole lot more exotic."

"How can the accidents be an epidemic?"

"These people had accidents because they were sick."

"As mayor I've never been faced with anything—"

"None of us have."

"I only took over the job to help out after Gloria left town. The biggest problem I've had so far is that squabble with the Army Corps of Engineers over our dikes. I wouldn't know where to start with something this complex."

Steve Haston had been timid in his day-to-day decision making, his leadership at the monthly council meetings alternately limp-wristed and carping.

His sole contributions to handling the fire department's problems were a single phone call to the station one day to ask if I was "okay" and then letting Stan out of his sight. Essentially, I was running the fire department by myself.

"We should have a meeting," I said. "Start with Brashears. He treated Jackie and Stan both. Bring in McCain's doctors. Get Eastside Fire and Rescue involved. It could just as easily be them next time. If it's a chemical hazard passing through our district, it's moving by truck, which means it's going through their district, too. The State Department of Transportation should be involved. The State Patrol."

"You believe this was something you folks got on the job?"

"I do."

"The city is self-insured. This is going to destroy our cash flow. Look, Jim, I'll clear the docket and we'll work on this full-time. I'll call the King County Executive. One of us will have to speak with the governor. Maybe we can get disaster relief from the feds."

"Who's there? Anybody home?" Karrie Haston walked into the room and stood awkwardly beside her father when she saw me.

It was easy to see the family resemblance. They were both tall, Steve around six-seven, Karrie five-ten. They both had long arms and lantern jaws. Although most people would have said Karrie was attractive, her father's face was just this side of ungainly, and the only thing you could say about his normal expression was that it resembled that of a man about to fall off a donkey.

Even though Karrie and I had been on a businesslike basis since the Christmas party, she flushed when she saw me in her father's living room.

At this late date, it was easy to see how improvident it had been to fool around with the daughter of the mayor. To trifle with the feelings of a probationary firefighter. For all I knew, she'd been on the couch because she thought it would further her career. Get her past McCain's critical reports. But more than that, attempting to seduce the daughter of the woman who'd seduced my wife had enough Freudian implications to keep a psych class writing papers for years. I didn't even want to think about it.

"Jim was just leaving," Steve said, flashing his bird-shit gray eyes at me as a signal that he didn't want Karrie to know what we'd been discussing.

I knew what he was thinking. If Stan had been sick, if Joel and Jackie were sick, Karrie might have contracted it, too.

As far as accepting this on a personal level, Steve was on the same page I was.

When I got home that night, the girls and I lit candles, set out the Monopoly board, and fell into a freewheeling discussion about life and our lives in particular, talking about why their mother wasn't with us anymore, a frequent conversation in our household and one I generally avoided. I answered Allyson's and Britney's questions more candidly than ever. None of us had laid eyes on Lorie since she left town three years earlier.

I felt I owed it to the girls to be as honest as I could. It wasn't as if they'd be able to ask later.

There wasn't going to be any later.

22. DON'T YOU HANG UP ON ME, YOU BASTARD

And now, this morning, I was on the floor.

A spectacularly ignoble way to begin one of my last days as a human being.

"Oh, Daddy. Quit horsing around. You have to get ready for work. Morgan's already here." Britney was standing behind me, her arms twined around my neck. I remained seated on the hardwood floor. I had no idea how long I'd been ruminating about last night, about Lorie. Or how long Britney had been in my bedroom.

"Not going to work today, sweetie."

"You're staying with us?"

"I'm going to spend as much time with you as possible." She hugged me closer, her tiny rib cage pressed against my back. Though I had a couple of days to work it out, I had no idea who was going to take care of her after I was gone. Their grandfather couldn't take care of himself. My mother was in Japan—or was it Shanghai?—going through an extended second childhood and in no shape to take on two girls. Lorie's parents were not the kind of people I wanted to leave them with.

"Want me to tell Morgan to go home?" Britney asked.

"Let's keep Morgan. I might have to run some errands."

"Oh, goody. Me and Ally and Morgan and you. This was too much to hope for. It's going to be like Morgan's our mommy, isn't it?"

"Britney? Don't—" But she was already out of the room.

The razor I shaved with every morning had been my father's. I hadn't thought about that in a long while. Yesterday's visit had shaken loose a lot of ancient feelings.

He'd been a hard disciplinarian in my early years. Punishment had rained down on me willy-nilly, even though as a child I'd bought into the Sixth Element of the Saints of Christ hook, line, and sinker. For years I believed I was headed for heaven and that if I died prematurely, I would meet Jesus Christ at the pearly gates. For years I'd taken a whack on the bottom for every little infraction.

The crack in my faith began the week my mother vanished, the week my father told me it was my fault.

Later, one night on a drive home from a Saints sojourn in Oregon, my mother asleep, my father and me listening to show tunes on some funky Oregon Public Radio channel—I was twelve and my mother had returned by then—I asked about his pronouncement four years earlier that my mother's departure had been my fault, since by this time she'd confirmed I'd had nothing to do with her leaving.

He swore he'd never said any such thing.

When I insisted he had, that he'd said it more than once, he dismissed my sputtering objections as absurd, yet I knew what he'd said. It hadn't been out of my mind for a day.

He said I'd been young and emotionally distraught after my mother's departure and that my memory was a child's and faulty. I didn't buy it. I'd memorized thousands of Bible verses without being accused of having a faulty memory. Although we never spoke of it again, his denial haunted me, had in fact been the linchpin in my decision to run away from Six Points.

"Morning, Mr. Swope."

"Morning, Morgan. I hope you don't mind; I'm going to be home today, but I'll be running errands and making phone calls. I would appreciate it if you could be with us while I'm doing that."

She blushed. "I'd love to." Britney began bouncing up and down and squealing. Allyson took it a little more calmly, though I saw her exchange a meaningful glance with Morgan.

We had breakfast together, the girls and I. Morgan, who was as skinny as six o'clock, claimed she'd already had breakfast at home, though I doubted she had. The girls babbled, while I pondered the end of my life and, for all intents and purposes, the end of theirs as they knew it.

Before we were done, Mayor Haston phoned. "Jim. The King County Executive wants to have a meeting today at the mayor's office. Twelve noon. Can you be there?"

"Absolutely." I was delighted things were moving so quickly. We were going to whip this rabid dog before he bit anyone else.

"I talked to Brashears last night. He'll be there. And one of McCain's doctors is coming."

"You've been busy."

"I'm worried."

"Good. I am, too."

We drove to the fire station, the four of us shoulder-to-shoulder in my pickup. The engine was in, but the medics were out, which left three people on duty. Ben Arden was working in Ian's spot, along with Karrie and a volunteer. In the event of a fire, more volunteers would pop out of the woodwork to help. At least that was the plan. They were all on pagers.

I went into the office and looked up the fire report Chief Newcastle had written for the truck accident last February. The report said the chicken truck was owned by Alsace Poultry, based in Kent, Washington. I already knew Holly had driven for Continental Freightways Associated, a company out of Seattle.

When I called Continental Freightways, I was connected to a harried-sounding man who answered, "Continental." After I began to explain who I was and what I wanted, he interrupted. "Last winter? What does that have to do with the price of tea in China?"

"We have someone here who's sick, and we think it's from that accident. We're just trying to figure out what the product is that's making our people sick."

"Hey, look. I'm busy here. Hazardous materials are not our gig. Why don't you go down the street to Consolidated? They might know something."

"It was your company's truck. Holly Riggs was driving."

"Just goes to show they shouldn't be letting girls behind the wheel." He laughed. "Call Consolidated."

The line went dead.

"Bastard."

"Daddy, you said a bad word." Having led the charge through the fire station, Allyson was behind me now, trailed by Britney and Morgan, who was trying to keep her cool, although it was clear she was overpowered by both the hardware and the stark immediacy of my profession. You could still smell smoke in the station from a fire we'd had three days ago.

We could look into the chickens if Stephanie found a cause for it, but until further notice, I was going to concentrate on whatever product or combination of products had been inside Holly's truck. I found it much more credible that a chemical had caused our problem than chickens. Our reports hadn't included a copy of the manifest for either truck. There had been no reason for it. I remembered a few things about the contents of Holly's rig and had been wracking my brain all day yesterday and last night trying to recall a specific logo I'd seen on one of the boxes.

I knew I'd read about the company in the *Wall Street Journal* just a day or two after the wreck, so it had stuck in my mind. The logo consisted of a winged lion inside a black circle. Today, without further thought, the name of the company popped into my head. Jane's California Propulsion. I looked it up on the Internet and found my memory was dead-on—Jane's California Propulsion, Inc. In San Jose.

Dialing one of the phone numbers provided on their Web page, I found myself getting shuffled from office to office. After explaining my problem to several individuals and then waiting for almost ten minutes while the earpiece spewed out easy-listening rock, I finally managed to get connected to a Mr. Stuart in their safety division.

"Mr. Stuart? I'm Lieutenant James Swope with the North Bend Fire and Rescue in Washington State. Some of our people are having health problems we've connected to a truck accident last February outside of town here."

"That's too bad, Lieutenant, but I don't see how that has anything to do with us. We work with rocket propulsion systems."

"There was a box on the truck with your company's logo on it. At least, I'm pretty sure there was. It was a big accident, and we know quite a few of the packages on board were damaged. Some of them were leaking. We're trying to ascertain what sorts of products you might have been shipping."

"Well, the first thing you need to recognize is that we weren't shipping anything last February. Most all of our trans-state shipping takes place during the warmer months."

"You sure?"

"Positive. All of that goes through our office here. Sorry we couldn't be more helpful."

"Sorry to bother you."

So much for slap-shot, hit-or-miss technique. I'd do the rest of this by the book. One step at a time. Making sure of my facts before I wasted any more time.

"Come on, guys," I said to the girls, who were still in the room. "We're going to take a little drive."

Seattle was thirty miles away. These days with all the new housing developments infringing on the green hills above Snoqualmie and Issaquah and with the traffic feeding off Highway 18, I-90 was a mess. Still, it wasn't until Mercer Island that we found ourselves stuck behind a mile of vehicles, the cab of my truck filling up with the odor of exhaust. My headache was worse than ever.

So this was it.

The last week of my life.

Sitting in a traffic jam. Terrific.

23. ALL THE CHICKEN STRANGLERS

ontinental was located in a dusty industrial section of town several miles south of Seattle's core, just off of East Marginal Way on Colorado Avenue, gray, dingy buildings and storage yards for blocks in either direction. We heard the nearby toot of a train whistle, and while I parked in the lot, Allyson and Britney watched a 727 coming in low for a landing at nearby Boeing Field.

I left the girls in the truck and went into a narrow building, where two men were sorting paperwork and slapping staplers at a long wooden counter. A woman sat at a desk on the far wall. Nobody looked up.

"North Bend Fire and Rescue. I called earlier?"

The man who spoke was maybe forty, husky, with thickset shoulders, knuckles like new potatoes, a wide face, and blue Steve McQueen eyes a susceptible woman might fall into. His curly hair was a faded rust color. He wore jeans and a plaid work shirt. His name was Cleve according to his name tag, and he didn't look at me. Not once. Not until I started in on him.

"What can we do for you?" he asked.

"I need to see a manifest for one of your trucks that was involved in a wreck outside North Bend last February."

"You the guy that called?"

"Yes."

"February? Jesus H. We're not librarians. I told you on the phone we don't transport anything that would cause health problems. Go over to Mainland Freight on Utah Avenue. They do hazardous materials."

"Holly Riggs was driving." I could tell the woman at the desk knew Holly by the way she raised her head. With a shrug of his shoulders, Cleve turned his back to me and began filing papers in a metal cabinet. "Listen, we have people in a nursing home over this."

"Try Mainland."

"Holly Riggs wasn't driving for Mainland. She was driving for you."

"Look, pal. What I want right now is to see you pucker up and skedaddle out that door."

"Holly Riggs is in a coma. I think there's a chance whatever put her in the hospital was on that truck." The woman at the desk was getting more and more interested.

"Out."

There was no reason for his intransigence, no reason other than hubris and lassitude—or else he was trying to hide something. I wanted to smack him. It was the first time in years I'd felt like hitting someone. The Sixth Element of the Saints of Christ followers had been taught to avoid altercations, to heal the severed ear, to turn the other cheek.

When two truck drivers entered the room, the other man behind the counter assisted the first one while Cleve finished up his filing and headed for the driver beside me. I'd been dismissed.

Their small talk was just warming up when I stepped into the prissiest voice I could muster and said, "Cleve, sweetie. I'm sorry about last night. I didn't mean to hurt your feelings." The room lapsed into a silence you could feel on the small hairs of your arms.

Cleve looked directly at me and said, "What are you talking about?"

"Cleve, come back to my pad tonight and nothing like that will ever happen again. Why, just this morning when I called here, I said to myself, Cleve is still thinking about me. I know he is. And that was good, because I was thinking about you, too, Cleve. Good thoughts, Cleve. Only good thoughts."

"What the fuck are you talking about?" Everyone had a trigger point, and, by some instinct I couldn't name, I'd put my finger on his.

"You and me, sweetie. You know what I'm talking about. Now don't get fussy. You know Doctor said fussy is bad for your LDL."

"What the hell do you want?" He turned to the others. "I don't even know this asshole!"

"What I want is the shipping manifest for the truck Holly Riggs was driving the night she had the accident."

Fists bunching at his sides, veins on the side of his neck distending, he strode to the end of the counter where I was standing and spoke through clenched and crooked teeth. Some of them looked like they were going to break. "What's this crap about *last night*? If you don't get off the premises in ten seconds, I'm going to climb over this counter and make you sorry you were born."

"You're actually going to lay hands on me?" I smirked lewdly at the others. "That would be so darn thrilling, Cleve. Don't count to ten. Do it now. Come over that counter and hurt me, baby. Hurt me bad."

The woman at the desk was shaking her head, warning him, all the while looking at me, curious, confused, and a little frightened. This office hadn't been so shaken up since the Nisqually earthquake.

"Trust me, you're not going to like it," Cleve said.

"Baby, I'll take what's coming to me, and I'll love you even more. You know that, don't you, sweetie?"

"Quit calling me sweetie!"

"Get the manifest and the MSDS."

"I'll knock you straight to hell."

"That would be soooo romantic, Cleve. I'll save the newspaper clippings for my scrapbook. 'Gays Duke It Out at Truck Yard.'"

I winked at the others.

Exasperated, Cleve glanced around the room. I had the feeling he ran roughshod over these people and that they were enjoying this. The men at the counter feigned disinterest and glanced away quickly. "What are you looking at?" Cleve barked at the woman.

"Nothing at all . . . sweetie."

All three men at the end of the counter laughed explosively.

Minutes later I had a Xerox copy of the manifest and the MSDS for the shipment Holly had been carrying last February. Cleve would have given his left nut and his firstborn son to get me out of there.

On the drive back to North Bend, we got trapped in traffic again.

On an impulse, I exited the freeway at 156th Street and drove to a nearby Toyota dealer. These guys had skinned me pretty bad a few years ago when Lorie and I bought the only new car either of us had ever owned.

Just to make the rest of them crazy, I picked the dumbest-looking salesman in the place, spent all of twenty seconds selecting the most expensive vehicle they had in stock, and bought it. If my life was going to fade out in a traffic jam, at least I could do it in air-conditioned comfort. It wasn't as if I was worried about making the payments. When they pressed me for extra insurance, I bought it all, including the disability insurance that paid off the car in the event I lost the ability to work. They thought they'd found a rube, but I would essentially have free use of the car for the week, and afterward my estate could sell it and put the money in trust for my daughters.

Morgan drove the truck with the Big Gulp container still glued to the roof back to North Bend. Allyson rode with her, while Britney rode in the new Lexus with me.

"Daddy, you always said we couldn't afford a new car," Britney said.

"We can afford this."

"It smells funny. Doesn't it smell funny?"

"That's what they call new car smell."

"We've never had a new car, have we?"

"We had one once. Your mother took it."

"Because she needed it more than we did, right, Daddy?"

"That's right. You know I love you, don't you, Britney?"

"You always say that when we start talking about Mommy."

"I guess I do, don't I?"

The salesman had thrown in some CDs, and Britney was playing Andy Williams's *Branson City Limits*, had taken a liking to "Moon River."

"I wish things could have turned out differently with your mother."

"Like you wish she didn't steal my piggy bank?"

"How'd you know about that?"

"She 'pologized. Told me not to tell you. She said she was going through a rough time when she left."

"When did this conversation take place?"

"On the phone at Easter. She said she would give anything not to have left us. Said if she had to leave us with anybody in the world, she wanted it to be you."

"You made that part up."

"Well, yeah. That last."

"You scamp," I said, running my fingers through her hair.

"Daddy. Morgan just fixed it."

"Looks nice."

"It would look nicer if it was like Audrey Hepburn's." A couple of nights earlier the girls had seen *Roman Holiday* and, like filmgoers everywhere, had fallen in love with Hepburn, as well as with her gamin hairstyle. I was still trying to decide whether they would regret cutting their hair.

On the drive into town on I-90 we passed the accident site where Stan Beebe lost his life. The only reminder that there'd been a fatality was a swatch of small trees his truck had knocked down. I imagined Marsha would come out and put up a white cross to mark the spot. Or maybe some members of the department would do it. Anyway, I wouldn't be around to see it.

At the fire station Ben and Karrie quickly took all three girls under their wing, while I went into the watch office and used my last few minutes before the noon meeting to glance at the shipping manifest I'd picked up at Continental.

The manifest sheets were all copies, but Cleve had handed me several other pieces of paper that were originals. I hadn't bothered to look at any of it on the way home or at the car dealership. Some sort of procrastination thing. Trying to hold back my own demise. It's harder to investigate your own end than you would think.

Holly's load had originated in Chattanooga, Tennessee, where she'd made several stops to pick up merchandise. I wasn't good at reading things like trucking manifests with all their columns and abbreviations, but I did manage to scribble down a list:

26 crated bicycles—Spears Bicycles Partners, to Seattle

44 boxes of bicycle accessories—Spears Bicycles Partners, to Seattle

32 boxes of paper towels—Bounty, to Seattle

16 boxes of hot sauce—Tamale Brothers, to Seattle

10 containers of Coca-Cola "product"—Coca-Cola, Inc., to Seattle

4 boxes books—Canyon View Systems, to Redmond

3 boxes miscellaneous—JCP, Inc., to San Jose via Seattle

3 bales comic books and assorted magazines—Spencer Publishing, to Bellevue

6 large boxes clothing—the Gap, to Seattle

8 small boxes miscellaneous—DuPont, Westinghouse, to Seattle

12 boxes assorted goods—Pacific Northwest Paint Contractors, to Tacoma

"Hey, Jim," Ian Hjorth said, peeking into the office. "The meeting next door is about to start."

"Sure."

What caught my eye on the list was that three of the boxes marked miscellaneous had been shipped from Tennessee to Seattle but were ultimately destined for San Jose. The shipper was JCP, Inc., which most likely stood for Jane's California Propulsion, Inc. But I'd already called them and they'd denied shipping anything through the Northwest last February.

"Jim?" It was Hjorth again.

"I'm coming."

When I'd called Jane's earlier, I'd wondered how Mr. Stuart could have been so certain without checking. People that cocksure, in my estimation, were frequently wrong.

I was now certain that our woes had originated in Holly's rig, not the chicken truck.

Surely we wouldn't have been the only people to contract this had our problems originated with the chicken truck. Wouldn't we have heard about zombie chicken stranglers at the local chicken plants?

As far as I knew, all the chicken stranglers were still wrenching heads.

At five minutes before twelve, I walked next door to the city offices, where a crowd of officials had gathered. It was almost intimidating to see what I'd triggered.

I was under immense pressure to sway these folks to my viewpoint, yet I had no physical evidence to present, nothing but stories and speculation that now began to seem outlandish. I would have felt a whole lot more secure in my arguments if Stan Beebe had allowed events to unfold on their own, so that we knew what would have happened to him. It was a selfish thought.

I couldn't help having misgivings about the outcome of this meeting. For one thing, Stephanie Riggs hadn't shown up yet.

Also, I'd been counting on the shipping manifest to include some exotic chemical or biohazard, had been hoping the Department of Defense had been shipping germ cultures for their latest secret weapons. That would have at least given our search for an antidote some sort of direction. I could hardly claim we'd been poisoned by bicycle parts or hot sauce. I wasn't happy that the guy at Jane's had lied about shipping in February, but there could be other explanations for that.

I was stuck with Stan Beebe's story, our fire department victims, and, of course, my own symptoms, which I was not planning to put forth for public review. Tell these people I was a goner, and inside of thirty minutes every busybody in town would know. Who wanted all the neighborhood biddies bringing over casseroles? People would want to pray with me. Could you imagine? The Toyota dealer would repossess the car. My phone wouldn't stop ringing.

Besides, I was still trying to figure out how to tell my daughters, and I certainly didn't want them to hear it through the grapevine.

Karrie, the two Bellevue medics on duty that day, and Jackie Feldbaum's common-law husband were all in attendance. I mingled with the fire personnel from other departments, making small talk until Steve Haston asked everyone to gather upstairs in the meeting room, where we found a long table surrounded by folding chairs. Latecomers, of which there were over a dozen, were forced to stand against the wall. Me included.

Mayor Haston took his place at the head of the table. He'd never been much of a commander, but he'd taken this task upon himself, his somber mood and height dominating the room. Introspective, prone to being overly fastidious in small things, when he did take charge of something Steve Haston was known as a control freak, so that city council meetings became almost unbearable as he flustered and quibbled endlessly over trivialities. He'd been like that as a volunteer firefighter, too. Had driven everyone nuts.

After Lorie and Gloria skipped town together, local gossips told me he'd been a domineering husband, that he'd thrown a fit when Gloria wanted to work outside his office, that he'd controlled family expenditures with an iron fist and hadn't allowed her to have her own friends, that every major decision concerning Karrie had been his. Without a shred of proof, I'm ashamed to say I believed every word of it. Which made me wonder what people believed about me and Lorie.

After introducing each of the principals and reading off their credentials from notes typed up beforehand, Haston thanked everyone for coming and introduced me.

24. BURY ME SLOWLY; I MAY HAVE A FEW LAST WORDS

By nature I was not a public speaker, yet I'd had enough experience in front of groups at Six Points that it didn't bother me.

What made it troublesome today was that I was trying to talk these citizens into saving my life.

I knew it. They didn't. And wouldn't.

I told the group about Chief Newcastle, about the autopsy report and the discovery that his hands were coated with an unidentified white substance that looked like candle wax but did not come off. I detailed the events and symptoms surrounding the accidents that Stan Beebe, Jackie Feldbaum, and Joel McCain all had. Using the grease board in the front of the room I listed the seven-day progression of symptoms as Beebe and Holly had delineated them. Anybody who noticed my hands were blemished was circumspect enough not to mention it. I told them about Holly, the truck accident, the fact that the only place all of these people's paths intersected was on I-90 in February.

Sadly, I could tell from the looks on their faces my discourse had not won them over. At least, not all of them.

Dr. Brashears spoke after I did. Brashears was a heavy man, balding, with a wide, flat, florid face and eyes windowed by black-framed glasses. After equivocating about doctor-patient privilege, he confessed he'd had two patients recently, Jackie and Stan, both members of the fire department, whose symptoms had not been dissimilar to the symptoms on the list on the board, that one of them had sustained massive brain damage that had presented very much like a stroke. One of Joel McCain's doctors spoke next, had discovered the same basic symptoms pertained to Joel and confirmed that his fall had not caused his brain injury. This doctor left for an appointment as soon as he finished speaking.

Through contacts he had at the University of Washington, Haston had brought an environmental chemist to the meeting, a wisp of a woman named Esther Mulherin.

When she wasn't at the University of Washington, Mulherin worked for Electron Laboratory Research in Kenmore. She'd previously made a name for herself researching polymer membranes for studies of ion selectivity characteristics. Ms. Mulherin wore wire-rimmed glasses and had a self-effacing demeanor and manner of dress that I felt sure made her next to invisible in any crowd. She was the only speaker who remained sitting, explaining that the Chem Sources book for this year listed 155,000 chemicals in use in the United States, that most of these had not been tested on humans. In other words, the list of possibilities for this particular offense, if it was chemical in nature, was boundless. One thing that puzzled Mulherin was the lag time between what we believed was the date of the contamination and the onset of symptoms.

Mulherin expressed a strong desire to be part of the core group studying this, saying she felt it was a wonderful opportunity to get in on the ground floor of a potentially deadly breakthrough. As ghoulish as it sounded, I had the feeling the more people got sick, the better she was going to like it.

When this one dragged on, I began to remember why I hated meetings. Some of the attendees were convinced we had a problem. Others remained dubious. What everybody did agree on was that if we did have a problem, it would affect other fire departments in the region as well as the public at large. On that basis it was decided to set up a committee to study and follow the events in North Bend, to make findings, to come up with recommendations, and, if any more cases came to light, to alert other state and county departments and the public. Everyone agreed it was too soon to make a media announcement.

No one wanted to spread needless panic.

No one but me.

I tried to argue the point. If we went to the media, maybe we would find somebody out there who knew something. I could have tried by myself, but I wanted the imprimatur of this group behind me. In the end, the panic argument won the day, as if the public were going to run screaming out of their houses and jump off cliffs when they saw this on the evening news.

Click and Clack, aka Ian Hjorth and Ben Arden, came in late and raised the possibility that our meth lab in the woods back in May might have triggered this. I didn't think so, but I couldn't stop them from talking it to death.

We'd responded on the North Fork of the Snoqualmie River, driving up a steep road used mostly by logging trucks. After a quarter mile of climbing, the road turned into gravel and dirt.

Two miles in we found a clandestine methamphetamine lab.

By the time we arrived, the cooks were long gone, although the lab was still brewing product. We called the county sheriff's office and roped off the area until an environmental cleanup company could dispose of the chemicals.

We'd hosed and scrubbed our boots thoroughly, but the possibility remained that one or more of us had dragged some poison back to the station. Holly had not been there. Nor had I seen her in person afterward. But what if, asked Ben Arden, the symptoms of exposure to a meth lab were similar to our symptoms?

The deputy chief for Bellevue said he'd researched drug labs after the Bellevue department found two inside their city limits. While the health effects of the various chemical compounds used in manufacturing methamphetamines were onerous—including, in the short term, headaches, nausea, dizziness, decreased mental function, shortness of breath, and chest pain, which none of us had experienced back in May—the longer-term reactions included cancer, brain damage, miscarriages, heart problems, and even death. The chemicals involved could range from toluene, anhydrous ammonia, and ether to even phosgene gas.

I had to admit some of those symptoms were chronicled in Beebe's seven-day cycle. All in all, though, it appeared unlikely that the drug lab was the cause of our problems.

It was suggested that there were any number of scenarios in which our loved ones might be potential victims, that our causal agent might be chemical, bacterial, or viral, that Jackie's husband, McCain's wife, and Beebe's children were at risk and should be examined. It hadn't occurred to me until that moment, but it was possible I had placed Britney and Allyson in danger. Morgan Neumann might have it, or Morgan's mother, Helen.

Was it possible I'd tracked a virus into the house on my shoes, that Allyson and Britney, who liked to traipse around the house barefoot, had picked it up on the soles of their feet? Could it be that I was going to be brain-dead in June, that my daughters would follow in July?

The thought paralyzed me.

For many long minutes I found it difficult to follow the discussion, unable to move or speak.

The fire department had been my life, as well as the source of a great deal of good in our family. It had given us the money to pay our bills and put food on the table, a roof over our heads. Now I was forced to confront the possibility that it might also be the worst thing that ever happened to us.

By the time I'd regained my senses, the discussion was waning.

A study group was formed consisting of Steve Haston, myself, a captain from Eastside Fire and Rescue, Ms. Mulherin, Dr. Brashears, and one other to be named later. Our first committee meeting would be on Monday.

By Monday I would be strapped into a wheelchair.

They could wheel me in as exhibit number one.

I don't know what I had expected. These people all had jobs and lives to go back to. I didn't have anything but waxy hands, a headache, and the dilemma of how to tell my daughters they were going to be fatherless. It was clear I was on my own here. These people weren't going to save me.

Steve Haston closed the meeting with a lengthy speech, the longest of the day, and it was while he orated that I began to suspect he had preselected himself as the next head of the fire department. Why not? All the rest of us would be over at Alpine Estates sucking mush. This was all speculation on my part, but it was so like Haston, who seemed to reinvent himself every five to ten years. He'd been a cop. A musician in a string band. An accountant. A cuckold. A mayor. Why not fire chief?

The syndrome seemed to have given me a sixth sense. Yesterday I'd known what Stephanie Riggs was going to say several times before she said it and had actually completed a couple of sentences for her. This morning at Continental Freightways I knew exactly how to terrorize Cleve. Now I knew Haston was angling for the chief's job.

As the meeting disbanded, Brashears motioned that he wanted to talk to me in private. After the room emptied, he said, "What day are you on?"

"You think anybody else noticed?"

"Not that I could tell."

"Day three."

"You seeing a doctor?"

"Yes."

"You need anything at all, get in touch. I mean that."

"I will."

The thought that he was speaking to a dead man made Brashears look at the walls, the carpet, anything but me. Then, without another word, he left.

25. WHAT WE GOT HERE IS A NICKEL HOLDING UP A DOLLAR

Outside on the sidewalk, Ms. Mulherin cornered me. She stood so close and was so short that she had to look almost straight up at me, her neck cranked back at an angle that reminded me of a worm on a hook. For a moment I thought she'd made the same observation Brashears had and was going to talk about it here on the sidewalk in front of God and everybody.

Ms. Mulherin said, "Organophosphates. Have you thought about that?"

"I've been kind of—"

"Because they're everywhere. If you think about it. Parathion. Malathion. Pesticides are everywhere. And if you think about it, organophosphates are readily translocated in living organisms. Have you thought about this?"

"I'm sure that's more in line with your expertise than mine."

"Yes, well, uh-huh. Hmmm. I'm sure you know generally with organophosphates you see symptoms within two hours. Difficulty swallowing, loss of appetite, nausea, vomiting, abdominal cramps, and even diarrhea. Was any of this reported?" She had a face that had seen too much sun, lines around her eyes, even around her ears. Her lips were almost nonexistent, as if she were trying to suck a straw some jokester had put a pea in. "You think I could visit your fire station with some of my grad students? We might be able to pick up traces of—"

"Be my guest. Show up whenever you like."

"Maybe at the end of the week?"

"Fine by me." She was going to write a paper on this. I could see it. She was going to gain prestige in the academic world standing on our dead bodies. To her, we were organisms to be studied, questioned, dissected, and eventually autopsied.

The King County Executive, who'd been glad-handing on the sidewalk with some of the other participants, came over and interrupted Ms. Mulherin, as if interrupting was something he'd been commissioned to do by the county. He was a tall man, almost as tall as my six-three, though easily fifty or sixty pounds heavier, most of it in his belly.

"Look, Swope," he said. "A couple of the Eastside guys were talking, and they seem to think you folks probably got into some rat poison or something. Don't get me wrong. It's not that I'm not backing you. Because I am. It's just that I need to see more evidence before I can commit to anything. Right now I'm about as convinced there's an epidemic as I'm convinced cows can fly." Mulherin gave him a dry look. "You get some proof, come see me. We'll take it to the governor, you and I together."

The combination of Mulherin's detached ghoulishness and this man's coldly reasoned incredulity lit a fuse in me.

"I get some proof," I said, "I'll take it to the news, and the first thing I'll tell them is you were stalling while the public health was at risk. That people turning into vegetables wasn't something you had time for."

"Now, now, now. What I said was—"

"Fuck what you said!"

I turned and walked away. Nobody concealed what they were thinking better than a former devout follower of the Sixth Element of the Saints of Christ, so the burst of anger surprised me almost as much as it did him.

I'd cooled off by the time I found the girls in the rec room, knocking balls around on the billiard table. Morgan was officiating good-naturedly. After a few words of encouragement, I went into the officers' room, where I dialed Holly's home number in Tacoma.

It rang eight times before I heard Holly on the answering machine.

The sound of her voice choked me up.

I left a brief message and dialed Tacoma General. After a few minutes, a woman informed me Dr. Riggs was no longer affiliated with the hospital.

"Her sister still there as a patient?"

"I believe so."

"She okay? I'm a friend."

"Her condition hasn't changed."

It was hard to realize how much hope I'd invested in Stephanie Riggs, a woman who really had no reason to help me.

She'd promised to call this morning.

Promised.

It was a bigger disappointment than it should have been. Between my dissatisfaction with the meeting and Stephanie's failure to contact me, I was feeling as forgotten as a puppy in a locked garage.

I dug through my wallet for Stephanie's cell phone number, but I'd misplaced it.

I sat down with the shipping manifest from Continental Freightways. DuPont was a possibility. They were a chemical company. But what bothered me more than the manifest was that I'd been lied to by the guy at JCP, Inc. I picked up the phone and called them back, asked for Mr. Stuart, was told he was out to lunch. No shit, I thought. He was out to lunch when I spoke to him. They took my phone number and promised he would call back.

In the officers' room I looked up Jane's on the Internet. It was a rocket fuel company, or had been. Now they were researching hydrogen fuel cell technology for all sorts of things: spacecraft, jets, automobiles, hovercraft, military vehicles, submarines. A quick glance at their literature told me they used platinum in their work. I didn't see how platinum could have caused our problems, but then, what did I know?

While I was on the Internet, on a whim, I went to my favorite search engine and began trying out various phrases: *downed firefighters, fatal firefighter illness, firefighter mystery casualty, brain-dead firefighters.* After about twenty-five minutes of experimenting, I came across an obituary for a firefighter in Chattanooga, Tennessee:

> *Vic Swenson, former all-state tailback for the Olewah Owls and twenty-year veteran of the Chattanooga Fire Department, died yesterday after a long, undiagnosed illness, the result of the controversial Southeast Travelers Freight fire three years ago. For the past three years Vic has resided in the Sunnyside Nursing Home, where he's made lots of friends. He was active in fishing and hunting and played golf at least once a week, and most of his friends said he was the smartest "cheater" they ever saw. Vic always had a smile for everyone and will be missed by his wife, Sally, and three children, Vic Jr., Echo, and Heather. Memorials may be made to the Citizens' Fund for Truth about Southeast Travelers.*

For many long minutes I found nothing else on the Internet about the Citizens' Fund for Truth, and then I came upon a Web site put up by a CFD firefighter named Charlie Drago called "The Truth about the Southeast Travelers Incident." Unfortunately, the site was bollixed beyond belief, so that there was only the home page. Lots of tantalizing promises of links and other pages, but none of it worked. I tried a different Web browser, but that didn't produce anything, either. Only the home page. No links. No contact information. No phone number. Also, the word *incident* had been spelled *incedent*.

I phoned the Chattanooga Fire Department main switchboard, told them I was a fire officer in North Bend, Washington, and was looking for Charles Drago. I was told he was on duty today and given a station house phone number, which I then called. "Yeah. Charlie's working today. Let me get him for you."

As did the woman who answered the phone, Charlie Drago had a Southern drawl so thick you could cut it with a chain saw. I explained who I was and detailed my situation. "You told anybody about this?" he asked. "Anybody at all?"

"Well, yes."

"Then you'd better watch your ass, buddy. They'll be coming after you. No shit. They're probably following you right now. They'll burn your home down. They tried to burn mine down. They'll blow you to smithereens. I mean this. No shit. They'll blow you to Kingdom Come. Your life ain't worth a plug nickel."

"Who will? Who will blow me to smithereens?"

"Them."

"Who's them?"

"Whoever was responsible for our incident at Southeast Travelers. Probably the same assholes who're responsible for what's happening to you fine folks. We lost three guys there. Well, one's dead. The other two only wish they were."

"Vic Swenson?"

"Yeah. He was one. How did you know that? You're not working for the insurance company, are you? You bastard."

"No, Charlie. I'm not working for the insurance company. I'm a fire-fighter in North Bend. What happened to these guys at the freight company fire?"

"They tried to burn my house down. You see my Web site? It's all on my Web site."

"I was just there. I couldn't find anything on it."

"Damn it! I posted that just yesterday. They trash my site. You know what else? I think they're following me again. Hey. Check it out. If they're not following you by now, they will be. Now tell me the truth. You're not one of them, are you?"

"Charlie, I'm not sure—" Even as I spoke, the house bells clanged. This guy was crazy. I wondered why they even left him on duty. Battier than bat shit. "That's our house bell, Charlie. We've got a call. I'll talk to you later."

"Vaya con Dios, amigo."

"Sure, Charlie."

I wasn't on duty, but it was a long-standing tradition that extra hands hanging around the station responded in the event of a fire call. Had it been an aid alarm, I wouldn't have bothered, but the tones were for a fire call, and when the dispatcher announced what we had, it came in as a trailer fire. Heavy black smoke reported by cell phone callers on the freeway. More calls were being received from neighbors out on Edgewick Road.

In our department most "smoke in the vicinity" calls turned out to be bogus, a yard crew burning brush, a hobbyist farmer tuning up his tractor, a woodstove stoked down too far.

At "working fires" our department relied on mutual aid from nearby departments and on volunteers, who would race from their day jobs or abandon their spouses at night to risk their lives backing us up. It was absolutely the best part of small-town America, and having been raised in the city, I loved every part of it.

Before I cleared the office, my girls rushed downstairs in a state of breathless agitation.

"A fire, Daddy! A fire!" Allyson yelled. It was funny to see her shed her matronly manner so quickly. "Can we go?"

Britney was so intoxicated with the thrill of it, she couldn't speak at all, just stood next to her older sister gasping for breath. Morgan pretended to be above it all, but I could see she was amped, too.

Any other day I would have said no, but this might be their last chance to see me doing one of the few things I did well.

I tossed Morgan the keys to the Lexus. "Do not go over the speed limit. Adjust the mirrors. Obey all the traffic laws. Don't worry about missing anything. If it's a good fire, it'll still be burning when you get there. Park off the roadway. Watch out for firefighters and incoming apparatus. Volunteers out here get pretty jazzed. Don't get in anyone's way."

"Yes, Mr. Swope," said Morgan.

Ian Hjorth, who had already kicked off his station boots and put on his bunking boots and pants, was climbing up behind the wheel of the engine. Without taking off my civilian clothes, I climbed into the cab next to him. Karrie and Ben Arden were seated behind us in the crew cab. They would finish dressing and don air masks while we drove, prepared to step off the rig and fight fire upon arrival.

Manned by the first arriving volunteer at the station, the tanker would respond to refill our pumper when we ran out of water. Empty, it would then be driven to the nearest hydrant to be refilled. Our engine carried a thousand gallons, enough to put out most structure fires in their incipient stages. The tanker carried an additional five thousand.

Just below Mount Washington, I spotted a pall of heavy black smoke rising from behind a low hill. The color and the speed with which the smoke was rising were indicators that we had a structure fire.

On the radio I confirmed that we had a column of black smoke. This would let our volunteers on Wilderness Rim know to bring the engine we kept parked up there at our satellite station. It would also let Snoqualmie, our mutual aid department from the next small town over, know we really had something. It would let the first volunteer to arrive at the station know that he should bring the tanker.

We exited the freeway and rolled up a narrow road shaded by trees on both sides. Here and there a driveway or an open yard fronted the road. Two horses in a field lashed out with their rear legs and galloped off at the sound of our siren.

Half a mile from the freeway, we found smoke coming from the rear of a large lot mostly hidden by trees and brush. "It's Caputo's place," Ian Hjorth said, swinging our engine into Caputo's driveway.

"I spotted a hydrant about two hundred yards back."

"I'll tell the tanker guy when he gets here."

Because I was the first officer on scene, I would automatically become the incident commander, which meant I would remain outside the fire building and coordinate fire-fighting efforts, remain in contact with incoming units on the radio, and dole out assignments to individual firefighters as they showed up in their private vehicles. It would be my responsibility to make sure everybody on the fire ground worked as a team, that rescues were made promptly, that nobody was injured.

The first rule of fire fighting was: Don't get hurt.

If all the civilians weren't out of the building, or if we didn't know for certain whether they were out, our priority would be rescue. Most of the time, though, rescue and extinguishment went hand in hand. You put the fire out—the victim was no longer in danger.

I can't tell you how much I loved this job.

Right away I needed to determine whether there were exposures we had to protect with hose lines, whether there were nearby structures that might be damaged by fire. As in all building fires, we needed to ventilate the occupancy at the same time we put water on the fire; otherwise the smoke and steam had nowhere to go. The oldest way to ventilate was to go to the roof and cut a hole over the fire, ideally about four feet by eight feet.

We would also need firefighters standing by in full gear with an extra hand line just in case our primary team got in trouble.

Ian would place the apparatus near the building but not so near as to get scorched if the fire got out of hand, nor so far away that the hose lines wouldn't reach inside. He would get the pump running, open the lines for the firefighters who would crawl inside under the heat, and help hook up a supply line from the tanker.

House trailers, even double-wides, tended to have fewer exits and smaller windows than wood-frame homes. They also burned hotter inside. In the past ten years, North Bend Fire and Rescue had lost two elderly home owners in trailer fires. You had to worry about losing a firefighter in one, too.

Karrie Haston and Ben Arden would take in the first hand line. Ideally, I would go in with Karrie, because she was still on probation and so far had been to only one good fire. Crawling inside alongside her would allow me to make sure she didn't get into trouble and would also give me a chance to see how she reacted to heat, stress, and lack of visibility. Her skills on aid calls were exemplary, and except for her constant questioning of authority around the station, something I viewed as a habit she'd picked up from years of bucking her father's heavy-handed authoritarianism, she'd acquitted herself well in most arenas. But so far I had yet to see her fight fire. It was pretty simple: you couldn't fight fire, you couldn't have the job.

"It's Caputo's place, all right," Ian Hjorth said again. As we pulled into the driveway and stopped, low-hanging branches tore at the paint on our fire engine and slapped loudly against the light bars on the roof.

A large maroon Chevrolet sedan blocked our approach.

The driver, a doughy woman of about seventy, stood thirty feet in front of the idling car pointing at the burning trailer as if we couldn't see it. It was impossible to hear what she was shouting over the sound of our motor and the stream of radio chatter crossing the airwaves.

"What we got here is a nickel holding up a dollar," I said, trying to push my door open against the bushes. Ian inched the rig forward to help.

"Caputo's mother," Ian said. "She was here when he hacked his toe off with the maul last fall."

Something first-in fire personnel always thought about was what the next-in units would see when they got there. Arriving at a fire, each unit got an indelible look at the structure and the work being performed or not being performed, and when the next-in units found us stuck in the bushes, they would laugh their heads off.

Stalling around outside a fire building was not a reputation I wanted to carry to my grave.

"You guys stay on board," I said to Karrie and Ben. Branches shrieked against the door as I worked it open.

Beyond the Chevrolet lay a small grassy swale and beyond that the trailer, black smoke pouring from a partially open window on the right-hand side. Less concentrated plumes of smoke issued from cracks and seams in the trailer.

Still facing the domicile, the old woman backed up unsteadily, tottering in a clump of weeds. I asked if this was her car, but she couldn't hear me over the rumbling of our diesel engine. When I spotted the keys in the ignition, I slid the seat back, got in, placed the car in drive, and parked on the sod just past her, leaving the keys in the ignition.

"I know he's in there," she said, her voice tremulous. "I came over to bring him some greens for dinner."

I, too, figured Caputo was in there, since his flatbed truck was parked where he always parked it on the north side of the driveway.

Our diesel roared past, and I missed the rest of what she said. Ian, Ben, and Karrie disembarked and went to work. I yelled that there was probably a man inside. Behind us, a volunteer jogged into the driveway. "Grab the next guy and lay a backup line to the front door," I said.

Then Morgan and my daughters showed up on foot. I caught Morgan's eye and pointed to the old woman in the bushes. "Don't move from there." The three of them went to their assigned position, as cute as porcelain dolls, all three in shorts, deck shoes, and pastel blouses. Too bad nobody had a camera.

Ian had already switched the transmission out of drive and into pump. The fire was beginning to rip, flame licking out the front door. We were on the verge of losing the trailer, and probably the owner, too. If he wasn't already dead.

"Look out for those dogs," Ian said as I walked around the fire engine. I hadn't heard any barking, but Caputo's Dobermans had been in the back of my mind since we arrived.

26. BEND OVER AND KISS YOUR BIG OLD WHATCHAMACALLIT GOOD-BYE

Ideally, the first-in unit at a structural fire would view three sides of a building as they roll up on it, always making sure to drive all the way past the front to see down that third side. This generally produced a fair idea of what was happening. Because the mobile home was capped at either end by thick brush, viewing three sides without a walk-around was not going to happen.

We had a couple of minutes before the rest of the units would be asking for instructions, so I set off on a quick 360 of the building.

The diesel engine, the whining pump, and the volunteers shouting at one another made it impossible to know whether there was anybody yelling for help from inside.

If you knew him as I did, you'd be as surprised as I was that Max Caputo hadn't torched his place before now.

Calamity rained down on the man—divorces, drunkenness, car accidents, multiple manglings prior to the table saw incident yesterday, traumatic loss of teeth in bar fights, skin rashes so severe they required hospitalization. Caputo was the only man I'd ever heard of who'd been attacked by both a bear and a cougar.

What he'd probably done, I realized in a flash, was wash down the painkillers the doctors had prescribed for his severed fingers with beer, a potent combination of booze and drugs that would disorient you or me or anybody. No doubt he set fire to his own place by accident.

Black smoke was jetting out the narrow vertical bathroom window and along the roofline. The windows were coated inside with a tarlike substance, a sign the fire had been burning for some time.

It was close to a backdraft situation, and I told Ben as much when I passed him. "I'll warn the others," he said. Under the right conditions a backdraft could throw a door into the street, blow a firefighter across the yard, kill him and all his unborn children.

I wore multilayered bunking pants, tall rubber boots, a bunking coat and helmet. I put on my heavy firefighting gloves, gloves you could pick up a hot ingot with, then gave my radio report.

"Dispatch from Engine One. We have smoke from a single-story double-wide trailer approximately twenty by forty. Brush on three sides. We're getting water on it now."

In my experience dogs tended to act predictably in a fire: There were those that pooped and those that ran away. Sometimes both at the same time. A third type of dog would bark and snap at anything that moved. I had the feeling Caputo's Dobermans weren't running and had, by now, about pooped themselves silly. That left only the third response.

Yesterday, they had been chained at the south side of the house, but now when I stepped through the brambles, there were no dogs to be seen. The paths back here were low tunnel-like affairs beaten down by the Dobermans. At the rear of the trailer I reached a clearing and found an abandoned dog chain lying next to a tree stump, food bowls nearby.

In an open space between the rear of the double-wide and the encroaching woods, two large oil drums were on their sides, each with a capacity of maybe thirty gallons, along with half a dozen large brown paper sacks. The area smelled of dog shit. I kicked one of the drums and got a hollow sound for my trouble; the oil on the spout looked fresh. We hadn't seen any of this yesterday, but then, we hadn't been back here.

The property sloped away from the trailer so that the back door was accessed via seven or eight wooden steps. The door was locked, the window blacked over on the inside from the smoke. There were no water streams inside, not yet.

Even though only a minute or two had passed since our arrival, it seemed to me as if we'd been jick-jacking around for a week.

I was rounding the corner at the far end of the trailer, headed back around toward the front, when something in the brush caught my eye.

Against my better judgment, I waded up to my hips in blackberries and dug deep into the prickly vines until I had my hands on a dog collar.

It was still attached to the animal.

He was breathing rapidly, more or less positioned as if he'd been thrown there. Dark lips curled off his canines as the Doberman growled at me. I saw no blood and figured he was either drugged or dying.

If somebody had come here to attack Caputo and his animals, Max wouldn't have been able to put up much of a fight with his mangled hand. Even if they'd reattached his fingers yesterday at the hospital, which I did not believe had happened, he wasn't going to be able to form a fist or hold a weapon.

After I waded out of the blackberries, my eyes fell once again on the oil drums.

There was something wrong here.

My thoughts turned to six dead firefighters in Kansas City back in the eighties, to another incident in Texas City, Texas, that happened long before I was born, where twenty-seven firefighters and almost six hundred civilians were killed when a ship blew up at dockside.

Dashing along the back of the mobile home, I picked up one of the empty brown paper sacks and sniffed it.

Fertilizer. Ammonium nitrate!

The combination of ammonium nitrate and diesel fuel was the same explosive compound that had been used to blow up the World Trade Center in New York the first time, as well as the Federal Building in Oklahoma City.

There was a good chance the trailer was going to blow up.

My daughters!

Before I could think the situation through, I found myself on the ground. On my butt. I'd landed hard. With no warning.

With even less warning, I was on my back, staring up at ribbons of black smoke in a blue sky. I hadn't fainted. Nor had I tripped. There had been no explosion. Not yet.

Struggling to a sitting position, I peered around to see what had taken my legs out from under me. There was nothing around me, no man or woman, no dog, no offending object.

I rolled to one knee and regained my feet, only to fall again.

Day 3: Worse headache, dizziness, falling down.

It was the second time today I'd fallen.

Taking a glove off and placing the radio mike to my lips, I said, "Dispatcher from Edgewick Command, we're going to evacuate. We have indications of large quantities of ammonium nitrate and fuel oil on the premises. All incoming North Bend units stand by one-half mile away. We have ammonium nitrate and fuel oil. Lots of it."

Reaching my feet unsteadily, I grabbed the sidewall of the trailer for support and then let go. The metal wall was as hot as a pancake griddle. I moved slowly at first, more confidently after a few steps.

When I reached the front of the trailer, I realized nobody on scene had heard my radio transmission.

Ben and Karrie were still in the smoky front doorway. I reached into the smoke and slapped Ben on the rump. "The place is filled with ammonium nitrate. Abandon the building. Now!" Twisting her head around, Karrie looked at me through the mask of her SurviveAir face piece. "I mean it! Out!"

Reaching up into the cab, I turned the siren on and switched it to the abandon building warning, a tone we'd never used except in practice.

I dashed to where my daughters and Morgan had been. The old woman was there, but my girls and Morgan were missing. Choking on my own dry throat, I called out my daughter's names. "Britney? Allyson?"

"Daddy?"

The three of them were watching me curiously from the other side of the maroon Chevrolet. Judging from the looks on their faces, I'd been bleating their names like a maniac.

I stepped between them, picking up Allyson under one arm, Britney under the other, adjusting their skinny little bodies as I ran. "Follow us, Morgan. You, too, lady. Everybody out of the yard. It's going to blow up."

Behind me, I heard the old woman complaining that her purse was in her car, that her Robitussin was in her purse. I didn't have time to quibble and was happy to see that despite the complaining she followed us.

On the other side of the street, I set my daughters down and looked back as Ben, Karrie, and Ian ran across the road behind us. "You girls hide behind that motor home. I'll be with you in a minute."

Something in my voice told them not to ask questions.

I jogged back to Caputo's driveway just as a black pickup truck pulled into the drive and plugged the opening.

I stepped around to the darkened driver's window and found myself confronting Steve Haston. He wore full bunking gear and a white chief's helmet. He'd never been a chief. For the last five years he hadn't even been a volunteer. Then, I noticed he had Newcastle's gear on, Newcastle's gear that had been hanging on a hook in the firehouse for the past month, the gear nobody had the heart to dispose of. The coat was too short in the arms by about five inches.

He said, "The fire's behind you, Jim. You got everybody going the wrong direction."

"Get your truck out of here. Even if this place wasn't a powder keg, nobody parks their personal vehicle in the driveway at a fire scene. You know better than that."

"Powder keg? What are you talking about?"

"The trailer is full of ammonium nitrate."

He laughed. "Ammonium nitrate? Isn't that fertilizer? By the way, you'd better tell Snoqualmie to get down here. They're back a ways pulled off the road."

"The trailer is on fire, and it's going to blow. Now get the hell out of here."

"No can do, buddy boy. I'm taking over as incident commander." By now everybody else was off the premises. Accompanied by a thick, fast-moving plume of black smoke, flame began to emerge out the front door of the trailer. The pump on Engine 1 was still running, although somebody'd shut off the siren. "I've decided, in light of how you people lost control of the department with the health issues and so forth, that somebody needs to get on board and take charge. I guess that's going to be me. Now you get those people back in here and fight some fire."

"Good-bye, Steve," I said, walking away. "I'll see you get the best funeral the city can afford."

"What?" he shouted out his window. "What?"

Moments later Haston's truck sped across the road in front of me. In reverse. He parked on the lawn in front of a ranch-style house about seventy feet beyond where my girls had taken refuge. The way he was driving, we were lucky he hadn't run over anybody.

We were not quite directly opposite Caputo's place, shielded by a motor home, as well as by a small hillock on the edge of Caputo's property. I figured we were almost two hundred yards away, but somehow it didn't seem far enough. I had no idea how much ammonium nitrate was in the trailer or how much of an explosion it might produce, or even if it *would* explode. Years ago in Kansas City, when a burning construction trailer blew up and killed six firefighters, windows were knocked out over a mile distant. The noise was heard ten miles away.

Like a mother bird spreading her wings, I opened my bunking coat and enveloped my daughters under the fire-retardant Nomex material. When I motioned to Morgan, she gathered close, too. "Is there really a bomb?" she asked in a small voice.

"I guess we'll find out."

As we huddled, I began to have misgivings. In my twelve-year career, I'd never seen *anybody* pull everyone out of a fire building. I was going to look either prescient or remarkably stupid. It was possible I'd misread the evidence. After all, what had I uncovered? An injured dog, some empty sacks, a couple of oil barrels.

And why would Caputo turn his trailer into a makeshift bomb?

Stump blasting. Of course. He'd been blasting stumps. Why hadn't I thought of that sooner? Now that I thought about it, stump blasting made a whole lot more sense than anything else. Whether or not the materials were inside the trailer was another story.

Beside us now, Ian Hjorth said, "Did I hear you say bomb?"

Ben Arden unbuckled his backpack and dropped his self-contained breathing apparatus into the grass. "We could have had it out in another few minutes."

"I'm going with my gut here," I said.

Ben and Ian exchanged glances. I knew they were both wondering whether I'd lost my mind.

The radio traffic was atwitter, both from the dispatcher and from the units waiting half a mile down the road. Everybody wanted details.

It was at this point that Mayor Haston stormed over to us. I had a feeling if not for the fact that my girls were with me, he would have thrown a punch. He was that angry. I'd heard a rumor that when Newcastle fired him from the volunteers, they'd nearly come to blows, that Haston had a hair-trigger temper. This was the first time I'd faced it. I knew he blamed me for the fact that our wives had run off together.

"I don't know much," Haston said, standing over me, his helmet akimbo, "but I know that trailer's burning like a box of kindling. It kind of makes me wonder about you, Swope."

"You're right, Steve. You don't know much."

"You got everybody into a lather at the meeting. Could be you're just one of those people likes to run around crying wolf."

It had been more than three minutes since we'd evacuated the property. "Steve, the way I figure it, this is a no-brainer for you. I'm right, you get to live. I'm wrong, you'll look good for wanting to go back in."

"Don't hand me any of your bullshit. I want your people back in there. Now."

"You're not going to make much of a chief if you don't know what ammonium nitrate and fuel oil do," Ian said.

At that moment, in the midst of the withering look Haston gave Hjorth, the world around us altered in a manner that few people ever experience.

The ground rocked. The air pressure all around loaded down in an instant. Our ears popped. A great gust of hot air rocked the motor home, nearly tipping it. The tops of nearby trees bowed to the ground and then flew back up like whips. Half a dozen birds came crashing to the earth around us, as if they'd been shot.

Mayor Haston, who hadn't been sheltered by the motor home with the rest of us, actually flew backward eight or ten feet and landed on his back.

In the eerie stillness immediately following the explosion, burning debris began sprinkling out of the sky. His face impregnated with tiny bits of blackened material resembling sand, Steve Haston slowly sat up on his elbows.

"That," Ian Hjorth said, "is a cheap lesson in what happens when ammonium nitrate mixes with fuel oil."

"What?" Haston was deaf now, at least temporarily.

"It means you just tried to murder about fifteen people," Arden said. "It's a good goddamned thing you weren't in charge. You dumb bastard."

"What?"

"He said you're a dumbass because you're on your keister while we're all safe here behind this motor home," Hjorth said, smiling. "Shit-fer-brains."

"Why don't you stand back up?" Arden said. "When the secondary blast comes you can do that little puppet dance again. Like Pinocchio jacking off. I kind of liked that."

Karrie stepped over to her father and said, "Shut up, you two."

I couldn't help recalling that Ben had been on the pipe back at the trailer, Karrie's rump wedged firmly in the doorway while Ben had been inside. It should have been the other way about, Karrie on the pipe, Ben backing her up. She needed to prove herself in the same manner as every other firefighter since time immemorial. And she needed to be aggressive about doing so.

27. FARTING NICKELS

"You okay?"

Allyson and Britney craned their necks up at me and nodded, their eyes like half dollars. I'd never seen them so frightened. Morgan had instinctively twined her arms around my neck when the blast hit, her body knocking us all up against the side of the motor home, and now she clung to me long after the danger was over. Embarrassed over our cheek-to-cheek position, she stood up and gave me a smile that was part chagrin and part conspiracy, as if we might have moved to a new level in our relationship. As if we had a relationship.

"You guys stay here," I said. "There could be another blast."

Morgan wiped her teary eyes with the back of her hand. "I don't think I like fires."

"Trust me, this was a freak deal."

I'd watched the blast send Haston's helmet flying a hundred feet across the yard like a lost prayer. Saw a crow with a broken wing on the roof of a house, having fallen out of the sky. Later, the doctors found particles of aluminum from the outer walls of Caputo's trailer embedded in Haston's face. They removed several small pieces of insulation from under his scalp.

Pieces of Engine 1 had become projectiles. Strips of metal and burning debris had rocketed over our heads across the yard, striking the house or landing in the woods beyond the house. Twenty seconds after the blast, heavy metal parts were still dropping all around us.

A large chunk shook the ground when it landed forty feet away. A second later a sliver of metal knifed into the ground where the four of us had been moments earlier, burying itself eighteen inches in the turf.

Morgan began crying. Britney and Allyson looked out from under the motor home where they were hiding, their eyes huge and round and curious, just a little bit pleased with the whole thing. They didn't want to miss any of this. I winked at them. Allyson winked back, but all Britney could do was scrunch up her face. In other circumstances it would have been hilarious watching her efforts.

When I figured everything that *could* fall out of the sky *had* fallen, I buttoned my coat, straightened my helmet, and stepped out onto the lawn to survey the situation.

Two of our volunteers dragged Haston back behind the motor home to protect him from a secondary blast, should there be one. On the radio, the Snoqualmie unit warned about the possibility of more blasts. We all knew from the antiterrorism classes we'd taken that planned terrorism events often came in pairs, the second explosion designed to catch the police and first-in rescuers off guard.

Trouble was, this wasn't an act of terrorism. At least I didn't think it was.

This was the work of a moron.

Except for Haston, whose face was almost as black as his truck, all the survivors on this side of the motor home looked pale.

Haston was shaking his head and repeatedly screwing his fingers into his ears, his temporary deafness a situation Hjorth and Arden were determined to exploit to the limit. "Trying to put another nickel in the meter?" Arden asked.

"Maybe it would work better if you shoved it up your ass," Hjorth said. "A guy like you should always keep a pile of nickels up his ass. That way whenever you need change you can fart nickels."

Hjorth and Arden laughed uproariously at the thought. Either they had gotten over the explosion more quickly than anybody else or they hadn't gotten over it at all and abusing the mayor was their way of coping. It was hard to know with them.

A quick survey of the fire-ground personnel told me that except for an assortment of ringing eardrums and a few minor cuts, Mayor Haston had sustained the only real injuries.

We'd started out with five civilians—Haston, Caputo's mother, my girls, and Morgan—along with eight firefighters, four paid and four volunteer, so it was a relief nobody had been killed. North Bend could easily have lost thirteen people.

Fourteen, depending on where Caputo was.

We waited five minutes. During that time the officer on the Snoqualmie rig got on the air to ask if we were all right. I gave a status report and added that they'd better start searching for spot fires, because from our vantage point we could already see at least one off in the trees. Nothing burned faster than a dry Douglas fir, and the area was well populated with them.

When I got off the radio, Caputo's mother confronted me, eyes empty, lips quivering. "What does this mean? Where's my son?"

"I don't know, ma'am. I don't know where your son is."

"What's this?" She gestured at a large chunk of pink insulation from the trailer's walls that had drifted out of the sky like a piece of cotton candy. "Tell me about this. Can anybody tell me what this means?"

Ian gave me a beleaguered look and draped his arm around the old woman's shoulders, walking her to one side and speaking softly. In twenty seconds he'd gone from mocker to grief counselor.

After I set up a perimeter to keep out neighbors and passersby, who were already showing up on foot, after I had assigned a team to check nearby residences for casualties and damage, Ben Arden and I walked across the road.

Aside from burning brush and two large maples that had been knocked half over so that their branches were knuckling the ground like football players waiting for the snap, the first thing we spotted was the still-burning hulk of the maroon Chevrolet. On the far side of it sat Engine 1, stripped down to the frame and six metal wheels, most of the rubber vaporized or blown off: no hose, no tank, no motor, no cab. The engine had been in a perfect line with Caputo's now-vaporized trailer, as well as with the motor home two hundred yards away. Combined with the small hillock, it had probably saved our lives.

On the far side of the decimated engine, Caputo's double-wide trailer had been replaced by a giant hole in the ground. As if a bulldozer had flattened them, the brush and trees surrounding the trailer were leveled for a distance of sixty feet in all directions. The oil drums and paper sacks I'd seen behind the trailer were gone. As were the blackberries. Not even the dog collar remained to convince me I had seen a dog.

Spot fires continued to smolder in the trees and brush around us.

After Snoqualmie and our second engine from the Wilderness Rim satellite station arrived and began lobbing water high into the firs, the Snoqualmie officer sent a runner to tell me they'd found an object wedged into the fork of a tree approximately a quarter mile from ground zero, that they'd tentatively identified the object as a human head.

Everybody at the scene remained on pins and needles, looking for more body parts, but all we found was a mangled hand—Caputo's—the hospital dressing still in place. Just as I thought, they hadn't sewn his fingers back on.

It took an hour to get loose of the scene. I fielded questions, gave orders, explained what had happened to at least twenty different individuals, all the while promising my girls we would have lunch soon.

Morgan seemed more distraught than anyone, and after a while I began to suspect she might be overreacting to garner attention from me.

Just after the media arrived, two Eastside Fire and Rescue investigators showed up and began snapping pictures, focusing their questions on Ian, Ben, myself, and Karrie—the four who'd gotten closest to the trailer.

They were particularly curious about the fact that we'd visited Caputo yesterday.

My personal theory was that, under the influence of prescription medication and alcohol, Caputo had left food burning on the stove. After all, his mother had been in the process of bringing over part of a meal. I figured the dog had gotten into rat poison or eaten some tainted roadkill. The ammonium nitrate, which Caputo probably kept around for removing stumps, had been stored inside and premixed with the fuel oil, although I didn't recall seeing it yesterday when we were cleaning up. The fire set it off. My theory held water until Caputo's mother insisted Max had never blasted a stump in his life.

Oddly enough, a volunteer had parked his extended-cab pickup truck in front of my new Lexus, so that the Lexus received no damage whatsoever, while the volunteer's truck lost three windows, a tire, and most of the grille. I put my bunking clothes in the trunk and left my knee-high rubber boots on. My civilian shoes had disappeared along with everything else on Engine 1. Either that or they were in a tree with Caputo's head.

28. GOING TO THE BANK IN A DIAPER

As I drove the four of us back into town, I couldn't help thinking about Charlie Drago's warning that we would be blown to smithereens. Had to be a coincidence. Charlie Drago was paranoid. Our explosion had been caused by Caputo, who'd been one of our resident nutcases ever since I was in the department. The only thing that bothered me was the dog. Caputo loved those dogs. He would never have hurt one of them, much less throw one into the blackberries. Even harder to believe that the mutt just happened to get into rat poison the day Caputo blew himself to hell. That part bothered me. It bothered me a lot. Everything about the explosion bothered me.

Sure, fire departments handled explosions, along with fires, car wrecks, first-aid calls, broken water heaters, you name it, but the last time North Bend had faced an explosion had been . . . I couldn't even remember the last time. Probably never. Certainly never during my tenure. They weren't that common.

"You girls like to see your grandfather?" I said as we drove back to town.

Britney was sitting beside me, Allyson and Morgan in back. "I'm hungry," Britney said.

Allyson leaned forward and looked at me suspiciously. "Which grampa?"

"Swope. Grandpa Swope. My father."

"I thought he moved away."

"He's living a few blocks from here. You want to see him?"

"Are you going to?"

"I thought I would."

"I want to see Grampa," Britney said. "I want to see him!"

Allyson nodded. I didn't know how to prepare them. After the explosion I didn't have the mental energy to come up with anything.

"Grandpa's been experiencing poor health," I said lamely.

"What's poor health?" Britney asked.

"Means he's sick," Allyson said.

"He's in a nursing home," I added. "He won't be able to talk, but that doesn't mean he doesn't love you."

"If he can't say it, how do we know he loves us?" Britney asked.

" 'Cause we're little girls," Allyson said sarcastically. "We're adorable. Everybody loves little girls."

"He's always loved you," I said. "Nothing has come along to change that."

My girls *were* adorable and funny and smart and always buzzing with plans. I would miss watching them grow up. Thinking about it brought a wave of sorrow over me as powerful as anything I'd felt since Lorie left. It hit me like the shock wave back at the trailer. I came close to bursting into tears right there in the car.

We parked outside Alpine Estates, and as we got out, Britney said, "I'm hungry."

"We won't be long, sweetie."

"But I'm hungry."

"Quiet up, Brit," Allyson said. "I want to see Grandpa."

"You don't mind, do you?" I asked Morgan.

"I'll wait out here if that's all right." I tossed her the keys so she could listen to the radio.

"Try that Andy Williams CD," Britney said. "It's smooth."

As I opened the door for them, I realized everything I felt toward my girls had been amplified a thousand times by the near miss up the hill. My health situation had already been having that effect, but the fire and explosion had magnified it even more. I wanted every minute to stretch into a week, found myself memorizing every move they made. It was as if I were seeing them for the first time, as if I'd been blind.

Or would be soon.

I'd been feeling it since I got home the night before, that my senses were sharpening. That I was saving up images and feelings to take with me into diaperland.

As we walked into the nursing home, I knew these were my last days with my daughters, my last hours to enjoy their innocence and spontaneity, their quick-witted banter. What hurt was that I couldn't give them all of my time, that I simply didn't dare stop searching for a cure, not while there was the least chance I might beat this monkey. I'd been deserted by Stephanie Riggs, trivialized and politicized by the committee, lied to by Jane's California Propulsion, outmaneuvered by Mayor Haston, and essentially left to face this alone.

Moving to North Bend after the death of his third wife, my father had been an immediate hit with the girls, two and four years old then.

They'd adored him, and at this late date I could admit their adoration had bothered me. Grandpa had poured all the affection he'd never given me onto them, and they'd reveled in it.

It had been petty beyond reason to keep them from their grandfather, to withhold my own visits because of slights or things not done twenty-six years ago, to hold my mother's actions and his reaction to them against him for so long, as if it were somehow his fault she had left when I was eight. Oddly, now that I thought about it, both of us had been abandoned and left with small children. I knew my father was a decent man who wanted above all to do right. Or at least that's what he'd wanted when he had a will.

We found him in a wheelchair in the hallway outside his room, head lolled to one side.

Exuding the brutal honesty of the very young, Britney let out an "Ugghh!" Her sister elbowed her and put her index finger to her lips. Both girls looked to me for signals.

I took a breath and said, "It's a little like he's asleep. You would still love me if I was asleep, wouldn't you?"

"Oh, we love you, Grampa," Britney said. "Don't we, Allyson?"

"You sure that's Grandpa?"

Neither of them had gotten close, standing like tin soldiers with their feet together and their arms at their sides. A thoughtful nurse's aide who'd been eyeing us showed up with a box of crayons and some scratch paper. We all went into the room, the nurse's aide wheeling my father in behind us.

"He doing okay?" I asked.

She was a diminutive Asian woman, no more than ninety pounds, with long, lustrous black hair wrapped behind her head. "He do jus' fine. I go every day a' four, but he do jus' fine. Every day. You from out of state?"

"No."

"Have nice visit." Smiling and nodding, she left the room.

"He ever talk?" Britney asked.

"No."

"If I throw him a ball will he catch it?"

"Why don't you throw him a rock?" Allyson said. "Don't be stupid. Of course he won't catch it. Look at him. Let's draw something. Like that stuff we mailed Mommy."

"I can't do *that* many pictures," Britney complained.

"Even one picture would be nice," I said.

Twenty minutes later, a bored Morgan wandered in and waited as the girls colored. A moment later, when I saw Dr. Brashears walking past the door, I called out. He came back, smiling quietly, eyes filled with my fate.

"What are you doing here?" Brashears asked.

I gestured toward the room. "My father."

"I just went over Jackie's records. She conformed to your list of symptoms even more closely than I thought. By the way, I called Tacoma General. Got some doctor named Philbert. Holly Riggs and Jackie? Their symptoms match perfectly."

"And neither one is coming out of it?"

"Doctors aren't God, but I don't think so."

When the girls finished their drawings, we tacked them up on the bulletin board on the end wall in my father's room next to the newspaper clipping about me. I gave Morgan some cash and sent the three of them over to North Bend Way to Scott's Dairy Freeze. The pictures were directly under a note that said: *There is banking and cigarettes at the floor dayroom every Mon & Wed & Fri at 10:00 A.M.*

As if my father was going to be doing any banking. Or smoking.

Alone in the room with him, I pulled up a chair and held his hand. He'd been a poor father some of the time, but then I'd been a poor son some of the time. Hell, he was human. Just like me. Like most of us, he'd done the best he knew. The princely manner with which he'd treated my daughters was a hint of how badly his own demons had tortured him in the years when he'd been raising me.

After a while, I called the fire station to see whether anybody had left any messages. No one had. I took a calling card out of my wallet and called JCP, Inc., in San Jose, asked for Mr. Gray in their administrative offices. It took a while to reach him.

Once I had him on the line, I went through the whole thing again, the accident, our health problems since the accident. I mentioned Mr. Stuart's denial that their company had been shipping anything in February. "I've got the shipping company's manifest right here in my hand," I said. "You guys shipped three packages, and they were involved in a serious accident."

"I'm sorry you and Mr. Stuart got off on the wrong foot," Gray said.

"There was no wrong foot about it. He said you guys don't ship in

February. I have a copy of the manifest right here in front of me that says you did."

"Stuart is very well thought of around here. If he said we weren't shipping in February, then that's what he honestly believed. Now, I'm not even sure that we *were* shipping last winter. I'd have to check the records myself."

"What we have is, we have a couple of dead firefighters up here."

"Dead?"

"A couple more who are brain-dead."

"What do you mean by that?"

"I mean their central nervous systems are shot. They can't walk, talk, or feed themselves. They're incontinent."

"I can assure you, Lieutenant . . ."

"Swope."

"Lieutenant Swope . . . that Jane's does not manufacture or ship anything that would cause symptoms like the ones you're describing."

"Are you sure?"

"Absolutely. Just out of curiosity, what symptoms were your people showing? I mean early on."

"Why do you want to know, if you don't ship anything that might cause a problem?"

"Just thinking out loud. Let me get back to you. I've got a meeting I'm late for."

I gave him the phone number at the station.

I was helping the nurse's aide change my father's diaper, a messy business at best, as well as a benchmark I was determined to get past, when a woman's voice called, "Jim?"

I turned around and found Stephanie Riggs staring at me from the doorway.

29. ALL THE WOMEN IN MY LIFE

We'd been pulling his trousers back on, were in the process of sitting him up, feats the diminutive nurse was ill-equipped to accomplish alone. Stephanie rushed in to help situate him in his wheelchair, then watched as the nurse left the room carrying a plastic sack. The odor of human shit lingered long after I found a citrus spray bottle in the bathroom and misted the room.

"I left messages, but you never got back to me."

"I didn't get them. I drove up, but I couldn't find anybody in the station. Finally a volunteer who was hanging around said somebody saw you over here. He also said somebody died at a fire today? Not another firefighter I hope."

"A civilian. By the way. Phone tag is something you play with people who have more than four days to live."

"I was working on your problem. I didn't think you needed the reassurance of knowing that."

"It looks like I did."

"I'm here now. I'm here for you. I'm sorry that wasn't clear."

I was annoyed that Max Caputo's bizarre death had stolen so much time from my own impending finish. I was annoyed also that Stephanie hadn't hooked up with me sooner, as promised. Or maybe I was just annoyed. "What did my tests show?" Stephanie took a deep breath and looked down at my father. It took me a minute to realize she wasn't going to reply, at least not right away. "Dad, this is Stephanie Riggs. Stephanie, my father, James Swope, Sr."

"CVA?"

"Little over two years ago."

"Same condition as Holly."

"The thought has occurred to me."

"You're a good son."

"That's one thing I'm not."

"No, you are. I saw you working with the nurse before you knew I was here. And you've kept him close to home. A lot of people would just ship someone in his condition out and never think twice about it."

That was exactly what I'd done and I felt lower than whale shit be-

146

cause of it, yet I could hardly point out my crimes to Stephanie. She already hated me.

"I'd rather be dead than have a stranger changing my diapers," I said.

"Don't say that."

"You haven't thought about that with Holly?"

"I don't even want to talk about this."

"Fine. Tell me about the tests."

She moved past me to the window, folding her arms across her breasts and gazing out at the sunshine. I'd read once that in wartime people were like rabbits, the proximity to death heightening their sexual awareness, exponentially increasing their drive to mate. I was beginning to feel that way myself. Stephanie was wearing Holly's perfume again, and that subtle aroma never failed to make me think of sex.

"The tests weren't conclusive. So far everything looks normal, same as Holly. That's what's so baffling. It's all so damn normal. Anything changed with you?"

"I've had a headache all day. I fell twice. It's pretty much what Stan and your sister reported."

She thought about that while I looked out the window over her shoulder. "You frightened?" she asked.

"Are you asking out of professional curiosity, or just for something to talk about?"

"I really want to know."

"I'm thinking I'm going to be like him in four days."

"No, you're not. We'll—"

"Find a cure?"

"Of course we will."

"In four days? Get real."

"You can't give up hope."

"I'm not giving up anything. I'm just being practical. The worst part is I don't know what's going to happen to my girls."

"Your ex-wife still in the picture?"

"She's wanted by the law." Two years ago I might have outlined the details of Lorie's misdemeanors ad nauseam; in the first years after our divorce I'd complained bitterly about Lorie to anybody who would listen and quite a few who didn't want to but couldn't get away from me. Ultimately, I ran out of listeners before I ran out of words. Now, more than anything else, she was a blot on my history. If she was a disgrace to parenthood, what did that make me for choosing her to be the mother of my children? She was just one more piece of evidence that I was an idiot.

I sat on the bed and picked up my father's limp hands.

I thought about how over the years I'd blamed so many of my problems on him, how I'd measured, infantile as it seemed now, each woman I'd dated by the impression I thought she would make on him. About how badly I'd needed to impress him with my companions. He must have chosen my mother for a lot of the reasons I was choosing women now.

I was the young male expelled from the troupe, wanting to come back and conquer, if only psychologically, the alpha male. As religious as he was, my father had frequently betrayed himself with a lingering look at a slim ankle or a prolonged gaze into a pair of pretty eyes. At fifty-seven, and still turning heads, my mother was a testament to his need to be surrounded by beauty. She'd been twenty-four when they married. He'd been forty-four.

Within the limitations of his life, my father had been good to me. Later, when he needed me the most, I had abandoned him, just as the rest of the world would abandon me at the end of the week.

"You're a good son," Stephanie repeated.

"I'm hungry. How about you?"

"Driving over here I saw a little Italian place on the corner. Any good?"

"Sure. Trouble is, my daughters—" Just as I said the word *daughters,* Allyson and Britney burst into the room. Morgan remained in the doorway, eyeing Stephanie with a malevolent intensity I could never have predicted. The girls were each towing a gas-filled balloon on the end of a long yellow ribbon, raving about a clown they'd seen down the hall. Britney had a pink mustache. "Strawberry shake, little girl?"

She wiped her mouth with the back of her hand.

"Allyson? Britney? This is my friend Stephanie. Stephanie's a doctor. And, Morgan? This is Stephanie."

Morgan remained sullen. The girls immediately let me in on their plot: they wanted to go to E. J. Roberts Park, a small public park a few blocks from the fire station. If they'd been scarred by our brush with death that morning, they weren't showing it.

"They're adorable," Stephanie said after they'd paraded out with Morgan. "You've done a wonderful job with them."

"They're great, but it's not all my doing. Lorie was a good mother before she left. At least part of the time. You interested in seeing somebody else with the syndrome?"

"Where?"

"Right down the hall."

In Jackie's room the television was playing to an audience of one. I turned the volume down and let Stephanie make a quick examination of the patient while I read some of the notes and cards on the bulletin board, some for her, some for her roommate, who was out. There'd been two unsigned Christmas cards on my father's bulletin board, both from the same insurance company. Somebody who felt sorry for him must have tacked them up. "She in an accident?"

"Crashed her car."

"She a firefighter?"

"A volunteer. Aid calls only."

"She's got the hands."

"Yup."

We ended up walking to a restaurant a block away.

As we started to cross the railroad tracks, I looked up and suddenly realized I was sitting on the ground. I had been walking alongside Stephanie one moment—on my keister the next. It was embarrassing.

30. HERE COMES ONE NOW

The Italian restaurant was across from the mountaineering shop and just up the street from the bike store.

After we ordered, Stephanie leaned toward me, pressing her torso forward so that the table put a horizontal dent across her as if she were a foldout paper doll. She was pretty enough to be a paper doll, her hair pulled back into a loose ponytail, her pale-blue eyes full of life, a slight swatch of freckles across her nose and cheeks. She was exactly the sort of woman who never would have had anything to do with me unless forced to. "I believe I may be on the verge of finding out what happened," she said. "At least a good portion of it."

"And?"

"I thought it would be something we found in the hospital, you know, the results of one of the tests we did on Holly, or on you, but your tests are all coming out normal. Just like hers. So last night I got on the Internet and began trying all sorts of things with various search engines. And there it was."

I must have done something with my face, because she said, "I'm sorry. I guess you want the *Reader's Digest* version and here I am giving you the unabridged version. I've found three cases in Tennessee that are almost identical to what we're seeing here. All firefighters."

"Chattanooga?"

"Yes. Did you find that, too? Happened after a fire in a shipping facility, which just happens to be where my sister's cargo originated the night she had the accident. Same city, different shipping facility. When I called this morning, they told me to speak to their lawyers. Their lawyers said if I had a suit, to file it; if not, they couldn't tell me anything. I've left a couple of calls with their fire department, but they're having some sort of conference, and everybody from the chief on down is out of the office."

"I spoke to a firefighter named Drago. I think we should call him back." Stephanie handed me her cell phone and I dialed the number from memory. It was one o'clock in North Bend, three o'clock in Chattanooga.

Drago answered the phone himself this time. I reminded him of who

I was and skipped the amenities. "Tell me why you warned me about a possible explosion."

"I don't know what you're talking about, man. Who are you?"

I ran through it all again. "Somebody called me earlier, but how do I know it was you? Start from the top. Tell me exactly what you got and how you think you got it."

The man was off his rocker. As I spoke, he interrupted repeatedly in an effort, apparently, to make sure I wasn't with the media or a private drug company, or an insurance company. You could tell he was nuts, not so much by what he said, although there were plenty of clues there, but by the staccato sentences and the up-and-down tone of his voice. I'd never heard anyone talk quite like that.

I told him as plainly as I could who I was and what had been happening to the North Bend Fire Department. When I gave him a list of the symptoms, he made me go over it twice, just like Santy Claus.

After I told him I was on day three of the syndrome, that my doctor thought I would be a zombie by the end of the week, that we'd just come back from a trailer explosion that could have wiped out the entire department, he said, "Lookit. Three years ago we had a couple of rigs respond to a fire at a place called Southeast Travelers. A freight outfit. They're still running trucks not two miles from here. What makes it so tragic is we could have pissed and put it out. It was just a silly little room fire. What we did was, we ran a line in with two guys on the pipe. Within two weeks those two guys plus one of our fire investigators were in the hospital. Pretty much the same symptoms you're describing. Brain-dead by the end of the month.

"All three had been at Southeast, and all three had moved packages and freight around. Those little shits at Southeast tried to deny it, but there was only one place it could have happened. Doctors around here thought they might have gotten into some insecticide. But that storeroom didn't have any insecticide in it."

"You say it was only two weeks between the fire and when they came down with the symptoms? That makes me think we're not talking about the same thing. It was longer up here."

"Your guys are turning into zombies? Just layin' there, nothing behind their eyes? Gotta feed 'em? White stuff on the backs of their hands?"

Rubbing one hand, I said, "How are your guys doing?"

"I hate to say it, but Vic is dead, and the other two are organ donors going to seed. Lost most of their weight. Their muscle tone. They got bedsores. The oldest is forty and looks like an embalming school has been using him for practice. They just started feeling sick, nothing earth-shattering, and then one day they either didn't wake up or collapsed where they stood. Two of 'em are in nursing homes. The other one, Vic, died of a heart attack about six months ago. His wife had already divorced him so she could marry somebody else in the department. Tell me that wasn't a scandal. I hope to Jesus cows are laying eggs and roosting in trees before anything like that happens to me."

"Has there been an investigation?"

"Our mayor appointed a commission to study it, and the state's working on it, too, but nothing's happened. I think after our senator got into the mix, that's when the investigation started going cow shit."

"What makes you say that?"

"They decommissioned one of the groups studying it and then seeded the other one with people from the chemical industry. You know there's politics in it when they actually put representatives from some of the companies we think caused it on the panel to investigate. After a year they put out a preliminary report which says basically diddly-squat. Then one of the guys on this eighteen-member commission has a heart attack and everything grinds to a halt while they spend four months scouring the countryside for a replacement. Four months!"

"Anybody narrowed down the cause?"

"Sure. Down to about, oh, twenty or thirty different companies. To about a hundred and fifty chemical agents, maybe ten thousand possible combinations. Southeast ships chemicals around the country. And every one of those companies wants to stall the investigation. There's a million theories floating around out there, but nobody knows for sure. We got lawsuits out the yinyang. We lost three good men, and we should be moving heaven and earth to figure out why, not hiding behind attorneys."

"Don't you guys have a union?"

"Yeah, but the leadership is basically hanging our guys out to dry."

"It doesn't make sense. You'd think the city would want to find the cause. What if it happens again?"

"That's just it. Everybody's saying it could never happen again."

"How can they know that if they haven't pinned down the cause?"

"Thank you very much. That's what I've been trying to tell them. The commission has identified over a hundred and fifty chemical compounds got spilled or opened at that fire. You mix one chemical with another, and all of a sudden you've got a substance nobody knows nothin' about. Truth is, we might never know what caused this."

"Nobody else caught the syndrome? None of the freight company employees or the truck drivers?"

"Nobody. Which makes us think it was a gaseous compound. The smoke goes away, so does the hazard."

"Or maybe some mixture of chemicals that doesn't remain stable very long."

"Coulda been."

"Anybody catch it and then shake it?"

"Not that I know of. You sure you got this?"

"I've had four coworkers go down."

"Like our guys?"

"Two are that way. Two are dead."

"Jesus, I'm sorry, buddy. I really am. You got your family stuff in order and all that?"

"Some of it."

"Far as I know nothing has ever changed with these guys, until one died from a heart attack. Vic was my best friend, so it's not like I ain't been keeping tabs. I'd like to say yes, they're getting better, but the truth is, these guys are zombies and always will be."

"God."

"Yes."

"Why did you warn me about an explosion?"

"I can't talk about that, man. I mean, I really can't. They're watching me. In fact, I'm pretty sure they're taping this phone call."

"Who?"

"That's just it. If I knew who, I could do something about it. It would take a month to tell you everything that's happened around here. I will tell you this. I went back to Southeast Travelers one night to look around. They've kept the building pretty much the way it was, all taped off and everything. There was a man in there in the dark doing something. I couldn't quite tell what. I could tell he didn't work there. The bastard threatened to kill me."

"What'd you do?"

"I got out of there, man."

"Call the police?"

"What I did was, I started packing a gun."

"You find out who he was?"

"No, man, we didn't become friends or nothin'. Scared the hell out of me. I really thought for a minute he was going to kill me."

I had some more questions for Drago, but I could hear the tremor in his voice. Charlie was coming close to losing his mind right there on the phone. I decided to change the subject and asked about the companies involved.

After much shuffling of papers and confusion on his end of the line, Drago told me he couldn't locate the list of companies with products in the fire room at Southeast Travelers. Instead he told me all the company names he could remember off the top of his head and everything he knew about them. I wanted to compare the list from Holly's truck with Drago's list. It seemed to me that if we found products on both lists, we should concentrate on them.

"How about a company called Jane's California Propulsion? Did they have anything at Southeast?"

"Jane's? Maybe. I dunno. It's a pretty long list. I can't remember all the companies. Listen, I'll get back to you when I find my complete list. And you get in touch anytime, day or night," Drago said. "I mean that. You want something, it's yours. I'll fly out there and sit with you, man. I mean that. I'm there for you. Anything."

"Thanks, Charlie."

When I hung up, Stephanie looked at me and said, "Did they?"

"Did they what?"

"Recover?"

"No."

We were still waiting for the meal when Mary Kay LeMonde approached our table with a look on her face that was half curiosity and half challenge. Through part of the winter and early spring, Mary and I had kept company, our time together overlapping Holly's entrance and exit in my life, as well as the second Suzanne's, the Suzanne whose existence had spurred my breakup with Holly. You can see how complicated things were.

I liked women, liked to be friends with them, liked to be lovers with them, and I especially liked to be friends with them *after* I had been lovers with them. I can't tell you why it meant so much to me, because I didn't know many other single men who were friendly with any of their exes, much less *all* of their exes. To me, it had always been pivotal that my lovers liked me after the heat of passion waned, which was ironic because Lorie barely spoke to me and certainly had not been back to visit since the night she left three years ago.

Joel McCain claimed it was almost as if I were forming a club of ladies I'd fucked.

Fucked. That was the word Joel had used. Could any term be more degrading, more gauche, more unpolished, or, in this case, more apt? Until the past few days, I'd never used the word. Not even back in the army. Oddly, Joel, with religion oozing out his ears, had used it all the time.

"Hello, Jimmy."

"Mary Kay. How nice to see you."

As with the others, after we stopped sleeping together Mary Kay and I remained on speaking terms—the last phone call about two weeks ago.

Grasping the table for support, I stood up, realizing as I looked into her dark-brown eyes that even though we still spoke on the telephone from time to time, I had been doing my level best to avoid her. Two weeks ago at the QFC I'd raced out of the store after spotting her. Childish, yes. Vintage Swope? You bet.

Mary Kay was unquestionably the best-looking woman on the staff at Mount Si High School and had often gone on about how handsome I was and what a nice couple we made and so forth. We had been a matched pair, neither of us ever appearing in public with unflossed teeth, a hair out of place, or lint on our clothes, two mirror addicts temporarily in love with the thought of coupledom. For years I'd been as shallow as a puddle of melted ice cream, and now all I could think about was how shallow Mary Kay had been, still was, and how glad I was to be shed of her.

Mary Kay was too busy with her machine-gun chatter to notice the way I gripped the table for support. Talk, talk, talk. Mary Kay had even nattered while we made love, a proclivity that had kept me from completing the business at hand on at least one occasion. She'd gabbed our breakup to death in much the same way Holly had, analyzing the smallest details until I wanted to bay at the moon.

I introduced the women, telling Mary Kay that Stephanie was a doctor, that we were working on a fire department project together. Don't ask me why I cared what she thought. Mary Kay and I would never see each other again. Before she left, Mary Kay ascertained that Stephanie was from out of state and would be leaving soon, all of this done in one polite exchange after another.

I couldn't help thinking how much of my life had been frittered away on women I knew were only passing through. It seemed such a colossal waste of time. But then, I'd always been misguided about what it took to be a man. It was no accident I ran away from home and moved directly into an army barracks, no accident, either, that within two years of my exit from the service I'd become a firefighter. One macho trade after another. And of course, Lorie had been gorgeous. Demented, but gorgeous.

My years of standing around on street corners handing out Bible tracts alongside timid females and gawky men had polluted my entire adult life. I was still trying to be a man's man. Anything but the sissy on a street corner.

After our waiter left, Stephanie said, "That must have been a tangled web."

"What?"

"You and Mary Kay."

"Not really."

"So why did you feel you had to make sure she knew you and I weren't romantically involved."

"I didn't say that."

"You did everything but pull out a grease pen and print *strictly business* across my forehead. You ashamed to be seen with me?"

"Absolutely not."

"You practically apologized to her for being with me."

"She's a little touchy, is all."

"Because of the way you broke up?"

"I suppose."

"It *is* over, isn't it?"

"It is, but she was having a hard time believing it."

"You didn't make it plain?"

"It's more complicated than that."

"How could it be any simpler? You don't want to see her anymore. You move on. She moves on."

"It's hard to explain."

"Selfishness always is. Were you seeing her before Holly or after?"

I picked up a piece of bread and broke it. "Before."

"You took a long time to answer. It was during, wasn't it?"

"I'm tired."

"*You* dumped *her.*"

"We decided to make some space."

"*You* decided to make some space."

"She wasn't fighting it. She—"

"You're not the kind to tell somebody it's over, are you? No. You're too passive-aggressive for that. You like women hanging around. Clinging. Making you feel wanted. Important."

"You drove up here today to attack me?"

"I'm not attacking you."

"Funny. It feels like you are."

I'd harbored some slim hope that Stephanie Riggs would remain my ally throughout this ordeal, that she would be there to the end, but it was a pathetic hope. Too bad there was no one else to hold my hand when I turned into a vegetable, not unless I wanted to resurrect my relationship with one of the Suzannes or Mary Kay or one of the others.

"She's still carrying the torch and you love it."

"Basically, we're just friends."

"If there's one thing you're *not*, it's friends. So what woman hurt you so badly you can't trust *any* woman? That you want to torture them all like this?"

"What's trust got to do with it? Is that what Holly wrote in her diary? That I'd been betrayed?"

"I'm guessing it was your mother."

The meal had been in front of us for some time. I sprinkled grated cheese on my tortellini and picked up my fork. "I'll be dead by the end of the week. What does it matter?"

"Dead?"

"As good as."

"You won't be dead."

"You think I'm a sonofabitch, don't you?"

"I think you're just like anyone else, a complex human being who doesn't quite understand all of his motivations. There's nothing wrong with that. Most of us don't understand what makes us tick. Look. I really am sorry I opened my big mouth."

"No. You're right. I've known a lot of women, and I'm not sure I treated any of them the way I'd want my daughters treated. I've never been good with relationships. Every woman I've dated in the last couple of years . . . I start off thinking this is the one, and by the time I have her convinced of it, I've lost interest." I broke off a hunk of bread and dipped it in olive oil.

"Did you cheat on your wife?"

"Why are you asking that?"

"You cheated on Holly and this other person, Mary Kay."

"I didn't say I cheated on Mary Kay."

"But you did, didn't you?"

"We were friends. It wasn't—"

"Did you cheat on your wife? Indulge me. I'm trying to get to know you. We don't have that long, and I want to know you."

"You know plenty."

"I don't, though. Not enough."

I didn't know what kind of game she was playing, but as uncomfortable as it made me, it also pleased me in a manner that was hard to describe. I'd never been with a woman as brutally honest as her. Nor one who could put a knife in my heart as quickly.

"Did you?"

"What?"

"Cheat on your wife?"

"Never even crossed my mind. Well, toward the end it crossed my mind. But it never happened. And it never would have. Marriage vows are sacred."

"Your baby-sitter was staring daggers at me."

I broke off another hunk of bread. "Was she?"

"She's got the hots for you."

"I suppose you think I engineered that, too?"

"I don't know how it happened, but it's easy enough to see what it does for your ego."

Oh, brother.

31. JANE'S CALIFORNIA PROPULSION, INC.

igging into my lunch while she perused the list of company names I'd scribbled on the paper place mat, I thought about the script that had already been played out in Chattanooga. Had the problem there been addressed properly, firefighters in North Bend wouldn't be dropping like empty shell casings under a drunken hunter.

Stephanie said, "Canyon View Systems. Is that what this says?"

"Yeah. Now that you mention it, Canyon View was on the manifest I got for Holly's truck, too. But they were only shipping books, as I recall. And according to Charlie Drago, they were the only ones who helped out in Tennessee. Everyone else stonewalled or fought them tooth and nail. Canyon View sent two specialists down to answer questions and assist with the investigation."

"My Aunt DiMaggio? You saw her the other night at the hospital. Her husband founded Canyon View Systems. She runs it."

"That would make sense. Your aunt said Holly shipped stuff for them from time to time."

"It also makes sense that they sent people down to help when nobody else would. Aunt Marge has always had a fairly well developed social conscience. She did a lot to help Holly get on her feet when she first arrived here in Washington."

"Was she running the company three years ago?"

"Phil was still alive then, so he was."

It was at about that point that I got a brainstorm and asked to borrow Stephanie's cell phone. Mine had blown up with the engine back at Caputo's trailer. On the first call I reached Mr. Stuart from Jane's California Propulsion, the same man who'd told me they didn't ship in February. I told him who I was and he said, "Lieutenant Swope? I guess you spoke to my colleague Ben Gray? It turns out we *were* shipping last February. I'm sorry about that. We very rarely send anything out during that time of year, and I could have sworn we didn't last February. My mistake. Now what can I do for you?"

"I wanted to know what you were shipping and if there might be any adverse health effects attached to it."

"We have a lot of materials we send by truck. Unfortunately, they're all classified. I'm not really at liberty to talk about them. You say somebody's been sick?"

"Quite a few somebodies."

"I'm sorry to hear that. Do the symptoms include dizziness?"

"Yes."

"Headaches? Ringing in the ears?"

"Yes. How did you—"

"You're sure?"

"Yes. What does it mean?"

"Nothing. Nothing at all."

"How could it mean nothing? Why ask if it means nothing?"

"Just please bear with me. This is a standard list of questions we're required to go over. What other symptoms are there?"

I listed them, and he seemed to be writing it all down. Afterward, he said, "Not us. It wasn't anything we have. We don't work with any product that would cause anyone to go brain-dead."

"What about the rest of the symptoms?"

"We don't work with anything that could cause brain death."

"What *do* you work with?"

"As I said before. Our work is classified. Lieutenant Swope, what if we were to send a couple of representatives up there?"

"Listen, if you have anything that might be causing our problems, tell me. There are people going through this right now."

"We'll have a couple of representatives up there in three hours."

"What? You have a company jet?"

"No. They'll be flying commercial. Good-bye, Lieutenant Swope."

"Wait a minute. Did your company have any products in a shipping facility fire at a place called Southeast Travelers in Chattanooga three years ago?"

"I really couldn't tell you. As I said, our representatives will be seeing you shortly."

We hung up and I related the conversation to Stephanie, who said, "They've probably been sued before and have instructions not to say anything. No doubt that's why they're sending people up here, too."

"It sounded to me like he knew what we had before I told him. I think these guys know what's going on."

"I want to talk to my aunt. If her company helped out with the investigation in Chattanooga, maybe she knows something."

"Apparently she doesn't know what the symptoms in Tennessee were, or she would have recognized them in Holly."

"Canyon View is a big company. She might not know anything at all, but somebody there will."

Stephanie picked up her cell phone and punched in a number, asked for Marge DiMaggio, and then listened for a moment and hung up. "Went to Portland this afternoon for a meeting. Staying overnight. She's got a meeting up here at eight-thirty tomorrow morning. She'll call beforehand."

DAY FOUR

32. THE CURVE OF HER THIGH

With all that was happening, you'd think insomnia would have robbed me of my ability to sleep, but you'd be wrong. Once again I slept like the dead. No tossing or turning. No tottering trips to the loo in the wee hours. No memory even of having gone to bed. Just a blissful sleep that seemed to last forever. Maybe my nights were a foretaste of brain death. Maybe I was going to be happier than I'd ever been.

Thursday. By Sunday it would be over.

It occurred to me as I contemplated these things that going to sleep at night couldn't be too different from death. Suddenly a great calm descended upon me.

I began to wonder why any of us feared death.

Last night had been a stretch in heaven.

I yawned lazily and glanced over at the clock. It was eight. I hadn't slept this late in years.

Although it would be an hour before we got any direct sunlight, the rooms in our small house were slowly filling with the early morning June dawn. The house was quiet, motes of dust drifting in the dead air. I was filled with the sheer wonder of being alive.

Because we were almost directly underneath the west face of Mount Si, the morning sun didn't reach us until ten-thirty or eleven in winter and not until nine-ish on the longest day of the year, which would be next week. In our stronghold under the mountain it was always a little cooler than the rest of the township, a little dewier, and in winter a little frostier.

I had slept in a pair of rumpled sleeping drawers and an oversize North Bend Fire and Rescue T-shirt, was now padding around the hardwood floors of our house barefoot wondering where everybody was. It was a small house with a living room, two bedrooms, and a dayroom that served as our family room just off the open kitchen.

They were on the futon in the family room, Britney, Allyson, and Stephanie Riggs, who'd spent the remainder of the day with us. We'd taken turns calling the companies that had been involved in the Chattanooga incident from the list Charlie Drago had provided and then on the manifest from Holly's truck last February, calling until anybody who could answer a phone had gone home for the day. If Charlie Drago was to be trusted, and I wasn't sure that he could be, there were dozens of suspects in the Tennessee incident, many more than on the list he was able to give me. Judging from what they might have been carrying, there were only three logical choices in our accident: DuPont Chemical, Pacific Northwest Paint Contractors, and Jane's California Propulsion, Inc. None of the three were on Charlie's incomplete list, but that didn't mean much.

DuPont was being as intractable as any large corporation could be. So far I had yet to talk to a single person in authority there. At lunchtime Jane's had promised to send a couple of people up in three hours, but as of that night they still hadn't arrived. I'd called Jane's five or six times since then, but neither of the two parties I'd spoken to earlier were in and nobody else seemed to have heard of me or a junket to North Bend. Pacific Northwest Paint Contractors had been shipping, among other items, toluene, which Stephanie looked up yesterday. The pathophysiology included effects to the CNS, euphoria, dizziness, confusion, CNS depression, headache, vertigo, hallucinations, seizures, ataxia, tinnitus, stupor, and coma. It was very close to the list of symptoms from exposure to organophosphates.

The list wasn't exactly in line with what I was going through, but it was close enough. It occurred to me that the reason Joel had fallen off the roof and Jackie had crashed her car might have had to do with some of those symptoms in combination with one another. Hallucinations and dizziness. Euphoria and stupor. It was scary thinking about it. Pacific Northwest Paint had promised to check to see whether their shipment had been damaged and whether any of their containers had been opened.

In addition, Stephanie made a half-dozen discreet calls to physicians and personnel at Tacoma General. We discussed and analyzed Charlie Drago and the situation in Chattanooga, agreeing it would be good to get a second perspective from Tennessee.

Allyson and I had prepared dinner together while Stephanie and Britney played Candy Land, and then, at Allyson's insistence, we set up candles on the table for dinner. The girls continued to treat Stephanie like visiting royalty. After dinner Stephanie and I were dragooned into a game of Monopoly, which we abandoned before it officially ended, when Allyson got so far ahead of the rest of us that Britney started to cry.

It was almost eleven when we unfolded the futon in the family room, insisting, all of us, that Stephanie forgo the motel and stay here. When the girls begged to watch a late-night movie with her, *The Whole Town's Talking,* with Edward G. Robinson and Jean Arthur, I objected, knowing Stephanie had been up late the night before, but Stephanie said a girl party would be fun, that I should go to bed and get my beauty sleep. Britney cackled, never having heard the phrase *beauty sleep* before.

As I stood in the doorway between the kitchen and the family room watching them, I felt so much love for my girls it almost hurt. Characteristically separated by half a body width, Britney slept by herself, while the other two were snuggled up together. It was ironic because during the day Britney was the clingy one and Allyson the slightly more standoffish of my daughters. When sick or asleep, they reversed roles, Allyson clutching, Britney off to one side. Britney had a whisper of perspiration on her brow, both feet sticking out from the blankets.

Mixed with Allyson's darker, heavier-looking mop, Stephanie Riggs's hair was so silky and lustrous, it seemed from another world.

Too bad Stephanie hated me. Had circumstances been different, I would have been thinking about the curve of her thigh under the sheet, the gentle jut of her jawline, her hair splayed across the futon. But Stephanie had pegged me like a lepidopterist pinning down a butterfly: conquer and abandon. A small-time prick working big-time hustles on unsuspecting females all over the valley. The supreme cad. A self-involved jerk.

That had been my unspoken, underhanded, and unacknowledged modus operandi for the past three years. Funny how knowing it was your last week on earth could open your eyes to things that should have been obvious all along.

Before the syndrome, I'd had little time for real life. I'd been chasing the perfect woman, the one who would look good on my arm, the one other men would envy me for, the woman who wouldn't leave me or get sick or go crazy or be anything but beautiful, the woman you could always count on with absolute certainty, the woman who existed nowhere on earth but in the deepest recesses of my brain.

After seducing each candidate with a sincerity that was believable primarily because I believed it myself, after earnestly convincing her of my fitness as a father, as a potential husband, as a lifelong friend, partner, and confidant, I would begin to discover minor aspects of her character that didn't suit me. Eventually these token flaws would pile up and grow in importance until, after some days or weeks of torturing myself with indecision, I would make the inevitable announcement that we were getting too close; I would tell her I needed space. In other words, as several women had told me, I'd had my fun and it was time to move on.

Convincing them we were still friends was my own sick little mischief, which in my own mind managed to lessen the injury delivered but in fact only prolonged their pain.

Sincerity was the key, I'd found, when dealing with women. If you could fake sincerity, you didn't have to fake anything else. My only defense was that I faked it so well that even I believed it was genuine. I was and always had been a genuine dope! As only a former Christian and a true idiot could, I believed my own patter.

Everybody has the capacity for self-deception, but I was the king.

Yesterday Stephanie made my jaw drop when she asked what woman had injured me so badly I felt the need to hurt all women. When you're playing the kind of games I'd been playing and found yourself in the presence of a woman with that sort of quick insight, you ran like a scalded cat. I would have, too, if I hadn't needed her help so desperately.

My mother had abandoned me at age eight. When she returned four years later, a meager two postcards and one belated birthday present in between, she became so self-conscious about relating once again to the religious rigmarole of the Sixth Element of the Saints of Christ, about fitting back into the hierarchy at Six Points, about being taken back by her husband, James, Sr., that she all but forgot me. I was twelve by then and not nearly the cute little button-nosed imp she'd left. In fact, I'd turned into something of a sullen brat. But then, even when her plate was almost empty, Mother had too much on it for me. By the time she returned, I was old enough to be bitter but proud enough to hide it, resentful enough not to forget but alienated enough to make sure it never happened again. I would die before I would put my trust in her.

Despite her cutting insights into my flawed psyche, I was surprised at how comfortable I'd been spending time yesterday with Stephanie. Not that I wasn't still scared of her, mind you.

Not wanting to disturb their slumber, I stepped into a pair of sandals and went out back to the pasture. The morning air was clear and crisp. Intent on making each moment last as long as possible, I stood in the field under Mount Si, which rose to forty-one hundred feet over our house in a steep wall on the far side of the Middle Fork, firs clinging to the south end of the mountain, ragged rock screes and crags spanning the north end. Nobody ever visited our place without expressing wonder at how close the mountain was, at how majestic and awe-inspiring and downright frightening it was. Like Yosemite, people said.

On summer evenings hang gliders launched off the top, taking advantage of the warm air currents that raced up the steep face, and each year thousands of hikers and tourists labored up the four-mile trail on the side of the mountain, scrambling to a lookout just out of view of our property. From the top you could see Seattle thirty miles away, the snow-capped Olympic Mountains across Puget Sound, and, directly below, the entire town of North Bend.

I could hear the river a hundred yards in front of me as well as the breeze in the trees.

After some minutes, I heard footsteps in the tall grass behind me. I'd been out long enough to be thoroughly chilled in my T-shirt and sleeping shorts, long enough to start feeling sorry for myself.

"We slept in," Stephanie said, coming alongside me and staring up at the mountain. "You have a good night?"

"Slept like the dead."

"I wish you wouldn't use expressions like that." She touched my hand.

"Realistically, what do you think the odds are of stopping this before I end up like your sister?"

"Realistically?"

"You're stalling."

"I don't know. I don't—"

"You don't think it's going to happen, do you?"

"I do and I don't. We basically know what's going on, which is an advantage Holly and the others didn't have. Except for your friend Stan, none of them suspected what this was. I'm speaking to consultants and specialists all over the country. You've got those people from California coming up. They might know what this is. And since Canyon View was helpful in the investigation in Tennessee, my aunt or someone working for her might know something."

"In other words, the odds of stopping this before I end up like your sister are slim to none."

"I didn't say that."

"I know. I said it for you."

33. THE HEATHEN UNDER GOD'S BED

"Damn it, Stephanie. You didn't pull any punches that first day I met you. I didn't like it, but I admired you for it. Tell me what you really think."

"I'm not God. I can't see the future."

"I can."

She sighed and wrapped both arms around my waist. I dropped my arm over her shoulders. The sky was pale blue except for a wispy pink-tinged cloud crowning the foothills to the south. The sun still hadn't come over Mount Si. "What an extraordinarily beautiful place," she said.

"I don't know if I ever truly appreciated it until now."

"You religious, Jim?"

"I used to be. These days I'm what you might call a heathen and proud of it."

"It seems to me religion has a place in life, especially a place for people who are in the situation you're in. Do you think it might help if you had some counseling—I don't know, a pastor or a priest to talk to?"

" 'And you shall know the truth, and the truth shall make you free'? That sort of mumbo jumbo? Or how about: 'Let the God of my salvation be exalted'—Psalms Eighteen, verse forty-six? Or: 'Lead me in thy truth, and teach me: for thou are the God of my salvation; on thee do I wait all the day'—Psalms Twenty-five, verse five. Or: 'Deliver me from blood-guiltiness, O God, thou God of my salvation: and my tongue shall sing aloud of thy righteousness.' Let's try Hebrews: 'Now faith is the substance of things hoped for, the evidence of things not seen.' "

"So you know the Bible?"

"I still remember about half of it."

"So you must have prayed in the past. Your prayers were never answered?"

"I figure if there's a God, he keeps pretty busy arranging natural disasters and destroying nations, maybe figuring out how to manipulate one population into cutting off the hands of another. What he does is a lot more fun than answering prayers from a nitwit like me. I spent sixteen years of my life hiding under God's bed. My parents thought they had the revelation of the absolute truth of the universe through the prophet William P. Markham; he was the con artist who founded the Sixth Element of the Saints of Christ. We kids got Bible assignments each morning. I think I had most of the New Testament memorized before I could read, before I could think, really, because when you're living in a cult, thinking is pretty much discouraged. We bragged about being free-thinkers, but come up with anything not strictly approved by William P. Markham and whoa. We weren't even allowed to *read* about another religion. Maybe that's why wherever I've lived, I ended up spending half my time in the public library."

"Who's going to be with you through this? You need somebody."

"I was hoping you would stick around."

Stephanie slipped her arms under my shirt, her bare hands hot against my flesh. "I'll stick around as long as you want me to."

"Just till I'm eating mush. After that I won't know who's here and who's not."

"I'll be here."

When we went back inside, arm in arm, the girls gave each other knowing looks. They'd set the table as formally as a wedding banquet, had come up with the idea of cooking breakfast, dollar pancakes, Allyson's favorite. Stephanie and I added juice and scrambled eggs to the menu.

I surrounded more than my fair portion of pancakes, feeling invincible the way Bill Murray felt invincible in *Groundhog Day*. Clog up my arteries? That would take years.

"So?" Britney asked at the conclusion of our breakfast. "Are you two getting engaged?"

"Brit!" Allyson shouted. "I told you not to say that."

Stephanie could see as painfully as I could the irony of my daughters trying to plot out the rest of our lives at a time when our family was on a countdown timer.

"What makes you think we might get married?" I asked.

"She stayed overnight," Allyson said.

"That was only to save her from a long drive. Honey, we're working on a project."

"You don't like her?" Britney asked. "Isn't she pretty?"

"Of course I like her. And she's very pretty. But there are other considerations."

"Like what?" Allyson asked.

"Ally," Britney said. "You're going to spoil everything."

"*You* started it."

Filled with emotion, Britney looked around the table and said, "Daddy never lets anybody stay over. This is a millstone."

"A milestone," said Stephanie softly. "I think you mean it's a milestone."

"Yeah, right, whatever. The second Suzanne never stayed over once, and he really liked her. Mrs. LeMonde never even came in the house. Holly was nice, but . . ."

"What about Holly?" Stephanie asked.

"Morgan saw them kissing in the car."

"I'm sure your father's kissed a lot of women in the car."

"No, he hasn't really," Britney said. "Just Holly, and the second Suzanne, and maybe Mrs. LeMonde."

The breakfast was sitting foully in my stomach, but I didn't heed the warning.

I barely made it to the bathroom, dropping to my knees in front of the commode and retching until there was no more to bring up. I couldn't remember ever vomiting so violently, or feeling my stomach walls actually connect with my spine. For a few moments in the middle of it, I thought I was going to choke to death, or die of heart failure.

From the doorway behind me, Stephanie said, "You all right?"

"I don't know why I don't read the symptoms for the next day before I go to bed." I'd barely gotten the words out when another round shook me. And then a minute later, as I was washing up, the wave of nausea vanished as quickly as it had arrived.

Day 4: Headache goes away, cannot keep food down.

Stan Beebe had been through this. So had Holly, Newcastle, Joel McCain, Jackie, and those three in Tennessee. I was joining a select brotherhood.

I must have looked ashen when I came out of the bathroom, because Allyson took my hand and said, "You all right, Daddy?"

"Fine."

"Did we leave eggshells in the pancakes? You get shell shock?" It was a longtime family joke.

"No. Everything was wonderful. I just have a bug in my stomach, that's all." I found myself kneeling in the living room, clutching my eldest.

Britney, who had been obsessed with death and abandonment issues since her mother left, rushed over and said, "You're not going to die, are you?"

"No, of course not." I caught Stephanie's eye from the other room. "We all die eventually. You know that."

"I know that. I'm not a baby," Britney said. "But I want Ally and me to be at least twenty-one before you die."

"I'll be twenty-three. You'll be twenty-one," Allyson said. "I'm two years older."

"And how could I forget that? You only remind me every hour."

34. TWO-DOLLAR MAP, TWO-DOLLAR WHORE

Morgan had left a message on the machine saying she felt under the weather and could not baby-sit today. I could tell from her voice she was trying on a fit of pique over Stephanie. She'd done the same after seeing me with Suzanne.

With the help of Karrie Haston, Ben Arden, and Ian Hjorth, the three paid firefighters on duty that day, Stephanie and I set up a base camp in the officers' room. In the end we had a computer with an Internet connection, three landlines, plus two cell phones. Karrie and Ben set up the office while Ian kept watch in the station and entertained Allyson and Britney with cartoon drawings on the blackboard. In a matter of minutes, Stephanie and I were fielding calls, Stephanie logging outgoing and incoming so that we didn't duplicate our efforts.

There was still no sign of anybody from Jane's. When I called them in San Jose, I couldn't get through to anybody. It was as if the plant had closed down.

Stephanie contacted two doctors, one in California and a second in New York, both specialists in diseases transmitted by poultry, while I tried to get hold of someone else affiliated with the Chattanooga Fire Department. What I wanted was the down and gritty, a confirmation or confutation of Charlie Drago's tale. Also, I wanted a confirmation that Jane's California Propulsion, Inc., had had packages at Southeast Travelers Freight. I didn't know that they'd had anything there, but I strongly suspected it.

Trouble was, the Chattanooga Fire Department was hosting a conference in town, and none of the administration or union people were in their offices.

Stephanie tried her aunt's condo in Bellevue and then her office in Redmond. Marge DiMaggio was in a meeting and had left instructions not to be disturbed.

It was just about then that Karrie showed up at the door to the office. "Two suits to see you at the front door," she said.

Stephanie followed me to the tiny watch office at the front of the station, where I met two short bald men who looked uncomfortable in their sport coats and brown slacks. Both men kept their hands in their pockets, although each had brought along a bulky briefcase and one had a laptop computer in a black bag. Their names were Hillburn and Dobson. They were pudgy and soft the way people who'd been indoors all their lives were.

"Morning," said Hillburn genially. He was bright as a button, and I had the feeling he had as many years in universities as I had in the fire department. They both claimed they were already full of coffee but drank more after Karrie offered it.

Out the window across the street I could see what looked like a rental car. These were the two from Jane's California Propulsion, Inc.

"Mr. Stuart said you guys would be here in three hours. That was yesterday."

"Did he?" Hillburn and Dobson looked at each other. "Did he say that? Odd. He knew we had to be in Denver yesterday."

"It *is* odd," added Dobson.

"Now let's get down to cases," Hillburn said. "First off. How many people have been affected?"

"Here?" I said. "Here in Washington? Five that we know of. One more with symptoms."

"And what are the symptoms? Exactly."

I listed them while Dobson opened his laptop and typed them into a document. He kept typing after he was finished with the list, as if recording our meeting. In fact, he did a lot more typing than we did talking, filling up all the empty spaces with his tap-tap-tapping.

"Okay," Hillburn said. "Now. I need to see the manifest."

I walked to the other room and brought it back. After he'd studied it a minute, he handed it to Dobson, who studied it also, then entered the complete list of materials and involved companies into his computer, typing like a high school speed champ.

I said, "Were you shipping a product that could have caused any of our symptoms?"

Without looking up, Dobson said, "No."

"No," repeated Hillburn reflexively.

"How can you assure us of that?" Stephanie said.

"And you are?" Hillburn said.

"Stephanie Riggs. I'm his doctor."

"A doctor of medicine?"

"Yes."

Hillburn and Dobson looked at each other for a second, and then Hillburn looked at Stephanie for a long while as Dobson directed his attention back to his laptop. Finally, Dobson looked up from his typing again and said, "We've never had anything even remotely like this."

"What *have* you had?" I asked.

"Well, unfortunately, company policy prohibits us from discussing that."

"Company policy," said Hillburn.

"And company policy would also preclude you from admitting you had something like this even if you did, wouldn't it?" I said.

"More than likely," Hillburn admitted.

"So what sorts of previous health concerns are you prepared to admit to? And did you have any products in a fire at Southeast Travelers' shipping facility in Chattanooga, Tennessee, three years ago?"

"Before we answer any of your questions, we'll need to see the materials," Hillburn said. "The actual materials from the crash site."

"You've got the shipping manifest in front of you."

"We know that. We need to look at the materials. The truck trailer and so forth."

"We don't have the truck trailer. I told you the accident was last winter."

"What do you mean, you don't have the trailer?"

"I mean all that stuff got hauled off months ago."

"So how do you know the accident had anything to do with these health problems you're talking about?"

"We don't. Not for sure."

"You sure you don't have any of the materials?" Hillburn asked.

"Just that manifest."

Hillburn and Dobson looked at each other; Dobson was already folding up his laptop. They were out the door before I could stop them. As the door closed behind them, Dobson said, "I guess that's all we need then."

"What the hell were you shipping?" I yelled at the closed door. I followed them outside.

"You have any more problems with this, give us a call," Hillburn said as if he were being helpful.

"Wait a minute!" I screamed at their backsides, but neither of them slowed, not until they'd reached their rental. "We've got people who are going brain-dead here. I'm one of them. You've gotta damn well tell me what you think is happening!"

For half a minute they looked at me like two owls in a thunderstorm, neither willing to concede anything. Then they quickly got into their car and drove away.

"Sons of bitches!" I said.

Stephanie was waiting for me at the front of the station.

I said, "They're assuming because we can't pin them down on it they can skate in a court of law."

"I'm not so sure they knew *exactly* what we were talking about," Stephanie said.

"They seemed like nice guys," Karrie said as we went back into the station. "I mean, they came all this way to help."

"They came all this way to cover their butts. When they found out they weren't in trouble, they packed up and left. They weren't here to help."

We went back to the office at the rear of the station, where Stephanie called her aunt, again without result.

Last night she'd updated me on Marge DiMaggio. After her husband died, DiMaggio took over the running of Canyon View Systems in Redmond, Washington, and put everything she had into it. Now the company was on the verge of being sold for a "staggering amount of money." I recalled Marge had tried to talk Holly into investing in their stock, telling her that in a matter of months the value would skyrocket.

Ben and Karrie went to the other computer to look up anything they could find on chicken-related illnesses, a channel of investigation for which Stephanie still held out hope. Karrie seemed along for the ride, which was strange considering she'd been in Holly's truck with the rest of us. I kept thinking about how abruptly Hillburn and Dobson had lost interest in us. Stephanie called an expert on industrial poisons and gathered more information on toluene. Nobody had any brainstorms.

At ten-thirty I took a call from Ms. Mulherin, the environmental chemist from the University of Washington, her voice sounding unoiled over the phone. "I understand the committee's being disbanded," she said.

"What?"

"I heard the committee's been canceled."

"Where'd you hear that?"

"I had a message on my machine when I got in this morning. Your mayor told me there'd been a mistake."

"Mayor Haston?"

"He told me he was sorry for the imposition, but we were to discontinue any work we'd started. Don't tell me there was never anything wrong with you people?"

"Nothing's been canceled, Ms. Mulherin. We're still as sick as ever."

"Good. Well, no, not good that you have this, but . . . Do *you* have this?"

"I'm afraid I do."

"I'm sorry. Well, I'm still gathering a preliminary team of graduate students. I won't be out to your station until early next week."

"I guess you'll see me then," I said, savoring the irony.

How many others had Steve Haston contacted, and why would he disband the committee?

Before I could give the news to Stephanie, a voice on the station intercom paged me to the watch office. I was barely out the door when my girls ambushed me in the corridor.

"Daddy, Daddy. Look what we got," Britney said, leaping into my arms. She had a stuffed animal, a grisly-looking creature that could only have been designed by someone on PCP. Allyson held a similar toy at arm's length, and I knew it wouldn't be long before Allyson's distaste would poison Britney's feelings for her own gift.

"Where'd you get these?"

"Grandma and Grandpa," Allyson said. "Grandma said you forgot to pick them up at the airport. Grandpa's mad, but he's pretending he's not. Grandma already pinched my face. She says I look like Natalie Wood in *Miracle on 34th Street.*"

"You do look a little like Natalie Wood."

"Really is he mad?" Britney asked, squirming out of my arms. "I'm gonna go see."

"Don't say anything, Brit!" Allyson called out as her sister disappeared. "Blabbermouth."

I said, "I forgot all about them."

"They're so boring."

"They love you, even if they are a little—"

"Don't say they're different, Dad, 'cause they're a lot more than different. I didn't want to see them last summer, and now it's already *this* summer, and here they are again. Omigod. My life is just draaaaaggging on. If it weren't for Stephanie and Morgan, this would be the longest of the nine summers I've had to live through. I suppose they're going to stay at our house again? Daddy. Can't you tell them we're contagious or something?"

"They've come a long way to see you."

"Grampa smells like BO."

"Let me put it this way: We can pick our friends. We can't pick our relatives."

"You picked Mommy."

"Allyson, you're getting too smart for me."

Wesley Tindale was retired from Alcoa Aluminum, and Lillian from retail sales. They had only the two grandchildren and doted on them, insisted on speaking to them on the phone once a week, an ongoing ordeal both girls had to be coached through. The Tindales saw Allyson and Britney as their second chance. They'd had two daughters themselves, my ex, Lorie, and Elaine. Elaine was doing drugs somewhere in New York, and Lorie, also involved in drugs, was wanted by the law. It was hard to tell which of Lorie's offenses was worse in their minds, the drugs, the forged checks, or the lesbianism. It drove me to distraction that they blamed Lorie's conversion to homosexuality on me.

Wesley was almost as tall as I was, saturnine, invariably in baggy slacks and today sandals with black dress socks worn so thin his toenails showed through. His long sideburns were left over from the seventies— or was it the sixties?—and his eyebrows were so overgrown, both my girls were frightened by them. He had severe dark eyes that were always a little blurry, yet he spoke in a commanding voice, his best feature.

Coming from a family of teetotalers, it had taken me years to realize Wesley was drinking before breakfast. He did most of his driving drunk, did most everything drunk. Lillian, on the other hand, was arguably the worst driver in the Western Hemisphere, drunk or not. The irony was that, with over a century of driving between the two of them, neither had a mark on their driving records. Go figure.

At less than five feet, Lillian was short enough she looked like a joke walking alongside Wesley, her torso round as a ball. Today she wore madras pants and a large loose-fitting blouse in a color I couldn't describe—a garish purple-mauve-yellow ensemble. They both wore straw hats. Each year it was a different *fun* gimmick. Last year for the entire week they'd worn matching bow ties with battery-powered blinking lights.

Britney and I found the blinking lights oddly amusing, but Allyson had not been happy about the extra attention while out in public.

"Sorry about the airport," I said, shaking hands with Wesley, holding it until he gave up. He trotted out the marine-sergeant death grip every time we met. "One of the men in the department died this week, so I've had a lot on my mind."

Putting on a false joviality that Karrie, always fascinated with the specter of bad relatives, was quickly picking up on, they mentioned the airport fiasco several more times, reassuring me after each reference that being old and abandoned in a strange airport hadn't bothered them at all, that they'd rather enjoyed the long line at the car rental place, and that being independent with their own vehicle would be a pleasant change from having me cart them around as in years past, that neither of them minded getting lost in Federal Way, and that they were finally learning how to read their two-dollar map.

I would be reminded of the two-dollar map again and again the way a sailor's wife reminded him he'd gotten the clap from a two-dollar whore. Had Lorie been here, the guilt factor would have whittled her down to nothing, but I had no time for it.

"Look," I said as Mayor Haston walked through the front door and greeted Karrie. "I understand you want to see the girls today. Fine. Take them out to lunch. Go to Snoqualmie Falls, whatever. Just have them back in time for dinner at five. We're going to eat at my place. Can you be there?"

"Of course we'll be there," Wesley said. "That's why we came."

"Just the three of us?" Lillian asked. Her table count always left out Allyson and Britney, a fact that Allyson never failed to take note of.

"If you bring the girls back, that'll make five. I'll be bringing a friend. So there'll be six."

The room filled with an uncomfortable silence as Wes and Lillian realized I was stepping out of my usual pattern—that I was taking charge.

After half a minute Lillian said, "Well, girls. I suppose we'd better shake a leg. We wouldn't want to be in anyone's way, would we?"

They were halfway out the door when I turned to Haston, his face still stained from yesterday's explosion, bandages on his chin and across the bridge of his nose.

"Did you cancel the committee?" I asked. "Because if you did, I'll have channel five out here. They talk to me, I guarantee you're going to end up looking like a jackass."

Ben Arden and Ian Hjorth must have heard the word *jackass*, because they were both in the room in a flash. Wes and Lillian were listening in the doorway, my curious daughters behind them.

"I formed the committee. I can disband it."

"God, Haston. Your only child was in the back of that truck. I don't know if she has any symptoms yet, but if she does she's on the seven-day timer just like . . ." I remembered my girls in the doorway and stopped myself. Motioning for my in-laws to leave, I continued. "Why did you call the committee off?"

Until that moment, this had been a contest of wills between the regulars in the department and Haston. That it hadn't occurred to him he might be endangering his own daughter's life amazed everyone in the room, him included, because when he began speaking he stuttered. Karrie stared at her feet.

"Do you?" he asked, turning to his daughter. "Have any symptoms?"

"I can't believe you canceled everything, Father. Why did you do that?"

"You have symptoms?"

"I want to know what difference it makes. Jim has them."

"He does?"

"Yes."

The room grew silent. My in-laws and daughters had left. I hadn't been aware that Karrie knew, but the look on Ian's face told me everyone in the station was aware of my predicament.

"I made a few calls," Haston said. "That was all there was to it. Some of those people must have misinterpreted what I was trying to tell them."

"Oh, get off it, Dad."

The room was quiet for a few moments. "You going to call them back?" I asked.

Haston turned to me. "I know about you and my daughter."

"What?"

"I know you've been taking advantage of her. She's twenty-two years old, for cripes sake."

Wes had put his head back in the doorway. A car outside was making noise, so it wasn't obvious how much he could hear.

"I haven't been doing anything with your daughter."

"You weren't kissing on her at the Christmas party?"

"Where did you hear that?" Karrie asked, outraged that our rendezvous on the sofa had become public knowledge.

"Never you mind, missy. You were acting like a whore."

"Oh, Daddy. Grow up. This is so embarrassing. Okay. So we were making out at the Christmas party. We had too much to drink. So what?"

"I can't believe you tried to cancel the committee," Ben Arden said.

"I'll make some calls. If there's been a misunderstanding, I'll put it to rights. But I'm not going to forget about Christmas."

Haston stepped out the front door, forcing my former father-in-law away from his listening post. After the door closed, Ben slapped his hands together several times as if he'd just cleaned up.

Karrie said, "Sorry about that."

"Do you?" I asked. "Have any symptoms?"

"No."

"Good. I hope you don't get any."

"Thanks, Jim."

35. GETTING SUCKED INTO THE HAY BALER

I called Jane's again, but Hillburn and Dobson must have gotten through to them before I did. Nobody would talk to me. When I asked for Gray or Stuart, I was told they would both be in meetings for the rest of the day. I called Southeast Travelers Freight in Chattanooga, but that remained a dead end. They referred me to their law firm, and from there I was asked to write a letter requesting an interview.

When we still hadn't heard from Marge DiMaggio by eleven, I said, "Does your aunt know I'm on a timer?"

"I don't know what she knows. I'll go see her. You stay here and—"

"No way. I'm coming with you."

Stephanie insisted on driving, but rather than squeeze into Holly's cramped Pontiac, we took the Lexus. Neither of us relaxed as we cruised up Highway 202 past lush farmland and treed hillsides, talking at length about our quest, painstakingly revisiting the details of our phone calls. I was virtually certain the source of our problems came from Jane's California Propulsion, Inc., even more so after the way Dobson and Hillburn retreated when they found out we didn't have any physical proof that their company was implicated. "Bastards!" I said.

"You may be overreacting simply because you didn't like them," Stephanie said. "I didn't like them, either. But don't let that affect your judgment. It might not be them."

"I'm not overreacting."

"I'm just trying to help you do this with your reason and not your emotion."

"Easy for you to say."

Much like the tough-nut farmer who cuts off his trapped arm with a piece of tin to keep the hay baler from pulling his whole body in, I was developing an incredible will to survive, to beat this any way I could.

After learning we'd spoken to Charlie Drago, the Chattanooga Fire Department PIO called us and handed out the official CFD account of the Southeast Travelers incident, sounding as smooth as melting butter and as sharp as a stomach cramp.

Her statement, which sounded as if she were reading it verbatim off a script, was riddled with buzzwords, evasive language, and carefully sculpted commentary. Yes, they did have three casualties, but whether or not those casualties were related to the Southeast Travelers incident or even to one another was still a question to be determined by law. Yes, the families were suing the shipping company in ongoing separate actions.

When I prodded for an off-the-record opinion, she would only say Charlie Drago had undergone psychiatric hospitalization after the incident and the last she'd heard he was still on Prolixin and Haldol, which I knew to be antipsychotic medications. I knew right away she was giving me this information to discredit Drago, and guess what: it worked.

"You need more help besides me," Stephanie said at one point. "If people are going to be playing games, you should have somebody to look out for your best interests. Someone able to speak to the media, too."

"Who would you suggest?"

"A friend. Somebody you trust."

There was a pitiful dearth of candidates. It was bad enough to die when everyone around me was going to keep on going, but to die realizing I had no *real* friends left was a patch of rough pavement I didn't need just now. Stan Beebe or Joel McCain would have been my logical choices. It would have been a perfect job for Chief Newcastle, but we were a month late.

Ben or Ian might watch my back, but they were both young, and I wasn't sure they could handle it.

The thought occurred to me that I might call one of the fifteen or twenty women I'd dated in the past couple of years, but I discarded that notion. I'd made a pretty good mess of all that.

As we drove, I spotted a kingfisher with a tufted crown sitting on a wire alongside the highway. The little bastard probably wasn't going to survive the winter, but he didn't seem to care, was intent on taking the summer minute by minute.

Maybe we could stop this syndrome; maybe we couldn't. Whatever happened, I determined not to go down in a panic. I would do this with dignity. Same as that kingfisher on the wire.

Suddenly a greater sense of calm descended on me than ever before. The one big mystery we all face—our own death—was right in front of me. My mood today was a strange mixture of detached serenity and introspective hysteria. Serenity because I finally knew my end. Hysteria because time was running low. And because I'd always been, down deep, prone to hysteria. Maybe that was why I'd become a firefighter, in order to confront my basic nature.

Canyon View Systems was on a tree-filled campus in Redmond, three large buildings, an artistic collage of steel and glass and neo-something-or-other architecture. It was situated on a hillside, but most of the property had been graded until it was nearly flat, three or four wooded acres, no structure older than ten years, a score of sixty- and eighty-foot Douglas firs to shade the buildings in summer and keep out the worst of the winter storms, two fountains, a pond, and a bewildered flock of Canada geese shitting in the parking lot.

Stephanie swung past the guard gate and parked. As we got out of the Lexus, we found ourselves pursued by a heavyset guard in uniform. I had the feeling if we'd been getting out of my pickup truck instead of a Lexus, he might have pulled his pistol.

"Guess we were supposed to stop at the gate," I said.

"I never have before."

A Jeep roared up behind us with two more guards. "You been shoplifting?" I joked to Stephanie.

"This is crazy," she snapped.

I kept quiet while Stephanie alternately chastised and argued with them. She was a doctor. Mrs. DiMaggio was her aunt. She had business here, and furthermore, if we weren't allowed inside immediately, she would make it her goal in life to ensure that all three men lost their jobs. I believed her. They must have, too, because they left us alone, though one of the men from the Jeep trailed us into the building, pretending to pick up litter on the grounds when I looked back at him.

Inside, a Muzak version of "I Got You, Babe" spilled from hidden speakers. There was a large atrium reception and waiting area with two twelve-foot bamboo plants and a tall oak-and-brass counter with a woman behind it.

After we got past the receptionist, we went up a long open staircase and along a corridor full of offices. Although DiMaggio's door was locked, we could see through a narrow, vertical window that nobody was inside.

"I think I know where she might be," Stephanie said.

I followed her to a room two doors down, paint-splattered canvas tarps on the floor, a ladder in one corner, DiMaggio standing alongside two men in coveralls, the three of them flipping through carpet samples on a metal ring.

"Stephanie!" she said. "Stephanie, darling. What on earth are you do-ing here? I thought you were flying today."

"We need to talk, Aunt Marge."

"Of course, dear. Of course we do."

Without a word to the painters, she led us out of the room and down the corridor to her office, unlocking the door with a key. She kissed Stepha-nie on the cheek and gave me a huge smile. Walking around behind her desk, she sat heavily in a large swivel chair and invited us to sit.

36. DONOVAN CATCHES AN AWARD

"What is it, Steph?" DiMaggio asked. "Is Holly all right? Maybe now's a good time to talk about moving her back to the nursing home."

"It's already arranged. She'll be there tomorrow."

"It's for the best, don't you think?"

"Of course it's for the best. Or I wouldn't have done it. Marge, I've been phoning all morning."

"I got your message a couple of hours ago, along with about ten others. By the time I'd worked my way through half my callbacks I figured you would be in the air. I knew you'd call again tonight when you got home, and I figured we could have a long, leisurely chat then."

"I'm not flying anywhere. It's the syndrome. More people are coming down with it."

"I was aware some people had been ill. Jim told me when I saw him at the hospital, but . . . I'm sorry. I've forgotten your last name."

"Swope."

"Aunt Marge. Jim has it, too."

"Has what?"

"The syndrome."

It took a few moments for DiMaggio to digest the implications of what her niece had said. "I can't believe this. How could he have it?"

"He's got three days left. If we don't find out what's causing this and stop it, he'll be just like Holly."

"How can you be certain?"

"We're as certain as anyone can be," I said.

We might have said a lot of things to shock DiMaggio, but this seemed what she was least prepared for. It was half a minute before speech returned. "I thought what happened to your sister was . . . I thought it was a freak deal. I thought . . ."

"We think Holly caught it the night she had the accident near North Bend. Holly and four firefighters. Jim will be the fifth."

"You've tested him? You know he has it?"

"Tested and normal so far. But we found nothing anomalous in Holly's workups, either."

"Jim *looks* fine."

"Yes, he does."

"I'm sorry," DiMaggio said, turning her dark-brown eyes on me. "If you have this, I really am so sorry."

"Aunt Marge? Three years ago your company was involved in an investigation in Chattanooga. Several firefighters came down with a syndrome similar to this after a fire in a shipping facility."

"Yes, I vaguely remember that. But I never knew the particulars. We had a small shipment in the building where they had the fire. So did dozens of other companies. Our involvement came about when we sent people down to help in the investigation. But these were firefighters who got sick after a fire. Holly was found in her kitchen. Holly wasn't exposed to any smoke."

"What about her symptoms?"

"Honey, I don't recall anything about the symptoms of those poor people in Tennessee."

"Aunt Marge, if you know something that might help, tell us."

DiMaggio leaned forward, touched a button on her intercom, and said, "Cathy, would you send Donovan in here?"

"Right away, Ms. DiMaggio."

She turned back to us. "All I know is that the episode in Chattanooga was precipitated by a fire. I never was conversant with the catalog of symptoms. If I'd had any idea what happened to Holly could even be remotely connected to Tennessee . . . Had the thought even occurred to me, I would have told you. You know that."

"I know, Aunt Marge."

Rapping on the half-open door, a large man came in quickly, glanced at me, and then gifted Stephanie with a much longer look. He was almost as tall as I was but thicker, more powerfully built, shoulders like a gladiator, neck like a professional football player. His hair was cropped short and he had bright blue eyes. A deep tan. A man who would attract his share of female attention.

"Scott Donovan, this is my niece, Stephanie Riggs. Her friend, Jim Swope." His handshake was as light as tissue, his voice soft and whispery. When I swung around after the handshake, I accidentally knocked a small statue off DiMaggio's desk, a gold obelisk that looked like an award.

Donovan caught it midway between the desktop and the floor, then put it back, smiling at me. The guy could move fast for someone his size, for someone anyone's size.

"Stephanie is Mr. Swope's doctor. She tells me Mr. Swope has three days before he lapses into a coma. They've come for information about the incident in Chattanooga three years ago."

"There were two of us working on it. Me and Hardy."

"Ah, yes. Hardy. He's gone now, isn't he?"

"Been gone awhile."

"Would you like to fill my niece in?"

Donovan began to talk hesitantly. "There was a fire. Three fire-fighters got sick. The fire had been in a busy shipping facility, so all together there were hundreds of products that had been exposed during the incident. Plastics, artists' paints, you name it. I could go dig up the paper-work and my notes, but we came out of it pretty much empty-handed."

Stephanie said, "We want to know everything you found. What we've got here is too close not to be related."

"Okay. Sure. But we were down there for weeks. I'm not sure I even know where all my notes are."

"Tell you what," DiMaggio said, swiveling back and forth in her chair. "I'm going to bring Carpenter in on this."

"Carpenter?"

"That all right with you, Mr. Donovan?"

"Oh, sure. I think Carpenter's a good chemist. In fact, I like working with her."

"Good. Because I'm going to assign you and Carpenter to do the same thing with these people that you did in Tennessee with Hardy."

Donovan's voice grew squeaky. "But the Fudderman project."

"I'm going to loan the two of you to Dr. Riggs. Give her any informa-tion she requests and put all of our resources at her disposal."

"Fudderman needs to be completed by Monday morning, Tuesday at the latest."

"This will take precedence."

"Sure. Okay. You know me. I'm just wondering who's going to pay. This isn't going to be part of our deal with Tananger, is it?"

"We'll pay for it. The company will."

"I just hope the board doesn't see anything wrong with that."

"Me, too," DiMaggio said, humoring him.

"It's just that Canyon View has certain commitments right now, and after dedicating myself to those commitments for the past six months, it kind of throws me off course when all of a sudden the energy is going somewhere else. I'll get Carpenter." He turned to DiMaggio. "Is that what you want?"

"That's what I said. Bring your notes from Tennessee and give Carpenter an update on the way in here."

"I can do that."

"Thank you, Donovan."

"My pleasure."

Donovan was one of those men whose faces flushed when they were nonplussed. Even under the tan it had flushed several times during our conversation, usually at the same time his voice got squeaky. It was hard to square up the impressive physique with everything else about him.

After he left the room, DiMaggio said, "He's a bit of a nervous type, but trust me, he's probably pound for pound the best chemist on the West Coast. He has an astonishing background. He was in the Army Rangers. He's a black belt in karate. There's a picture in his office of him breaking a whole stack of boards with his head. Unbelievable. And Carpenter is nothing less than a genius. Entered college when she was fourteen, got a degree in chemistry by the time she was seventeen, then a master's in molecular biology. She was halfway through med school when we outbid four other companies for her services. MIT would have held on to her if they could. She doesn't have much experience, but I think this combination of the savvy in Donovan and intellectual in Carpenter will be just what you need.

"I want you to pull through this, Jim. And I want you, Steph, to find anything you can that will help your sister. Call me. Day or night. I mean that. I'd put the whole company on it if it weren't for this merger."

"Thank you, Aunt Marge."

The room grew quiet. I said, "What is it your company does exactly? Holly told me once, but I've forgotten."

"We're researching a new type of liquid metal." She went on but soon was talking about complex helical molecules and negatively charged DNA crystals, and it was all I could do to keep my eyes open. She was so enthusiastic about her work and the prospects for new discoveries, I quickly discarded the idea that she was trying to hide behind a facade of doublespeak. In her building, this was the lingo.

A noise in the corridor cut her talk short. She stood, smoothed her skirt, and walked around her desk. "You can use my office." When I stood, she grasped both my hands in hers and said, "Jim. You run into any roadblocks, call me. I can make phone calls, use my connections in the industry, whatever." Tears puddling her eyes, she tightened her grip. "I'm so sorry about this. Nobody deserves this. Especially not somebody with the heart you have. I really am sorry."

Not knowing what else to do, I nodded dumbly. She left the room in a swelter of emotion, then stuck her head back in and said, "I thought it was them, but it was the painters. I'll go see what's holding up the show."

I had no idea where she got that business about my heart, whether it was something Holly told her or a trait she thought she'd detected on her own. People were dying, you said all kinds of silly crap hoping they would buy into it. Much as I hated to admit it, I didn't have any kind of heart. The petty details of my life had swallowed every waking moment of my days. I'd been consumed with details since I was born. Except for my daughters, I'd never had time for others. Stephanie—working her ass off for a man she barely knew and didn't like—now that was heart.

After we were alone, Stephanie said, "At least we won't be overwhelmed by technicalese if this all turns out to be chemical in origin. I've had plenty of chemistry, but not like them."

"And we can ask them about those people from San Jose."

She reached over and patted my hand.

37. ACHARA

Twenty minutes later Donovan came back carrying a fat manila folder. The young woman accompanying him carried a yellow legal pad and a pen.

With a name like Carpenter you'd expect Anglo-Saxon roots, perhaps a tall Nordic blonde, but she was Asian. Later, we learned her father was an American serviceman who'd married a Thai woman. Achara Carpenter was five-five and slim, in a hip-hugging purple skirt and red silk blouse, a daring color combination that was stunningly beautiful on her. Her black hair was cut short and was incredibly thick. She didn't look the way I thought a genius should look, but then, what did I know?

Smiling graciously, Achara Carpenter stared at me half a beat too long, a sign that she'd been told I was dying. After a few moments of shuffling papers, Donovan said, "Oh, shoot. This won't take long. Don't start until I get back."

His reticence from the earlier meeting seemed to have evaporated.

"If you don't mind," Carpenter said, picking up a purple pen that looked huge in her delicate brown fingers, "I wonder if you could go over the symptoms. I understand they're not flulike?"

"Not at all," Stephanie said.

"One would expect headaches, nausea, dizziness, shortness of breath, possibly chest pains in the short term. In the long term, cancer, brain damage, miscarriages, heart problems. Maybe death."

"Why would you expect that?" I asked.

"Environmental diseases are wide-ranging, but their effects always center around just a few ailments."

Giving a detailed account of her sister's current condition, Stephanie salted her sentences with medical phrases, some of which I understood and some of which I did not. Nobody stopped to explain them to me. The more high-tech this got, the more left out I was going to be. "I'm assuming the other patients are in a similar state to my sister," Stephanie said, "although I've only seen one at this point."

"How many other patients are there?" Achara asked.

"Not counting Jim, three here and two in Tennessee."

"I'd like to visit all of the patients . . . eventually," Carpenter said, darting her dark eyes in my direction. We both knew by the time she got to Tennessee and back I'd be in a warehouse for the dim-witted. "Scott filled me in on the thing in Tennessee on the way over. You said you've seen one patient already?"

"Yesterday I visited a woman named Jackie Feldbaum in a North Bend nursing home."

"Her condition was similar to your sister's?"

"Identical."

"And you said all the victims have a skin condition on their hands?"

I showed her my waxy hands and said, "You got the hands, you got the syndrome." Without touching them, she looked them over carefully.

"What about fainting? Loss of consciousness? Syncope?"

"Not yet," Stephanie said. "He's fallen several times, but he hasn't lost consciousness."

"Ringing in the ears?" Carpenter asked.

I showed her the three-by-five card Stan Beebe had written and said, "Day five. How did you know?"

Head low, Achara Carpenter printed diligently on her legal pad, the hunch in her back and neck that of a longtime student. "And where are you in this progression?" she asked, her teeth white against her copper skin.

"How did you know about the hearing?"

"While I was waiting for Scott to get his papers together, I logged on to our computer. I found several lists of symptoms for various off-the-wall environmental maladies. Ringing in the ears was one symptom.

"Also, Scott told me there may have been chickens involved, so I found some contacts for a researcher in Hong Kong who studies poultry-human disease transmission. I would have called already, but it's, uh . . ." She glanced at a gold wristwatch on her delicate wrist. "Two in the morning there. If I'm hitting on your symptoms, I'm doing it by accident. Believe me, I'm shooting in the dark here. Is it possible one of the symptoms is depression? The thought of ending up in a nursing home must be depressing. Do you think maybe this person who went off the roof and the people who had car accidents might have been depressed and deliberately trying to hurt themselves?"

I said, "Jackie I don't know about. Joel McCain *fell* off his roof. It took him another four days to lose the rest of it. I don't think he knew what was coming. Stan Beebe did know and may have killed himself. I don't want to speculate."

It was another twenty minutes before Donovan returned.

When he did, we told him about Jane's California Propulsion and asked if they'd been involved in Tennessee. "Not that I know of," he said. "But then, I wasn't working it from that end. I don't know that anybody was. I was involved with the science of it. Matching the symptoms with known chemical hazards. Matching known chemical hazards with what was found in the building."

"And what was found in the building?" Stephanie asked.

"Want the whole list?" Donovan pulled out a computer printout that was at least three feet long.

"My God," I said.

"Yeah. The way I like to work, we eliminate the possibilities one by one. Sooner or later we'll narrow it down," Donovan said.

"That could take forever."

"Not really. You'll be surprised."

"I've only got three days left."

"Well, that's the way I work."

"Why don't we start at the other end? JCP, Inc., had a shipment in our truck accident. If they had stuff in Tennessee, the odds have to be pretty good they're involved. I mean, there wasn't that much in our truck that this could be linked to. DuPont had a couple of packages. A painting company. JCP."

"All I know is how I work. I can't work any other way."

"I can," Stephanie said.

It was nice to have somebody on my side.

DAY FIVE

38. BLURRED VISION, RINGING IN EARS, SYNCOPE

I could feel them trying to wake me up, a mass of femininity, soft hands, warm bodies, voices trying on my name like a sweater that was too tight, Allyson, Britney, and Stephanie, whose low, anxious tone stood in contrast to the fun the other two were having.

My girls were bouncing on the bed, climbing all over me, while Stephanie had morbid thoughts, and even in my semiconscious state I detected the anxiety in her voice. She clearly thought we'd slipped up in our countdown. That I was gone.

I could hear Britney's voice in my ear, but I couldn't respond. It was the most incredible feeling of powerlessness, worse even than one of those horrible dreams you have where you can't wake up even though you realize you're in a dream.

When I finally opened my eyes, I was unable to move my limbs or even roll my head to one side. In a flash of terror it occurred to me that my life was over. As of now.

Right now.

Then Britney walked across my thighs on her knees, and I jerked my legs involuntarily. A moment later I was able to sit up, nerves and reflexes intact.

I inhaled deeply.

Slowly, the events of yesterday afternoon and evening came back to me.

We'd stayed in Redmond for hours.

As a student, Achara, it turned out, had researched Legionnaires' disease. Donovan had at one time worked for the Pentagon studying the effects of biological weapons on chimpanzees. Odd they would both end up at Canyon View, where the focus was on liquid metals.

I noticed Achara was quieter with Donovan in the room. It was a societal given that young women tended to defer to men. Because of this, I'd been considering sending Allyson and Britney to a girls' prep school in Bellevue, had been trying to work out how I could afford it.

After we'd gone over the syndrome ad nauseam, Stephanie asked Donovan to tell us what happened in Tennessee.

Riffling through the file he'd brought with him, Scott Donovan began his story with a call he'd received three years ago from Phil, Marge's late husband and the founder of the company. Achara sat with her hands in her lap. Donovan spoke at his own pace, giving a blow-by-blow account of the second phone call, and the third, going so far as to include what he was thinking before, during, and after each call. Donovan had a way of dragging a story out that made you want to scream. Had he not been the individual who was probably going to save my life with his attention to detail, I might have strangled him. Believe me, I was still tempted.

It was apparent as the story unfolded that he believed if he'd been given free rein in Tennessee, he might have solved the riddle, that the only thing preventing it was the interference of inept government officials.

Somehow, after listening to Donovan outline the events in Tennessee for almost an hour, most of which was taken up with the politics in Chattanooga, I came to the conclusion that if one of these two was going to come up with a solution, it would be Achara.

Everything was moving along too slowly, considering the clock I was on, but to make matters worse, when he learned about the North Bend explosion, Donovan begged me to tell him every little detail. Before I knew it, I had squandered twenty minutes laying out Max Caputo's bizarre history and ultimate end.

On the way home we'd picked up sandwiches so that when Wes and Lillian showed up with the girls we'd have something to eat. I knew from experience they would be twenty minutes early to their own funerals, and I wasn't disappointed when they were already waiting for us in front of the house at ten to five.

Lillian let loose a couple of snide cracks about a *cold dinner*. When she'd been a mother, *her* girls always ate a *hot* meal. That's right, both her drug-addict daughters ate hot meals when they were growing up.

I skipped dinner, not yet confident enough of my stomach to put food in it. Afterward, Wes and Lillian insisted we sit in the living room like grown-ups, the four of us desperate to forge a conversation. I told them about the girls' latest exploits, though it turned out there wasn't much in my daughters' lives they approved of, not the spring softball for Allyson nor the karate classes Britney had begged for. Not even the Monopoly games.

Even when Lorie had been around to finesse things, talking with these two had been difficult, but on this particular night we plumbed the depths of discomposure. Scooping my eyeballs out with a spoon would have been more fun. Time wasters. First Donovan and Carpenter, and now Wes and Lillian. But for the disturbing fact that they would be my daughters' guardians in three days, I would have gotten rid of them.

When Stephanie left the room for a moment, Lillian turned to me and whispered, "Who is she again?"

"A friend."

"Oh, I see," Lillian said, raising her eyebrows to imply she certainly saw *everything*.

By the time they'd left, it was too late to make anymore calls. The girls and I started another Monopoly tournament. These would be among my last evenings with them, and I wanted to do whatever they wanted. As we played, we could hear Stephanie in the other room, alternately on the phone and then on the computer. Frankly, I was too exhausted to help. Turning into a half-wit was fatiguing. When it was time to get ready for bed, Allyson showed Stephanie a toiletry kit that included a new toothbrush she'd conned Grandpa into buying by intimating that she didn't have one of her own. No wonder they wanted to take the girls away from me.

Physically run-down almost to the point of collapse, I'd showered hastily and crawled into bed. Stephanie followed me and bedded down on top of my covers like a cat. You had to admire the confidence with which she addressed our relationship. We talked for a few minutes and then, in the middle of a sentence, I nodded off.

Couldn't stop myself.

"Aren't you ever going to wake up?" Allyson asked, sitting on her knees beside me. Britney was cross-legged on my stomach. It was morning.

"I'm getting up."

"You always wake *us* up," Britney said.

"Well, I thought I'd make you feel important, let you get me up for a few days."

"We're already the most important things in your life. You always tell us that," Britney said.

"You sure are, honey."

"Can we get Stephanie some clothes from the spare bedroom?" Allyson asked. "That way Steph won't have to drive all the way back to Tacoma."

"I thought you were saving your mother's clothes."

"Mom will never know."

"Sure."

In the blink of an eye she was gone. Still sitting on my stomach, Britney looked me over carefully. I bounced her up and down with my breathing, but she wasn't in a mood for play. "Daddy?"

"Yes."

"Does TB make you die?"

"TB? You mean tuberculosis?"

"I guess."

"Why do you ask?"

"Do you have TB?"

I sat up, the movement tumbling her over backward. When she'd righted herself, I held her hands and said, "No. Of course not. Why do you ask?"

"Because Ben told somebody you have a com . . . communicable disease. When I asked Grandma what that was, she said it was like TB."

"You didn't tell Grandma I had a communicable disease, did you?"

"I don't think so."

Stephanie was staring at me soberly.

"I don't have TB."

"Promise?"

"Promise. Why don't you go help Allyson pick out something for Stephanie?"

After Britney left, Stephanie said, "You're going to have to tell them."

"I've got three days."

"You leave without saying anything, they're going to be hurt for the rest of their lives."

"I know that, but you don't have to see the look in their eyes. I do. I've already done this once. Remember, I'm the one who had to tell them their mother wasn't coming back."

Stephanie walked to the door, then turned back to me. "I thought you weren't going to wake up."

"This is day five," I said, realizing my vision hadn't cleared yet. That my left ear was ringing. "I guess I don't have three days, do I? Only two."

You can't believe how scared I was. "If we don't beat this . . . I'm going to be . . ."

"I know."

While Stephanie was in the shower, Allyson came into the room, draping a flower-patterned dress over her shoulder. "How's this?"

"Very summery."

"Daddy?"

"Yes?"

"Are we going to live with Grandma and Grandpa?"

"No, dear."

"They said we were."

"They say that every year."

"I don't want to live with them."

I had to think about what I was going to say next, because Wes and Lillian, once they found out how sick I was, wouldn't stop until they had custody of my girls. I'd delayed thinking about this, and now that I couldn't avoid it, it was almost too much to process. I could live my life as a vegetable. I could die. I was growing accustomed to the thought of either.

What I could not grow accustomed to was the thought of Wes and Lillian raising my daughters. I'd been dealing with it by not thinking about it, but putting my head in the sand wasn't going to do my girls any good. I had to figure out something. To the outside world Wes was a successful building contractor and Lillian a loving housewife and saleswoman, yet they'd already botched the job with their own daughters. As far as I was concerned, Wes and Lillian were morons.

"They really love you, your grandparents."

"We don't have to be with them today, do we?"

"Tell you what. We'll let them do something with you today, just to appease them, and then that will be that."

"What does *appease* mean?"

"It means to make someone happy by giving them something they want."

"Oh, Daddy. I can't bear to spend more than half an hour with them. And you have to be there."

"How about two hours? And they'll want you to themselves."

"I want *you* there."

"I know you do, but they want you alone."

"Okay. Two hours. One minute more and I'm running away and joining the circus."

"It's a deal, squirt."

39. TWO LITTLE GIRLS LIVING BY THEMSELVES

Donovan and Achara were slated to show up at nine. Stan Beebe's funeral would start at the Lutheran church a few blocks north of the station at eleven. The engine was draped in black crepe and festooned with bunting and flags and would carry the coffin to the local cemetery.

The buzz around the station was that Joel McCain's wife had decided Joel needed to attend Beebe's funeral. Let me tell you, when I became a zombie, the last thing I'd want was to get wheeled around in front of my old friends like a mummy on tour. It seemed so unlike Mary McCain, who until now had kept Joel under wraps.

Maybe he *was* getting better.

On our way to the fire station, I told Stephanie to drop us off at the playfield at North Bend Elementary two blocks from the station. Realizing what I was planning, Stephanie gave me a sorrowful look through the windshield as she drove away.

After the girls burned off some of their breakfast, I found myself on my back upside down on the slide, staring up at the clouds, just like a kid. Britney was at the top on her back, the soles of her feet resting against mine, both of us suspended by my grip on the cold rails. Allyson sat at the very top playing with Britney's hair. Above us was a mostly blue sky, a battery of cumulus clouds rolling over the lip of Mount Si, wispy clouds I couldn't name streaking the middle of the sky, and corroded contrails from jet traffic to the west above Sea-Tac.

It had been years since I'd taken the time to lie on my back and watch clouds. The absolute grace of the atmosphere astonished me. After a while, I could almost feel the earth moving, could certainly see the clouds shifting in the sky. A private plane traversed the horizon silently. A thousand thoughts ran through my mind.

To have had these girls for as long as I had made me the luckiest man in the world.

"I have something I need to tell you," I said, finally.

"What is it, Daddy?" Britney and Allyson both had slipped into that same lazy summertime cadence I remembered as a youth, when everything slowed down and you had no worries and it seemed as if there were no such thing as clocks or teachers or homework.

Too bad their lives were about to implode around them.

"Does this have something to do with Stephanie?" Allyson asked, failing to conceal the note of hope in her voice.

I let go of the slide and slid to the bottom, sat up as Britney scooted into my arms. Allyson followed, slamming into us. "Stephanie's here because she's my doctor. I'm sick. I'm getting sicker every day. If we don't find out what's causing it, I won't be with you by the end of the week."

"What's the end of the week?" Britney asked.

"Sunday."

"Sunday?" Allyson flicked a lock of hair out of her eyes. "What do you mean, Sunday? Where are you going on Sunday?"

I'd violated my own philosophy of dispensing bad news, the same philosophy I'd used just a few days ago with Marsha Beebe. The rule was: Spit it out quickly and concisely and in clear, unequivocal language.

"If we can't stop this, I'll end up like your Grandfather Swope sometime on Sunday. I might even be in the same nursing home with him."

I still hadn't said it.

"You mean you're going to get old?" Britney asked.

Allyson had tears streaming down her face. "No, dummy. He's going to get sick."

"Neither one of you is a dummy," I said. Britney looked from Allyson's tears to me and back to Allyson, her lower lip beginning to quiver. This was exactly what I couldn't bear to watch. "My body will be here and my heart will be here, but my brain will be gone. I won't be able to talk to you. Or look at you. And after a while, I'll probably lose weight the way Grandpa did."

"You don't love us anymore?" Britney asked.

"Sweetheart, I'll still love you a hundred years after I'm dead. Anytime anything happens to you and you feel like you need someone, you can know that my love will be there alongside you. I love you both more than anything."

"Then why are you going to the nursing home?" Allyson asked.

"It's not for sure. But if it happens, it will be because I don't have a choice."

"How did you get sick?" Britney asked.

"Nobody knows. It's something to do with the fire department. I got sick at the same time Joel McCain and Stan Beebe and some others did."

"What if you get well?" Allyson asked.

"I'm hoping I will. That's why Stephanie's been working on the computer so much. A lot of people want to help. We're going to be seeing some experts today."

Allyson leaned her head against my chest. "So, Daddy? You shouldn't be goofing off with us. You should be with Stephanie."

"Right now I want to be with you."

"If you're not living with us," Britney said, "how are we going to get to school? And who's going to take care of us?"

"We'll take care of ourselves," Allyson said, knowing the alternative was at that moment registered eight blocks away in a motel.

"We'll figure something out."

"I'm going to miss you," Britney said.

"I'm going to miss you, too. Both of you. More than anything."

Seconds later Britney was wailing so hard and so loud, Allyson and I thought she was acting. She cried so hard, she went blind with it. A moment later Allyson started up. Then I shed my first real tears in years.

It was fifteen minutes before we ran out of water, another fifteen before we were composed enough to walk to the fire station hand in hand, talking about little things, anything but what was on our minds.

At the station telephones were ringing, firefighters and volunteers rushing to and fro. A few people were there to help out with our research on the syndrome. Most were there for the funeral. It was nine o'clock, and Donovan and Carpenter had not arrived. I was surprised by how much their absence irritated me. Even my alcoholic in-laws were punctual.

Ian Hjorth and Ben Arden had organized a squadron of volunteers to run errands and do the busywork. They'd even recruited children to keep Allyson and Britney company.

When the kids disappeared into the game room upstairs, I located Stephanie at the computer in the officers' room, Ben Arden's wife, Cherie, behind her, fiddling with a pot of coffee. "I found some stuff," Stephanie said.

I sat down, rubbing an ear to clear the ringing. Stephanie looked at me full on. "You told them?"

"Yeah."

"How'd it go?" When I didn't reply, she said, "Sure. I know. But you did it, and now you can move on."

"Right."

"Try not to be despondent, Jim."

"Lieutenant? We're going to stop this right here," Cherie added vehemently. Just what we needed, a new cheerleader fresh from the wings.

40. DIG UP THE CHIEF, QUICK; HE MIGHT NOT BE DEAD

"You heard from Donovan and Carpenter?" I asked.

"Huh-uh," Stephanie said. "But I think I'm on to something. For a month now I've been on various Internet medical forums asking doctors if they'd had any patients with symptoms matching Holly's. After we found out about that fire in Tennessee, I narrowed the search to the southeastern United States. This morning a general practitioner from Biloxi wrote back and said he recalled something from a couple of years ago. Two patients. Brain-dead. Waxy hands. Both much younger than your average stroke victim."

"What'd he say about them?"

"They were patients of a doctor he'd heard speaking at a seminar, a specialist in Knoxville. He claims this specialist had a theory about what'd caused it. Also there's a man named Carl Steding from Chattanooga left a phone message for you."

"From the fire department?"

"A newspaper guy."

"What about this specialist?"

"I've got a call in to him."

Cherie Arden spoke up. "I don't understand this thing, whatever it is. I mean, if you were all exposed back in February, why didn't you get sick in February? And why isn't everybody getting sick at once?"

Stephanie said, "People's immune systems are different. Some are strong. Some are weak. We don't know what might be affecting the way people react. As far as the lag time between exposure and onset of symptoms, apparently this syndrome has a long incubation period if exposure was minimal. I'm guessing the firefighters in Tennessee had a greater level of exposure than the people here, and that's why their symptoms came on so much quicker."

I said, "A guy came through town a year ago. From Montana. Ex-fireman. On disability. He'd had a stroke. He said they fought a fire out in the dingles somewhere in a store that carried everything you could think of: pharmaceuticals, ammunition, painting supplies, dynamite. Afterward, people who'd fought the fire started going down. In nine months four of them had strokes and three had heart attacks. They never proved it was caused by the fire, and they never got any money out of the pension system, either, even though they all knew it started with that fire."

Cherie said, "I never thought it would happen here. I sure hope Ben doesn't have it."

"Me, too, Cherie."

"I didn't mean it that way."

"I know. I really don't want anyone else getting it."

Two King County fire investigators in jeans and button-down shirts appeared in the doorway behind me, the first looking dwarflike beside the second, taller man, who had ruddy, baby-butt cheeks on an otherwise pale face he worked hard to keep unexpressive. These were the two who'd responded to Max Caputo's place after the explosion—the short one was Shad; the taller, Stevenson. Shad didn't look tall enough to be a firefighter, but then, most departments in the area had relaxed their guidelines on height in order to recruit more women.

"Need to talk to you," said Stevenson.

"I've got a funeral I'm about to go to."

"And we've got a man up on the hill came down in itty-bitty pieces," said Shad.

"We're still trying to fit it together." Stevenson planted a wan smile on his mug, delighted at his own witticism.

Ian Hjorth came up the hallway, peered over their shoulders, and said, "Sorry to bust in, Jim, but Karrie brought in some doctor from out of state who claims he's going to talk to the TV guys after the funeral. Says this syndrome is all in your head."

"What?"

"That's what he says."

"How could he know that without talking to me?"

"I don't know. He spoke to Karrie, though."

"Karrie doesn't know her ass from a sack of apples!" I glanced at the two fire investigators, who'd backed off in the face of my outburst. "Wait in the front office. I'll be there as soon as I can."

"Just don't be skipping out on us," said Stevenson.

"For God's sake," Stephanie muttered. "Where do you think he would go? A Mexican clinic?"

Just then, Karrie walked past the doorway in her black dress uniform.

"Karrie? What's this I hear about you bringing in a doctor to debunk our syndrome?"

"Dr. Perkins. I didn't bring him in. Not actually. I found him on the Internet and called him. He said this sounded like an interesting phenomenon and would we mind if he flew out. When he showed up yesterday, I took him to see Jackie. I was just trying to help."

"He's not even a real doctor," Ian said. "All he does is write books, get on talk shows, and play kiss-kiss with celebrities."

Karrie brushed a speck of lint off her coat. "I would think you'd be relieved. He's already proved you don't have to worry. Or hasn't anyone told you the syndrome's a figment of your imagination?" When the room and corridor had been quiet for a few seconds, she added, "Doesn't that make you feel better?"

"It would if I thought it was true."

"Oh, it's true."

"Wow!" Hjorth said. "I guess there's nothing wrong with Joel, then. And the chief must not be dead. Maybe we should go dig him up."

I gave Hjorth a sharp look. "Why hasn't he spoken to Dr. Riggs, who right now probably has more medical information about this than anyone?"

"He doesn't have to talk to another doctor to reach an opinion. He examined Jackie. He said as far as he could tell she was a typical head case from a car accident."

"He saw Joel, too?"

"No. I told him about everybody else, and he says they're all within the realm of the normal." She glanced at Stephanie, who was still seated at the computer behind me. "He said he's almost positive this whole thing is hogwash. A sad and wonderfully illustrative case of collective delusion."

"He's *almost* positive?" I said.

"You look like you believe him," Stephanie said to Karrie.

"Well . . . sure I believe him. He's a doctor."

"Listen, girl. *I'm* a doctor. My sister's been in a brain ward for two months because of this nonexistent syndrome. Trust me, it exists."

"But Dr. Perkins is internationally recognized."

"Karrie," I said. "What if he's wrong?"

"He's written books. I found one in the library."

"A lot of idiots have written books that are in the library. Why not wait a couple of days before making an announcement? If this gets in the news as a fraud, nobody'll help us. By Monday either I'll go down or I won't go down, and you'll know once and for all."

"All I did was phone him. He's researching a new book. *Modern Medical Myths: The Hazards of Self-diagnosis and Mass Delusion.* It's so perfect, don't you see? It fits in perfectly with what's going on here. You don't have it. Stan didn't have it."

"Is this why your father was trying to disband the committee?"

"I don't know anything about what my father is doing."

"You took this doctor to the nursing home," Ian snapped, "and then you told him about Jim's wife leaving him and every other irrelevant piece of gossip you could think of."

"You told him about my wife?"

Karrie backed away. "It's not like you own the story, Lieutenant. I mean, she left town with *my* mother." Having unexpectedly wandered into the mother lode of small-town gossip, Shad and Stevenson began rolling their eyes at each other. "I told him so he would have some background. And it's a good thing I did, because your personal history works into all this. Dr. Perkins says all this womanizing you've been doing has finally come to a head with the delusion about the syndrome, because this woman from Tacoma you were dating, Holly, got sick, and now you've transferred your guilt about the way you treated her and whatever else you were feeling about women in general to this syndrome. I should really let him explain. He's out in the other room gathering background material. When he puts you in his book, you're going to be famous."

"As a jackass." I turned to Stephanie. "You know Perkins?"

"He's written a couple of pop culture books. He specializes in exposing fad diets and exercise crazes."

"The chief died out in the woods," Karrie said. "Happens to hundreds of people every year. Jackie had a car accident because of her alcoholism. Of *course* Joel has brain injuries. He fell off his roof. Stan got so worked up about this syndrome, he made himself have an accident. Dr. Perkins said he wouldn't be surprised if you had an accident, too."

"Karrie. Let me see your hands." When she tried to rush out of the room, I grabbed her left wrist and held on. She pulled, sticking her feet out like a balky horse, and we played it like a kids' game until I reeled her in. "Jesus Christ, Karrie. What day are you on?"

"Perkins says it doesn't fit any syndrome he's ever heard of."

"Karrie, you need to decide what you're going to do."

"Perkins says the only thing wrong with us is we're caught up in a form of sympathetic hysteria. Show me one person of all these people where there isn't another perfectly suitable explanation for how they got hurt."

I nodded at Stephanie. "Her sister. She dropped on her kitchen floor for no apparent reason. Her hands look like yours. She's been in a coma for over a month. Exactly like Joel."

"Let Dr. Perkins see her. He'll get to the bottom of it."

"Where is he?" I asked.

"In the watch office interviewing some of the volunteers. He says in most major mass delusion cases there are precursor episodes that weren't as severe. He's trying to uncover those now. He wanted to know if that explosion the other day had been a delusion, but I told him I thought it was real."

"You *thought* it was real? Karrie, listen to yourself. If it had been any more real, they'd be burying us in thimbles. You're hobnobbing with a quack."

I stomped toward the watch office, Karrie riding my heels.

An imposing man with a shaved head met me in the watch office. "Dr. Perkins?" I said.

"And who may I have the pleasure of—"

"Get your hairy ass out of this station before I throw you through a wall."

A moment later Karrie and the good doctor were on the sidewalk out front; he was already explaining away my actions in terms of his theory: ". . . understandable reaction to having the delusion exposed and—"

"Wow," Ian Hjorth said as I slammed the door behind them. Mouths agape, the volunteers Perkins had been interviewing stared at me.

"Put Karrie on disability leave. I don't want her falling off a rig on a response." I pulled out the three-by-five card I'd been carrying. "Here. These are the symptoms. Make sure she gets a copy. In fact, make copies and pass them around. Who knows who else might need it."

"Yes sir, Lieutenant."

I found the two county fire investigators, Shad and Stevenson, outside the empty chief's office. Judging by their faces, they'd been hugely entertained by our melodrama.

As if he owned the place, Shad, the short one with scrub-brush eyebrows, entered Newcastle's office and plunked down in the swivel chair with a familiarity that offended me. Shad wasn't fit to carry Newcastle's jockstrap to the laundry. Stevenson hunkered on the corner of the desk, while I leaned against the file cabinet.

Shad said, "Buncha things. First, tell us again what made you suspicious when you got to the trailer yesterday."

"I found Caputo's dog dying in the blackberries. After that the empty ammonium nitrate sacks and oil drums."

"Yeah," Stevenson said. "How come nobody else found that stuff? Just you."

"I was the only one with the time to look."

"Trouble with what you're telling us is, we can't find any of it," said Shad.

"You didn't find much of the trailer, either."

"We know explosions tend to diffuse materials over a large geographical area," Shad said. "But we want to look into an alternate explanation for why we can't find this stuff."

"What would that be?"

"That those items never existed."

"Sure. Maybe the trailer didn't exist, either. Maybe Max Caputo never existed. Maybe there was no fire. Maybe that head we found in the tree fell from outer space. In that case, you boys might as well go home. Aloha."

"The head belonged to Maxwell Devlin Caputo, born in North Bend in 1970. They found one of his legs, well, the bones from one of his legs, and a cap with his scalp in it. Pretty grisly stuff. His record was not exactly clean, but he was no master criminal, either. He had some drug convictions after he got out of the army. Other than poaching arrests and somebody accusing him of stealing a tractor and some riding lawn mowers from a store here in town, that was pretty much it."

"I can understand the sacks disintegrating," I said, "but those drums probably went half a mile. You'll find them."

"Yeah," Stevenson said.

"Yeah," Shad said.

For a moment or two I didn't realize what they were getting at, and then it occurred to me this was their version of the third degree. Sarcasm. They sat back and stared, waiting for me to crack, both of them. I stared back. I was going to be a vegetable in three days. It was hard to think of anything they could threaten me with that came anywhere close. It was even harder to figure out why they were going after me.

"All that evidence," Stevenson said. "And now it's gone. Don't you think that's amazing?"

"It is unfortunate. The whole thing is."

"Oh, hey, that's right. You're the guy our chief was talking about. You're on some sort of final countdown. Got a week to live or something?"

"That's right."

The two of them looked at each other. "We're in the process of narrowing our list of suspects. We're pretty sure it wasn't Caputo."

"And?"

"We think it might have been you."

"What?"

"We think you might have set the fire."

"I was on the goddamn rig. I was one of the responding firefighters. I'm the one who figured out it was going to blow. If I hadn't been there, a whole bunch of people would be dead right now."

Shad said, "One: We can find no record of Caputo buying any fertilizer or fuel oil. We spoke to everyone else who responded to his accident the day before, and they said it wasn't in the trailer then. Two: We found his other dog in a ditch outside the property. He'd been poisoned with enough phencyclidine to drop a cow. We're assuming that's also what happened with the dog we can't find."

"What's phencyclidine?"

"PCP, angel dust, crystal," said Stevenson.

Shad added, "Also known as hog. Or rocket fuel. Everybody says Caputo loved those dogs."

"I agree. Max loved those dogs. So go find somebody who didn't like the dogs."

"We heard *you* didn't like Max or his dogs," Shad said.

"You heard what?"

"We heard you didn't like Max Caputo."

"You had trouble with him in the past, didn't you?" Stevenson said. "Didn't his dogs bite one of your people?"

"I never even thought about him."

Shad said, "We got a phone call said you were depressed about your physical health. Said you were thinking about killing yourself and you were planning to take some people with you."

"That's ridiculous."

"You are sick, though. Aren't you?"

"Well, yes."

"Is it terminal?"

"It's not good."

"You thought about suicide?"

"No," I lied. "Hell, no. Who called you?"

"Can't tell you," Stevenson said, but Shad gave it away with his eyes.

"You don't know, do you?"

"Maybe it was anonymous," Stevenson said. "Maybe it wasn't."

"You got an anonymous call from some crackpot, and now you're jumping all over me? Why don't you go after the caller?"

"Pay phone," Stevenson said. "You know any women in Tacoma?"

"Not any who could make the call."

"You sure? You see, the trouble is we know about firefighters. Lots of times they start fires. We also know about terminally ill patients. Lots of times they want to die. It all fits. You're depressed. You want to die. You know how to set a fire."

Stevenson might have done a better job of staring me down if he hadn't had those Clara Bow lips and those baby-butt cheeks with the pink circles in the center. "We figure you planned on wiping out the whole fire department," Stevenson said. "Even taking your kids with you. Then at the last minute you got the touchy-feelies and decided to let them live."

I got up and walked to the door. "They actually pay you guys for this?"

"You trying to get rid of us by walking out?" Shad asked, kicking the swivel chair across the room behind him in a display of toughness.

"Take it easy with the furniture. It was Harold Newcastle's."

"You're not walking out of here."

"Unless you're planning to arrest me, I am."

That would come back to haunt me.

41. THE LPG DISASTER

t was nearly nine-thirty when I walked through the door of the officers' room at the rear of the station. Stephanie looked up. "Line two."

"We've been paging you," Arden's wife added.

"You hear from Donovan and Carpenter?"

Stephanie shook her head. "Maybe this is them."

I picked up the receiver. "Lieutenant Swope."

"Hey, Lieut. This is Carl Steding at the *Chattanooga Times Free Press*. I had a chat with Scott Donovan. Apparently he spoke to you yesterday?"

"Yeah."

"He claims you folks are in the middle of some sort of plague related to an alarm you went on."

"If you're calling out of idle curiosity, I really don't have time. If you know anything about those three firefighters who went down three years ago or the Southeast Travelers incident, that's a different story."

"Funny you should mention Southeast Travelers. I followed that for our paper. It was the *Chattanooga Times* then."

"You know a firefighter named Charlie Drago?"

"For a while Charlie Drago was one of my primary sources. The last year or so, he's been a little less than reliable. What Donovan told me about you was intriguing, though. Especially in light of what I saw on the wire service yesterday. I understand you folks had an explosion a couple of days after you found out about this syndrome. We had almost the same thing happen three years ago."

"Okay. You've got my attention. What happened?"

"Three of our firefighters turned into vegetables after that Southeast Travelers fire. About a week after that, just about the time we were gearing up to start an investigation, the fire department got called to an LPG tanker accident. Big explosion. Six firefighters died. These were the same guys who'd worked with the three who went down after Southeast Travelers. Same shift. After that everybody was talking about the tanker incident, not Southeast Travelers. You could almost say somebody'd planned it that way. At least that's how it looks from this perspective."

"So you think somebody caused your tanker explosion in order to get rid of the rest of the people who were going to get sick?"

"All I'm saying is you people start talking about this syndrome, then a day or two later you come within a cat's whisker of losing everybody who's left. Isn't that what happened?"

"Basically."

"Same thing happened here. That's all I'm saying. Now we get a pretty big explosion in this area maybe once every twenty-five or thirty years. How often does your department respond to something like that?"

"I don't even remember one."

"If everybody had died at your trailer fire, how much time do you think the authorities would have for the syndrome? For one thing, there wouldn't be anyone left to get the syndrome. They establish a cause for your trailer?"

"Ammonium nitrate was the agent. It's beginning to look like it was not an accident, either. What about your LPG tanker?"

"Never really figured it out. Driver died in the fire. Impeccable driving record. A family man with kids. Nondrinker. Never used drugs. That we knew of. No reason for a wreck. It's funny how much stuff happened right around that time. This isn't really on the point, but the daughter of one of the downed firefighters died in a house fire during all the investigations. Pretty gal. Anastasia was her name. I guess she'd been doing a lot of legwork, kind of an unofficial private investigator for the families. Cops found her in her burned-out apartment. Somebody torched it with gasoline. Never found the perp."

"You say Donovan called you?"

"Sure did. I know Scott from way back. Him and some other guy stuck around for a coupla weeks. Top-notch. Both of them. Couldn't ask for a better pair. We had many a Scotch together. Those two slaved away from six in the morning until midnight. Canyon View was only one of a couple of dozen firms had packages in that fire. And hey, nobody else sent help. You see Scott, tell him 'hey, boy' from Carl in Chattanooga, will you?"

"I'll do that. Did Scott happen to mention JCP, Inc.? Jane's California Propulsion—"

"I know who they are. Why do you ask about them?"

"Did he mention them when he called?"

"Not that I recall."

"They have any packages at Southeast Travelers? Anything that might have broken or spilled?"

"Why are you singling them out?"

"They had some stuff in the truck we think caused our problem."

"I honestly don't know. Only saw the complete list of companies once. I think I could get it for you, though. Might take a couple of days."

"I would appreciate that, Carl. In fact, that might be about the best thing you could do to help."

"You got it, buddy. I'll call back when I find out something."

"Thanks. Oh, and one other thing. Charlie Drago mentioned he caught somebody prowling Southeast Travelers sometime after the fire, maybe destroying evidence or looking for something. He said the guy threatened him."

"Never heard that, but I wouldn't doubt it. For a while here we had private investigators and legal aides crawling all over the place. And Charlie has a way of failing to ingratiate himself with people. It's just a way he has. I wouldn't put too much stock in what Drago says. He's a little over-the-top these days."

"I gathered that. Thanks."

42. WE'RE A LITTLE LATE TRYING TO SAVE YOUR LIFE, BUT WE GOT THE CAR WASHED

Minutes before the funeral, Wes Tindale found me in the fire station. "Mamie and Lill ready?" he asked.

"Who?"

"Mamie and Lill."

I'd forgotten my in-laws penchant for renaming our kids, forgotten that their need for control was so overwhelming they couldn't bear to utter the names their daughter and I had given their grandchildren.

"*Allyson* and *Britney* have a couple of hours free this morning. After lunch I'm going to need them back."

"Really?"

"I'm going to need them back." For someone who often blustered like a whale coming up for air, Wes was easily hurt and nursed grudges for years. I'd always assumed his thin hide was one of the reasons for the drinking.

More surgically than any family I'd ever known the Tindales could express disapproval with a look or an exhalation or a mere twitch of the lips. The expression they used most often on my girls, sometimes mouthed in perfect synchronicity, was, "That's a no-no."

Disapproval of those around them was constant. Living in Arizona with them would be worse for my girls than being in a seventeenth-century Moroccan prison.

Crazed with the thought that I'd uncovered a conspiracy of some sort, or that Carl Steding from the *Chattanooga Times Free Press* had, that somebody or something was orchestrating the events of the past week, I sought out Stevenson and Shad. I found them in the kitchen munching doughnuts meant for the volunteers who'd come in to empty the hose beds and decorate the fire engine that would serve as Stan Beebe's hearse. Bloated with sugar and grease they'd washed down with free coffee, Shad and Stevenson shrugged off my news about the coincidence of explosions in Tennessee and Washington.

"That's what fire departments are about," Shad said. "They respond to emergencies."

"I don't think you can equate this trailer explosion with an LPG incident three years ago in Tennessee," Stevenson said. "An LPG truck that rolls over on the highway is an accident. What we have up the hill there was a triggered explosion. You sure you don't know anything about how it started?"

"Wait. Let me try to remember. Yeah. I killed Caputo and then almost blew up my little girls."

"You did?" Shad asked.

"You guys need to lay off the junk food."

Stan's funeral was held in the white wooden-frame Lutheran church on Northeast Eighth, a few blocks north of the station.

When Karrie Haston spotted me on the church steps, she ran over and hugged me until I could feel my own ribs against her small breasts, the buttons of her dress uniform coat pressing against the buttons on mine, our shared grief dulling the hard feelings between us.

Stephanie, who hadn't known Stan and who said she had a million phone calls to make, skipped the service. Along with a group from Beebe's church, Ian and Ben and Jeb Parker acted as pallbearers. I'd been asked to help but was afraid I'd fall while we were packing the coffin out of the church.

Mary McCain arrived at the church without her husband, sparing us all the sight of a former coworker with a brainpan full of mush. I knew the spectacle would have been too much for me and certainly would have been devastating for Karrie, who was still balancing on a tightrope of denial. When I asked Mary how Joel was doing, she replied, "There are definite signs of improvement."

Maybe this wasn't terminal after all. Maybe Holly and Jackie and I had a chance. Maybe with time and therapy . . . or with Christian Science. At this juncture, I would eat dirt to have a healing. "Can he talk?"

"Not exactly. But he tells me what he wants."

"He blinks? Taps his fingers? What?"

"Well, no."

"So how do you know what he wants?"

"I just know."

I had the feeling that Mary, like her mother, was an optimist almost to the point of criminality. "You think I could visit today?"

"I think he'd like to have visitors."

"Good. I'll be over later. That all right?"

"I'll be there."

Absent the mainstays of Stan's life, it was the most dreadfully executed funeral observance I'd ever attended, filled with sour notes, miscues, unprepared participants, and poorly written eulogies. I knew it had been orchestrated by the widow, Marsha, who'd called the station repeatedly over the past two days to fine-tune the arrangements, sending over lists of demands she said were nonnegotiable. She asked for twenty firefighters to ride the apparatus with his coffin. She wanted a white riderless horse led by a marine in dress blues—Stan had been a marine. Later I called her back and told her the rig wouldn't hold twenty firefighters even if we had them and the marines had turned down our request for the riderless horse and the man to lead it.

At that point she demanded *two hundred* bagpipe players to march the three miles with her from her house to the church on foot. As if Marsha could even walk three miles.

What was saddest of all was how few of Stan's close friends reached the podium. I tried to let it go, knowing Stan was beyond caring and that, as easygoing as he was, he probably wouldn't have minded even if he'd been there.

It was a short service, with four hymns and a lone bagpipe solo. There were funerals that magnified men, but this one, sadly, had shrunk Stan.

Afterward, I was getting ready to return to the station when I bumped into Linda Newcastle, whom I'd last seen a month earlier at her husband's funeral. She wore the same black dress, her long blond-gray hair in its familiar casual wave. "They're telling me Harry might have had this syndrome you have." Everybody in town must have known about me for the word to have reached Linda, I thought.

"That's our working hypothesis."

"You no longer think he had a heart attack out there in the hills?"

"No."

"You think he was on the ground for a day or two with nobody to help him? Paralyzed or whatever?"

"I'm no authority, Linda. This is all speculation."

"Harry liked you, Jim. He said you had your head up your ass where your private life was concerned, but he liked you. Excuse my French. I shouldn't have said that."

"No. He was right. I did have my head up my ass. I know that now."

"He also said you were kind to others, and being kind to others counted for a lot in Harry's book."

"Thank you."

"By the way, if things don't get better for you, what's going to happen to your girls?"

"I don't know."

"Because I would be more than happy to take them. They're wonderful kids."

"I'd love to consider that, but we have family."

"Sure. Good luck, Jim." She squeezed my hand.

I went back to the station, and as I was walking through the open apparatus doors, Donovan and Carpenter showed up in a shiny black Suburban. It was twenty minutes after noon, which made them tardy by almost three and a half hours. What pissed me off more than their lack of punctuality was the beads of water on their vehicle, as if, after pulling into town, they'd stopped to get it washed. I knew those buttons of water sitting on the wax job weren't tears for me.

I walked into the building alone.

When I poked my head into the computer room, Stephanie looked up. "How was it?"

"Like a funeral. Any word?"

"Charlie Drago left a number for you. It's a four-two-three area code."

"Chattanooga. I'll call him in a minute. I'm going to change."

"Still no sign of our friends from Canyon View?"

"They're outside."

On my way upstairs, I heard Donovan and Carpenter at the front door, Donovan's squeaky, high-pitched voice a distinct contrast to his bulky physique. "Hello? Heeellllllooooooo?"

Moving almost in slow motion, I went to the second floor and opened my locker, changed into my civilian clothes: jeans and a navy-blue North Bend Fire T-shirt. The next time anybody saw me in my blacks, I would be in a coffin, same as Stan.

It had occurred to me that there were two big ifs in my life right now. The first: Would I make it past this week as a viable human being? The second: If I wasn't going to make it, was I willing to kill myself in order to avoid thirty years in a diaper? I didn't have the answer for the first and couldn't decide on the second.

Beebe's death would allow his wife and children to carry on in a way that wouldn't have been possible had he been relegated to a nursing home. Marsha wouldn't have the nagging worry about whether Stan was being cared for and wouldn't have to feel guilty for failing to visit a man who didn't even know she was in the room. Nor would she have to go through the anguish of divorcing the poor bastard if she found someone else to be a father to her four children.

Downstairs, I found Achara sitting in a chair in the watch office, Donovan alongside, Stephanie in the corridor doorway in the sundress Allyson had picked out for her. Achara had a briefcase and papers laid out on the table beside her. As I walked into the room, we all heard a car door slam outside, a child chattering away. Britney.

"Thanks for the call," I said sarcastically.

"What call?" Donovan asked.

"The one telling us you weren't going to be able to make it by nine as arranged, but that you'd be here by . . ." I made a production of looking at my watch. "Twelve-twenty."

"We called," Donovan said, "but your lines were busy."

"I have two days left, and you show up three and a half hours late."

The room grew deathly quiet. Donovan didn't hold my gaze, turned to Achara and then Stephanie for succor. I'd been getting angry at people all morning, more surprised with each episode.

The voices outside grew louder, and then the front door opened and Wes and Lillian Tindale burst in. My daughters ran past them and into my arms. Smothered in kisses, I held them in my arms for a few moments, and then let them slide to the floor.

Sensing the tension they'd walked into, Wes said, "We got them back in time for lunch."

"It's nice to know somebody's punctual."

After they left, Allyson whispered to me. "Grandpa said he had to go to the rest room, but he went to the tavern instead."

"Thanks."

Achara introduced herself to the girls and said, "Would you two like to show me around? I don't know that I've ever been in a fire station."

After they left, I turned to Donovan. "So what the hell's going on?"

"We were late. It's not the end of the world."

"Not for you."

"We've been working on it. I'm sorry if we weren't in touch the way

222

you would have liked. I remember this from Chattanooga. People get emotional. I should have been on my toes. I'm sorry." Donovan turned his blue eyes to Stephanie, as if she were an ally, or as if he wanted to make her one. "I was at Canyon View at five this morning. Achara was there all night. I brought her up to speed on everything we'd done in Tennessee, and after that she wanted to do some records searches. She's a better chemist than I am—I'm mostly administrative these days—and she wanted to go over the list of chemicals we'd come up with in Tennessee to see if there were any that might have produced your symptoms. After that we were waiting for phone calls, mine from London, hers from Hong Kong. With the time differences and everything, it took a while."

"Did you find anything?"

"Unfortunately, not yet. We have two more people back at the plant going through the lists of chemicals we know were involved in Tennessee. We're doing everything we can think of as fast as we think of it."

"And what about Jane's California Propulsion, Inc.?"

"I still haven't been able to find out if they were involved in Tennessee."

My cell phone rang. "Yes?"

It was Olefson, one of the county chiefs from our committee. He told me they would be organized and working by Monday morning. "Fine," I said. I should have told them all at the meeting that I had the syndrome. Everybody was working in slow motion while I was dying at sixteen frames per second.

"Look," Stephanie said, sensing how irritated I still was. "Why don't you go break Achara free while Mr. Donovan and I compare notes."

"Sorry I went off on you," I said.

"Call me Scott. And don't worry about it. One thing, though. We'd like to see as many of the victims as possible. That would certainly help a lot."

"Mary McCain is expecting me this afternoon."

"Who is?"

"Her husband's got it. She's expecting only me, but I think I can get you all in."

I found the three of them sitting in the front seat of the tanker. When I opened the door, Britney giggled and leaned past Achara, who was on the outside. "We were hiding."

When Achara smiled, it was clear her heart was breaking for me. I could only surmise what spending five minutes with my daughters had done to her, because either one of them could have charmed the scales off an alligator.

"We're finished in there," I said.

"Everything resolved?" Achara asked.

"More or less."

"Achara thinks we should get our hair cut," Allyson said.

"So do I."

"Really, Daddy?" Britney was so excited she was about to burst.

"Yes."

"Grandma said short hair wasn't ladylike."

"Grandma has short hair," I said.

"That's what we told her," said Allyson, still indignant about it.

"You want out?" I said to the girls, who both shook their heads.

"You want to come over for dinner tonight?" Britney blurted. Allyson elbowed her and whispered in her ear. Britney added, "Stephanie won't mind."

"Thank you, but I'm afraid I'll be busy," Achara said. As I helped her climb down out of the rig, she said, "Maybe we should sit down and talk one-on-one about what's happening. I have some ideas."

"Sure."

"Later?"

"Yeah."

43. JOKESTERS WHO PUT ZOMBIES IN MOVIE THEATER SEATS

We caravanned to Joel McCain's house, Stephanie navigating the route by memory, having followed the fire engine there earlier in the week. On North Bend Way, in the middle of town, we passed a couple of high school girls in shorts and halter tops holding cardboard signs for a car wash. I figured this was where Donovan's Suburban had gotten wet. The thought made my blood boil all over again. They seemed helpful enough and indicated that they were working on the problem day and night, but every little thing was making me irritable.

Stephanie parked the Lexus in front of the McCain homestead while Donovan pulled his Suburban into a spot behind us in the cul-de-sac. The neighborhood was resplendent in the June sunshine, the lawns green and manicured.

A perplexed expression on her face, Mary opened the front door while we gathered at the end of her walkway. "Listen," I said. "Let me go first. She wasn't expecting all of us."

"No, it's fine!" Mary shouted. "Company will be good. I'm sure he's ready to see people. Whoever you want to bring is fine." As we drew closer and I made the introductions, Mary said, "If Dr. Riggs was here to treat Joel, I would veto it, but this is a matter of public health. Scientists always want to cooperate with the medical authorities. It's in the manual. Mrs. Eddy was very explicit."

I wondered what was going on with Joel that Mary wanted him to have this many visitors. Was it possible the syndrome really was transitory, that Holly was going to get better, and that Karrie and I weren't doomed? That Stan had killed himself for nothing?

"Thank you, Mary." My daughters were behind us in the cul-de-sac, Allyson walking across the street toward a girl her age, Britney lagging behind. "You two going to be okay out here?" I shouted.

"I'm going to play with Crystal, Daddy. We'll be okay."

"Don't lose track of your little sister."

"I'm not going to get lost," Britney said, annoyed.

The four of us crowded into the McCains' foyer, our numbers, my height, and Scott Donovan's girth making the rooms smaller. The last time I'd been here, Joel had looked like a CPR dummy, but today Mary was so buoyant and confident, I began to get my hopes up.

Mary escorted us into the stripped-down living room, where Joel lay on a tall hospital bed. His eyes were open, but other than that he looked like a man who'd just been thrown by a bull elephant, limp, dazed, broken. He wore a white T-shirt, a bedsheet obscuring whatever else he might have had on. To my great disappointment, he was pretty much the same glassy-eyed Joel we'd left four days ago.

Stephanie walked over and spoke his name, took his pulse, temperature, blood pressure, felt his brow, and began checking his extremities for signs of conscious or reflexive movement. I thought about trying to speak to him but couldn't get myself to do it in front of this many people. Anything I said would only make me look fatuous and show Joel off for the zombie he'd become. In fact, all I could think about was how full of life and humor Joel had been only weeks earlier.

I slipped out of the room and stepped onto the front porch, gently snicking the front door closed behind me. Across the street my girls were running in circles with two other children. Coming so soon after Stan's funeral, seeing Joel again had been ruinous, his twisted body dressed by somebody else, his facial muscles slack, the part in his hair crooked.

It would be a good many years before Joel got a funeral or the accolades Stan had received that morning. Not unless his mother-in-law fed him another apple. By the time they buried him, he would have spent a decade, perhaps several decades, lying in musty rooms by himself. It was the worst way to die.

A day at a time.

Alone.

Forgotten.

Joel and I had joined the fire department the same year. After my divorce he used to tease me about my dating habits, joking that I'd never met a woman I didn't want to dump. He claimed I had a pathological need to make each woman in the room fall in love with me so I could break her heart. It wasn't true. At least, not to the extent he claimed.

Standing alone on his porch, I thought about what he'd been trying to tell me. Joel had been relentless in trying to force me to see myself from a different perspective.

What hurt was that all those years I'd treated his comments as jokes and all those years he'd been right.

Joel had seen through me.

He'd said once I must have been a lonely child. How he'd come up with that diagnosis was beyond me, because everybody else in the department thought I was a happy-go-lucky guy, assumed I always had been.

Now, standing on his front porch, for the first time in years, perhaps ever, I was able to look at myself as an outsider might. I *had* been a sad kid. Life at Six Points had been infinitely depressing and had worn me down physically, while suppressing my spirit, too. One only had to look at my choice of reading material during those years.

I'd spent hours each day in the school library or the downtown Seattle Public Library, usually when I was supposed to be out on the streets proselytizing. The Sixth Element and William P. Markham had the longest list of banned books on earth, essentially any book Markham hadn't written, yet once I broke the tenet and began reading from outside sources, once I discovered the library, I found a whole new world. Hundreds, if not thousands, of new worlds.

I absorbed as much information about the universe outside our religion as possible.

I loved reading about war pilots, from the First World War right through Vietnam. There was something immensely compelling about the thought of being up in the wild blue while the rest of the world fought like barbarians below.

In addition to flying stories, I read every WW II escape memoir I could lay my hands on. I read about fliers slipping out of POW camps, about soldiers escaping from the Wehrmacht, about Jews, Communists, and gays escaping from the Gestapo. I read with relish and identified completely with men and women relating tortures at the hands of the Nazis, and swore that if I was ever tortured, I would do everything in my power to survive and exact my revenge. What I hadn't realized until years later was that I had been tortured every day of my young life, and that my pitiful reprisals would eventually be launched against an old man in a nursing home.

Ironic that I should identify with prisoners of war so completely. Ironic also that I should dream incessantly of escape from a prison camp. It was my spirit that had been in prison.

Cultists lived in a fantasy world, and according to Joel I'd fallen into a fantasy world after my divorce, too, seducing and discarding women like a fisherman seducing and discarding trout in a "catch-and-release only" stream. What an incredible bastard I was. It had probably been one of my exes who'd made the anonymous call to Shad and Stevenson accusing me of blowing up Caputo's trailer.

I was still thinking about all my exes when the front door opened behind me and Achara stepped outside. "He was like that when you saw him before?"

"Yes."

"Exactly like that?"

"Not exactly. When we saw him, he was choking on an apple."

"Oh, God. How many others are there?"

"Two still alive in Tennessee that we know about and two more up here. Stephanie's sister and a woman over in the nursing home. Joel makes three. I'll be the fourth. Karrie? The young woman at the fire station? I don't know if you saw her. She'll be the fifth, although I doubt she'll talk to you about it."

"I suppose it's possible Joel is the way he is because of his fall?"

"It's possible, but that's not what happened."

"So you expect to be . . . ?"

"By Sunday." I dropped my hands limply, made my facial muscles go slack, and feigned brain death. It was fun to watch the look of horror in Achara's eyes. Then, in case one of the neighbors thought I was mocking Joel, I relaxed the pose.

"That's not funny."

"I thought it was hilarious." Her brown eyes held my gaze. Somehow during our explanations yesterday at Canyon View, the magnitude of the tragedy had not impressed her. For all of his scientific distance, Donovan actually seemed more attuned to the personal impact of the syndrome, perhaps because he'd seen it up close in Tennessee. I'd sensed all along that he knew my pain.

"I feel dreadful about this."

"Join the club."

"No, I mean . . . If there was something we could do right now, this minute. I just . . ." She was whispering now and the ringing in my ears forced me to lower my head to hear.

"What are you two conspiring about?" Donovan had opened the door without a sound.

"I was just telling Jim I've turned down two offers to teach at Stanford."

"Don't worry, Jimbo. We'll figure this out."

Donovan's arrogance was almost as comforting as Achara's deception was puzzling. Why lie to Donovan? Weren't we all working on this together? I was beginning to wonder if she had her own agenda, if she was really committed to this quest.

"How can you say we're going to figure this out when there's so little time?" Achara said.

"Don't you worry. You're good at what you do. I'm good at what I do. Don't forget. I went through this once before and got stumped. It's not going to happen again."

Gazing across the immaculate lawn at the black Suburban, I said, "Nice rig. You stop to get it washed on the way into town?"

Donovan said, "On the drive out here some idiot teenage kid threw a tomato across three lanes of freeway and just about took out our windshield. I tried to get his license, but they took the exit to Highway 18 right after that."

When she spotted me watching her from across the cul-de-sac, Allyson jogged halfway across the quiet street and shouted, "Do we have to go now?"

"Not yet."

She ran back to the game, laughing. I found myself looking to see whether her hands were clear, but my vision was blurred, and at this distance I would have needed binoculars even if it wasn't. Jesus. My kids might have it. Somebody was responsible for this. I didn't know who, but somebody had to be. Thinking about my kids getting it made me want to kill whoever was responsible.

Eight minutes later Stephanie came out of the house deep in conversation with Mary McCain, their sudden camaraderie odd, considering Stephanie was a doctor and Mary had always taken pride in the fact that she'd never visited a doctor in her life.

A few minutes later, Donovan and Carpenter were locked into a heated discussion in the Suburban, the windows rolled tight.

44. YOU HAVE FIVE SECONDS TO MEMORIZE THIS: 754018241863O846

Positioning the vanity mirror so that I could watch the argument in the Suburban behind us, I missed all but the gist of what Stephanie was telling me, something about how much faith Mary had that her religion would bring Joel back to his old self. Despite what Mary thought, Joel was gone. He was an idiot and would be for the rest of eternity. Just as I would be.

The speed limit was thirty-five, but we were doing closer to forty-five; behind us, the Suburban quickly matched our speed.

Without warning, the Suburban swerved across the yellow line and nearly struck an oncoming vehicle, overcorrected, and went off the road on the right, a sheet of dust flaring up as it crossed the dirt.

"Achara had an accident!" shrieked Allyson, who'd been watching the Suburban with me.

"Stop," I said.

"What?" Stephanie glanced into her mirror and pulled onto the parking strip, reversing until we occupied the stretch of roadway directly opposite the accident. The Suburban had center-punched a small tree. The vehicle the Suburban had so narrowly missed was backing up, too.

"You girls stay inside," I said.

"Can't we go see?" Britney asked.

"No."

The tree, about five inches in diameter, had creased the front bumper of the Suburban. Other than that, there wasn't much damage. The windshield was intact.

"Oh, God," said Donovan when I reached the vehicle. He was cupping his nose with both hands, blood leaking through his fingers. The deployed air bag had popped him good. I reached inside past Donovan and turned off the ignition.

As I moved around the vehicle to see how Achara was doing, one of our volunteers, Andre Stiles, climbed out of the pickup across the street, still wearing his uniform from the funeral.

He peered around the vehicle to see where I was headed, spotted

Achara, and rolled his eyes. As a group, the guys in the department indulged in a lot of adolescent humor about my homing in on the best-looking woman at any accident scene—some of them even claimed I'd elbowed them aside to get to particularly pretty victims. I almost always let them run with their joke.

Achara was on the passenger side of the Suburban, hands on her knees, staring at the ground. "You all right?" I asked.

The ringing in my ears obscured her initial reply. When I asked her to repeat, she said, "Got a pencil? I'm going to give you some numbers. Don't tell Scott."

"Why not?"

"Write this down. I want you to have this before I tell you anything else."

"I don't have anything to write with."

"There's no time to get it. Just listen. Seventy-five, forty."

"Seventy-five, forty."

"That's the first part. The rest goes, eighteen, twenty-four, eighteen, sixty-three, oh-eight, forty-six. Write it down first chance you get. Don't let anyone see it until you need it."

"Need it for what?"

"Give it back to me. Do you remember it?"

"Seventy-five, forty. Eighteen, twenty-four, eighteen, sixty-three, oh-eight, forty-six."

"Not too many people could do that."

"Bible school."

She wasn't bleeding, but she would probably end up with a black eye from the impact of her air bag. "You sure you can remember that?"

"I can remember anything."

"Jesus Christ! You could have killed somebody," Donovan whined, rounding the rear of the Suburban holding a four-by-four inch gauze pad to his nose, his tieless shirt dappled with red.

"It was *your* fault."

"My fault? You grabbed the wheel. You don't *ever* grab the wheel when somebody else is driving."

"You were in the wrong lane, Scott. You were going to kill somebody."

"The only person was going to kill anybody was you."

"Look who's talking. Mr. Ethical."

"Now don't get into *that*."

"I'll get into it if I want to get into it."

"This is my last warning. Don't go there." His voice was surprisingly calm considering what they'd just been through.

They glowered at each other, and before anybody could react, Achara stepped forward and kicked Donovan in the shin. He stepped back and held his leg. The contrast in size between Achara and Donovan made the skirmish almost funny. I doubted she weighed a hundred pounds. At the least, Donovan weighed two-forty.

None of this kept her from kicking him a second time.

I stopped her before she could do anything else. "No, you don't. That's the end of it. It's over."

"Get out of my way. You don't even know what this is about."

"Sure I do. It's about somebody going to jail."

"Don't even make me tell you how many martial arts I know," Donovan warned, over my shoulder.

Donovan's jaw was clenched, his blue eyes glued to Achara. Yet, strangely, he seemed afraid of her. In a physical altercation he could take Achara, together with me and probably Stephanie and Stiles, all of us at once. Because of the calluses on Donovan's knuckles, I had no doubt his martial arts skills were impressive. Yet he hadn't made a move to defend himself.

Stiles picked up his aid kit and marched across the street to his pickup truck. Stephanie took Achara by the arm and led her behind the Suburban. I gestured for Donovan to step over to the Lexus.

"What's going on between you two?"

"You saw her. She caused that accident."

"What were you arguing about in the truck?"

"It's pretty simple. I'm in charge and she's not. She was in school so long, she never learned to take orders."

"You two better straighten this out."

"She'd better straighten herself out." Donovan looked off in the distance toward Snoqualmie Pass, where billows of black smoke from the state fire academy were rolling across the foothills. We'd all trained up there at Exit 38, everyone in the department, probably every firefighter in the state. "She just needs to stay on track. She gets out of the lab so infrequently, I don't think she knows how to behave in public."

"I have a feeling there's more to it."

"Hey, listen. *She* assaulted *me*."

"You drive back with Stephanie. I'll go with Achara."

"Not necessary. We'll be fine."

"You sure?"

"It's a lot of strain, you know?" Donovan's eyes held mine. I figured him for a real Lothario, a heartthrob with the ladies, or maybe the guys, the ones who liked that type, big, thick, muscular, the boyish haircut, the baby-blues behind the wire-rimmed spectacles. "Trying to figure this out and get the work done before we lose you. And now we have that other firefighter, what's her name?"

"Karrie."

"I know this is a lot of pressure on Carpenter. I tried this once before in Tennessee and we weren't successful, and you know what? It really bummed me out. I think the same thing's happening to Achara. You know what I'm talking about. You do emergency work all the time. We don't get out of the office. This is just a lot of strain."

"Yeah. Well."

Stephanie came around the vehicle and said, "I think she'll be okay now. Why don't we switch cars. You drive with Achara?"

Donovan said, "Forget it. We've got work to do. I'll go with Achara."

For a split second Achara looked at me, and I had the feeling she was afraid I might tell him about the numbers she'd given me. She stepped forward and put her talon of a hand out, and she and Donovan shook.

Moments later Donovan managed to extricate the Suburban from the ditch without the assistance of a wrecker. There was no telling what was going on between them, perhaps a tinge of professional envy, Donovan finding himself upstaged by the whiz kid from MIT, Achara rankling under the yoke of a boss she knew had lesser skills than she. Or maybe it was seeing Joel. Visiting him had shaken me up, too.

What bothered me even more than Achara's sudden show of temper was the numbers she'd given me. I had no idea what they meant or why she'd offered them. Or why she didn't want Donovan to know about them. I had the feeling they were part of a chemical formula, but what did I know? Sooner or later I'd get her alone and we would have an interesting conversation.

45. DON'T ASK ME WHAT I WAS DOING IN A MOTEL ROOM WITH STEPHANIE RIGGS

Wracked with guilt for not being with my daughters, I thought about fleeing before she came out of the bathroom. I was stretched out on the bed, hands clasped behind my head, doing deep-breathing exercises, while the smartest, most attractive woman I'd ever met was taking her clothes off behind the bathroom door in a sleazy North Bend motel room.

Outside, it was nearly as dark as my heart.

My girls and Morgan had left a note. Although I'd given her the keys and told Morgan she could use my truck for whatever came up, I was surprised when she took me up on it. They'd gone to a movie I'd seen with them already, one they knew I didn't care to sit through again.

After we decided to go to the store to pick up groceries for supper, Stephanie, instead of turning left off Ballarat and heading toward the QFC, had turned west on North Bend Way, swinging into the parking lot at the Sunset Motel. When the motor stopped, she gave me a long look.

"What?" I said.

Without a word, she went into the office, got a key, and proceeded to a room off the second-floor balcony. Suspecting I was soon to become the recipient of what my army buddies used to call a mercy fuck, I followed with the aimless hankering of a stray dog trailing a garbage truck. Not that Stephanie was anything like a garbage truck, even if I was exactly like the stray dog.

It might have been my imagination, but I thought she'd been looking at me differently all day. It was even possible we'd had a few tender moments of the kind you get with someone you're beginning to fall in love with.

Despite my reputation as a womanizer, I was always confused when it came to women. I never knew what they were thinking, not unless they told me, and most of the time even then I didn't *really* know.

As I followed her up the open stairs and along the walkway, she turned back and ambushed me with a kiss. Right out there for the birds to see, and the three Hispanic kids kicking a soccer ball against the wall of a nearby garage door. Ridiculous and dewy-eyed as it sounds, it was the kind of kiss you always want to be your first with a woman, the kind you never get except once in a blue moon, when one of you is just a tad drunk or a lot exhausted and you know the relationship is not going to extend past the exchange of phone numbers.

We weren't drunk, but we both knew the relationship had two days, three at the most, and that must have added spice to it.

Stephanie resumed her ardor as soon as we were in the room, her body small and slender and taut in my hands, her arms twined around my neck, her lithe stomach pressed against mine, as she stood on tiptoes clinging to me. Every part of her body felt hot against my cool skin. She kissed the tips of two fingers and pressed them to my nose, then turned and disappeared into the bathroom.

I closed the door with my foot and reached out and flicked on a dim light. The drapes were already closed. The room had a queen-size bed, a vanity, one chair, and a cheesy painting of a moose in a swamp.

I lay on the bed without a thought in my head except . . .

Mercy fuck.

I was about to get one.

Joel McCain once told me my crimes against women were a control issue, that I needed to be in control of every little aspect of every relationship. I only half wondered how he knew that about me. He hadn't endeared himself to me by calling my relationships with women crimes. I'd bridled at the thought. Hell, I was still friends with all of my ex-girlfriends.

But he was right about control. As a child I'd had zero control over my life or even the hours in my day. At Six Points every waking minute was accounted for, booked in advance by the church, by my father, by William P. Markham, and by the Lord Jesus Christ. If you were a kid, there was no time for riding a bike or flying a kite or painting by numbers. Nobody played cards or read fiction. These activities were all blueprints offered up by the devil to take your mind off God's work. Since birth I'd had the principles of austerity and compliance pounded into my brain. Okay. So I had control issues.

I suppose I must have been a control freak with Lorie as well, though specific examples escape me. Lord. Maybe I had driven her away! Maybe her parents were right about me. Maybe I'd turned my ex-wife into a lesbian.

Now I was in a motel with Stephanie Riggs.

And she was in control.

And you know what?

I kind of liked it.

My life had been taken out of my hands, my days orchestrated by our panicky quest to track down the origins of the syndrome. If she wanted to come out of the bathroom and make love, fine. If she wanted to come out and tell me to scram, that was fine, too. At this point I refused to let anything bother me.

When I heard the shower running, I knew I was in for a wait.

The funeral had been hell. Sitting between Karrie and Ben Arden's wife, Cherie, I could only wonder why I hadn't believed Stan Beebe's story back when there'd been a chance to save him.

The world had mobilized to save my butt, but without lifting a finger I'd let Stan drown in a sea of desperation.

The visit to Joel McCain's house and the bizarre interactions between the chemists from Canyon View had been puzzling at best. Achara's quiet conference with me and desperate anger at Donovan had been even more puzzling. Thinking to catch her alone, I'd been on the lookout for her all day, but it hadn't happened.

Back to the station after the accident, I was standing outside in the sunshine dialing various media outlets on a cell phone when the black Suburban pulled into the gravel lot across the street from the firehouse, Donovan and Carpenter peering out the open driver's window like an old married couple out for a Sunday afternoon drive, the issues between them seemingly resolved.

Side by side, they walked across the street just as Stephanie came out of the station. After eavesdropping on my phone conversation for a moment, Donovan said, "You're not calling a television station, are you?"

Placing my palm over the phone, I said, "Yes. Why?"

"That's crazy. You should stop!"

"I'm—"

"Trust me on this. I was in Chattanooga, where the news guys came in like a herd of elephants and raised so much dust things never got right again. The investigation ground to a halt! I'm telling you. We've got a couple of days to move like lightning. Don't gum up the works."

I told the folks at the TV station I would call back. Maybe Donovan had a point. He'd been through this before; I hadn't. I had a strong inclination to hold a press conference, but maybe he was right.

Donovan interrupted my thoughts. "I'm planning to run down some leads here in the valley. I want to look over the accident site from last winter. I also want to interview McCain's friends. And Feldbaum's. Maybe yours, too. Sometimes you can get something verbally that you can't dig up with test tubes and science."

"I told you before. It's got something to do with Jane's California Propulsion, Inc. It has to."

"I know. I know. And we think there might be something to that. I've already done a quick read-through of my lists from three years ago, and I can't find their name. I'm going to have Achara work on that this after-noon. She'll check out the various components to rocket fuel and see what the health implications are. She'll also make some calls about Jane's. We have a few contacts in the industry, so we might be able to learn something."

"Thanks."

"Don't mention it. We want you well, pal."

"Thanks."

He winked. I glanced at Achara to see what her take on this was, but she didn't seem to be paying attention.

"If you're still thinking about calling the media," Donovan said, "don't. I'm telling you. They show up, they'll turn this into a circus. You want to give a hundred interviews a day? That's what the chief in Chattanooga was doing. And they didn't get one pertinent piece of infor-mation from the public. Not one."

Stephanie came out of the station in time to hear this. "You're *not* go-ing to call the media?" she asked.

"I was. Donovan's got another take on it."

"I think you should."

"What do you think, Achara?" I asked.

She turned to me. "It's your call. I'm not going to vote on a thing like that." Everybody waited for my decision, Stephanie, Donovan, Carpenter, Ian Hjorth, who'd also come outside and joined our group.

"I'm going to talk," I said.

Stephanie patted my shoulder. "Good. Somebody out there might know something."

Shaking his head with a conviction that almost changed my mind, Donovan said, "It's your call. But first give us a twenty-four-hour period without interference."

"I don't think so. Tomorrow's day six."

"You don't know that for certain."

"Tell you what, Scott. When you contract this, you take a chance on which day you're on."

"You're right. Sorry. Forget I even said that. Jesus. I don't know what I was thinking."

I set up a press conference for ten o'clock the next morning outside the fire station.

Soon after my decision, Achara took her briefcase and notes and walked the two blocks to the North Bend branch of the King County Library; she said she was looking for a place to spread out her notes and work. Donovan climbed into his Suburban and drove off without telling us where he was headed.

Stephanie and I dropped the girls off with Morgan at my house, exchanging tearful kisses with both. Morgan, who'd been all but unreachable for almost two days, was suddenly eager to baby-sit.

The most frustrating task that afternoon was locating firefighters from the Chattanooga Fire Department willing to speak candidly. Already one firefighter was being sued by one of the litigants for speaking out in public, and just about everyone and their mother had been subpoenaed to the trial.

Once again, I found myself in a long, rambling conversation with Charlie Drago, who now filled me in on the LPG disaster that happened two weeks after Southeast Travelers, the explosion he'd forgotten to tell me about during our first conversations. The fact that he'd forgotten to mention it the first time around spoke volumes about his mental acuity.

He also said there'd been a fire in his garage shortly after he began looking into the syndrome, blamed it on powerful unnamed forces, said he'd been followed by men in black for weeks, that his phone had been tapped, that they might be listening to us that very minute. The more we spoke, the more I realized Charlie was a full-blown paranoiac.

"You gotta listen to me," Drago said. "Whatever anybody tells you about that LPG incident, it was *not* an accident. It was a *trap*. You know who responded? The same group of guys went to Travelers. It was only luck it didn't kill more than the six of them and the two civilians. You wipe out half a battalion and you suddenly no longer have anyone who cares about Southeast Travelers. Specifically, you wipe out the guys who responded to Southeast, and you got no one left to come down with this syndrome and start suing. That was the plan all along."

"Carl Steding told me the same thing. That it was a trap. Or at least that's what he hinted."

"Trouble is, we're practically the only two people in town who think that."

"Wasn't the LPG incident ruled accidental?"

"Sure it was. That's what they wanted."

"That's what *who* wanted?"

"The people who lit up my garage."

"And who were they?"

"Whoever stands to lose their pants over Southeast Travelers. It could be any one of thirty corporations. Or their investors. Thousands of investors. In fact, investors are usually the worst. I should know. I was an investor once."

Toward evening a battalion chief from Chattanooga named Frost called in response to messages I'd left. He told me I could cheerfully disregard anything Charlie told me, that Charlie had been spouting nonsense about Southeast Travelers for so long, nobody listened to him anymore. When I mentioned Charlie's garage fire and his thoughts on the LPG truck accident, Chief Frost said, "Charlie started it hisself, left a sack of hot ashes from his woodstove too close to a wall. And that LPG truck driver? He reached over to change the radio station, got a bee in his briefs, whatever. Nobody but Charlie and some asshole works over at the paper ever thought there was anything odd about it.

"The tank itself must have ruptured with the crash, which would have weakened the double-wall construction. Burned real hot. We went in like we're taught, hard and aggressive, two teams on two hose lines, each spray pattern protecting the team behind it, but the tank blew before we got it cooled. The explosion was unbelievable. Hey. Out of those eight guys, six died, which was a miracle in itself, because they all should have been blown to Kingdom Come. One escaped with minor burns, and one had to retire. Helluva deal. We also lost the truck driver and a news photographer who happened to be in the way. I didn't get there myself until minutes later, but I saw it from a distance and believe me, I thought twice about turning around and heading on outa there. You ain't lived until you've seen an LPG tank go up. It hadn't been mostly empty, we would have lost a lot more people. Damn lucky."

"The same shift had the LPG fire as went to Southeast Travelers?"

"Yeah."

"The guy at the paper seemed to think that was significant."

"I don't know why."

I spoke to several more fire officers who either had been at the tanker fire in Chattanooga or were intimate with the details. Unfortunately, the details shed little light on our problems in North Bend. Even though Drago told me at one time he had a complete list of the companies involved in the Southeast Travelers fire, he couldn't confirm or deny JCP, Inc., had been involved. So far, neither could anybody else.

We fielded several calls from people in the upper Snoqualmie Valley asking to confirm Scott Donovan was working with us, so we knew he was making the rounds.

At five-thirty people began disappearing to go home and have dinner with their families. By six-thirty there were only three of us left, myself, Stephanie, and Cherie, God bless her. She'd been with us all day.

Stephanie looked across the conference room table at me and said, "None of these doctors has called back. I told their people this was a matter of life and death."

"They'll call."

"Know what else?"

"What?"

"I sure wish we could have done an autopsy on your friend."

"Why not wait and do one on me?"

"Not funny. And please don't talk like that."

"Yes, ma'am."

"I spoke to the CDC today. I was honest with them. I shouldn't have been. I told them most of these cases had been officially attributed to something other than a syndrome. For instance, your chief dying out in the woods. Or the two car accidents. They're real busy. They need more conclusive evidence of a syndrome before they'll send someone out."

The girls called every half hour or so to make sure I was all right and to find out when Stephanie and I would be home. Later they called to tell me they were going to a movie with Morgan.

At a few minutes after six o'clock we got a call back from one of the doctors Stephanie had been waiting on, a neurologist in Biloxi who'd treated a young woman who had been brain-dead for three years; after complaining of dizziness and ringing in her ears, the woman had gone down in a matter of days, her only outward symptom waxy-looking hands. Stephanie kept the doctor on the line for half an hour.

When she hung up, she turned to me. "She's exactly like Holly and the others."

"They ever track down the source?"

"Nope."

"Do they know anything?"

"Nope."

46. THE DEEP BLUE DREAD

The shower shut off with a bang of the pipes in the wall, and for some minutes there was no sound from the bathroom. When the door finally opened, Stephanie's silhouette was limned by the light behind her. She walked toward me as relaxed as if she were shopping for groceries.

She padded barefoot across the room, stood beside the bed for a few moments before I felt her weight on the mattress. Slowly, she crawled next to me, smelling of soap, toothpaste, and shampoo, pressing the length of her body against mine. It was at times such as this that I usually came up with my dumbest comments, as if the occasion inspired the idiocy. Tonight was no exception.

"This is a mercy fuck. Right?"

"Yes, it is, sweetie."

"Then it's not going to happen."

"What? You don't want to help out a socially maladjusted doctor who's been so busy putting herself through med school and residency and establishing a practice, she never had time for a social life?"

"You're only doing this because you feel sorry for me."

"No. You're doing it because you feel sorry for *me*." Her faulty logic forced a laugh from me. I could see by the look on her face that she liked me. It always came as a surprise to discover a woman liked me. Any woman. Maybe my reluctance to accept love came from those years after my mother vanished, for whatever else was going on in her life, my mother had certainly abandoned her only child. Lorie's disappearance probably didn't help. Or maybe somewhere down deep, all guys felt that way. I'd never talked to another man about it, so I couldn't say for certain.

Running my fingers over the silky skin of her hips and stomach, cradling the hint of her belly with my palms, wrapping my hands around her waist, encircling her girth with my hands, I tried to lose myself in the moment. It would be the first time all day I'd stopped thinking about the syndrome.

She began helping me off with my T-shirt, then unbuckled my pants and began wrestling them off. I was so ready to make love, it was embarrassing.

"I can see there's going to be no mercy here," she said.

242

I took her in my arms, rolled over, and kissed her. As we played, I began having flashbacks to all the times I'd made love with Holly. Holly had been more relaxed in life, more uptight in bed, more serious making love, while Stephanie, so solemn in life, took immense delight in every little nuance of our bodies.

Still, I couldn't shake visions of a naked Holly from my brain.

Holly lay in some dank nursing home, alone and forgotten the same way I would lie alone and forgotten in just a few days. I had treated her terribly, and now I was about to pop her sister. Looking at it in this new light, our tryst seemed wrong in the worst of all possible ways.

"What's the matter?" she asked.

"I can't."

"Oh, it's pretty obvious you can."

"I don't think so."

Grasping me, she said, "What's this?"

"Some sick cosmic joke."

She rolled on top of me.

"Stop."

"Hey, don't turn this into a big moral issue." She hovered over me and stared into my eyes. "Let's not analyze this. I'm sick to death of analyzing every little thing in my life. It's the reason I don't have a life. I think it's the reason you don't have one, either."

Thinking had always been my downfall, and I found I couldn't stop now. Ironic, because in three days I wouldn't be able to think. "I feel so bad about my life. The way I—"

"Shush," she said, her hair tickling my face as she leaned over, her small breasts brushing my chest. "Don't talk. That's the secret, big boy. Just lie back and enjoy the night."

"Did you call me big boy?"

"Okay, medium-to-slightly-above-average boy."

"Let's go back to big boy."

"Sorry. You lose what you question."

Later, lost inside her, I felt her hot, moist breath on my ear, her legs wrapped around mine, her hands on the back of my neck. It was an animal thing making love, but it was magnificent, too, and I wanted it to be so deliciously slow, we would both explode with desire before it was over.

And then, just for a moment, I thought my heart stopped.

Afterward, twined together, wet and sated and full of warmth we'd each appropriated from the other, I found myself beginning to drift off. I struggled to remain alert but failed. Lately, each time I went to sleep, I was just a little afraid I wouldn't wake up. Then Stephanie was shaking me, and I was half-awake but still dreaming. A weird sensation.

It seemed forever before I got my eyes open. "I was worried," she said.

"It was as peaceful as I've ever been. Like I was dead."

She'd turned on a lamp, her hair down around her face as she watched me. I had no idea how long we'd been here: one hour, two, a day? While I was rapidly coming to terms with my fate, I could tell by the deep blue dread in Stephanie's eyes, she was not. Wouldn't. Couldn't.

Making love with Stephanie had been penny fun and pound foolish. Worse, it had been diabolic. After I joined her sister in the mental ether, the pain of Stephanie's consanguine betrayal would only be that much greater for her.

Ironic. Just as I was recognizing my own unhealthy need to inflict suffering on the women around me, I went out and did it again. The fact that it had been her idea didn't make it any easier to stomach.

We dressed in silence, kissed briefly at the door, and stepped out onto the walkway. It was almost eleven-thirty. Two doors down, a man and a woman, half-crocked from the sounds of their movement and slurred voices, quarreled over which of them had the room key. A moment later I realized we were listening to Wes and Lillian Tindale.

Our meeting surprised me, but it *shocked* them. Mouths agape, they both turned and stared.

For a few moments the four of us looked at one another and then, without a word, Stephanie pivoted around and began walking away. I followed. Downstairs, we climbed into the Lexus, while a dumbfounded Wesley and Lillian gawped down at us.

As we headed out of the lot, two men in a rental car headed in. "Stop," I said. The two men parked next to us and headed toward a room on the ground floor. "I thought you two were leaving town," I said, rolling the car window down.

The two balding men looked startled. Hillburn and Dobson from Jane's California Propulsion, Inc. I'd been suspicious of them for pulling out of town after our chat, but now I was even more suspicious because they hadn't pulled out of town at all.

"What are you two doing?" I asked, getting out of the Lexus.

They looked at each other and headed for their room without answering. I ran over to them and grabbed Dobson by the arm. "No. I want to know what you two are doing. I thought you said your company couldn't possibly have had anything to do with our syndrome. If that's so, why are you hanging around?"

"Doesn't have anything to do with you," said Hillburn, who had the key in the door.

"You two are up to something." They just stared at me. Before I could say anything else, they opened the door, went in, and slammed it in my face.

"Did you see those bastards?" I said, getting back into the car.

"I don't like them, either, but it doesn't necessarily mean anything. Achara was going to look into rocket fuel products. Maybe she's found something."

"I'm surprised we haven't heard from her. The library closed hours ago."

We stopped at the fire station, where Stephanie retrieved some personal items out of Holly's Pontiac, which was still parked there.

It was hard for me to look at our fire station, a place I'd loved for so many years, a home away from home, a place I was destined never to inhabit again.

Just as we were about to leave, a black Suburban pulled around the corner, Scott Donovan at the wheel.

"I've been looking for you two," Donovan said. He had a strange look on his face, as if surprised to see us.

"Here we are," Stephanie said.

"Do you have some news for us?" I asked.

"You guys . . . I just want to meet with you in the morning. Before the news conference. That all right?"

Stephanie turned to me. "Sure."

"I just . . . I've been looking all over for you. Where were you?"

"Out and about," Stephanie said cheerily.

"We ran into Hillburn and Dobson. From JCP? They're still in town. Doesn't that seem odd to you?"

Donovan rubbed his chin. "It seems very odd. Where'd you see them?"

"The Sunset Motel."

Donovan gave us a look. "I'll go check it out. And don't look so glum. We're going to lick this."

"I'm not glum," I said.

"No? Is there a reason you have a room reserved over at Alpine Estates?"

It took a moment to realize what he was talking about. He seemed disappointed when Stephanie explained the room was my father's.

After we left, I said, "He look like he's been drinking?"

"Maybe."

"That newspaper guy in Tennessee hinted that he was quite a drinker."

The street lamps on Ballarat complemented a gigantic moon dangling over the south corner of Mount Si.

My girls would be wondering where I was. Once again I'd fobbed them off onto a baby-sitter and was ashamed of myself. Tomorrow was little enough to give, but tomorrow was theirs. We were getting nowhere with this quest, and I wasn't going to waste my remaining hours struggling like a wild horse in quicksand. It seemed the more I fought, the more hopeless things looked. Tomorrow I would hold the news conference, gather my family around, and wait for somebody to throw a rope over my neck and save me.

If somebody produced information that altered my lot, so be it. If not, my destiny was in the hands of God.

If there was a God.

Spooky.

I didn't believe in him, so why was I invoking his will now?

I began deep breathing again.

In my mind there was no longer much hope that I would be cured. It was a weak trail, and we were moving slowly. The fact that I had someone to share this with meant a lot to me. It meant even more that it was a woman who'd once reviled me.

We were on Ballarat, just past the library, when Stephanie pulled to the curb. My ears were ringing, and for a moment I couldn't figure out why she'd stopped. Then a fire engine raced past, siren squalling, red lights whirling. The ground seemed to shake as it passed. A moment later Jeb Parker raced past in his Volkswagen. I wasn't wearing my pager, so I had no idea what they were responding to. It must have been a fire call rather than an aid response, because moments later another volunteer sped past at seventy miles an hour. The engine could have handled an aid call by itself.

The moonlit road out of town took us north, then veered east directly toward the base of Mount Si, then north again paralleling Si toward my house, three legs, each about half a mile long. My place was in a small enclave of treed properties next to the Middle Fork of the Snoqualmie River.

Across the fields a plume of fast-rising black smoke rolled upward. The smoke, highlighted as it was by the moon's light, looked like an act of war.

"Step on it," I said, irritated that I wasn't driving.

Stephanie followed my gaze and accelerated.

"A grass fire?" There had been two nuisance grass fires outside of town that afternoon.

"More likely a structure fire. Or a vehicle. Smoke from vegetation is light-colored." Even as I spoke, I caught another glimpse of the column. It was close to my property, too close, and hot, with orange streaks high up in the black smoke.

"Hope it's not one of your neighbors," she said.

"Me, too."

During the minute or two it took to complete the trip, my mind went blank, which was odd, because when I was riding the engine my mind never went blank. I would have been mentally running over the list of things to do when we arrived.

From 428th S.E. you took a dirt and gravel spur road, passing Helen Neumann's place, to reach mine. A little farther along was Fred Bagwell's homestead, Fred a confirmed bachelor, an acknowledged alcoholic, and a lifelong misanthrope. The odds were about a hundred to one the fire was Fred's place.

As we approached the long gravel drive that led to my house, I saw the flashing red lights of the engine in front of us, the dust from Jeb Parker's Volkswagen running along the center of the dirt road like a huge gray hedgehog, volumes of thick black smoke rising up off a structure partially hidden behind the trees.

"Oh, God," I said, the words as dry as day-old toast.

"What?"

"It's my house."

"How could that be?"

"I don't know. Drive in. I need to make sure my girls got out."

47. INTO THE INFERNO

The confusion at the site could have been worse, but not by much. The engine clogged the one-lane driveway, Parker's vehicle having swung around them. The engine had stopped too far from the fire. There were two trees next to my house and they were both alight now. The roof was burning, smoke pouring through the broken-out living-room window. Caution was one thing, but they were too far back.

I didn't like the speed of the smoke. Or the color. Or the fact that some of the windows were already broken out. I didn't like anything about it.

I motioned for Stephanie to drive around the engine and into the field, which she did, heading for a spot between Helen Neumann's house and mine. It was good to have a partner who didn't panic, a woman used to working in emergency rooms.

Before the car stopped rolling, I opened the door and leaped out, running past Jeb Parker as he donned his bunking clothes next to his Volkswagen. Anonymous volunteer firefighters in bulky yellow turnouts were climbing down off the engine. Helen Neumann stood in front of my burning house, a rumpled sweater thrown over her shoulders, looking small and frail, her thin gray hair in disarray, a woman in her forties who seemed seventy.

What I did *not* see was either of my daughters.

Or Morgan Neumann.

Several hours earlier they'd gone to the movie in my truck, but the truck was back now, parked by the side of the house.

I touched Helen Neumann's shoulder. "The girls, Helen? Where are they?"

She gave me a blank look and turned back to the fire building. An hour ago I thought going brain-dead was the worst thing that could happen.

I'd been wrong.

This was the worst thing that could happen.

Watching your family burn in the fires of hell.

Though we were sixty feet from my house, the heat on our faces was enough to make Helen wince. From the blackness and speed of the smoke

I knew the interior was boiling over. As if to confirm my judgment, another living-room window cracked open, and sections of plate glass fell into the flower bed.

Things were moving in slow motion. I felt as if I were trapped in a dream. Maybe it *was* a dream. Maybe I was still back at the Sunset Motel and this was a nightmare.

I grabbed Helen's shoulders. "Helen? Where are the girls? Where is your daughter?"

"She's . . . why . . . she's baby-sitting for Mr. Swope." Helen's mind was always slow, but tonight it had stripped all its gears.

"Are they at your house? Have you seen them?"

Two couples from the other end of our small enclave stepped in front of me, the women in nightgowns and tennis shoes, the men with their shirts hurriedly thrown on, one of them barefoot. Nobody had seen my daughters. A car full of teenage girls was parked to one side, having driven up the lane to gawp at a stranger's tragedy. People needed to see others in pain. It was like a circus act.

I'd wasted half a minute unmasking the obvious.

If my daughters had come out, they would have been next to Helen Neumann. They hadn't and they weren't.

I ran to the Lexus, popped the trunk, kicked off my shoes, pulled my bunking boots-trousers ensemble out, and stepped into the boots, pulling the suspenders up over my jeans and T-shirt. I slipped into the bunking coat and picked up the face piece and helmet as I walked. The helmet slipped out of my fingers. I'd never been this nervous at a fire. Not even my first.

I'd wasted too much precious time.

I ran to the engine, where two firefighters from the Snoqualmie department were dragging hose toward my house. I pulled a spare backpack out of the compartment and onto my shoulders, fastening the waist buckle and shoulder straps as I walked. I tugged my facepiece over my head, put on my helmet, and twisted the main air valve behind me on the bottle, all of this done on automatic pilot.

Two unmasked firefighters from Snoqualmie were in my front yard directing a hose stream through the broken-out front window. They were thirty feet away, but still, the heat was forcing them to duck low. It was pretty obvious everything in my front room was cooked.

Unless they were in one of the back bedrooms, my girls were gone.

"There are kids inside!" I yelled at the firefighters. "Get in there! Move up on it!" One of them glanced over his shoulder at me, but neither budged. I don't think they heard me.

Masked up, flashlight in my gloved hands, I jogged toward the front door. Before I could go in, one of the firefighters on the hose line, a large, pale man with a black mustache and crooked teeth, grabbed my shoulder and held me back. "You'll never make it. Let us knock it down from out here first."

Their line was directed horizontally into the rolling ball of orange but was having almost no effect. Over two hundred gallons a minute making no dent in the heat. Failing to darken the flames.

I stepped close to the house, knelt, opened the front door—it should have been locked—and felt a searing blast of heat on my face.

I crawled into the house on my belly. "Allyson!" I called. "Britney! Where are you guys?"

In my mind they were dead, having hidden under their beds or in a closet, long since having given up on their father. I could think of nothing worse than dying by fire, especially when you thought your hero firefighter father was going to save you.

And didn't.

It became apparent quickly that I wasn't going to bring them out through the front. The heat was so bad my wrists were burning where the gauntlets on my gloves were pushed up into my sleeves, the back of my neck feeling like the worst sunburn of my life. I tried to get lower, slithering along on my stomach for another few feet. I was breathing cool air from the compressed air cylinder on my back, but the room was as hot as anything I'd ever endured.

I backed out just as the hose stream hit the ceiling above me and a great billow of steam descended all around, burning my cheeks around the edges of my face mask, scalding me so badly I wanted to scream.

Just before I cleared the front door, something opaque came down across my vision and slapped my facepiece so I could see only out of my left eye. I wondered for half a second if my face was burned. There was so much adrenaline pumping through my veins, I couldn't tell.

When I got outside, the firefighters in the yard cut down the volume of water from their nozzle and arched a stream of water onto me. We could hear the sizzle of evaporating water on the plastic Cairns helmet, on the metal parts that held the shield up. Steam rose off my coat and backpack.

As they cooled me off, one of the tires on my pickup truck exploded with a dull pop. A male bystander scampered over to it, opened the door with a T-shirt wrapped around his hand, released the brake, and tried to push the vehicle to safety. Two other men ran over to help but found the sheet metal too hot to touch.

When I swiped at the object across my facepiece, I realized a piece of my helmet had melted onto my air mask. Only by taking my helmet off could I peel the melted plastic off.

"God, you're burning up, man," said the nozzleman. "I didn't think you were going to come out."

"Don't shoot it into the rear," I said. "I'm going in the back door."

"It's not going to work. It's—"

Maybe they would be back there somewhere—my girls—hiding in one of the back rooms.

As I reached the still-intact window of the family room in back of the house, I could see flame rolling across the kitchen ceiling toward the back door.

I opened the door and was met by a dull roar of orange bursting out over my head. Stupid bastards. The firefighters in front were using their hose stream to push the flame and heat at me from the front. They hadn't listened to me.

I dropped to my knees and crawled inside, flashlight in one hand.

Another burst from the hose line in front of the house pushed a gigantic ball of yellow-orange across the ceiling toward me. I flattened out on the floor for a moment, feeling the heat on the back of my neck and through my heavy protective Nomex clothing.

Knowing the pain had just begun, I inched forward into the inferno.

48. RICE, SOUP, AND KIDS IN THE CUPBOARDS

I moved along one wall sweeping my arms under furniture, under the futon, behind the chairs, anywhere a child might hide or an adult might fall. On hands and knees I made a quick and thorough circuit of the family room keeping my nose on the floor. Walking upright, I would have lasted all of ten seconds. Our bunkers were fire-resistant, not fireproof, and even on the floor I could feel the incredible heat.

As I crawled, I felt blisters forming at my wrists and on my ears, where the heat knifed under my bunkers. House fires didn't often get this hot, especially with the building's windows broken out and water being applied.

In the kitchen, I reached under the table and heard the familiar sound of chair legs scraping across linoleum when I bumped them, the sound I heard every night at dinner.

Remembering my daughters sometimes liked to conceal themselves under the sink, I opened every one of the lower cupboards. Britney often leaped out at me when I swung the cupboard door open to get cat food for Eustace.

Unnerving her dad was about the most fun Britney ever had.

I would give anything to have her leap out at me now.

She didn't.

As I passed the refrigerator, I heard the clatter of plastic and knew I'd upset the cat's bowl. It was all so normal. Under the scrim of smoke and heat, everything was the same as always.

Visibility was marginal in back of the house, growing worse as I moved forward under volumes of thick black smoke. The farther I moved toward the front of the house, the hotter the air grew. The flashlight in my hand didn't help much. I couldn't see it. Water streams pouring through the front windows produced hundreds of gallons of steam, which descended to the floor and burned me. From time to time I swiped the steam off my facepiece with my glove.

In my panic my inclination was to speed straight through to the bedrooms, but years of training took over and I searched each room as I came to it in an orderly manner. Hit-and-miss searches had been the precipitator of more than one civilian death. Especially with children, who tended to hide; it was too easy to scoot right past them and not know it.

My prayer was that my daughters were in their bedroom, door closed, rags stuffed around the cracks. That they were safe and waiting for me. Wouldn't that be any father's prayer?

Approached from the front, our house had an open floor scheme, the only sealable rooms the bathroom to the left of the front entrance and the two bedrooms, also to the left of the front entrance. If you went right, you came into the living room, where I was now, then the kitchen and the family room, both of which I'd just now searched.

Our living room was burning like the inside of a woodstove.

The interior walls had half-inch shiplap on them, knotty pine nailed over older shiplap also half an inch thick, both sides identical, two inches of wood to drill through for our TV cable. The guy who built this place must have been pilfering from a lumberyard at night. To make matters worse, one of the previous owners had varnished all the knotty pine with an oil-base sealant.

Cozy-looking house.

Total firetrap.

The girls and I might as well have been living inside a can of gasoline.

The water stream hadn't knocked down much, if any, of the heat. The others should have been inside fighting the fire. Aggressive, up-close attacks worked best in a residential fire. Too many of our volunteers liked to keep their distance, and God knows we didn't have many regulars left. Click and Clack, but I hadn't seen them outside.

An interior attack was the game plan you wanted when searching for victims. But that's not what they were doing.

Moving along the left wall, I reached out to my right, expecting to find one of my girls, inert, helpless, but all I found were familiar objects, the antique cedar chest Lorie had bought at an estate sale and refurbished, where we kept our old calendars, tax records, and school papers. The chest was charred on top but intact, feeding my hope that my daughters were still alive. I opened the lid and felt around inside.

"Britney? Allyson?" Nothing.

The fire in the attic space above me produced a dull roar. I'd never been below an attic that was going quite like this. The roof would cave in soon.

Again, the sound of the hose stream drowned out all other noise, alternately pounding outside on the roof, then slapping the walls through the windows. When the water hit it, the fire on the shiplap walls would go out momentarily, then spring back, growing steadily hotter all the while.

Through the open window I heard men shouting, the airy burp-burp of alarm bells on self-contained breathing apparatuses as firefighters activated them. People were getting ready to come inside and help.

Then, for whatever reason, whether they'd run their water tank dry or simply reversed strategies, the hose stream shut down. Immediately the atmosphere around me became hotter.

Using my gloved hands, I felt underneath the low coffee table in the living room just opposite the gas stove, touched something, a piece of clothing, a stray shoe. When I moved the table, I realized the shoe was attached to a foot.

Pulling the table out of the way and feeling with my gloved hand, I knew I'd found someone. Not either of my daughters. Too big.

Morgan!

She wasn't moving, nor did she react when I touched her.

I felt around on either side to see whether my girls were nearby but came upon bare hardwood floors and nothing else. Morgan must have been sleeping on the sofa when the fire started, must have slept through the initial phase. Why the smoke detectors didn't arouse her was another matter. They weren't beeping now, but they must have been before they melted.

Too often civilians woke up, smelled smoke, jumped up out of bed, and dropped dead right there because they'd inhaled a lungful of air so hot it cauterized their lungs. Had Morgan rolled off the sofa and kept her face near the floor, she would have been out of the worst of the heat and able to suck up enough oxygen at floor level to get out of the building. Even during the late stages of a fire, there was almost always an inch or two of breathable air on the floor.

For a split second I contemplated leaving Morgan where she lay, going after my girls. But I couldn't do that.

I could only hope the men outside with the hose lines would get their act together and tap the fire, that my daughters were in their room with the door closed.

At night, closed bedroom doors were standard policy in our house, as they were in most firefighters' homes, yet a bedroom door didn't hold off a fire for long. Theirs was a standard hollow-core interior door rated for twenty minutes in a fire. Worse yet, it may have been open or partially open, because when my daughters were upset they wanted their door open, Allyson as a rule more claustrophobic than Britney. Morgan would have given in to their request in a heartbeat.

Tortured by doubts, I dragged Morgan's body back through the house, through the kitchen, awkwardly around the corner into the family room, then out through the utility room door to the back porch. I might have taken her through the front, a shorter trip, but I chose the route I knew to be safe.

Morgan was a delicate creature. So precise in everything she did. Always with that awkward grace of a yearling. So thin. Pulling her along the floor was like pulling a stick doll.

When I reached the back porch, nobody was there to assist me. It was still too early in the fire for the legions of volunteers who generally helped out in the yard.

I got to my feet, picked her up, carried her away from the structure and out onto the cool grass of our backyard. I was still looking around for somebody to take over when I realized she wasn't breathing.

She had no hair. No recognizable face. Her clothes either had burned off or were melted beyond recognition. Char everywhere on her body. No identifying marks, just a stiff, doll-like figure, arms clenched in front of herself in the classic pugilistic burn victim pose. The only color anywhere was on patches of clothing that had been against the floor. This was an obscene and grotesque caricature of the sweet young woman Morgan had been. The body on the ground in front of me looked more like a Hiroshima bomb victim than my baby-sitter.

When I returned to the back porch, I found my pathway blocked by one of the firefighters I'd seen in front, Christi, who stood deliberately in the doorway, black smoke pouring out over his head.

"Good work," he said. "You got her out."

"Move!" I was still "on air," breathing through my face mask, clean compressed air instead of hot, filthy smoke.

"Don't chance it again, Lieut. Anyone else in there is dead."

"My daughters are in there."

It wasn't clear whether he heard me or not. "Nobody could do it now. We didn't think you were going to make it out the first time."

"Move."

"I can't let you do that. You'll be burned."

"I'm already burned, you stupid bastard."

I tried to push past him, wrestled with him for a moment, and then found myself on the ground next to the porch. Whether he'd pushed me or I'd tripped, I had no idea. As I climbed to my feet, he ducked low and ran from the doorway, racing away in front of a surge of flame that rolled out after him like the boulder at the beginning of *Raiders of the Lost Ark*. The family room had become a furnace. Nobody would make it in there now, not even with a hose line.

I sprinted around the other side of the house to my daughters' room. The window was intact, but the inside shades were burned off, the space beyond that filled with boiling flame. Jesus Christ, I thought. The fire's consumed my babies.

I'd been a damn fool to waste time searching for them in the main rooms of the house.

The canniest tactic would have been for fire teams to have taken their line through this window; had they done it soon enough, they might have been able to protect my kids from the flames, which, as far as I could tell, had been largely in the main section of the house. We might have gotten my kids out this window.

Had I come to this window first thing, I might have rescued them.

The front yard was filled with neighbors, police, volunteers, a news photographer I recognized from the local paper, even old Fred Bagwell, standing off to one side as if we were all contagious. Another engine was wedged into the drive behind the Lexus, a tanker farther back in the trees. Yellow helmets everywhere.

A hose team worked bravely on my front porch, even though everybody involved could see flame leaping out over their heads like huge farts from Satan himself. A moment later the interior gave off a low, rumbling sound and a torrent of smoke and flame belched out the doorway, knocking both firefighters off the porch and into the yard. Another hose team cooled them off with a water stream.

As I stared in disbelief, part of the ceiling in the living room dropped, splashing a million hot embers into the interior. My experience and survival instincts told me anything I did now would only get me killed.

My heart told me to go in.

Crouching low, working along the floor, I began to fight my way through the wall of flame. Even as I tried to move forward, something or somebody grabbed my boots and began dragging me backward. I was sliding out of the house on my face, inexorably moving away from the flames as if on a conveyor belt. I was being yarded out by a team of firefighters.

I struggled, but they knelt on my arms and chest and legs, pinning me to the earth.

"You bastards!" I yelled through my facepiece. "You're killing my girls!"

I twisted and kicked and fought, but there was half a ton on me. My alarm bell had been ringing for some time now, but nobody paid any attention to it. The bell signaled I had five minutes of air remaining. Maybe. Moments later the ringing stopped, along with my air supply.

I began choking on the rubber facepiece, unable to get my arms free to disengage the mask. I was suffocating. Like a madman, I jerked and thrashed, trying to reach the facepiece so I could release the rubber straps holding it against my face, fighting to get the smothering rubber seal away from my nose and mouth. They wouldn't let me up. I'd never been in a worse panic. Thrashing my head from side to side, I knocked the facepiece against my tormentors, hoping to dislodge it, anything to keep from suffocating.

There were six men on me now, nailing me down the way you'd nail down a tent.

The facepiece was fogged over from the inside. I couldn't see them and they couldn't see me.

And then my girls and I were at the playground where I was explaining the syndrome had been a mistake, that I wasn't going to leave, that everything would be as it always had been. I was no longer on the fire ground. In fact, I probably wasn't even on earth. Sure. This had to be heaven. I was dead and united with my daughters.

Who were dead, too.

And we were all weeping with joy. We were dead, but we were joyous. Who would have thought?

Of all the damnable luck.

49. THINK AGAIN

"They came close to killing you."

I took a deep breath, my first conscious inhalation in some time. A nasal cannula was dangling off my ears, the prongs in my nose. I felt the compressed air bottle I was wearing, as it dug into my spine. I rolled over and managed to get an elbow under me. "I wish they had."

Tears trickling down her face, Stephanie knelt beside me. "Are they in there? Are your girls inside?"

Viewing the conflagration the house had become, I refused to answer. My home was a mountain of flame now. Nothing could have survived. Not the sharpest firefighter in full bunkers on air. Not a dog. Not a flea on the ass end of a dog. Certainly not a seven-year-old and a nine-year-old in cotton shorty pajamas.

The house was a fireball. The roof had caved in over the living-room area. As we watched, another portion of the roof collapsed, sending up a shower of sparks thirty feet into the night. Angels going to heaven, I thought. Little angels going to wait for me.

There were now five hose lines shooting water into the building.

But it was too late.

My house was destroyed. Morgan was dead. Everything I owned or ever would own had been obliterated. Everyone I loved was gone.

"Allyson," I said weakly. "Britney." Once again, I tried to get to my feet. Whether I'd been injured in the melee, was half-dead from oxygen starvation, or had simply used up my reserves I had no way of knowing. But I couldn't get up. I wondered if I'd been without oxygen long enough to incur brain damage. As if it made any difference.

In two days I'd be the all-American poster boy for brain damage.

"They *might* have gotten out," Stephanie said. "Don't you think there's a chance?"

"Same chance as a Popsicle in hell."

There is no way to estimate how long I wept. I cried a river, while the radiant heat from the fire warmed the left side of my body and dried my tears. Stephanie whispered to me, but I didn't hear what she said. There was no consolation. Nobody could save me now.

I'd made my own hell.

I'd traded sex in a motel room for my daughters.

I'd swapped two innocent lives for fifteen minutes of lust.

I was still weeping when one of the volunteers came running around to the front of the house, exclaiming loudly, "I made a rescue. I got one!"

He was behind a cluster of people, moving quickly, a bundle in his arms.

I got up and began moving.

A moment later he was behind a pair of burly volunteers, and then I couldn't see what he had in his arms because the stack of flame behind him was so bright I was blinded by it. The man who'd made the rescue was Gil Cuthousen, one of our volunteers. I was pretty sure Gil didn't know I lived here. I also found it odd he'd made a rescue I couldn't. He'd never been much of a firefighter. When I saw what he had cradled in his arms, I actually felt my heart beating behind my Adam's apple.

Gil was laughing.

He held Eustace, our cat.

Dead and stiff. The hair on his back singed.

Black humor often took bizarre turns at a fire, and in the past I may have been guilty of similar insensitivities myself, though right now I hoped not.

Stepping close, I doubled up my gloved fist and coldcocked him. Cuthousen fell to the ground, as stiff as the dead cat, which landed on top of him.

This time nobody grabbed me.

In front of us one of my outer bedroom walls collapsed inward with a fiery roar. We all turned to the house, transfixed. Five minutes later, water streams began getting a toehold on the flames. Ten minutes after that, the rubble that had been my home was pretty much extinguished.

North Bend Fire and Rescue had saved another foundation.

I knew we wouldn't find my daughters without digging through a significant amount of debris, just as I knew I wasn't going to be able to stand to look at my girls when we finally found them—still, I could think of no way to stop myself. In fact, I would have a shovel in my hands when we went into the back bedroom. I felt as if I'd been repeatedly clubbed senseless and was about to have it happen again.

Analyzing the sequence of the fire, I knew they had probably been dead before we arrived, probably before we even left the motel. Death by smoke inhalation frequently occurred in the early stages of a fire.

I stumbled around the periphery of the house in a daze. Anything to keep my mind off my daughters.

Somewhere under all that char and rubble, investigators would find two tiny bodies, most likely huddled together. Perhaps hidden under the lower bunk. Or below the window.

I struggled to avoid thinking about their final moments, but the visions came crashing in anyway.

My only consolation, feeble as it might be, was that my failed efforts at rescue had not been the cause of their deaths, that they'd probably died before I entered the structure. Jesus, I was such a fool! Had I not been screwing a woman I'd just met, I would have been home with them.

If I hadn't been such a slut, my daughters would be alive.

I was a crappy father, a whore, an inept firefighter. In short, I was an asshole, and this syndrome was exactly what I deserved.

I walked to the backyard, past Morgan's corpse, past a pair of solemn volunteers standing guard over her body, and when I got far enough out in the field where nobody would hear me, I wailed in the moonlight.

I knew now what I had to do.

It was early Friday morning.

Sometime before Sunday, before I lost my mind, I would kill myself.

50. THE KIND OF GUY I AM

I was sitting on a stump sixty feet from where my front door had once stood.

It was after midnight, and the trees and field beside my house had turned surreal with the blinking red lights and the ghostlike waves of smoke rolling over everything, my terrors complemented by the rumble of diesel motors, the sleep of the dead punctuated by the staccato bark of radio traffic. By now everyone on scene knew my daughters were inside. Clusters of firefighters, friends and coworkers alike, avoided me while they awaited directions from the fire investigation team on where and when to begin digging. Normally, I suppose, people would have come around to offer their condolences, but I'd been rude to the first couple of people who'd tried it, so the word had gone out: Leave him alone. He's not feeling too good. Wisps of toxic smoke snaked off the remains of the house. Digging them out was going to be a long, arduous task. A gruesome one. Everybody was thinking about it.

I'd been told Helen Neumann was being comforted by neighbors, but I knew that to be a lie. There would be no comfort for Helen, just as there was none for me. Besides, Helen didn't know any of our neighbors.

Everything else on the fire ground took a backseat to the investigation. Even if my girls had not been buried inside, the half-collapsed structure would have been dismantled piece-by-piece in an effort to understand how the fire had started and why Morgan failed to escape.

Until fire investigators deemed otherwise, my home would be a crime scene.

Just my luck—the county fire investigators who caught this case turned out to be Shad and Stevenson. They asked me a series of questions before going into the ruins. How many in the house? Where did I think their bodies might be? Where was I when the fire broke out? Who was with me? Why had I slugged Gil Cuthousen? Where had I found Morgan's body? Why had I moved it? Did I have any enemies? Had anybody ever threatened me?

Then they went in, Shad and Stevenson, with four firefighters to do the grunt work, garbage cans and shovels in hand, picking through the living room, working the area where I'd found Morgan. Forty minutes later Shad and Stevenson came out, having cleared the floor where I'd found the body, taken photos, and removed large amounts of debris one shovelful at a time. They went around the periphery of the smoking ruins with Captain Pulaski from the Snoqualmie department and stopped in the backyard to examine Morgan's corpse. They were back there for a while.

From time to time others approached and asked questions. Could they get me something to drink? Was I warm enough? Was there anyone I wanted called? I shrugged off the questions without answering. When asked whether I had a place to stay, I mumbled, "The Sunset Motel."

I was a fool for leaving my daughters. But then, I'd been a fool all my life. I'd been a fool to invest so much faith in the teachings at Six Points. I'd been a fool to join the army. A fool to marry Lorie Tindale. I'd been a fool to screw around with all those women, and I'd been a fool to sleep with Stephanie. I'd been a fool to let my daughters out of my sight.

When anybody blocked my view of the smoldering house, I stared through them. I'd been helped off with my bunking clothes, my Nomex hood, my heavy coat, the thick trousers and suspenders along with the knee-high rubber boots. The jeans and T-shirt I'd worn underneath were still wet with sweat. Somebody found my civilian shoes and put them on me—Stephanie, I guess.

It was cool now, that middle-of-the-summer, nighttime chill that descends on towns near the mountains, yet I remained sopping, sweat trickling along my brow and off the tip of my nose.

In the next few days there would be four funerals. Allyson. Britney. Morgan. Me. My friends at the firehouse could arrange ours. God knows Wes and Lillian weren't up to the task. Besides the alcohol problem, Wes had already suffered a myocardial infarction and Lillian a minor stroke, precipitated, she said, by a visit from an FBI agent with a bad hairpiece, who'd talked endlessly about her daughter's check-kiting scams in the Midwest and in Florida.

The fire department put up a portable generator in the front yard, a light string plugged into it, so that the black guts of what remained of my house were lit up like a picture shoot, while the investigators continued to poke around the periphery. They still hadn't gone into the bedroom area.

Both my kids had been emotionally traumatized today, and in hindsight I could see I typically had bungled it. Six months earlier I'd found

Britney playing with matches, as it happened, not long after one of her mother's erratic phone calls. We'd talked about it, and I'd made it clear how dangerous playing with matches was.

What if she had started this, lit a book of matches in the closet, lost control of the flames, closed the door, and tried to pretend it didn't happen? She wouldn't be the first kid to play out that scenario.

Or maybe Morgan had been smoking on the sofa and fell asleep, dropped a lighted cigarette into the cushions. I'd seen Morgan sneak cigarettes behind her mother's house.

And then it struck me.

My ex was the one with the hidden agendas. She'd been gone three years, but what if she'd chosen tonight to return? Was it possible Lorie held enough of a grudge against me to do this? Was it possible she'd sneaked inside using her key, which still fit the locks, and torched the place? I'd spoken to her on the phone as recently as Easter and believed we were on amicable terms, but I thought we were on amicable terms when she scrammed out of town with the original Mayor Haston.

One of my greatest weaknesses was not knowing when people were pissed at me.

Was Lorie angry enough to have done this?

Generally, an amateur torch uses an accelerant, most often gasoline. I'd never seen that much heat in a house that hadn't been torched. Two winters ago we'd responded to a stubborn house fire that turned out to be fed by five gallons of high-octane gasoline splashed around liberally by the ex-husband of the resident. The resident survived; her canaries, pet llama, and house didn't. Neither did the ex, who lit a match while he was still enveloped in the fumes. Blown into the backyard by the initial blast, he died in the hospital four days later. Burned all to hell. Poetic justice, we thought.

Two shadows stopped in front of me. "Need to ask a few questions," said Shad, the shorter of the shadows, the one I didn't like. What am I saying? I had no use for either of them.

Without averting my gaze from the house, I said, "You find any trace of my daughters?"

"We were just working in the living-room area. But we came up with a few questions."

"I answered your questions."

"We got more."

"When are you going to start digging for my daughters?"

"Where were you tonight?"

"I already told you. When are you going to dig?"

"Listen," Shad said. "We're going to cool the place off and go in carefully. We don't want to disrupt the evidence. This was an arson."

"How do you know?"

"Hey, numb nuts. We're asking the questions." I looked up. It was Stevenson, the tall man with the pale face and the Cupid's bow mouth. The grin made me want to hit him.

"How do you know it was arson?"

Sensing that there was some bad history between us, a third man, a homicide detective, walked over and interceded. His name, I later learned, was Ron Holgate. He was of medium height, had short, curly brown hair and a rotund torso. He wore a suit and tie. He said, "The neighbors think they saw it start. They heard a vehicle leaving out of here at a high rate of speed. When they went outside to investigate, all they could see was a dust cloud. At that point there was only a small orange glow in the front window. They went inside and called nine-one-one. By the time they came out again, maybe a minute later, there were flames shooting out both sides of the house. You know as well as I do a house fire doesn't progress like that unless an accelerant was involved."

Stevenson said, "You keep a five-gallon can of gasoline around?"

"No."

"We found one in your living room."

"You're shitting me."

"Not far from the clean spot on the floor where the body was. Burned everything around but the outline of that girl. Too bad. The question is, where were you when this went up?"

"He was with me," Stephanie said. "We got home late. He had a babysitter staying with the girls."

"We saw your baby-sitter," Holgate said. "You have any enemies?"

"Just these two." I looked at Shad and Stevenson.

"What were your daughters up to tonight?" Holgate asked.

"Went to a movie with the baby-sitter."

"In her car?"

"My truck." We all looked over at my truck, which had caught fire from the radiant heat and was now a burned-out hulk.

"You've got two days left, and your kids are with a baby-sitter?" Stevenson asked.

"That's the kind of guy I am."

"That girl in there have any reason to be angry with you?"

"What girl?"

"The dead girl. Neumann. Morgan Neumann. Your baby-sitter."

"Of course not."

"No reason? You sure? People say she had a crush on you. You weren't fooling around with her, were you?"

"Shut your mouth."

"Just a possibility that had to be raised."

Holgate stepped forward, the voice of reason. "Why don't we tell him how we think it went down?"

Shad and Stevenson looked at each other. Shad said, "You got a natural gas stove in there in your fireplace? You keep the pilot light on in the summer, or do you shut the whole thing down?"

"On. Every once in the while the girls get cold in the morning."

Holgate said, "So the baby-sitter takes a five-gallon can into the house, douses gasoline all over everything, and before she can exit, the fumes reach your pilot light and . . . va-voom!"

"It didn't happen that way," I said.

"Why not?"

"Because Morgan wouldn't do that."

"Did she or did she not have a crush on you?"

"I don't see how that makes—"

"It gives us a motive, that's what it gives us."

"She didn't do it."

"So tell us who did."

"I don't know who."

The three of them walked out of earshot and conversed. After a few moments, a King County Police deputy I'd seen them speaking to half an hour earlier showed up and joined their powwow.

Periodically, Stephanie mopped me with a towel. "Oh, God, Jim," she said. "I'm so sorry."

"I just don't believe Morgan would do anything like that. It's crazy."

"I only met her those few brief times, but I don't think she would, either."

I thought about the way Morgan had been looking daggers at

Stephanie, thought about how hormones raced around inside a teenager, and then I wondered if I hadn't underestimated her feelings for me. Was it possible Morgan had been so upset about Stephanie she'd decided to kill herself, and take my girls with her? Was that possible?

"It's my fault," I said. "This whole thing is my fault."

"Don't say that. You don't know that."

"And yours."

"How do you—?"

"This was never about saving me. You wanted to alleviate all that guilt you felt for not being part of your sister's life. This has been about you from the beginning."

"That's not true. That's—"

"Taking me to bed was about you, too. If we slept together, you could off-load some of that guilt you felt for all the crap you threw at me when we first met. I veg out and you're guilt-free."

"That's an awful thing to say."

"You fucked me in every way possible."

"I'm sorry if you see it that way, but I was—"

"Keeping me from saving the lives of the only two people on this planet I ever loved."

You had to give her points for sticking. I would have flown out of there like a broken promise. But then you already know I'm a stone-cold bastard. More and more I was realizing it, too.

A moment later we heard a disturbance in the dark field behind us, a volunteer from Snoqualmie's department trying to turn back someone who was traipsing toward us across the grass from the paved road several hundred yards away. The interloper, a small, slender figure, went around the volunteer and proceeded directly toward our gathering.

It took me several moments to recognize her.

It was Morgan. My baby-sitter.

Morgan was alive.

Some yahoo blinded her with a spotlight from his pickup truck, causing her to stumble the last thirty yards. For the first time in almost an hour, I got up off the stump. When she got close, I hugged her. Out of gratitude, I guess, gratitude that she was alive. She hugged back with an uncertainty that was clear to all of us.

"Why weren't you with my girls?"

"I . . . had to . . . What happened?" She was as confused as a butterfly at a cockfight. The fire investigators and the homicide detective approached, and all five of us began shooting questions at her simultaneously.

"Morgan," Stephanie said, taking charge of the interrogation by virtue of her gender. "We thought you were in the house."

"I was." Morgan stepped out of my embrace and stared at the hulk that had been my home, her lower lip quivering. I knew what she was thinking, because I'd been thinking the same thing. She was thinking she'd just made the worst mistake of her life.

"Why did you leave my girls? And who did you leave them with?"

Turning to me in tears, Morgan said, "I didn't leave them with any-body. We thought you were going to be home pretty soon. I didn't mean to do anything—"

"If this is your baby-sitter, who the hell is in the backyard?" Steven-son asked.

"You have anything to do with setting this fire, young lady?" Shad glared at her.

"No. Of course not."

Obviously Morgan had left my children with a friend while she'd gone off to be with a boyfriend or to a beer party or some such teenage nonsense. My girls were dead. I'd dragged the substitute baby-sitter out of the fire.

"Who was baby-sitting?" I asked.

"I was."

"Who else?"

"Nobody else."

"You didn't leave my girls alone. I know that. We found her."

"You found who? I didn't leave them. I would never leave them."

"Then where were you?"

"I was—"

"Daddy! Daddy!"

I turned around so fast I almost twisted an ankle.

Like broken-field runners, the two of them raced through the line of vehicles in the long driveway leading to our house, Britney barely able to keep pace with Allyson, Allyson sprinting in and out of the various groups of firefighters, who were drinking Gatorade and chucking down cookies. I wasn't sure if I was hallucinating or not.

When I started to run toward them, Shad must have thought I was trying to flee the scene, because he leaped in front of me waving both arms. I knocked him down so fast I didn't get to see the look of surprise on his face. Later, they told me he went down like a mousetrapped stop sign under a truck.

And then they were in my arms, Allyson and Britney.

And I was swinging them around and hugging them, and we were all alive again. The three of us.

We were a family again. I couldn't believe it.

51. RECONSTITUTED PIZZA AND COKE

"Where were you?" I asked, setting them on the ground and kneeling between them, holding them. I was afraid this was another hallucination. During the last hour, had I renounced my atheism and prayed to God, I would have given anything in exchange for my daughters. Instead, here they were free of charge. Maybe there was a God.

"Daddy, what happened to our house?" Allyson couldn't tear her eyes away from the smoldering ruins.

"I don't know."

Wide-eyed and mute, Britney refused to let go of me. I held her close, Allyson alone in front, her eyes vaguely accusatory, as if I or someone else on scene were responsible.

"It's all burned up," Allyson said.

"Yes, it is. And you know what? I thought you were in there."

"Daddy, that's silly. We were at a movie."

"Why did it burn up?" Britney asked.

"You were at a movie until . . ." I glanced at my watch. "Almost one in the morning?"

"We had a flat on the freeway," Morgan said. "We had to wait for the patrol. We waited, like, forever."

"The *State* Patrol," corrected Britney. I gave her another little squeeze. She squeezed back, as if I were the one in need of comfort. What a paradise I'd fallen into, embracing her skinny little body, feeling her bony ribs expand and contract as she breathed. Life was such a goddamn miracle. I gazed into Allyson's eyes. Her mother had been able to read my feelings, too, often before I knew them myself. Allyson stepped forward and kissed my sooty cheek.

"You must have been worried." With those words of comfort from a nine-year-old, life began to flow back into me.

"Yeah, and they never came," said Britney. "The State Patrol never came."

"Why didn't you guys take my truck? I left the keys with Morgan."

"We started to. We drove all the way into town, but Brit threw up in it," Allyson said.

"She what?"

"I think she had too much pizza and Coke."

Britney made a face. "It was the Coke. I can eat any amount of pizza without throwing up. At Lindy's party I ate three and a half slices. I held the record."

"You threw up there, too," Allyson said.

"Yeah. From the Coke."

"You all right now, pumpkin?" I asked.

"I'm fine. We didn't want to take the truck after I threw up in it."

"You guys must have been off in the truck when Stephanie and I came by the first time. You get the flat fixed?"

"Morgan didn't know how," Allyson said. "Finally one of the boys on Morgan's tennis team saw us, and him and his mom gave us a ride. Then we saw all these fire trucks." Britney put her cheek against mine.

"Where's my stuff?" Allyson said. Always ready to stick up for herself, Allyson wasn't inclined to let this affront to her perfect summer slide.

"I'm afraid it's all inside, sweetheart. Everything's still in there."

"Not Miss Squiggly?" Britney said. She'd been dragging Miss Squiggly around since she was two. The doll was a mess. No hair. One eye. One leg.

"Even Miss Squiggly. We're going to have to start from scratch."

"I don't want to start from scratch," Allyson said defiantly.

"I need Miss Squiggly." Britney burst into tears.

When I hugged them both again, Allyson started crying, too. "Look, you guys. We're all together and nobody got hurt. Right now that's the important thing. Nobody got hurt."

Even as I said it, in my mind's eye I saw the corpse in the backyard. If it wasn't Morgan, who was it? Could it have been one of my old girl-friends, someone who'd come carrying a grudge and a can of gasoline? Maybe one of the Suzannes?

Or Lorie? For the corpse to have been Lorie's, she would have had to lose some weight, but then, I hadn't seen her in three years. She could have lost plenty of weight in that time. I wanted to go around the building and look at the corpse again, but I wasn't about to let go of my daughters.

"What about my new sandals?" Allyson asked.

"We'll get you some more."

"I was going to wear those tomorrow."

"I want my Miss Squiggly," said Britney, slipping her thumb into her mouth. She hadn't sucked her thumb since just after her mother left.

"Allyson," I said. "Did you guys have anybody over at the house?"

Measuring the question, Allyson stopped crying and arched a look up at me. "No."

"You sure?"

"Nobody."

"Morgan, you didn't have any friends visit?"

Morgan said, "No. We got pizza and headed out for the movie. Then Brit threw up. We came back and took my mom's car, and then on the way home we got that flat and waited for the patrol."

"*State* Patrol," corrected Britney.

A shadow fell across us as Stephanie approached, eyes moist. She hugged the girls. I said, "Stephanie, I'm so sorry for what I said. Can you forgive me?"

"Forgive what?"

Clasping her to me, I said, "I'd give anything to erase what I said."

"Forget it."

"At least let me plead temporary insanity?"

"Stop apologizing. Your daughters are safe. That's what counts."

"Okay, okay, okay," Stevenson said, stepping forward. "This is all peachy keen. Hi, girls. Glad you could make it." He fixed his dark eyes on me. "Mind if we ask some questions without this circus breathing down our necks?"

I stepped off a few paces into the field with Shad, Stevenson, and Holgate. It was so dark, I could barely see their eyes. Holgate said, "I'm glad your daughters showed up."

"Thanks."

"The question now is, who's the prizefighter in the backyard? You originally thought it was that young lady over there, right?"

"My baby-sitter, yes."

"I can see they're about the same size. Easy mistake to make. But who's in your backyard, really?"

"I don't know."

"We're going to have to question the baby-sitter. And your girls."

"Like hell."

"It's a matter of routine that—"

"Ain't going to happen. You're not talking to my girls."

"At least your baby-sitter," said Shad, more irritated with me than ever.

"You'll have to see her and her mother about that." As he gawked at Morgan's bare legs, a shriek came from that direction. Helen Neumann had just come out of her house and spotted her daughter. Why Helen had thought her daughter was in the fire when she hadn't yet returned her car was beyond me, but then, Helen had always been prone to panic.

"You want to know how we think this went down?" Shad asked.

"I do. Yeah."

"You did it."

"Here we go again."

"No, bear with me. We got a telephone call from a woman. Maybe two hours ago. Said you were real depressed. That you guys weren't getting anywhere trying to find a cure for whatever it is you think you've got. That right?"

"We haven't found a cure. That part's right."

"Said you were going to take yourself out. That you might want to take your family out at the same time."

"Another anonymous caller?"

"A woman. I think she was the same one I spoke to after the trailer explosion. Only this time she called from a pay phone in Bellevue. You know anybody in Bellevue?"

"Who doesn't?"

"It fits your MO perfectly."

"What does? Setting my house on fire? Give me a break."

"No," Shad said. "Not setting the fire. Chickening out. You've done it once already. With the trailer. You set it up to kill yourself. And then at the last second you get the butterflies and run away."

"Look. Surely you can figure out who made the call."

"Wish we could," Stevenson said. "It was a pay phone."

"You got an explanation for all this?" Shad asked.

"Sure. Somebody's setting me up."

"Why?"

"I don't know."

"We're going to go through the rest of the house," Stevenson said. "And then we're going to come back and talk to you again."

"He was with me," Stephanie said. "You're barking up the wrong tree."

"You guys really got a call about me tonight?" I asked.

Shad tipped his head toward his taller partner. "He did."

"But you didn't do anything about it, did you?" I said. "You didn't believe her, did you?"

"I believe her now. Stick around. We're coming back."

"Anyone who knew two hours ago that my house was going to burn down was in on it."

As I spoke, an evidence technician from the county approached, a young woman with short chestnut hair and heavy eyebrows. She wore the green-brown uniform of a King County deputy and held a partially burned driver's license by the edges.

"Anybody know this person?" she asked.

52. MISS SQUIGGLY HEADS FOR THE BEACH

Without taking it from the technician's fingers, each of the three investigators leaned forward in turn and examined the license: *Carpenter, Achara. Sex F. Height 5′0″. Weight 95 pounds. Eyes brn. Birth date 090969*. Along the right side of the license on a blue background was a picture of Achara.

A wave of nausea flooded my stomach. Things had made a horrible kind of sense when I thought the corpse belonged to Morgan, but what on earth had Achara been doing in my house?

Maybe Donovan was somewhere in the burned-out hulk, too. But if that were true, their black Suburban would have been outside. Besides, we'd seen Donovan minutes before the fire.

Carl Steding had told me the story of the daughter of one of the downed firefighters in Chattanooga, who'd coincidentally died in a house fire. They never caught the killer-arsonist. The assumption had been made that it had been unrelated to her investigation of the syndrome. Unrelated to the downed firefighters. But it hadn't been. This was too damn similar. It was those two bastards from Jane's we'd seen at the motel.

"You know her?" Shad said.

"Works as a chemist at Canyon View Systems. In Redmond."

"You want to explain what she was doing on your living-room floor?"

"I have no idea. As far as I know, she didn't even know where I lived."

"Somebody knew."

Stevenson pulled out a toothpick and put it into his mouth. "She have any reason to burn you out?"

"No, of course not."

"What about that vehicle the neighbors saw?" Stevenson asked no one in particular.

"Talk to the neighbors."

"What about the ladies?" Stevenson asked.

"What are you talking about?"

"I hear you like the ladies."

"I like all sorts of people."

"How long have you known this Achara Carpenter?" He mispronounced her first name, calling her *Akra*.

"Two days."

He smirked. "From what they tell me, two days would be about all you would need."

"He *says* he was with the doctor," Shad reminded him.

"That wouldn't stop an operator, would it, Jimbo? From what they tell me, you're a first-class operator. How did you have it figured? You bang the doctor in the motel and then come home and pork the chemist?"

"Why don't you go wash your mouth out with soap?"

Stevenson's Cupid-bow mouth pursed into what some would have called a shit-eating grin. The others stared at me in the dark. Then all three stepped back and conferred with one another, glancing from time to time at the fire building, at my charred pickup truck, and at me.

I walked back over to the girls and gave Morgan a long hug. I gave Helen Neumann one, too, the first time I believe we had ever touched.

"We were scared waiting on the freeway," Morgan said.

Karrie Haston approached the investigating team, handing a sheet of paper to Stevenson, who held it aloft and read it by the fringe light from a spotlight on a King County deputy's car. When he was finished, he gave it to Shad.

After Shad read it, he asked Karrie a question and then all four of them looked at me. Touching my back from behind, Stephanie said, "What's that all about?"

"No idea."

When they reached us, Shad and Stevenson stood a little too close. Karrie kept her distance. Holgate hung back, too.

"We were just wondering what this was doing pinned to the firehouse door," Stevenson said, stretching the sheet of paper gingerly between the index fingers and thumbs of both hands. When I reached for it, he jerked it away and said, "Uh-uh. No touchee. Just read it."

The note was typewritten.

To whom it may concern,

    I, Jim Swope, being of sound mind and clean heart do solemnly swear that I have killed myself and my family on this night of June 19. For reasons best known to myself, I'm taking

Achara Carpenter with me. It is better this way. My life has come
to an end and my children's lives will never be what they should.
Nobody should be an orphan or live the kind of fucked-up life
I've led. To those behind, I apologize for any trouble I may have
caused.

J. Swope

"You can see right away any fool could have written this. It's typed.
Even the signature."

"It's only got one fool's name on it."

"It could have the president's name on it and it wouldn't mean shit."

"Funny coincidence, wouldn't you say?" said Shad, stepping closer,
"that this note was found the same night your house burned down."

"There's nothing funny about it. It's a frame-up."

"That woman you dragged outside, the one only *you* seemed to
know was in there? How did you know?"

"I didn't. I went in after my daughters."

Ron Holgate straightened his rep tie with one hand. "Where was the
note found?"

"On the front door of the firehouse," Karrie replied.

"Logical place to put it if it was legit," Holgate said.

"Logical place to put it if it was a frame-up," I said.

The three investigators stared at me with various degrees of indictment clouding their eyes. "It's pretty obvious," Shad said. "You wrote the
note, set the fire, and then got out of the house at the last minute."
Stevenson nodded. Holgate pursed his lips and looked at his feet.

"Wouldn't be the first time somebody backed out of a murder-
suicide after the murder part," said Stevenson. "You probably did the
same thing two days ago with the trailer."

"What are you talking about?" Stephanie said. "He was with me all
night."

"You got any independent proof of that?" Stevenson asked.

"The Sunset Motel," Stephanie said. "Go check their records."

Shad looked Stephanie up and down. I wished she hadn't been wearing one of my ex-wife's summer dresses, the material thin enough that
lights behind her worked as X rays.

"You got a phone number for the motel?" Holgate asked. Stephanie dug through her wallet and pulled out a receipt, while Holgate pulled a cell phone off his belt.

Meanwhile, the two fire investigators stared me down. From the moment they met me at Caputo's, neither of these guys had liked me.

Holgate rejoined the group. "They checked in all right. At least she did. Nobody saw him."

"My in-laws saw me leaving a few minutes before we got here."

"Your in-laws?" Shad said. "Cute."

"They with you the whole time?" Stevenson smirked.

"Of course not."

"I was," said Stephanie. "Up until he went into the fire."

"You'll swear to that?" Holgate asked.

"Absolutely."

"Not good enough," Shad said, squinting at Stevenson. "Not with everything else that's been going on."

"Are you calling me a liar?" Stephanie asked.

Stevenson said, "We expect you to lie for him."

"I just met Achara yesterday," I said. "I don't have a motive. Are you guys even listening?"

"When did you meet the good doctor?" Shad asked.

He had me on that.

"Other thing we're thinking about, King County just told us a woman matching the description of Achara Carpenter filled up a five-gallon can at the Texaco station a couple of hours ago. She was with a man, but nobody could give a description. That wouldn't be you, would it?"

"How many times do I have to tell you?"

"I think we're going to have to take you in for questioning," Stevenson said.

"Without finishing the house?"

"Just go over there and sit in the back of our vehicle until we're through."

"Not bloody likely."

"You want me to arrest you? Is that it?" Shad asked. "Consider yourself under arrest."

"On what charge?" Stephanie asked.

"Suspicion of arson."

"It's not going to stick," I said.

"Then we'll hold you as a material witness. You've been disappearing on us all week. This way at least we'll know where you are. Maybe this will encourage you to answer a few questions."

"I answered your questions."

"Yeah?" Shad said. "Why was this Achara person in your house at midnight?"

"I told you, I don't know. You guys really get paid for this?"

Before I could stop him, Shad slapped handcuffs around one of my wrists. As he reached for my other wrist, Stephanie said, "What the hell is wrong with you? Can't you see he's burned?"

Shad examined my left wrist. There were more burns on my right wrist. Removing the handcuffs, he began walking me toward the King County deputy's car, his intent to lock me in the cage in the backseat. Britney ran in front of us. "Where are you going, Daddy?"

Bending low, I spoke softly. "Tell Stephanie to look for me at Miss Squiggly's favorite spot."

"But why, Daddy?"

"Shhhh. Tell you later." I winked, gave her a kiss, and walked to the squad car with Shad.

He opened the back door, then reached up to force my head inside. Instead of moving with him, I grabbed his wrist, threw a quick elbow lock on him, and levered him into the backseat on his face. It was the last thing he expected. To tell you the truth, it was almost the last thing *I* expected.

I ran thirty paces in the direction of my house before I heard the first shouts of alarm behind, oddly enough from my own daughter.

53. CATCH ME IF YOU CAN

Nobody warned me Stevenson had been a running back on his high school football team or that Ron Holgate, who looked overweight, jogged five miles a night and competed in 10K races, that in the past five years he had twice run down suspects on foot. I found all this out later, after I dashed past the rubble that had been my house, past the two sad-eyed volunteers standing guard over Achara's fire-stiffened body.

Lurching into the darkness in the field behind our house, I plotted a path toward the bank of the Middle Fork two hundred yards away. The moonlight was hazy under a pall of smoke that represented our vaporized house and belongings. There were firs in the middle of the field and a few more at the south end, but I was headed for the small cluster of deciduous trees on the riverbank.

The riverbed of the Middle Fork was mostly rock at this time of year, and you could wade across the stream in a multitude of places, although if you got caught in the deeper sections, the current could sweep you away. About once a summer we pulled a body out, usually some hapless local teenager who got trapped under a log and couldn't escape because of the immense pressure of the flowing water.

"Stand in your tracks, asshole!" yelled Stevenson. I ran faster. He yelled twice more, as did Holgate, their voices giving away their positions. Both were close and getting closer, especially Stevenson, whose last words sounded as if they'd come from my hip pocket.

I swore to myself that if he knocked me down, I was going to fight. I had one day left on the planet, and I wasn't going to let small-minded suspicions and bureaucratic megalomania steal those precious hours from my girls. I'd already robbed them of enough time myself.

I wasn't the swiftest runner, but I was flying tonight.

Toward the center of the field, we would cross a series of furrows. Obscured by tall grasses, they would be hard to see even if you were expecting them. They were perilous during the day, worse in the dim moonlight.

I stepped into the first furrow, stumbled, righted myself, and leaped up onto the ridge beyond it, then down into the next ditch, quickly establishing an up-and-down rhythm, as if riding a miniature roller coaster. I was panting now, gasping for air, windmilling my arms wildly to maintain balance.

Behind me, one man screamed, "Oh, shit!" and I heard the *thwack* of a body striking the soft earth.

The other voice was still close. "You asshole!"

Stevenson didn't sound nearly as winded as I was, but even so, I had gained ground on him. I could swear I was breathing so hard my lungs were bleeding. My legs were about to buckle.

I was almost to the riverbank when I heard him closing in on me again.

Barely visible in the moonlight, the path ran downstream along the bank for maybe a hundred fifty yards before it came to a dead end. On hot summer afternoons teenagers jumped off the steep dead end into a deep greenish-blue pool, skinny-dipping and drinking beer. For years a rope swing had dangled over the pool. I could only hope it was still there tonight. Behind me, I heard Stevenson cursing as branches and blackberry vines slapped at him.

I was breathing so hard, I could hear only two things now, the air rushing in and out of my throat and the slap of Stevenson's shoes on the rocky path as he closed in.

"Thought you were . . . going to . . . get . . . away . . . didn't . . . you . . . ?" he said as I reached the end of the pathway and launched myself out into space over the river. I couldn't see the rope swing, but I knew where it should be out there in the dark over the river, and as I sailed out on faith I reached out for it, clawing at the air like a drunken Superman, just as if I could see it, the rope, hoping some Good Samaritan hadn't tied it up out of the way.

By some miracle I got a grip on the rope and swung almost in slow motion out over the black, moonlit pool. I could feel Stevenson brushing my backside. And then I was free. Free and swinging. Below, I heard him splash noisily into the pool. I could still hear him shouting and wallowing in the cold water long after I jogged downstream along the bank.

Forty minutes later I found myself in the brush off Reinig Road near Miss Squiggly's favorite spot on earth. We locals called it Unemployment Beach; the county called it Three Forks Park. Easily one of the most panoramic sites in the area, Unemployment Beach was a sandy spot where the three forks of the Snoqualmie fed into one another; another mile and a half downstream, the river dropped almost three hundred feet over Snoqualmie Falls.

Several vehicles came past, including a volunteer fireman returning home from my place, a fire engine, and the tanker that had responded from Snoqualmie.

When I saw Holly's red Pontiac, I stepped out into the headlights and waited. As the car pulled alongside, I leaned down to the half-open passenger-side window and greeted my sleepy daughters in the backseat. I looked at Stephanie, who said, "I know. I agree. Totally. Your time is too short. They knew that. They were being assholes. Excuse my French, girls. Where to?" Stephanie asked, after I climbed in.

"The Sunset Motel."

"Oh, no. We're not going to—"

"Just a visit."

"You're not going after them?"

"They have to be the ones."

"Why can't we just go to a hotel? What are you going to do? Beat them up?"

"I have no idea. Just go by the Sunset."

We headed toward Snoqualmie on back roads. I was sore all over but hadn't felt it until now. I had five or six smallish burns, including my knees, where I'd crawled over hot spots in the fire. My left knee was aching as a result of our footrace in the dark. My feet were wet and cold from crossing the river.

I turned around and peered into the backseat. Tilted against each other like stuffed animals on a shelf, both girls had fallen asleep under the blanket I'd tucked around their legs.

"They out?" Stephanie asked.

"Sawing z's."

"We were so damn lucky. Somebody tried to kill us. All of us."

"I think I know who."

"You think Hillburn and Dobson killed . . ." Stephanie looked over the seat back to ascertain whether the girls were really asleep.

"You saw them tonight. They looked guilty as hell. And Donovan was all over town asking questions. It wasn't like they wouldn't have known about her."

"Jim, if you go there tonight, they'll find you. You'll be arrested. I don't want you to do anything you'll regret."

"You mean something I'll regret for the rest of my life?"

Stephanie followed my directions and drove through Snoqualmie, past the high school, and back to North Bend on the old highway. I would be surprised if they hadn't checked out, but if they hadn't, I had no idea what I was going to do.

The Sunset Motel was lit up like a carnival ride, three county police cars crowding the street and entranceway, along with our own North Bend aid unit. Stephanie drove past while I slid down in the seat until only my eyes were above the window ledge. Hillburn and Dobson were standing outside in slacks and T-shirts, talking to the female evidence technician we'd seen at the fire.

"Maybe they're arresting them?" Stephanie said.

"Not likely." I saw a Latino man with blood on his shirt, a couple of hysterical Latina women screaming at him from across the courtyard. "There must have been a fight."

"What do you want to do?"

"I don't know why those bastards are still hanging around."

"Let's go to Seattle and put the girls to bed."

"They must have figured their frame-up was perfect."

"We'll find a nice hotel with a pool."

"It has to be them. The coincidence of the events in Chattanooga and here is too much. The syndrome is discovered. An explosion wipes out most of the survivors or, in our case, almost wipes us out. There's a house fire in which key investigators are killed. Jane's lies to me every time I talk to them. It's gotta be those bastards."

"We don't have proof."

"I don't need proof."

"Besides, if it's Jane's, those two are probably just errand boys. The real culprits are a thousand miles away."

"You're right. I'll fly to California."

"Jim . . ."

"I'm kidding. Let's find a place to stay."

"Jim? I love you."

"Where did that come from?"

"We might not have a lot of time. I wanted to say it."

I could have returned the sentiment, but right now I didn't feel anything but relief that my daughters were alive and an irrepressible anger at the men who'd tried to take them from me.

"I wish things were different for you."

"I've got one day left. A day is all I need. Most people don't really live twenty-four hours. I never did. One day will be plenty."

She didn't say anything else, but it wasn't too much later before I heard her crying in the dark.

DAY SIX

54. A BREEDING GROUND FOR NEUROTICS

In the morning I found her watching me with something akin to amuse-ment in her dusty-blue eyes. There was no telling how long she'd been awake. I remembered we'd taken a suite at the Warwick in downtown Seattle. We'd situated the girls in a king-size bed in the other room in front of a television and an episode of *Love Boat*, one of their favorites; they wanted so much to believe in romance, particularly after the failure of mine with their mother. And also perhaps after the failure of mine with a long line of women after Lorie. Still, they were both asleep inside of a minute.

Stirring under the sheets, I quickly became aware that pajamas for the adults hadn't been on the "to buy" list the night before. I glanced at the clock: nine-thirty. I was waking up later each morning. Tomorrow was day seven. I might not wake up at all tomorrow.

Stephanie's skin was like liquid silk, her body warm when she rolled onto me, warm everywhere except her cold feet. Our lovemaking was ferocious, even more so than last evening at the Sunset Motel. This morning we had the added impetus of being on the run as well as the knowledge that time was running out. Afterward as I lay there recovering from the exertion, I said, "Me, too. I love you, too."

She rolled her head over to look at me. We were lying side by side. "You don't have to say it."

"I'm a guy. Believe me, I know I don't have to say it. I want to say it."

"You know, you're a lot nicer than you think you are."

"Don't count on it."

"But you are."

My ears were ringing louder than ever today. Besides the burns, there was a tweak in my right knee and another in my lower back. Minor quib-bles. Except for these, I felt like a million bucks.

"Jim, I've been thinking. Do you still want to spend the whole day with your girls?"

"I do and I don't. We need to work on this if there's still a chance, but I can't let my girls down, either. They need time with me. Especially if this is my last day."

"Let me call Donovan and my aunt. This is Saturday, but I have cell phone numbers for both of them."

"When you talk to Donovan, find out if he has Achara's papers or if they were with her in the fire. I think she was on to something before she died. She gave me a string of numbers to memorize. They may be part of a chemical formula, maybe for an antidote. And I need to call Steding in Tennessee. He must have proof by now that JCP, Inc., was involved there. For me, that's the final part to the puzzle. If Jane's knows all about this, maybe there's an antidote and they have it."

"If they haven't given it to us by now, they're not likely to."

"No."

"Can I ask a favor, Jim?"

"What?"

"I know a lawyer here in town. I treated his son in Tacoma at the hospital. I've called him and he's agreed to come out and write up some papers for us to sign."

"What sort of papers?"

"I know how worried you are about your girls. . . . Well, if you don't make it. I'd like you to assign me as their guardian."

"You'd do that?"

"Listen. I've lived my life pretty much in a vacuum. I don't go out. I don't see people. I work and then I work some more. It's been like that since high school, when my parents died. It took Holly and now you to open my eyes and make me realize I haven't been living any kind of life. I love you. I love your girls. I want to be part of your family."

"And you've got this attorney on tap?"

"He's already drawn up the paperwork. All we have to do is sign it."

"You've been a busy girl."

"Yes, I have."

For myself, I'd come to terms with my fate, and whether it happened today, tomorrow, or in two minutes, I was good to go. What I had not come to terms with was abandoning my children. I especially did not want to leave them with Wes and Lillian Tindale, whose home was now and always had been a breeding ground for neurotics.

"You realize this will be forever?"

"I'm fully aware of that."

"You planning to take them with you, or relocate here?"

"I've had an offer at Tacoma General."

"You got a deal, babe."

We kissed and then, charged with the excitement of the moment, she leaped out of bed and began trotting out purchases she'd made while I slept. "I found most of this stuff downstairs in the gift shop, but I had to go down the block for the swimsuits. I got red sandals for Ally. A doll for Britney, a teddy for Ally, and a Monopoly game. What do you think?"

"I think if you keep parading around like that, you're going to have to dole out another MF."

"MF?"

"Mercy fuck."

She laughed, crawled over the bed and kissed the tip of my nose, and was gone before I could grab her. After we showered and dressed and she'd applied Silvadine to my burns, we woke the girls. She'd purchased haircutting utensils and fingernail polish in the same shade Achara Carpenter used, Stephanie's covert tribute to a woman who'd befriended us at the cost of her own life.

Within half an hour both girls had bobs matching Achara's, were sitting on the edge of the tub in the bathroom painting their fingernails and toenails, jabbering away about Achara, who they didn't yet know was dead.

Their house had been leveled. Every personal possession they'd ever owned had gone up in smoke. The family pet was dead. Any sense of security they'd ever felt was compromised. They didn't need to hear about Achara. Not today.

We had a leisurely breakfast delivered from room service, and after that it was a race to see who got to Boardwalk first. As sick as I was of Monopoly, I was glad to be alive to play it. Glad my girls were alive to play it. "This is good," Allyson said, "because we lost the old wheelbarrow, and I always wanted it."

"I like the thimble," said Britney in a tiny voice.

"What do you like?" Stephanie asked me.

"Whatever's left."

"I'll take the little dog, then."

We played for an hour, Stephanie and I making cell phone calls in between our moves, she to her aunt, who'd heard about the fire in North Bend and was sick with worry for all of us, and me to Carl Steding in Chattanooga to get the final word on Jane's. Steding could not be reached. We changed into our swimsuits and went downstairs and swam, nearly two hours of cavorting in the pool, interspersed with telephone calls trying to track down Steding or, at this point, Charlie Drago or anybody else in Chattanooga who might know what was going on. Stephanie taught Allyson to dive while Britney and I floated around in the shallow end. Except for the constant ringing in my ears and the chlorine biting my burns, I felt pretty darn good.

Later, in the suite, I noticed Allyson, who was not ordinarily given to neatness, had arranged the toothbrushes and hand towels in the bathroom in perfect descending order, mine, Stephanie's, hers, and then her little sister's. I knew Allyson had done it, because Britney would have arranged it with the mother and father toothbrush at either end. Poor girls. They so much wanted the one thing they were destined never to have, a real family.

It would have been a perfect day if it hadn't been for the fact that I would be brain-dead in less than forty-eight hours, maybe less than twenty-four, a thought that wedged itself into my brain like an ax blade every five minutes. Just around the time I managed to stop thinking about it, it came back again.

I wondered if I was going to feel *anything* for the next forty years.

After a snack downstairs in the Brasserie Margaux, Stephanie and I led the girls to a private room off the lobby. There we met the attorney she'd befriended in Tacoma and she and I signed the legal documents, having already consulted with the girls about our plan.

Attorney Davies was a tall, plum-faced man with a bad toupee—his wife, who'd come along as a witness, was a short, bulging-eyed woman with crooked teeth and a personality wound tighter than copper wire on a stick. We'd bought bouquets from the gift shop for the girls, trying to make this more of a celebration than a wake.

Every once in a while Allyson would get a look in her eyes as if she were about to cry, but Britney was contained in the event, grinning ear to ear.

The rest of the afternoon was spent in our rooms either making phone calls or in a chatty marathon four-handed game of Monopoly. The girls were losing their father tomorrow and you might think we'd be talking about that, but none of us did. With a smidgen of help from Stephanie and a wink from Allyson, Britney won the Monopoly game and declared herself queen of the world.

It was three when I finally reached Carl Steding. "Carl. Jim Swope here. From North Bend. You were going to look for a complete list of the companies that had packages at Southeast Travelers for me?"

"Yeah, yeah. I said I would do it and it's done. I've been calling your fire station all morning. Had a long chat with a young woman there. She's kind of wigged out. Says she has the syndrome."

"That would be Karrie."

"Yeah, that was her name. Does she really have it?"

"I think so. What'd you find?"

"No JCP, Inc., involved. Nowhere. I even went as far as to find out if any of their two subsidiaries might have been involved. Or anyone who ships to them. Near as I can tell, they didn't have a thing to do with it."

"Are you absolutely sure?"

"As sure as anyone can be. If I were you, I'd start looking someplace else."

I felt as if I'd been hit with a two-by-four. Everything had pointed to JCP, and now on my last good day I find out they had nothing to do with it and I'd been looking in the wrong direction all along. I was on the verge of panic but knew I had to think this through calmly. My brain was cycling through everything I knew about the Southeast Travelers incident and our own accident response in February, trying to sort it all out. "Tell me something, then. That young woman you said died in the house fire?"

"Which young woman?"

"You told me the daughter of one of your firefighters died in a house fire around the time you guys were investigating this."

"Oh, yeah. Anastasia Brown. Sure. What about her?"

"Did Scott Donovan know her?"

"Yes. Of course. In fact, they were working together right before the fire."

"Thanks."

Stephanie looked at me after I hung up. "Jane's didn't have anything there?"

"Nope."

"So what do you think?"

"I think if it wasn't Jane's, it was somebody closer."

Stephanie and I looked at each other for a moment. Allyson said, "So what are you going to do, Daddy? Is there no hope? No hope at all?"

"There's always hope, sweetheart."

Twenty minutes later Stephanie contacted Donovan by phone for the first time that day. She'd left half a dozen messages on his voice mail, but he hadn't returned any of them. I listened at the earpiece, the warmth of our cheeks mingling. "Good God," Stephanie said. "Have you made *any* progress? Have you figured out this syndrome?"

"No, I'm sorry to report. I've been consulting with people from the company about Achara's death all day. It's shaken people up pretty bad. There's so much going on. The sale of the company. This business out in North Bend. What happened to Achara. I still don't understand it. Say . . . where are you guys? I'd like to come over and see how you're doing."

"We'd better not say right now. So what do you think happened to Achara? When was the last time you saw her?"

"Last time I saw her was the last time you saw her. She was headed for the library. I was supposed to go pick her up, but I never got the call."

"Listen," Stephanie said. "I'll leave my cell phone on. If you come up with something, call."

"Oh, you bet I will, Dr. Riggs. I'm not giving up on this. No way I'm giving up on this."

After she hung up, Stephanie and I looked at each other. I said, "A young woman investigating the syndrome dies in a house fire in Tennessee. Another one dies here. There's an explosion in Tennessee. There's another one here. Somebody was in both places."

"Orchestrating it."

"Daddy? Who died?"

"What?" Allyson had asked the question and Allyson wasn't easy to fool.

"You said a woman died here."

"Nobody you know."

"She died in our fire, didn't she?"

"Yes, dear."

Stephanie and I finished the conversation in the other room. "If it wasn't JCP, Inc., who was it?" I said. "How many possibilities are there? There is only one other company involved in both incidents. You rule out the possibilities one by one, and then, no matter how unlikely, you're left with the culprit. Those are Donovan's words."

"I don't want to believe my aunt was the cause of my sister's problems. I can't believe that. Besides, Canyon View was only shipping books in Holly's truck. How could books have caused this?"

"The manifest said it was books. Maybe it wasn't. After all, books aren't exactly their business."

"That's true, but I assumed they were industrial manuals or research textbooks or something."

"So did I. Achara wanted to meet with me. She wanted to tell me something about those numbers she gave me. I think the main purpose of getting rid of her was so we would not have that meeting."

"What are we going to do?"

"I'm going to wait until it gets dark."

Stephanie looked at me for a long moment. "That cuts your time down even more."

"My time's been running out all week. I'm getting used to it."

At dinner downstairs, Britney said, "This place sure is 'spensive."

"What makes you think that, honey?" Stephanie asked.

"The man in the lobby said it was so 'spensive they were billing him twenty-five cents every time he cut a fart." We laughed so hard the table rocked, and then one of the girls farted and we really went to pieces.

After dinner we went upstairs so the girls could check out the TV fare, but they fell asleep before we got through the schedule. It was seven-thirty.

Stephanie left quietly while I tugged off their shoes and tucked them in, kissing them good night. Or maybe it was good-bye. I knew Stephanie had done me a favor leaving me alone with them, that she'd wanted desperately to stay and be part of my final farewell.

Later, we made love one last time. It was as gentle as a whisper at a wedding.

And then I was asleep.

I'd had a lot of stress along with a series of long days. Or maybe it was a guy thing. You had sex. You nodded off. Or . . .

Maybe my time was up.

55. HERE'S THE KICKER

Everything appeared to be shaking.

It took a few moments to realize it wasn't an earthquake, that somebody was jiggling the bed. My ears were ringing or I would have identified the sound sooner. A woman crying.

I was on my back, the blankets tight around me, as if I'd been tucked in by a mortician. When I lifted my head ever so slightly, I spotted our baby-sitter, Morgan Neumann, hands clasped in front of her, standing at the foot of the bed, tears staining her pale cheeks. Stephanie was beside me, one arm thrown across my chest as if playing out an Elizabethan melodrama.

When I reached out and touched her hair, Stephanie stopped crying and crawled higher on the bed, kissing my cheek repeatedly. Still sniffling, she laid her head on my shoulder.

"Oh, God. I tried so hard to wake you. I even stuck a pin in you. I'm sorry."

"You can take it out now."

"It was just a little prick."

"Just like me."

"Don't joke around, Jim. I know ten or fifteen more hours aren't all that much, but I was counting on every one of them."

I might have climbed out of bed, but I was naked and Morgan was watching. "Hey, Morgan. What are you doing here?"

Wiping her wet cheeks with the sleeve of her shirt, she said, "I was going to sit with the girls."

"Sit with the girls? Where were you going, Steph?"

"Morgan, would you mind waiting in the girls' room?" After Morgan was gone, Stephanie said, "I'm going to Canyon View."

"Alone?"

"I thought you were . . ." She kissed me. "I talked to a librarian at the North Bend Library who said Achara had been there until closing. Know what she was doing?"

"Tell me."

"Sitting in front of that big wall of picture windows. Sitting and staring at the mountain for hours. Does that sound like a woman researching a problem?"

"That sounds like a woman trying to make a decision."

"That's exactly what I thought. You don't think she took the gasoline to your house and torched the place, do you?"

"I think she was deciding whether or not to betray her employer. Donovan must have caught wind of her intentions. *He* drove her to the gas station, gave her some song and dance about needing the gasoline can filled up, then took her out to my house and did whatever he had to do to make it happen. Knocked her out. Strangled her. Dragged her inside. Poured gas all over. Remember how surprised Donovan was when he saw us last night? He thought he killed us—or me at least—in that fire."

"Then he's the one who left the note on the door of the fire station. He had some woman call the fire investigators and leave those messages."

"That's what I think," I said.

"I can't believe he would do that. I can't believe my aunt had anything to do with this."

"Maybe she doesn't know about it. You said she hasn't been in charge that long."

"When you met my aunt at Tacoma General, did you tell her about the syndrome, that there were other people who had it in addition to Holly?"

"I told her there were people in North Bend going down. She could have figured out the rest—"

"—If she already knew about the syndrome and what causes it."

I threw the covers off and swung my feet over the side of the bed. "I'm going. You stay here."

"You don't know what to look for."

"You stay here with—"

"You want to get stubborn? You've come to the factory. There is no possible scenario where I stay."

"Why not?"

"For one thing . . . I already paid the baby-sitter."

We looked at each other for half a minute. I could love this woman like I'd never loved any woman. I could love her until we were both a hundred and five. I could love her until the earth crumbled. "At the first sign of trouble, I want you out of there."

"I never bail out. It's my trademark."

"At the first sign of trouble. That's an order. As the designated guardian of my children."

"Okay. Yes, sir. You feel strong enough to do this?"

"I'll make it."

56. EXCEPT FOR BURGLARS AND LOCKSMITHS

After ten minutes of driving around the wooded neighborhood, we ascertained that Canyon View was locked but empty, found a strip mall abutting the back of the property, parked the Pontiac behind a row of buildings, shimmied up a rockery, and climbed a low fence. Below us was the roof of the strip mall, which consisted of ten or twelve single-story occupancies fronting a busy thoroughfare.

Stephanie produced a five-battery flashlight and other paraphernalia from a small gray bag. "Where'd you get all that stuff?" I said.

"I went to a store down the street from the hotel while you were sleeping."

"A burglar store?"

"Yeah."

Blundering through the darkness, we found a culvert with a small stream trickling along the bottom of it, then a natural embankment at the top of which was a Cyclone fence with a sign, red lettering on a white background: PRIVATE PROPERTY—KEEP OUT—VIOLATORS WILL BE PROSECUTED. The fence was far enough from the road that we could no longer hear the occasional car, nor see the glow of lights from the auto dealership across the street.

Stephanie had brought latex gloves for both of us, along with an assortment of tools: a small pry bar, flashlight, wire cutters, duct tape, and a screwdriver. I climbed the fence and used the wire cutters to sever the razor wire running along the top, cutting my thumb in the process.

Managing to get both of us over the fence and onto the Canyon View campus without further bloodshed, we worked our way through the trees and past the elephant-sized rhododendrons. I think at that point we both felt a little like Alice in Wonderland. What we were attempting was so far from our normal lives, it didn't seem real. But then, nothing seemed real these days.

We came to the smaller building first, two dark stories with a small loading dock on one side, a shipping and receiving facility.

The next building was the size of a small college campus administration building. All the lower windows were wired for security. Stephanie tried one of the back doors while I tromped through the flower bed along the wall of the building and searched for an unsecured window.

I couldn't shake the feeling the Redmond police were about to come barreling around the corner and arrest us.

If there was one thing I knew, it was breaking into buildings. Except for burglars and locksmiths, firefighters broke into buildings more often than anybody. An ordinary residence had a door most firefighters could kick in with their boot or, at the least, one they could jimmy with a Halligan tool. You could also take an ax and knock off the lock, remove the guts, and kick in the door. We didn't have a Halligan tool or an ax, and the doors on this building were built to withstand an atomic blast. Even if they weren't, there would be a security system in place that would trigger an alarm if we broke in.

I sat on a small cookie-cutter concrete curb that ran around a flower bed to think things out. After a while, I heard some clicking. I turned around and found Stephanie fumbling with the door. "What are you doing?"

"There's a number pad here. If we could only figure it out."

Just below the knob was a numerical code pad with ten buttons lined up vertically. "Try seven, five, four, zero."

She punched the numbers, pushed the door open, and gave me an astonished look. "How did you know that?"

"Isn't that your aunt's birthday?"

"Oh, you're a genius." I stepped inside in front of her. "Wait a minute. She wasn't born in July. She wasn't even born in 1940."

"She wasn't?"

"No."

"You have your cell phone?"

"Yes."

"We get separated, go straight to the car and get out of Dodge. I'll call you later, and you can pick me up."

"I'm going to stick with you."

"No dice. We've already been over this. First sign of trouble: run."

"Why don't we just both go to the car?"

"I'm telling you the way it's going to be."

"Okay."

"One more thing. When I'm gone—" She touched her fingers to my lips in an attempt to stop me. "However it happens with me, I want you to open yourself up to the world. Marry if you find someone who you can love and who'll be a good father to the girls. I want you happy. I want the girls to have a family. They deserve it. You deserve it."

"Oh, Jim."

"Maybe after a couple of years you could shoot some air into my veins. You don't have to promise or anything, but it would be nice if I knew I wasn't going to spend four decades staring at a lightbulb thinking it was God."

On that cheerful note, we tugged on our latex gloves and commenced burgling.

57. A STACK OF LETTERS FROM A DEAD MAN

In the atrium by the reception desk a smattering of red, yellow, and violet floor lights shone from the bottom of the shallow fish pool, but most of the light in the building came from street lamps outside in the parking area.

We checked Margery DiMaggio's offices upstairs, her old office, which was unlocked and filled with cardboard boxes, and then her new office, which was locked but which had glass in the door, an unlikely amenity for such a security-conscious company.

Knocking out the glass with the pry bar, I reached inside, unlocked and opened the door to the smell of fresh paint. The spacious office suite had oak furniture and a tall oak cabinet at one end of the room.

The cabinet turned out to be a bar. Cognac seemed to be the drink of choice here. I took a sip of soda water and looked around while Stephanie riffled through the papers in her aunt's desk. The file cabinets were unlocked. Switching on a small lamp, I pawed through them and found routine business mail, records of meetings, financial statements, copies of letters concerning various research grants, letters to vendors, bids for work on the campus, contracts for janitorial service, letters to universities asking about various metallurgy projects and research.

"Most of this is personal," Stephanie said, slamming a desk drawer angrily. "Pictures from her trips to Hong Kong. A boyfriend in New York City. I didn't know she was seeing anybody. Some married guy, works for *Scientific American*. What'd you find?"

"Nothing pertinent."

It was a luxurious office, designed to display power and ease. It even had its own adjoining sitting room and spacious shower facility with sauna, both with separate exits leading to the corridor. I went to the window and gazed out at the parking area below. The trees directly in front of the building had been cut down so that from this office and the one on either side the view was unimpeded as far out as the dark guard kiosk by the street.

"Hey. Check this out," Stephanie said. "There's a folder on some guy named Armitage got fired for embezzlement. He wrote them a letter about my uncle's death. Claims Phil DiMaggio got sick downstairs in the lab and died the next day."

"Is that true?"

"They told me he was driving down I-405, got into a road rage thing with some other driver, had a heart attack, and drove himself to Overlake Hospital. Armitage claims he got sick from chemicals he was handling. Apparently, he's been making this allegation for a while, because he says here: 'Despite your assurances to the contrary, I cannot help but feel Dr. DiMaggio's demise can't be directly attributed to anything other than the materials he was working with on the twelfth of October. Nor can it anymore be deemed a coincidence or an accident that Ms. Janet Beechler, who had been in the room when Dr. DiMaggio was handling said materials, suffered a fatal automobile accident the night following his death.' "

"A fatal accident? You think they were killing witnesses two years ago right here in Redmond?"

"Could be sour grapes; they'd already fired Armitage when he wrote this letter." Stephanie glanced back at the papers. "Here's a letter from my aunt saying Beechler's car accident happened because she was distraught over her boss's death. She says they had the best physicians in the Northwest caring for her husband. That he had a bad heart. I don't know if that's true, but why bother to answer a crank letter from a man you've just fired for embezzlement? The next set of letters are copies of letters to Armitage from Canyon View's attorneys. They'd apparently threatened to turn evidence of embezzlement over to the Redmond Police Department if he didn't go away. I wonder if Armitage was talking about Uncle Phil's death *before* he got fired."

Stephanie handed me a newspaper clipping. "This would have been four weeks later."

Puyallup Man Dies in Car Wreck

Last night at 2:20 A.M. witnesses saw a tan and gray Bronco leave the roadway on I-405 and roll down an embankment, where it burst into flame. By the time the fire department reached the Bronco, it was too late to rescue the occupant, who died at the scene. The driver was William Atherton Armitage, 42, of Puyallup. Police said the vehicle had a number of empty alcohol bottles inside. It was not immediately known whether Armitage had been drinking.

A spokesperson from Canyon View Systems, Armitage's employer until last week, said Armitage had been distraught over the death of a coworker and had recently lost his position at the company amid a flurry of charges and countercharges involving the theft of $300,000 from the firm.

"There's more. She's got files on five former employees who are all either dead or in nursing homes. All . . . yeah . . . two are dead and three are in nursing homes. It doesn't say what's wrong with them, but I have their ages. Twenty-seven, thirty-three, and thirty-five."

"Not your normal nursing home clientele."

"Neither was my sister. Neither are you."

"A nursing home's not a bad way to go. Especially if they serve you pudding every day." I made an idiot face. I was getting pretty good at it.

"Stop it."

I'd noticed industrial eyewash stations in the hallways. Also, Marge DiMaggio's shower was no ordinary shower facility. There were three stalls, each separated by a berm and a wall, so that an individual could step from one to the next, working his or her way down the line. At the end of the row there was a stack of operating-room blues, face masks, and a box of latex gloves. It was the same type of wash-down arrangement the fire department would construct to run people through after a hazardous materials exposure.

"Check this out," Stephanie said, calling me into the main room. Near the office door, she switched on an ultraviolet lamp. The room lit up, but not by much. "Remember black lights? What do you think this is for?"

"So they can paint each other with phosphorescent finger paints and run around in the dark nude?"

Stephanie was not amused. I was getting goosey. My time was running out, and instead of becoming more and more nervous, I was looser than I'd ever been. Almost slap-happy. It was as if I were inebriated.

Downstairs, we found enough eyewash fountains and shower facilities to clean up a rugby team. We broke into three more offices and found work areas—labs, chemicals, machinery, spectrographs, a miniature smelter in a room with concrete walls. All of it was tidy. All of it was ready for a white-glove inspection by a prospective buyer.

Stephanie found the labs fascinating, flipping through notebooks she found and examining the high-tech equipment. We broke into several locked cabinets, but they contained nothing but standard lab supplies.

If we were right, these bastards had infected innocent people from Tennessee to Washington State and now were covering their tracks like a blind cat burying shit. Ironically, there were SAFETY FIRST signs in every corridor.

Stephanie had turned on the lights and was peering into a microscope. I could tell by the way she gripped the dustcover, she was nervous as hell.

I said, "Let's go back to your aunt's office."

"I want to look around here. This is where they work. There's got to be something."

Somewhere in the building a telephone rang. We looked at each other, and Stephanie stopped breathing. The phone rang eight times before it stopped. "A telemarketer," I said.

"At eleven o'clock at night?"

I shrugged. "I'll be upstairs. Somebody shows up, you scream. I'll do the same."

"Sure you will."

Upstairs in DiMaggio's office, I circled the room trying to figure out what was bothering me. They had to be keeping it on the premises, in either this building or the one we'd bypassed outside. They had to have a substance that turned people into zombies. A product potent enough that they maintained shower facilities on all three floors. A product that might be neutralized with something as simple as soap and water—for I'd found nothing else in any of the showers. Where would they keep this product? Better yet, where would they keep an antidote for it?

Sitting with my feet on DiMaggio's desk, I paged through the letters Stephanie had unearthed. I'd been there a few minutes when visions of Achara's charred corpse popped into my head. It was hard to put something like that completely out of mind, particularly if the victim was someone you'd known and liked. Achara had taken a risk giving me those numbers. The first series had been the combination to the keypad on the downstairs door, but what about the second series?

Without consciously thinking about it, I walked across the room to the liquor cabinet, went into the bathroom behind the wall, and found a void behind the cabinet. I'd seen it earlier but hadn't guessed the significance.

It took a few minutes to figure out that the liquor cabinet was on wheels and that moving it to one side would expose a tall gray door to a hidden vault. Somehow Achara had known I might be here before the week was out.

In giving me the combination to this vault, if indeed that's what the numbers were, she'd accurately gauged the urgency of my desperation as well as the depth of her employer's obfuscation. There had to be something in here she needed on a regular basis, something Achara needed to access when the boss wasn't available.

Sixteen years of memorizing Scripture finally paid off in something more meaningful than being able to take down women's phone numbers without a pen and pad.

18-24-18-63-08-46.

I worked the dial carefully and at the end of my troubles heard nothing. If I'd dialed the correct combination, there had been no confirming click to acknowledge it.

However, when I pulled on it, the heavy vault door swung wide.

58. HEY, LADY-KILLER; GET RELIGION; SAY YOUR PRAYERS; DON'T SPILL

The vault interior was eight feet tall, five feet across, and maybe three and a half feet deep. There were five shelves, a gray cash box the sole squatter of the upper shelf, notebooks and manuals stacked on the two shelves closest to eye level, vials in racks on the shelf at belt level, a collection of dust balls on the first shelf above the floor. On the floor were two large corrugated cartons, one taped shut, one open.

I examined the notebooks and a manual, but the jargon contained so many formulas, they might as well have been authored by aliens.

The first three vials were labeled hydrochloric acid, sodium azide, and sodium cyanide—not the ingredients you wanted to drop in Aunt Maud's tea. I was no chemist, but I'd had my share of hazardous materials classes for the fire department and knew hydrochloric acid and sodium cyanide shouldn't be mixed. Sodium azide was a poison if taken orally and lethal enough that even contact with your skin was to be avoided. Two years ago it had been the centerpiece of a shocking story about a pair of teenagers who'd broken into a factory in Massachusetts and gotten it on themselves while looking for cash and drugs. Both died. God only knew why Marge was keeping it in this vault or what they used it for here.

Dangerous as they were, these weren't chemicals that would send your brain back through twelve million years of evolution. No. We were looking for something else.

I knelt and peered into the open cardboard box on the vault floor. I don't know what I expected, but it wasn't a carton of Bibles. I pulled the first three or four out and examined the black leather bindings in the dim light.

Last February Holly's truck had been carrying Bibles.

I picked out a book and leafed to a random passage, something William P. Markham had taught us to do. My index finger fell on Ecclesiastes 2:20–21: *Therefore I turned my heart and despaired of all the labor in which I had toiled under the sun.* Yeah, me, too. According to Markham, a random opening of the Bible would be directed by God; thus, whatever passage you turned to was given to you by God, meant for you specifically, a message from above, the word of God out of his mouth. Before his stroke my father often let his Bible fall open at random. If he happened on a passage he didn't like, he continued the process until he found something more to his taste.

I recited the next verse in Ecclesiastes from memory. " *'For there is a man whose labor is with wisdom, knowledge, and skill; yet he must leave his heritage to a man who has not labored for it. This also is vanity and a great evil.'* "

The passage was about two emotions I had come to know well: despair and vanity. I was in despair because of my situation yet had enough vanity left to think I counted for something in the grand scheme of things, that I was more than a molecule on the ass of a flea crawling across a map of the universe. There was only one problem.

I wasn't.

I was the same as every other human on the planet, and when the final random asteroid came hurtling through space to take us all out in one big flash, to pitch us into the inferno, our destruction would no more be directed by William P. Markham's God than by a finger randomly placed in the Bible.

How I wanted to believe in a God. I envied believers, no matter what their persuasion. Maybe that was the despair the passage in Ecclesiastes had spoken of. But wasn't it the ultimate vanity for me to think I was important enough that a God a billion light-years away had enough interest to orchestrate my days and nights, mine, Jim Swope's?

There were probably countless habitable planets for a God to keep track of, and here he was letting little old me have this fender bender, giving me a good job, giving me a wonderful pair of daughters, letting my wife leave me, turning me into a veggie—all because it was part of some grand scheme that would make sense somewhere down the line.

What if God had put a single germ on the planet Earth a billion years ago and was coming back in another billion years to see what had come of it? What if that was all there was to his plan?

It wasn't as if I didn't want to believe.

More than anything I wanted to believe in a Lord who would rescue me. Yet, no matter how hard I wanted it, I couldn't convince myself there was a God or that God provided an afterlife.

I opened six or eight Bibles from the open box, then ripped the shipping tape on the second box, which, according to the label, had been freighted in from Tennessee.

Fancy that.

More leather-bound Bibles. I took one out and turned it upside down, flapping the pages as if to dislodge a bookmark. Something broke on the floor at my feet and I heard the hollow, tinkly sound a shattered Christmas tree decoration might make.

The floor around my feet glinted with tiny jewel-like shards of glass. I'd dropped a small glass ampoule. Pieces of broken glass were everywhere, on my shoe, in my pant cuff, on my sock. Alert not to cut my hand through the latex glove, I brushed them away.

When I inspected the inside of the Bible, I found a section of the Old Testament cut out with a razor knife, just enough to accommodate the vial. I opened four more Bibles before I found a second ampoule. When I had six of them, I lined them up on a nearby chair.

Each was stoppered with a tiny synthetic cork and half filled with a greenish-gray powder that looked like ground pencil lead. None of the ampoules were labeled.

Canyon View appeared to have more use for religion than I had.

There were another thirty or so Bibles in the boxes, no telling how many more ampoules. When you thought about it, a book made a relatively secure container. After all, it had taken a whole lot of mishandling to burst the boxes in Holly's truck.

Moving to the desk across the room, I sank into Marge DiMaggio's plush leather swivel chair and pulled the telephone across until I could read the dial pad from the light of the street lamp outside. Stephanie answered her cell phone on the first ring.

"You all right, Jim?"

"I think I found the mother lode."

"What is it?"

"You have to see it."

"Be there in a minute."

She was breathing heavily when she burst through the door, her hair tossed back with the speed of her movement. "Don't move from the doorway," I said as she started into the room.

"Why not?"

"I spilled something."

"What?"

"I don't know."

"At least let me switch on a—"

Before I could stop her she'd turned on the lamp near the door. The black light. She turned it off as soon as she realized her mistake. I suppose, as had I, she'd forgotten the lamp was ultraviolet.

"Turn it back on."

A moment later we were looking at a green phosphorescent glow coming from the floor in front of the vault and from my feet. It was stronger in certain spots, weaker in others, as if the black light were tracking footprints. My footprints. And my left foot, the one I'd dumped the ampoule on. Now we knew what the black light was for. Whatever was in the ampoules had been laced with phosphorescent matter to make it show up under ultraviolet. I'd noticed ultraviolet lamps in the offices downstairs, too.

"Jim. Look at yourself." For the first time I looked down at my lap and the desk in front of me. A greenish glow came off the telephone I'd used to call her, smatterings of green on the desktop, a stronger glow from my right hand and shirt. "It's on your face, too. What is it?"

"Holly had Bibles in her truck. Canyon View was shipping books. They ship this shit in Bibles."

"What's that on the inside of the safe door?"

"Oh, crap. I didn't see that." I walked across the room to the vault and moved the door until the combination of ultraviolet and outside light made the notice readable. "They call it DiMaggio number fifty-six, or D number fifty-six. Your aunt related to Joe DiMaggio, the baseball player?"

"By marriage. Phil was."

"He hit safely in fifty-six consecutive games. D number fifty-six: *'Avoid contact with skin. Avoid contact with eyes. Avoid flame. Avoid breathing vapors in the event of fire. Rinse thoroughly in a series of staggered showers. Use cold water and at least fifteen minutes of heavy soaping. Destroy clothing and anything else that comes into contact with number fifty-six.'*"

Circumventing the green glow on the floor, Stephanie took a couple of steps into the room. "You go take a shower. The way you are now you can't even sit in the car."

"Don't come in."

"Push that door back toward me. I'll turn on the light and read it. There might be something about an antidote."

"Okay, but don't walk over here."

"I won't."

I swung the heavy vault door so Stephanie could read the instructions; then I stepped into Marge DiMaggio's shower facility. The room had two exits. Now I knew why. You went in one end contaminated, came out the other clean. Or so you hoped. There were three shower stalls, with rinse-off areas outside each, glass doors arranged so that you stepped in one side, then out the other, making a kind of S as you worked your way through. A diagram on the wall presented the steps.

I took off my clothes, then rendered the latex gloves I'd been wearing inside out, one into the other, and stepped into the first shower stall and turned on the water. It was heart attack cold—warm water opened the body's pores and allowed the absorption of foreign substances. I soaped up, scrubbing every part of my body with the sterile mitts provided, scrubbing until I ached all over from the cold. I found the shampoo and lathered my hair. I shivered under the cold spray for fifteen minutes and found myself beginning to go hypothermic. I stayed in the second shower ten minutes, as suggested on the wall diagram. Ten more minutes in the third shower.

After toweling off, I stepped into a too-small set of blue hospital scrubs and a pair of paper slippers that fit perfectly. DiMaggio had big feet. Or maybe these were leftovers from her husband.

Back at DiMaggio's office the overhead lights were on. Stephanie was on the other side of the room, her back pressed firmly against the wall. I wondered for a split second whether she'd somehow gotten into the D#56. She seemed frightened, no, petrified.

But D#56 wasn't the problem.

The problem was standing next to the closed vault door. Scott Donovan was the problem. An even bigger problem was the nine-millimeter semiautomatic pistol he held in his right fist.

"Hey, lady-killer," he said, grinning at me. "All clean now?"

59. TUB-O'-LARD

"Don't be shy," Donovan said, waving the pistol around in a mock orbit of greeting. His voice was as calm and soothing as it had always been. "Come in and join the festivities."

I stepped into the room, but not so far that I wouldn't fall back into the corridor when he shot me. Had Stephanie not been there, I would have fled. Or tried to. Now Stephanie and I were stuck to him and to each other as if he were a strip of flypaper and we were hapless insects.

Standing near the vault, Donovan turned his head to examine it, and Stephanie took the opportunity to gesture at me with her right hand. She held a small object behind her hip, but I couldn't tell what it was. A handheld heat-seeking missile launcher would have been nice, but it looked more like a syringe. I had no idea where she'd found it. She hadn't brought it with her. After Donovan made certain the safe was locked, he turned to us, his eyes as blank as a cod's.

"Too bad you're not safecrackers," he said, his tone reasoned and mellow, his demeanor so nonchalant you would have thought we were discussing the weather. "I never thought you'd get this close."

"You going to call the police?" Stephanie asked.

"At this point, that is not an option."

"Why not?" I asked.

"Because there comes a time in business and commerce when somebody backs you into a corner and you find yourself forced to do something you never would have done under normal circumstances, something you don't want to do but which needs doing. I've found myself in that predicament several times in my career. Unfortunately, I'm in that predicament right now. You two shouldn't be here. I don't know what all you've found while you've been poking around, but we can't afford to take a chance you've uncovered any of our trade secrets. It wouldn't be fair to the people who work here."

"Let me get this right," I said. "You're going to kill us because you want to be fair to the people who work here?"

"Don't be twisting this all around. You people are the ones who made the mistake. Breaking and entering, I think it's called. It's a form of sabotage. Espionage, you might even call it. You've heard of Julius and

Ethel Rosenberg. No different. The work we're doing here has implications for national security."

His voice was soothing. It was hard to believe he had a gun and was saying what he was saying. The man who is about to kill you is supposed to be a maniac, not someone with the demeanor of a shy pizza delivery boy.

Stephanie must have heard him in the hallway while I was in the shower. I could visualize the scenario. She would have had time to warn me or shut the vault door, probably not both. She must have found the syringe inside the vault while I was in the shower. I wondered what was in it.

Showing up Monday morning to an office redecorated in blood and brains wasn't going to please DiMaggio, especially if the blood and brains belonged to her niece. Tonight Donovan's job was to get rid of us with the least amount of disruption to the office surroundings.

Maybe I was guessing, but his look wasn't one of moral quandary; it was more that of a man facing a conundrum: how to get these two yokels outside, dead, and into the trunk of his car with a minimum of fuss.

Donovan scratched the tip of his nose with the barrel of his chrome semiautomatic, pondering, looking us over, checking out Stephanie. I didn't know anything about guns, but his looked well oiled and cared for, like something he might use to take down bull elephants when he wasn't bumping off burglars.

"How did you find us?" Stephanie asked.

"The building's got a silent alarm. All the key officers are automatically notified."

"You all drive in together?" I asked.

"You'd like that, wouldn't you? If we had some witnesses."

He looked at me meaningfully, and his tone began to take on a hard edge. He was working himself up to this. I could see in his eyes behind those wire-rimmed glasses that he was trying to steel himself to the task at hand. At the commune once I'd watched my father butcher a live chicken. He'd made the same shift in attitude right before he picked up the chicken by its legs, laid its neck across a block of wood, and swung a hatchet down hard.

"You killed Achara, didn't you?" I said.

"You think because I'm standing here with a gun I'm the bad guy? Don't get confused. *You* broke in. *You* snooped through our building. I saw the offices downstairs that you ransacked. You're the ones who did this to yourselves. Don't be blaming it on me."

"Achara did that to herself, too?"

"Not me. You burned your house down."

"You're going to kill us, Donovan, at least have the balls not to lie while you're doing it."

He considered just long enough to give me a glimmer of hope that maybe he wasn't going to kill us. It didn't last long. "Okay. That's fair. I killed her. I poured gas around your living room. I thought you were inside. I thought it was over right there."

That he was willing to admit culpability in the burning of my home meant he thought we weren't going to tell anybody. That we were as good as dead already. I said, "Three years ago you flew to Tennessee pretending to help while you were pulling strings in the background to make sure nobody learned anything. You did the same thing in North Bend."

"I can't deny there was some strange stuff happening in Chattanooga." He laughed.

"And who called the fire investigators and told them I set up the explosion? And last night, my house? Somebody you know?"

"Mrs. DiMaggio insisted on doing that herself. She used to be in summer stock. Loves playing a part. Practically begged me for it."

I was sparring. Wasting time. Holding out for a miracle.

Any minute now he would shoot us, wrap us in a big plastic tarp, and drag our bodies downstairs to dispose of.

We might stall him for five minutes, but in the end he was going to shoot us.

Running wouldn't work—he would easily line me up in his sights before I reached the end of the corridor. And Stephanie didn't have a chance standing along the far wall of DiMaggio's office under the Paul Klee. For her, running was not even an option.

I'd been facing my own demise all week, and now that it was here, panic gripped me in a way it hadn't during the past seven days. I laughed aloud. I was destined to turn into a vegetable tomorrow, and here I was panicking over the thought of getting shot. I guess I was really panicking over the thought of Stephanie getting shot. My life was already over— Donovan would be doing me a favor—but Stephanie was being robbed of the next fifty years. I had an ugly vision of Morgan and my daughters waiting in the hotel room for days before contacting the authorities.

"As long as this is all settled and you're not going to change your mind," I said, "maybe you could clear up a few things."

"Like what?" You could tell he didn't mind the stalling—the more delay the better. He was still trying to work himself up to this.

"I don't understand why you dragged Max Caputo into this," I said.

"Who? Caputo?"

"Remember the trailer on Edgewick Road?"

"Oh, him. I followed the fire engine the day before. After you packed him off to the hospital, I did some reconnoitering and decided his property was ideal for what we had in mind."

"You mean for wiping out the whole department."

"Well, yeah. Anybody who might have been exposed in the truck accident."

"So you killed Max and filled the place up with ammonium nitrate?"

"I didn't kill him."

"Who did?"

"I'm assuming it was the explosion. I left him in a closet."

"I don't understand any of this," Stephanie said. "Why were you shipping D number fifty-six without precautions? Especially after that first accident in Tennessee. Why take another chance?"

"The odds were one in a million that anything would happen. Maybe one in ten million."

"That clearly wasn't true," I said. "You'd already had an accident right here in the plant. Another one in Tennessee. Who knows what else that you won't tell me about? It's got to be easier to take precautions than it is to run around murdering people."

"We took precautions."

"Putting it in Bibles?"

"That and having our own driver handling it. The mistake was hers. Your sister's the one who screwed up."

"Like hell she did," Stephanie said. "You even tell her what was in there? Did you bother to tell her how lethal it was? She didn't know anything about it. I've got her journal. She never mentioned it."

"You're still shipping it in Bibles, aren't you?" I said.

"It was a fluke. That accident. It'll never happen again."

"You're a piece of work, you know that?" I shifted in the doorway, more to see what he would do than to make an escape.

"You're the ones who don't get it. This is what always astonishes me about people in your position. If you could see this from my point of view, you'd realize if it was you with the gun you'd do the same thing I'm doing. It's just how it is."

"You're really so blind you think that?"

"Abso-fucking-lutely."

"Jesus Christ. You need a psychiatrist."

"Why did you kill Achara?" Stephanie asked.

Donovan tensed and then relaxed, as if once again deciding it didn't matter what we knew. I had the feeling he was happy to brag about it, to tell someone, anyone. It must be tough to pull off a nice murder and not be able to tell anyone. His tone grew gruffer, like a preacher working himself up to a bout of cussing. "Bitch needed killing."

He laughed, but it rang false. He was trying his best to be The Great Evildoer, but somewhere deep down he knew it was wrong and twisted, and he wasn't proud of himself—even though he was trying to convince himself he was. I don't think villainy came naturally to him, although self-deception certainly did.

"She made the wrong choice. It was as simple as that." He clearly regretted killing Achara. He stared at the floor between us, and his voice grew softer. "What happened after she made that choice, well, that was out of my hands."

"Please let us go," Stephanie said.

"Sorry. Letting you go is not an option."

"Sure it is," I said, moving toward the telephone on the desk. "I'll call the police. We'll turn ourselves in."

Donovan stepped forward and centered the pistol on my chest. We were fifteen feet apart now.

Stephanie was at the outer edge of his peripheral vision. I took another step toward the gun.

"Just stay where you are," he said.

Donovan wanted to kill us both in a civilized manner, but I was determined not to make it easy for him. He killed me, he was going to remember it. He'd already made the transformation, and now I was, too, reverting to the primordial, moving backward through evolution, returning to a time before civility, a time when men brained each other with rocks.

A man as large as Scott Donovan didn't spend his spare time lifting weights and practicing karate because he felt he was in control. He was compensating. I had no idea what he was compensating for, but it was for *something*. And a man compensating as hard as he was didn't take goading well.

So I called him a tub-o'-lard.

Okay, I know, but I was under a lot of pressure, and I couldn't think of anything else. Besides, it seemed to actually work. The natural pink in his cheeks began turning bright red.

"If you think calling me names is going to get you anywhere . . ."

"Jesus. You'd fall into a barrel of tits and come out sucking your thumb. I bet your karate works great against a mattress tied to a post."

"You don't think I could take you?"

"Not if I had one arm tied behind my back."

Donovan sneered and tucked his pistol into the waistband behind his back. This was too good. He began rolling his shoulders, flicking his arms back and forth like a swimmer on the starting block, warming up. You were about to kill someone with your bare hands, there was no point in pulling a muscle.

Stephanie crept along the far wall toward the corner. "Don't do it, Jim."

Donovan and I locked eyes, mimicking the prefight ritual of a couple of over-the-hill club fighters. I tried to look mean. He did, too. It must have been hilarious.

Before he could make a move, I turned and sprinted out the door.

You can imagine his surprise.

60. A MINOR SCUFFLE; OR, THE DAY I LOST SOME OF MY MOST VERY FAVORITE TEEFFS

"You crazy fuck!" Donovan shouted. "Come back here."

Too late. I was around the corner. In the corridor. Moving fast.

And then . . .

Bullets began tearing through the wall. He hadn't bothered to chase me, was shooting through the wall at where he guessed I might be. A stream of bullets.

Fragments of wallboard whizzed behind me in staccato ruptures, lead chasing me up the corridor like a zipper. Though each missile was closer than the last, by some miracle none of the slugs nicked me.

Instead of continuing down the corridor, I ducked through DiMaggio's shower room. When I opened the door that led from the bathroom back into DiMaggio's office, Stephanie and Donovan were in the doorway I'd just exited.

I stepped back into the office in time to see him hit her with an elbow. She went down hard but managed to slip her arms around one of his ankles, anything to hamper him.

Neither noticed me.

I ran across the room and launched myself through the air, striking Donovan across his midsection, using shoulders and fists and all the momentum I could generate.

The collision propelled us both away from Stephanie and against the wall in the corridor, where we crumpled into a heap.

I weighed a hundred ninety-seven pounds—or I had at the beginning of the week—yet hitting Donovan had been like butting my head into the bole of a two-hundred-year-old tree.

While he was still trying to get up, I struck him at the base of the nose with my palm. The blow tilted his head backward and yielded a spurt of blood. He cocked his head back and gave me a hellish look. His glasses were askew, the frame broken.

"Out of here, Stephanie!" I said. "Get out! Now!"

Before I could step away, Donovan swung his heavy leg around in an arc and knocked me off my feet.

316

Ian Hjorth, who studied martial arts, had once brought in a video that showed a karate expert killing a steer with a single blow to the head. Donovan's hands looked capable of that, thick and heavy and callused. I'd learned a couple of tricks from watching Hjorth's videos; one was that if you could help it, you didn't want to get into a fight with someone who'd trained for street fighting. I certainly didn't want my elbows, wrists, or fingers broken backward, my eyeballs gouged out, my ears ripped off. I didn't want my lungs collapsed. I didn't want anybody inserting his fingers into my nostrils, yet I had a feeling I was headed for some or all of it.

Before I could regain my feet, Donovan clubbed me across the side of my skull. It felt like I'd been hit with a four-by-four chunk of lumber.

The blow lifted me off the ground; it also silenced the ringing that had been in both ears all day, silenced my left ear completely, so that I was now hearing in mono.

"Run, Jim!" Stephanie called out, a note of hopelessness in her voice.

"*You* run," I said, the words coming to my ears with a weird little echo as if from inside a jar. "Get the hell out."

Donovan and I were on our feet now, squaring off. Somewhere along the line he'd lost the gun, though the room still reeked of gun smoke.

It took fifteen seconds to figure out what he was waiting for. Then it occurred to me. He was waiting for me to regain my senses. He wanted me alert and aware. He wanted me to feel each blow.

I was three or four inches taller than Donovan, yet he outweighed me by a muscular forty pounds. On his side he had bulk, power, strength, cunning, years of training, and a desire to inflict maximum damage; on mine I had reach, leverage, and a willingness to suffer. He was a black belt in karate; I had walked away from any schoolyard challenge reciting: " 'Whosoever shall smite thee on thy right cheek, turn to him the other also.' " In other words, I was accustomed to being laughed at but not to fighting.

Extending his fists, he spoke softly. "Now you're going to hurt."

I didn't even see the blow. It knocked me into DiMaggio's office, where I staggered, tripped, did a backward somersault, and got to my knees and then to my feet in one motion.

I stood up in time to take a blow to the face.

Inside the office, Stephanie was cowering behind the door, a hypodermic syringe clutched in her hand.

Taking short, quick steps, Donovan stepped forward and hit me in the face again, hard. There was no telling how I kept my feet under me. I was seeing stars now. Lots of them.

My jaw and mouth were numb and felt watery.

Something hit the floor at my feet. At first I didn't want to look down because I was afraid it was one of my teeth. When I did look down, I found I was wrong.

It was *two* of my teeth.

More loose teeth were floating around in my mouth.

When he threw his next punch, I ducked and his fist connected with the top of my skull. I wanted to drop to the floor and scream in pain, but by sheer force of will I kept my feet under me, swaying in place like a drunk.

"Shit!" he said, cradling his fist with his free hand. He threw another punch with his uninjured hand, but I stepped back and he missed. He missed another punch, this also with his undamaged hand. Maybe he wasn't going to kill me after all.

Then something hit me in the mouth.

I landed heavily on my right side, rolled, managed to get to my hands and knees. After choking for a few seconds, I coughed up an object that had been lodged in my throat.

A molar.

The left side of my face was swollen and tight. My jaw was broken.

I recalled once reading about a man in a bear attack who'd been besieged by the same feeling of disbelief that was now gripping me. In his wildest dreams he'd never imagined himself getting eaten by a bear. In my wildest dreams I'd never imagined getting beaten to death by a chemist.

61. STEPHANIE GETS INTO DONOVAN'S BRAIN

knew after he finished with me, he would start on Stephanie. I knew also that there wouldn't be a thing I could do to stop him.

Not that I was having much luck stopping this.

The thought of Stephanie forced me to my feet. Broken and bleeding, the least I could do was keep him occupied. Give her time to flee.

He stood well back while I propped my legs under me like a newborn calf, wobbly and wet and trying not to stumble.

Stephanie said, "For God's sake, stop it. You're killing him."

Startled by the nearness of her voice, Donovan relaxed his martial arts stance for a moment and turned toward her. "Baby, you haven't seen a thing."

"Leave him alone, you big creep."

"Your boyfriend broke my hand. It'll be a while before I'm through with him."

Their brief exchange distracted Donovan long enough for me to run at him, head down, building up speed.

I tackled him just above the knees. My thought was that he'd go over backward, but it was like hitting a wall. If I'd had any teeth left, I might have sunk them into his thigh, but there was only wind and fluid where my choppers had been.

And then, without warning, he toppled over and I was on top of him, my fists moving like a blur of jackhammers. Or so I wanted to think.

Eventually one of my blows found the family jewels. Donovan yowled and curled into a fetal position.

Stephanie took a step toward us. "No," I said. "Stay back."

He rolled over and grasped me with both meaty hands, tearing at my clothes. The hospital top ripped apart. I might as well have been wrestling a gorilla—one of those big boys turning truck tires into pretzels behind the glass at Woodland Park Zoo.

Somehow he got one arm around my neck, and his grip grew tighter. We struggled, rolling across the floor, crashing into the desk, knocking over a chair, rolling across the room to the vault.

When he tightened his arm around my neck, the pain became unendurable.

It was a strangely intimate position, his breath warm and moist on my face, the blood from his nose trickling into my eye. I could feel the warmth of his arm around my neck. Could hear his heartbeat thumping on my back as he slowly closed off my airway.

He cinched his arm tighter, crushing my windpipe a quarter inch at a time. After some moments of this, he loosened his grip enough for me to get a snatch of air. He didn't want me to die too quickly.

We were on the floor, my eyes bulging, face itchy, limbs shuddering like a dying wildebeest. Big cats didn't kill their prey by ripping them apart. Not like you'd think. They clamped their jaws on the victim's throat and waited while the kicking victim exhausted the air in its lungs. It was revolting to watch, but not nearly as revolting as when you were doing the kicking and shuddering yourself.

"Run, Steph," I gasped.

As I began to black out, a shadow passed over us. For a moment I entertained a feeble thought that Stephanie was going to stab the bastard with the hypodermic she'd been holding. Or that she'd located his gun and was moving closer so she could put a slug into his brain stem.

Instead, she stabbed me. Hard.

In the buttocks. The needle went in so deep, I swear it hit bone. Despite the fact that I was on the brink of death, it hurt like hell.

A moment after the pain in my butt subsided, Donovan screamed.

Realizing his grip had slackened, I wrenched myself out of his arms and rolled free. Climbed to my feet.

My neck was so stiff I could only turn a few degrees in either direction, and even that produced pain. I'd never had a broken neck, but if pain was any indication, I had one now. Along with the broken jaw.

On the floor, Donovan whimpered. Strange to hear him actually whimper. It was easy to see why. Stephanie had buried the syringe in his right temple. It was hanging there like an errant dart.

When Donovan grabbed the syringe and yanked it out, the needle broke off in his skull.

He looked up at Stephanie, his pale eyes burning, and for the first time since I'd met him, his tone of voice actually sounded menacing. "I'm going to keep you alive, doc. I'm going to keep you alive all night."

By now I was at the desk searching for a weapon. I was clutching a pen when he grabbed me from behind, knocked me down, got hold of my scrubs, and, as I kicked at him, pulled one pant leg off, then the other.

The cloth caught on my foot and he dragged me across the room by the pants.

Once clear of the mess around the desk, he stood over me like a big-time professional wrestler, The Chemist, arms held high. Then he fell on me. It was almost in slow motion. And there wasn't a damn thing I could do to stop him. I had only enough time to raise the pen before he landed on me like a sack of steer manure.

Oddly, his weight sagged. It took a moment for me to realize what happened.

I pushed him off and rolled across the floor.

His breathing was heavy and ragged.

Propping himself upright on the floor, he peered about the room with one eye. The pen was protruding from his other eyeball, a good four inches of it buried in his socket. He hadn't quite figured it out yet. I was finding it difficult to believe, myself.

When he began crawling toward me, I noticed a trickle of clear fluid dribbling down his cheek.

"Stop right there," I said. "It's over."

"Not bloody likely. I'm gonna tie your guts around your neck and use 'em for a choker," he whispered, reaching for me.

A single Bible lay on the floor between us. I grabbed it with both hands and hit him in the face with the flat of it.

The blow drove the pen in, so that now only the tip showed.

"Shouldn't have done that," he said, toppling over sideways. He stopped breathing for a while and then started again.

I turned to Stephanie. "You think he's going to make it?"

"I've seen people take that much trauma to the brain and live."

We stood on either side, watching his chest heave.

My own breathing was rapid and shallow, my voice hoarse, my pulped mouth dripping blood and saliva. Two fingers of my left hand were beginning to stiffen at unnatural angles. Several of my remaining teeth teetered back and forth when I ran my tongue over them. No matter. After tomorrow only a numbskull would feed me solid food.

"Why'd you stick *me*?"

"I had to give you the antidote."

"You have the antidote?"

"I found it in the vault while you were in the shower. Right before I heard him coming."

"Couldn't you have used a smaller needle?"

"It was the only one I could find."

"Are you telling me I'm going to be okay?"

Stephanie held up a bottle of clear fluid. "The instructions on the inside of the vault claim it's ninety percent effective if taken within the first hour of infection. Eighty if taken on day two. Seventy on day three. And so forth. It's a linear progression."

"I'm afraid I'm not up to the math," I said, leaning against DiMaggio's desk.

"You're on the evening of day six. That gives you a forty percent chance. Maybe thirty."

"They must have gone through a shitload of victims to have it worked out so meticulously."

"Or a trainload of chimpanzees."

"Does it say anything about afterward? For people like Holly?"

"Zero cures after the first seven days."

"They had the antidote all along. Your aunt. This clod. Any of them could have handed it to us."

"I'm sure that's why Achara was killed. I know she wanted to help you."

Donovan was crawling across the floor now in what appeared to be a random pattern. Like a slug on a sunny sidewalk.

"What about him?" Stephanie asked.

"After we get out, we call the police. Anonymously."

Except somebody had already called the police.

We heard sirens and reached the window in time to see Marge DiMaggio and two coworkers leap out of a Ford Expedition below us. They dashed through the front door of the building just as a police cruiser pulled to a stop behind the Ford, blue lights flashing. A second and third cruiser were coming in fast. When I stepped back from the window, my foot touched Donovan's semiautomatic on the floor.

"Hide in the other room," I said, picking up the gun. "Once I get them in here, go out the back way."

"I'm not going to desert you."

"We get in a dither with the police, what do you think is going to happen to that?" I gestured to the vial Stephanie was holding. "Karrie needs it. Maybe you, too. That stuff is all over the room."

"I didn't touch any of it."

"Let's hope not. I'm going to keep your cell phone. When I know you're safe, I'll surrender."

Sixty seconds later DiMaggio and two underlings I recalled from our earlier visit popped into the doorway, huffing and puffing as if they'd run the whole way. Stephanie had concealed herself in the smaller room off to the side. The police remained outside.

"Good God!" Marge DiMaggio said, bursting into the room.

"Stay out. We've got D number fifty-six all over the place."

"What *are* you talking about?"

Donovan moaned. The coworkers, a woman and a man, followed DiMaggio through the spill area, muttering about getting out of the building, that I had a gun, that I was berserk. After the fight with Donovan and the threats to Stephanie's life, I felt berserk.

"What's wrong with his eye?" DiMaggio demanded, kneeling next to Donovan. "What did you do to him?"

"Just a little less than he was trying to do to me."

62. EXECUTIVE ANNIE OAKLEY ENDS MADMAN'S MIDNIGHT TERROR SPREE

I pointed the gun at Marge DiMaggio and told all three of them to stand in the corner behind the desk, an area I knew to be free of the chemical. The coworkers complied, but DiMaggio was the kind of woman who could get herself killed over a two-for-one pizza coupon. And she wasn't about to take orders from me.

"Over behind your desk, Mrs. DiMaggio."

"You go to hell."

"He's got D number fifty-six on him. By now you have it all over yourself."

Neither of the coworkers could take their eyes off the puckered puddle that had been Donovan's eyeball.

If the police were inside the building, I couldn't hear them, but then I was stone-deaf in one ear, so it wasn't likely I'd hear the sound of footsteps. "I was in your safe. Some of the D number fifty-six spilled on the floor."

DiMaggio got up and tried the vault handle, then smiled. She had the encyclopedia of smugness down pat. "You don't expect me to believe you've been inside this?"

"Achara gave me the combination."

"Did she now?" Amusement flitted in her dark eyes.

I might have recited the combination, but my head was ringing so badly I couldn't have spelled my middle name. Could barely remember it. Jerome. James Jerome Swope.

"If you're going to prevaricate, Mr. Swope, at least be reasonable. Achara didn't know the combination any more than the security guard out at the front gate knows that's a Paul Klee on the wall. Try again. I don't believe you."

There was more police activity in the parking lot below the window, men giving orders, car doors slamming, the sounds of radios. The office walls jumped with blue lights.

"Fine," I said. "Kill yourself. In the meantime, go over to the window and tell the police you three are hostages and we need a medic unit. While you're at it, tell them to stay out of the building."

"The police have been instructed to remain outside, at least until our security personnel call them in."

I caught my reflection in the office window.

The too-small hospital blues I'd put on after my shower had been shredded and torn during my combat with Donovan, so now I was naked. I pulled the remaining strands from around my hips and off my neck. The clothes I'd worn from the hotel were contaminated. There were more hospital blues in the shower facility, but I wasn't going to turn my back on DiMaggio to get them. I would just have to be naked.

I figured she had a gun hidden either in her desk or on her person and would use it on me the moment I looked away. What better opportunity to silence a critic?

EXECUTIVE ANNIE OAKLEY ENDS MADMAN'S MIDNIGHT TERROR SPREE. She would be a heroine.

There was a 40 percent chance the substance Stephanie had injected into me would reverse the syndrome, which meant there was a 60 percent chance it would not.

I'd been living with this syndrome for six days, but it felt like six months. Or six years. Time had sped up and slowed down, compressed and expanded. I was prepared to leave this world, conditioned to give up the ghost through either the death of my body or the loss of function in my central nervous system.

No matter what happened, my view of life on this planet would never be the same. I would take nothing for granted. Not after burying Harold Newcastle and Stan Beebe. Not after seeing Joel McCain, Jackie Feldbaum, and Holly Riggs turn into nerveless lumps. Not after escaping Caputo's trailer explosion, watching my house burn down around my ears, not after thinking my children were dead. After hammering a writing utensil into a man's brain. Nothing would be the same.

Life was a matter of time. If I'd learned anything this week, I'd learned time was what you made of it.

When I looked away from my image in the window, I caught DiMaggio staring at my hands. "That's right. They're waxy. I hear it's big this season."

"When did that start?" She joined the others behind the desk.

"My hands? I told you about it. Six days ago. Which makes tomorrow my last day, doesn't it? I may drop at any second."

The room grew silent. I knew if I did drop, one of them would pick up the gun and shoot me. No need for the world to try to figure out why I was brain-dead. Better to shoot a maniacal ecdysiast in the middle of the night than to have people listening to my theories about Canyon View Systems. I waved the gun in the air. The man seemed most frightened, possibly because he thought I was going to shoot him first.

He was wrong.

DiMaggio would be first.

"I was in your shoes," I said, "I'd stand around and wait me out. That's what you've been doing all week, isn't it?"

"I have no idea what you're talking about," DiMaggio said.

63. A HISTORY RIFE WITH UNUSABLE BRAINS

It occurred to me that the man and woman with DiMaggio thought Donovan was on the floor with a pen hammered into his eye socket because I'd run amok, not because I'd been defending myself. That they thought I was naked and holding a gun because I was stark raving mad, not because my clothes had been shredded off during our struggle.

That I had arrived this way.

That I'd been running around Redmond bare-assed all night. For all they knew, the last stage of the syndrome was insanity. Or nudity. Or both. Hell, for all *I* knew, the last stage of the syndrome *was* insanity. Or nudity. Or both.

In fact, for all I knew, I was as crazy as a shithouse rat. I wondered if anything I'd been saying made sense. I wondered if Stephanie had actually found an antidote and stuck me with a hypodermic or I'd imagined it.

DiMaggio wasn't afraid of me, perhaps because she had a built-in arrogance that staved off self-doubt, just as it staved off second thoughts. We didn't have a woman here who second-guessed decisions. No. This was the sort of person who could leave a litter of kittens in the woods, justify it in her own mind, and never think twice about it.

"I don't know how much money you guys are going to get when you sell the company, but I'll be rooting for you from the nursing home. New cars. Fine houses. Hire your own architect. Do it up right. Get yourself a Ferrari. What's it like to know you're responsible for so many broken lives? You murdered Chief Newcastle in North Bend and two others in Tennessee. Probably six more, actually. My friend Stan committed suicide when he found out what was happening to him."

"That's not how it is," said the woman to DiMaggio's right. "That is not how it is at all. We were not responsible."

"That's right. You're not responsible. But you *are* to blame."

"Shut your trap, Clarice," DiMaggio said.

But Clarice wouldn't keep quiet. "We never meant for any of this to happen. None of us even knew it was happening until a day ago."

"Who told you that? Marge knew last February. Her niece called her and told her."

Clarice turned to DiMaggio. "You told us—"

"Shut up!" Smoothing the front of her blouse with her palms, DiMaggio maintained perfect posture, unflappable. "Hush now, Clarice. I'll handle this."

But Clarice hadn't resolved herself for any moral ambiguity, didn't want to be in the wrong ethically, even if she might be legally. Her thin eyebrows bobbing to her words like broken windshield wipers, she appealed to me. "This is no different than when an airline carrier has a plane go down. People in business do their best, but despite their best, they have accidents. People die. It's not because somebody wants them to die. It's just the way the world is."

"Shut up, Clarice," DiMaggio said, not unkindly.

"No. Go ahead," I said. "Talk to me. I'm on day seven. It's Sunday by now. I get arrested, the earliest I'd get bail would be Monday morning when the courts open. By that time I'll be in a big white diaper. In fact, I think I can feel my mind slipping even as we speak." I rather liked the effect this last sentiment had on them, particularly on Clarice, who hunched her shoulders and tried to make herself smaller.

Even though I'd warned them to keep away from it, the man turned his back on me and looked out the window. Maybe he was too embarrassed to face me. Or maybe he was trying to signal the cops outside. Then, like a strutting bird of prey, DiMaggio stepped forward, defiant and, even at her age, still striking.

"You don't understand what's going on. This is groundbreaking. For some time now we've been working on a way to encode DNA into liquid metal. I don't expect a layman to understand why we're doing this or what it will accomplish, but I'll tell you anyway. We've been working with positively charged metal complexes that are known to liquefy substances. Because DNA has an innate capacity for recognizing complementary sequences of itself, it's the perfect tool for making electronic circuits. I won't bore you with the details. I will tell you we're not the only ones working on it, although we were the first. As you might suppose, one of the problems in a new field is that you end up handling chemical compounds nobody's used before. You take precautions, you do everything you can to ensure the safety of your workers and of the general public, but accidents happen. To say that we meant for them to happen, that we provoked them, is just plain myopic. If there was anything we could do, we would have done it."

I wanted to tell her I knew about the antidote, that I had a dose of it in my ass. But I needed to give Stephanie time to get away. "My brain turns to mush, and all you do is turn up the volume on your doublespeak."

"Mr. Swope, we've been running on a shoestring since the day my husband died."

"I can see that," I said, glancing around the redecorated office.

"Philip was the one we counted on to bring in funding, and after he was gone it began to dry up. Any lawsuit against Canyon View would have bankrupted the company—probably before we even got to court—stopped the project cold, forever ended any hope of those people recovering. You see, we're not only working on practical DNA applications for microelectronic circuitry and genetic engineering, but even though there was no profit in it, we've been working on an antidote for D number fifty-six."

"You admit it was your company caused those brain deaths?"

"I'm assuming Achara told you about D number fifty-six."

"I found it in your vault over there."

"You do persist, don't you?"

"A character flaw."

DiMaggio said, "Tananger Bryers is all set to buy our company. They will be in a position to make sure this never occurs again. They have the funding to—"

"Bribe and corrupt all over the world. They were the ones responsible for that chemical spill in Pakistan where twenty-eight hundred people died. Tanager Bryers won't make sure this never happens again. *You* should have done that."

"Freak accidents," DiMaggio said. "One in a billion."

"Go tell that to your niece in Tacoma General."

I stared hard at DiMaggio.

DiMaggio stared back, basking in the confidence that science and law were on her side. I kicked the Bible that had gone unnoticed. It cartwheeled across the floor until it hit Donovan's leg. He groaned. "You were shipping this stuff across the country in Bibles," I said. "You had accidents in Chattanooga and North Bend and God knows where else. You lost people right here in this plant. Right under your nose."

"Books make good insulators," Donovan said, from the floor. We all looked down at him in astonishment. "Phil found a warehouse full of 'em. Got 'em for a song."

"Why don't you tell us how your husband really died?" I asked.

The room grew silent. Clarice froze. The bald man's pate was beginning to shine with perspiration. I had the feeling they'd all bought into the heart attack story, that Marge's hesitation in the face of my accusation was giving them pause.

DiMaggio sat down in her padded swivel chair and began tidying her desktop, as if keeping busy would fend off my interrogation. "My husband worked himself to death trying to make Canyon View a success. William Armitage was a thief and a liar."

"Who you had killed."

"This has all been for Phil."

"He got some of that crap on his skin, didn't he? Phil did. Back before you knew how it affected people. Back when it was in a more potent form. When it didn't take five months to make someone sick."

"Took about five days," Donovan said, gasping for breath.

DiMaggio leaned forward, licked a finger, and turned a page on her desk calendar. "Our hands were tied. If we'd talked about it publicly, the sale would never have gone through."

"There's a letter on your desk says your husband died from D number fifty-six. Others in the company got contaminated, too, didn't they?"

DiMaggio scanned the papers strewn across the top of her desk until she found what I was referring to. "Armitage was a criminal."

I looked at Clarice and the man at the window. "I'm guessing you guys don't know about the antidote?"

"You want the truth?" DiMaggio seemed to be speaking more to her coworkers than to me, but it was obvious from Clarice's reaction that this was the first she'd heard of an antidote. "We had a deadline. We didn't have time to file affidavits and watch federal inspectors crawling all over the office. Mr. Swope, I don't expect you to understand, but whenever science makes breakthroughs, there are casualties. I warned Holly. I warned her, in the event of an accident, she was to call before she let anybody inside that truck. But by the time she called, you'd all been inside. There wasn't enough antidote for that."

"There really is an antidote?" The man at the window was sweating even more heavily now, his shirt stained with it.

"We'll talk about this later." DiMaggio took a deep breath and picked up the phone on her desk.

I said, "Did you know what they had planned for Achara?"

"Scott handles the cleanup operations."

"That's what you call murder? Cleanup?"

"Achara's dead?" Clarice was dumbstruck.

"In a fire," DiMaggio said. "The police think this man set it."

"Donovan set it. He told me as much. He thought I was inside with my kids. He killed Achara."

When all eyes in the room froze on something behind me, I turned slowly and saw two SWAT team members in black jumpsuits and Kevlar vests. They had rifles pointed at my chest.

"Drop it, buddy!" one of them shouted.

"Shoot him!" DiMaggio screamed. "He's got a gun. He's going to kill us. Shoot him."

"Drop the gun, asshole! Drop it now!"

There was only one way I could think of to stall them and at the same time to avoid getting killed on the spot.

I pointed the pistol at my temple and pulled my swollen and bloodied mouth into the most addlepated grin I could muster. "Make a move, I'll pull the trigger. Swear to God."

64. DON'T BURY ME UNTIL I GIVE THE SIGNAL

It took a few minutes for the standoff to move outside, the two SWAT team members, joined by six more men and one woman, all pointing rifles or shotguns at me, another eight or ten uniformed police officers dispersed behind trees, and in the darkness additional gun-happy officials arriving each minute.

As for myself, I held a cocked pistol in one hand, Stephanie's cell phone in the other. It wasn't easy to scramble up onto the roof of a police cruiser with both hands full, but I managed. Bare-assed.

Wingdoodle flapping in the breeze.

I almost felt as though I were playing a role in a film, a part in which a flubbed line could precipitate my death. Forget the nursing home. If everybody here fired at once, I could easily catch thirty bullets before I hit the ground.

When a couple of the SWAT team boys tried to move in closer, I said, "Back off, kids. I'll do it! Swear to God!"

"Come on, buddy. We've got you for illegal entry and assault. That's nothing. You might get three months. Let's not make it worse."

"Stand back, ladies and gents! Stand back and pray for me!"

I'd come to terms with the fact that tonight was my last night. Now I was coming to terms with these as my last minutes.

Strange as it seems, I was all right with it.

I really was.

Sounds dumber than a fence post in the rain, but I was *always* going to die.

Everybody dies. It was simply an event most of us never really gave much thought to. Now that I knew when, or pretty much thought I did, the terror had been stripped away. There was a genuine serenity in knowing. In fact, the knowledge was almost comforting as I stood on the roof of the police car, a dozen rifles trained on my chest, Donovan's pistol pressed to my brain.

I hadn't seen Stephanie during our tense procession out of the building. No telling whether she had fled or was still hiding upstairs. It worried me. I needed her to be safe and free, so she could take care of my girls, so she could administer the antidote to Karrie, but most of all, so that someone would be around to tell the truth after this was over. If DiMaggio had her way, this would go down as a mental patient caught in a burglary.

The nearby police cars were empty, but had they arrested Stephanie, they would hardly have placed her where I could see her.

The police had yet to ask about an accomplice.

And why would they?

I had all the characteristics of a classic maniac, and classic maniacs operated alone.

I was armed. Bloodied. Naked. Toothless. Berserk.

And now word had gotten around that I'd stabbed a man. I could hear them talking about it, rumors buzzing about in the darkness like mosquitoes. The cops were like big-game hunters wondering who was going to get the privilege of turning me into a rug, discussing my dementia in the same breath they discussed the best way to make the shot. They all thought I belonged in Western State Hospital. A woman cop cracked a joke, something about not having a camera.

DiMaggio and associates had remained upstairs, observing the festivities through the window. Sooner or later, tired of cupping their hands to the glass, one of them would turn out the overhead lights.

That's when the real entertainment would begin.

The thought made me laugh aloud, and of course, laughing made me look loonier than all the rest of this put together.

"Shoot him," said the bald man through the now-open upstairs window. "For God's sake, shoot him, so we can all go home. Can't you people please just shoot him?"

The officer with the megaphone told him to shut up, then told me he had doughnuts and coffee on the way—as if they could appease me with twelve dollars' worth of lard, sugar, and coffee beans. And why didn't I make things easier for myself, he said. If I gave myself up, I would be treated with dignity. They would provide clothes. I would be fed. Didn't that sound like a fair trade-off?

The phone in my left hand rang.

"Hello?"

"Jim?"

"Stephanie."

"You all right?"

"Yeah. You?"

"I'm at the hotel."

"The girls okay?"

"Everything's fine. It took longer than I thought. What's going on there?"

"We're just chatting."

"You and my aunt?"

"Me and the police."

"What happened after I left?"

"Nothing. I'm just getting a little air."

"Is that a loudspeaker I hear in the background?"

"They're practicing plan B for talking psychos down. Don't worry. It's not working."

"What do you mean? What about my aunt and her friends?"

"Still upstairs."

"Are they contaminated?"

"They are. I told them. They didn't believe me." At that moment, the overhead light in DiMaggio's office went off. From the parking lot I could see the greenish glow on the faces in the window. Green radiated off the side of the bald man's cheek. More green scattered through Clarice's hair, on DiMaggio's face. A troika of Halloween goblins.

"You still there?" Stephanie asked.

"Yeah."

"What's happening?"

"They just turned off the overhead light upstairs."

"Anybody else been up there?"

"That was one of my conditions for coming out of the building. Nobody goes in, and your aunt and her friends stay up there."

"You get some clothes yet?"

"Not exactly."

"You're still naked?"

"No."

"What are you wearing?"

"Slippers and a cell phone."

Clarice's scream pierced the night like a siren. DiMaggio glared down at me. I'd never seen so much hatred focused in a single pair of eyes. I could almost see the churning gears as she strained to figure out exactly what had happened. I'd been in her vault. I must have, or I wouldn't have had access to the D#56. What else was in the vault? Soap and water was the first part of the cure, but after that, it was the hypodermic.

She vanished from the window.

"What was that noise?" Stephanie asked.

"I think they finally figured it out."

"What are they doing?"

"Clarice is standing in the window crying. The guy disappeared right away. Headed for the showers probably. DiMaggio's gone now, too."

"Bet she's headed for the safe."

"If you're right, she should be back in about—there she is."

Leaning so far out the window I thought she was going to lose her balance and fall, DiMaggio yelled to the nearest police officer, "Don't shoot him. Whatever you do, don't shoot him. He's stolen a top secret chemical formula!"

This time when DiMaggio and Clarice disappeared from the window, I knew they were headed for the showers.

"The girls around?" I asked.

Allyson came on first, doing her standard imitation of a grown-up, the pose she adopted after her mother abandoned us. "Father. Are you coming back?"

"I don't know, sweetheart."

"Tomorrow's the last day, isn't it?"

"Yes, sweetie."

"After tomorrow are you going to be like Grandpa?"

"I might be."

"Stephanie said she gave you a shot."

"Right in the behind."

Allyson laughed nervously. "And it might make you better?"

"Just in case it doesn't, I love you, sweetie. Always remember that. You've made my life a joy."

"Daddy, you're starting to make me cry. I love you, too. I want you here."

"I want to be there, but I'm tied up. Can you put your sister on now?"

At the far end of the building an ambulance crew had been waiting for a signal from the police before going inside for Donovan. Now a medic unit pulled up behind the ambulance, and from the looks of things they were going to move in without my permission.

I caught the eye of the police officer with the megaphone. "There's been a hazardous material spill inside the building. Shows up green under a black light. The patient upstairs is covered in the stuff. So are those other three. So am I. Highly contagious. They call it D number fifty-six. Lethal as hell."

Brother, did that start a commotion.

65. NOW YOU BE A ZOMBIE

Certain theoreticians have conjectured that more than one universe co-exists with ours, that there may be dozens of parallel universes coexist-ing at the same time.

I believe in it more now than I used to. I believe I may be living lives in separate universes at the same time. Trick would be to jump from one of the bad ones, where you've somehow ended up in prison or crippled or blind, where you've ended up stupid or ugly, to a different universe where you're a rich kid from New Hampshire and have impeccable man-ners and a brown-eyed girlfriend.

In one universe you sprain your ankle stepping off a curb and go to the doctor's office, where you meet your bride-to-be in the waiting room, and afterward you go on to make her life miserable because she's an en-raged people pleaser and you're never pleased.

In another universe you're hit by a car in the parking lot outside your high school graduation ceremony, your leg is fractured in twelve places, and you limp for the rest of your life. You grow alienated and sarcastic, cannot hold down a job, and become a druggie and a drunk. Your best friend is whoever happens to be sitting on the next bar stool.

Or.

Your second-grade teacher decides to run off to Alaska to be a bush pilot; your class is taken over by Miss Bermeister, who lives and breathes teaching and who picks you out as her pet project—the effect she has on your life is profound. She instills a confidence and an enthusiasm for scholarship that propels you into higher education and, from there, into the ministry. You marry an ex-nun, remain childless throughout your life, and die of old age working in Africa in a save-the-children venture.

Or this.

Which really happened to my father. You're twelve, and one of your acquaintances shows up with his dad's revolver, which he's swiped from his old man's closet and which he swears is unloaded. He laughs, and be-fore you can duck or even blink, he points it at your head and pulls the trigger.

The hammer falls on an empty chamber.

He points the pistol at your best friend. This time the pistol goes off

337

with a loud crack. A bullet pulverizes your best friend's skull. You go on to live a long life—your friend wastes away in a curtained-off room and expires at twenty-six.

It all ends in death. Nobody gets out alive.

After all is said and done, a hundred years after you're dead does the length of your time here really make the tiniest bit of difference?

Is a life with 5,110 sunsets better than one with 27,000 sunsets? Or 40,000? And anyway—how many of those sunsets can you remember when you're on your way to paradise? Fifteen? Twenty? I can ask the questions, but I can't furnish the answers.

When all is said and done, perhaps fewer years are better years.

In one life I'm a man with a skull full of pudding.

In another I've survived the narrowest escape possible, have become the centerpiece in dozens of newspaper and magazine articles—a man who's come back from the brink.

I had stumbled through a lot of crossroads in my life, and except for our divorce and the way Lorie left me, which I'm not certain I didn't deserve, I lived a fairly decent life. It started with a father and a mother who loved me in the best way they knew how and ended with me loving my girls in the best way *I* knew how. Wasn't that as good as it could get? For anybody?

EPILOGUE

These days I don't get too worked up about things. Trouble washes over me like a warm and gentle tide. I do what I can to keep in a good frame of mind and try not to let outside events I cannot control frazzle me. I soak up love and sunshine where I find it. I shrug off aches and Arctic blasts.

It feels like afternoon. I no longer live by clocks, so I have no idea what time it is. I am sitting in a low chair staring out the window, my eyes refusing to focus. Sunbeams streaming through the window warming my arm and leg. I am luxuriating in one of the simplest pleasures on the planet. Sunshine. Warmth. Vitamin D free for the taking.

After a while a woman enters the room and speaks softly to me, kisses my cheek, strokes my mussed hair with a gentleness reserved for newborns, puppies, and the rest of those helpless souls most people overlook.

Without turning, I know who it is—from her scent and from the lovely sound of her voice.

Stephanie. Glued to me for the rest of her life by legal and moral obligations. Poor baby.

She picks up my cold, limp hand, pats it between her palms, and holds it for a while. Later, I sense rather than see she is moving across the room to my father, speaking in a normal tone of voice as if he might actually reply, just as she has spoken to me. As if I might actually reply.

My father says exactly what I said, which is nothing. Nothing at all.

Those of us who'd been involved in the North Bend Syndrome, as the world press came to name it, had never really brushed up against evil until that freezing night in February, not true evil, not the sort of wickedness that discards the lives of strangers over a casual meeting at corporate headquarters. By earthly standards I'd lived a fairly uneventful thirty-four years. One marriage. Two daughters. A home. A few close calls as a firefighter. On the other side of the world there were countries, entire regions, where a child was beating the odds to live past age five, where young girls died giving birth at fourteen, where children worked as slaves until they escaped or grew into shrunken adults, their minds atrophied from years of mindless drudgery and lack of proper nourishment.

Thirty-four years of healthy, productive living was nothing to gripe about.

It wasn't as if the world were going to clunk to a halt without me.

I'd gotten over that notion long ago.

Life was a river. Remove a cupful of liquid and the river never even knew you were missing.

I sit in the sunshine and know a lot of things. Some of these I know instinctively, some through the vexations of memory, some through a sort of spiritual process that I would have denied the existence of prior to that week last June.

I know Stephanie has moved from Ohio to North Bend, that she will probably remain in the area for the rest of her natural life. I know she is with my girls and that they love her and she loves them, that she shows it to them every day. I know there will be problems because there will always be problems in any family. But they will be minor problems, and life will go on. The river will continue to flow.

My cupful, your cupful, notwithstanding.

When they are ready, the North Bend Fire Department will hire a new chief, perhaps even Steve Haston, Mr. Disaster, but it is not a debacle I trouble myself over. Things have gone well for others, or so I've been told. Karrie Haston's body has accepted the antidote; she has resigned from the fire service and given herself over to social work in the South Bronx.

There is a peace in me I've never known before, and that peace involves knowing that no matter what happens in this room, or whatever room I end my days in, my daughters will remain forever bound together as only sisters who'd gone through great trauma can be. I see them as college students, still friends, still close, still doing things together. They will be heartbreakers. The thought warms me as much as the sunshine through the window does.

Their nights will be tinged with sadness because of what might have been, but the Swope family will move on. Life is for the living. In time, one or both will have children. If I am fortunate, the sounds and smells of babies will invade my space, talcum powder, cries for mother's milk, for missing toys. As long as my heart beats, love will surround me.

Stephanie will continue to fetch news of the outside world to this room. She will read pertinent newspaper articles aloud, such as the one about the indictment of eight officers of Canyon View on charges ranging from manslaughter to murder and arson.

340

She will bring further news of civil suits and of former employees ratting out the Canyon View bigwigs. She will continue to investigate the occurrences of that week and learn that Hillburn and Dobson of Jane's California Propulsion really did stay on in North Bend for a couple of extra days on other business.

As the years pass, Stephanie will find her own niche in the medical world. She will grow old gracefully, as her sister had not been allowed to do. She will come to understand better the demons that drove her early years. Maturity and serenity will take over her countenance. And I hope she will come to know me in a way that includes forgiveness as much as it does love.

The river will continue to flow. A single cup of water means nothing to a rain squall. It means even less to a waterfall.

Somewhere in the sky a cloud passes over the sun, and the radiant heat on my body dissipates. Behind me, I listen as Stephanie speaks to my brain-dead father. And then the girls come in, Allyson and Britney. And they are a little older now. A little different. Oddly, Britney now seems the more mature of the two. It's almost as if Allyson's skipped backward two or three years, playing catch-up on the missed summers of her childhood, while Britney has skipped ahead.

They are turning into outstanding young women.

Staring out the window, I feel each of my daughters step close in turn and kiss my cheek.

"Daddy?" It was Allyson. Close now, her breath on the back of my neck.

From the other side of the room, Britney calls out, "Don't bother him. He's resting!"

"Daddy?"

"Don't bother him. You know he needs his rest."

Slowly, so very slowly, I turn my head from the window. "Daddy? Can we have a picnic at Unemployment Beach with you and Stephanie? The weatherman says it's going to be the last nice weekend of September. Over eighty. Can we?"

I glance across the room to where Stephanie sits with my father. I put my arm around Allyson, slowly pulling my oldest into my lap. "A picnic? What would we eat?"

"Potato chips, Cheetos, corn chips. Chocolate pop."

"Chocolate pop?"

"Andrea Yates says it's god-awful delicious."

"And bean dip?"

"You know that gives you gas."

Britney rushes over and clings to my arm. "I think it's funny when Daddy gets gas. Can we go, Daddy?"

"Funny you should ask. I was planning a little trip out there myself. But now that I know you want to go, too . . . hmmmm, maybe I'll take you along."

"Silly," Britney says. "We always want to go with you."

"I know you do."

Life couldn't get any better, I think as Stephanie smiles at me from across the room. A few minutes later, we all get up and head for the store to stock up for the picnic. We have a lot to prepare for.